THE CASE OF MR. CRUMP

The Case of

MR. CRUMP

BY

Ludwig Lewisohn

WITH A PREFACE BY

Thomas Mann

FARRAR, STRAUS & GIROUX   NEW YORK

Publisher's Note: 1965

The appearance of Ludwig Lewisohn's greatest novel, *The Case of Mr. Crump,* in the Noonday Masters of Modern Literature series reflects the place this unique work has come to occupy in world literature. Mr. Lewisohn wrote his novel in the mid-twenties, but for legal reasons involving libel it could not be published in the United States at that time. In 1926 Edward Titus, an American living in Paris and a patron of avant-garde literature who admired the book profoundly, published a limited edition. From France, the book made its way in translation to every country in Europe, to Africa and the Orient, but it was not until 1947 that the work could be sold in America. In that year Farrar, Straus and Company published the first authorized edition, which was received with praise. An abridged version, retitled *The Tyranny of Sex,* was published by the New American Library and sold more than a million copies.

The Case of Mr. Crump is now recognized as a literary classic, one of the truly significant naturalistic novels of our century. This new printing, available in cloth and, for the first time, in an unabridged paperback edition, is acknowledgment of its enduring merit.

Preface

By THOMAS MANN

According to its form this book is a novel. It operates with fictive personages, narrates their actions, expresses their relations in dialogue and points these in such a manner that the absorbed and fearful reader perceives on every page the development of that criminal catastrophe which is the book's disastrous ending. It is, then, fiction, well and astutely composed, utilizing all the methods of modern technique, a work of art, in a word, in so far as it preserves its coolness of tone, keeps its distance, permits things to speak for themselves and sustains that severe and curbed and almost serene silence which is peculiar to all art and especially to the art of speech, and leaves it to the reader or beholder to draw his own conclusions. But simultaneously and at every moment the book is both more and less than a novel; it is life, it is concrete and undreamed reality and its artistic silence seems in more than one passage desperately like a cry. There is about the book something stripped and naked and so terribly immediate that it seems at every moment to negate its own form from within and to be ready to shatter that form. This circumstance will depress the book's value in the eyes of those who still demand a purely aesthetic impression. But one cannot fail to observe the book's indifference — an indifference that belongs to our time — toward such disapproval; its voluntary renunciation of mere aesthetic distinction, its readiness to make far-reaching aesthetic sacrifices in the service of documentary vigor. And it is notable that this indifference, this readiness and this renunciation are transformed unawares into artistic values of an ethical order and by a moral means elevate and ennoble the book again as a work of art — a process that illustrates the human oneness of the ethical and aesthetic categories by means of a most moving example.

We have here, then, a novelistic document of life, of the *inferno* of a marriage. That word exhausts the book's horrifying and infuriating subject matter — a marriage that should never have been contracted nor would have been save for the man's weakness and youthful inexperience — a marriage which, under the protection of cruel social hypocrisy and of a cruel social fear for the abstract institution, becomes an *inferno* — first through the scandalous legal advantages possessed by the woman as such, finally and hopelessly through the passional crime that brings to ruin the gifted and promising protagonist.

vii

It is American conditions that are delineated. Lewisohn is an American. He lives in Paris, since he cannot well live in America, where this book of his has been forbidden too. It was forbidden the mails in the name of that national morality, which plays so horrifying a part in the story, and has appeared only in a limited edition printed in France. And it is well that it has now been translated and may freely circulate among us. For there is no doubt that it genuinely enriches our store of foreign literary goods. The author declares that the book arose from his determination to tell "as well and as entertainingly as he could the true story of Herbert Crump." One must grant him that his power to stir and entertain us is very great. His book stands in the very forefront of modern epic narrative. His style is manly, sincere, precise and strong; there is in it a high determination after compact and direct truth and one is impressed and enchanted at once. At times he has the dry and desperate humor of Strindberg, as the subject itself leads one to be frequently reminded of Strindberg. The characters are human beings — even the woman, Anne Crump, remains human in all her repulsiveness. And this is meritorious. For without the corrective of creative justice and insight, the author's feeling of solidarity with his hero might easily have made of the woman a mere demon.

Finally the publication of this book is to be welcomed because it may thus extend its influence back across the ocean and contribute to that Europeanization of America that should be the counterpart of our much discussed Americanization and which is indeed the aim of the best Americans of our time. Among these, though living in temporary exile, Lewisohn must be numbered. These men, Lewisohn, Mencken, Sinclair Lewis, Judge Lindsay, the groups that gather about the *American Mercury* and the *Nation,* are striving to transform the handsome, energetic children of American civilization into beings of a ripe and adult culture. We Europeans, in the meantime, have no right proudly and indifferently to disregard such problems as that in this book merely because our social morality is a trifle more mature. The world has become small and intimate and there has arisen a common responsibility which only the malignant reactionary dare repudiate. Lewisohn declares at the close of his story that he desired to appeal "to the heart of mankind itself." He shall not have made, nor would I willingly suffer him to have made, this appeal in vain.

Contents

Book One

ANNE

1 THE fortunes of her family, her mother's life and her own earlier years were among the things about which Mrs. Crump liked to talk. She did not do so very often. The hour had to be quiet; the children had to be, so far as she could tell, safe and contented. On such occasions, especially after a good dinner, Mrs. Crump would unfold her reminiscences. She was fond, at such times, of sitting in a low armchair, holding a book on her lap. She would take off her reading-glasses, which were at no time very steady on the small fleshy bridge of her nose and lay them on the book. In such hours she was, in her favorite phrase, "taking a little comfort." Her imperfectly hennaed hair would be carelessly wadded on the top of her head as it had been since morning; she would be dressed in a slightly soiled, preferably yellow kimono. A fleeting touch of peace in her gray eyes, a sense sometimes of the pathos of the past, would soften the lines of the sudden bunchy forepart of her nose and of her formidable jaw.

She seemed, especially in their later years, together, most human at such hours to Herbert Crump. The world of her reminiscences was an unfamiliar yet not an uninteresting world to him. He was her second husband and nearly twenty years her junior. This fact, of which there were an hundred irrefutable evidences, including the obvious ages of her children, Mrs. Crump had never admitted. She said that

3

she was nine years older than Mr. Crump. Under artificial light and in evening dress, well rested and not unskilfully made up, she would produce this mathematical misstatement suddenly, irrelevantly and loudly. At such moments it was not wholly incredible. She used and treasured and laid up these moments as though she meant some day to confront the world with their accumulated evidence. In her after-dinner home moods of quietude and reminiscence this hard effrontery of assertion dropped from her unconsciously. She did not name the names of years. But not as a matter of prudence. All things that had to do with numbers, save one only, were naturally vague in her mind. She talked out of a thick, characteristic world of tenacious memories.

With never varying satisfaction Mrs. Crump would picture the ancestral home of her mother's people, the Bronsons of Frankfort, Kentucky. They belonged, according to her, to the best people of the town. "There were the Bronsons, the Howards and the Jacksons," she used to say. There was a big roomy old-fashioned Southern house with great bins of sweet potatoes and apples. There was a meadow with sheep. The grandparents were indistinct. Somewhere in the picture appeared and reappeared a Major Guineau, a Southerner out of the picturesque past with long gray locks straggling from beneath a tall beaver hat, a belated white stock and a silken waistcoat. On economic questions Mrs. Crump was vague too. Her grandfather had a business that had something to do with "the locks," with "the levee." Boats on the Ohio River were mentioned, even on the Mississippi. Concrete facts began to emerge with the admitted degeneracy of the family in the generation of Mrs. Crump's mother. There was no money after the "wah." Mrs. Crump said "wah" with studied un-affectedness. The Bronson boys couldn't go to college. Joshua Bronson wandered to Chicago and became a sign-painter and paper-hanger. Poor Uncle Anthony had the worst luck of all. Climbing in his boy-hood after a neighbor's grapes he fell and a wire, according to Mrs. Crump, cut so deeply into his leg that it had to be amputated.

Thereafter Anthony Bronson wore a wooden leg and took to drinking out of discouragement. He, too, drifted to Chicago in the middle

4

sixties, married a washerwoman's half-witted daughter and begot two girls, Lou who was a moron and on the streets before sixteen and Josey whom, up to a certain day in 1908, Mrs. Crump called "poor little Josey—she was such a pretty girl," but since that certain day "that God-damned whore" . . .

Mrs. Crump idolized her mother. She treasured a daguerreotype taken about 1860 which showed a slim young woman in a black silk bonnet and a black silk gown with very tight bodice and very flaring crinoline. A long oval face, large eyes, pathetic yet determined; the unnaturally high forehead, narrow but domed, which gave to all the women of the Bronson blood the air of old men even in their girlhood, was carefully concealed. Of her mother's character Mrs. Crump would give at different times two contradictory reports. "Poor Mamma, she was gentle and yielding and always did what she thought was right. And did you ever hear of anyone who had a worse fate?" And again: "I'm all a mush of concession. Mamma had a will like steel. She always used to say to me: Anne, you let men put it all over you. You've got no sense of the dignity of your sex!" Herbert Crump had known old Mrs. Toohey, as she was then, during the last years of her life. He could not solve the contradiction. Neither did the many stories of his mother-in-law's earlier life help him to do so.

These stories were sad and sordid enough. At sixteen Anne Bronson had married a man named Cyrus, captain of a steamboat on the Mississippi. This was in 1850, ten years before Herbert Crump's father had been born. Cyrus, a roystering yet sullen brute of those rough days, had infected his young wife with syphilis. He learned that she was pregnant and promptly kicked her in the belly. She fled home to the Bronson house in Frankfort. Cyrus was never heard of again. Of her mother's life during the next twelve years Mrs. Crump had no account to give.

With the entrance of her father into the story Mrs. Crump would introduce a touch of romance. He was an Englishman named Farrel. The Farrels had been in England before the Conquest. John Farrel had been converted to the sect of the Agepemonites by the Earl of Norwich's daughter. Mrs. Crump had her own idea of the relations of those two. He appeared in Frankfort in the very early sixties, tall, handsome, English, with hair and beard prematurely white. He had had yellow fever in New Orleans and the disease had left him thus. What his precise business was Mrs. Crump didn't know. But he had always made money; he had always been lavish. Sometimes Mrs. Crump in her more human hours would reveal the suspicion that the Agepemonite connection had turned into a taste for occultism and the earliest type of faith healing, coupled with a magnetic influence over moneyed women. There was a pamphlet by John Farrel in the New York Public Library. Mrs. Crump had once pointed it out to Herbert in the card-catalogue. Its title was *Mind, the Master of the Body;* it had been printed in Cincinnati. Whether Anne Bronson ever told Farrel of the Cyrus episode is not known. It is perhaps not without significance that she and Farrel were not married at the Bronson house but at the home of Major Guineau. Immediately thereafter they sailed for England.

2   TWICE in the course of the years at moments when, in another favorite phrase, she was "outraging her own feelings," Mrs. Crump had swayed her body to and fro and tonelessly sung out: "I'm a bastard! I'm a bastard!" On all other occasions she left her parents' marriage in a decent obscurity dimly adorned by Major Guineau. In all her accounts of the past she combined a similar relish for coarse and vital facts with a stale but stubborn romanticism. Startling stories would come out concerning her uncles, Joshua and Anthony. Nevertheless they were represented as Southerners of the old blood-and-thunder chivalric tradition. "If the Bronson boys had heard a man say to a woman of their family what you've just said to *me,* Herbert Crump, they'd have filled him chuck full of lead!" . . .

Legally married or not, the Farrels had settled temporarily in England and there in a maternity hospital "on the Surrey side" Anne Bronson Farrel, later Anne Bronson Farrel Vilas Crump, was born early in 1862. "I was conceived in Covington, Kentucky," she was fond of saying, "and born in London, England." All through the years her English birth was a source of endless satisfaction to her. Though pretending to unpretentiousness and condemning, especially in her first husband and his family, snobbishness and false refinement by an appeal to what she called the "corned beef and cabbage" of life, Mrs. Crump never neglected an opportunity to declare that she was an Englishwoman. Many people, to be sure, did not need to be told. They had, according to her, at once observed that she "looked English." Herbert Crump had never met any such people. He took Anne's word for their existence. What he did know from immediate experience was this, that whenever colleagues or friends of his spoke French or German in Anne's presence, she would say with a harsh superciliousness rendered grotesque by ignorance: *"Je ne comprong pas; je swee oon Anglaise,"* or *"Ick nick versteh; ick bin einer Englaender."* . . .

The Farrels remained in England for four years. Old Mrs. Farrel-Toohey had once told Herbert with genuine feeling that she loved England and that the four years there had been the happiest of her life. To Anne the period was naturally a blank. Her earliest recollections were of the Bronson house in Frankfort, of her mother and herself there, of her mother's bitter tears because John Farrel was not there and because she herself was once more dependent, this time with a child, upon the charity of her relations. Though always rather gaily proud of her rascally father, Anne Crump was no less indignant over the wrongs her mother had suffered at his hands. "My earliest recollection is of poor Mamma crying because Father had left her. It darkened my whole childhood—that sense of wrong and division. No, no, every child is entitled to a father and a mother." Why Anne hadn't taken this lesson more practically to heart remained for years a mystery to Herbert Crump.

John Farrel seems to have reappeared intermittently, always suave, lavish, rather dashing, but never showing a desire to be united with his wife. The "Bronson boys" despite their reputed fiery sense of the honor of their family had obviously remained passive. When Anne was about six years old, however, Farrel had suddenly taken her mother and herself to New York. But there in rented rooms over a bakery in Greenwich Street he had soon abandoned the woman again and finally, but had spirited the child away and put her in charge of a Shaker colony in upper New York State. Poor Mrs. Farrel had naturally been frantic. She had, according to Anne Crump, fallen into a profound and desperate melancholy which had been mistaken for madness. She had been removed to a public asylum on Blackwell's Island. There she had tried to hang herself. A wild and sordid turbulence came to Herbert from this story, though his interpretation of it changed greatly in the course of time. "Poor Mamma," Mrs. Crump would murmur, "Did you ever *hear* of such a thing? Luckily Andrew Stone Stevens, a very rich and prominent New Yorker, had fallen in love with her. He asked Mamma to get a divorce and marry him. She wouldn't do it, of course." At this point Herbert would find it hard to suppress the obvious comment that Mrs. Farrel was not in a position to pursue such a course, her marriage to Farrel having no legal standing. But he would let Anne go on: "She wouldn't. Mamma was always so pure-minded; I think she was the purest woman I've ever known. Anyhow, Stevens helped to get her away from Blackwell's Island and helped her to find me. She was in love with him too. But she had such a high sense of duty. So she took me and we went back to Frankfort."

For two or three years thereafter Farrel had sent clothes and money for the child, who had been placed in an academy for girls and young ladies at Hagarville, Kentucky. There, Anne declared, she had been a universal favorite. She had been called "little English Annie;" she had publicly recited a poem by Phoebe Carey, who lived or had lived in that neighborhood; she had learned to play a little on the melodeon. She would sometimes exhibit a picture of herself taken at this period—a little tinted daguerreotype which showed a small girl in a white apron whose chin and forehead already bore evidences of an abnormal development, in whose eyes there was already a dull yet fiery and unseeing look, a look that was turned inward upon an ungovernable will. . . .

Abruptly the Farrel money had stopped coming. Years later it was discovered quite by accident that John Farrel had married again, as he was to do several times more. On two occasions in later years Mrs. Crump had come upon groups of half-sisters and brothers of varying ages in different sections of the country. In spite of her sympathy for her mother, she regarded her father's inveterate habit of marrying and procreating with humorous tolerance. That attitude had not yet arisen of course when, as little Anne Farrel, she had had to leave the pleasant school at Hagarville and had come back to Frankfort to see her mother the poor relation and drudge in a confused and impoverished house. She felt her mother's dependence and unhappiness keenly, suspected the slights and humiliations to which she was subjected and with childish enthusiasm embraced her mother's scheme of going to Chicago. In that city Anthony Bronson had set up a household now; there, in addition, lived a sister of Anne's grandmother Bronson, Aunt Effie, who was married for the second time to a Dr. McWhirter, originally of Philadelphia. It was indeed this aunt, Effie McWhirter, who wrote and asked poor Anne Farrel and her fatherless child to seek refuge in Chicago.

Mrs. Crump never in any set terms described the Chicago of 1872 or 3 to which she went with her mother. Nevertheless it seemed to Herbert Crump that he could see those endless flat streets of inhospitable wooden shanties, that he could feel the atmosphere of raw sensuality and stentorian cant, the very reek of liquor and the clamor of booming. He could visualize with intense precision a few of Anne's frankest and most characteristic anecdotes: the one, for instance, about a certain preacher and quack, Camillus P. Quimby, who, collared, booted, frock-coated, got up out of a wench's bed and said with an oratorical flourish: "Louisa, this is the cream of existence". . . .

9

3 THE McWhirters lived in a big bleak frame-house on a big bleak street. The house was scantily furnished, and what furniture there was, especially on the second or bedroom floor, was being constantly shifted about. People came into the house; people disappeared from it. Queer people: fat women in rusty widows' weeds, heavily moustached men with pasty, pimply faces. Dr. McWhirter believed in vegetarianism, free love, magnetic healing and brotherhood. The people who drifted in and out were patients and fellow-believers. No one was ever asked to pay for bed or board or treatment. McWhirter got a small stipend from his family in Philadelphia, Mrs. McWhirter one hundred dollars a month from the sons by her first marriage in Dayton. Whatever his faults "Doc" was careless of worldly goods. Every morning he could be seen in his tall gray beaver hat with long ill-cut hair straggling out, clad in his shabby frock coat, setting out with a huge basket on his arm. He went to buy vegetables and stale bread for his house. His long scrawny figure leaned forward; his nose seemed to reach out scenting and estimating the world.

At breakfast, an hour later, there were eleven people. There was a new guest, a tearful youngish woman. Doc grasped her and pressed her close to him. "Sister, have you been true to me?" The forlorn female wept. A belligerent light came into Doc's small gray eyes. "Aha!" he shouted. "What you need is a change of polarity. Get up your positive, you slut! There, that's better, sister." Mrs. McWhirter would interpose. "Leave the sister alone, Doc; she's just lost her husband." "I know that, Effie." He did, in fact, have unexpectedly intuitive perceptions. "That's the reason I'm going to polarize her." Polarization, getting up the positive—these were Doc's cure-alls. He had once, if his account was to be believed, gone to the bedside of a man paralyzed for years. He had stigmatized the man and his female ancestors to the third generation in the foulest terms. The man had "gotten up his positive" and walked out of the room. "Be positive!" Doc would yell in his exuberant moods. "As for me, sir, I'm going to raise hell at my own funeral." A later anecdote had it that McWhirter made good his threat. The hearse that carried him lost a wheel; the coffin burst open; his thin dead lips curled in a wild ironic grin.

People wondered why the small, neat, apparently refined Effie Mc-Whirter had ever married the Doc; why she endured his eccentricity and grossness. Her sons in Dayton were profoundly chagrined by the connection. Yet it was precisely for the sake of her sons' good repute and peace of mind that Aunt Effie—Mrs. Crump would always lower her voice at this point—put up with Doc McWhirter. He had known her in Dayton; he had prowled about the house; he had come upon her and the handsome mulatto coachman in an unmistakable situation. The year was 1868. Poor Effie Roche became McWhirter's slave. She had to marry him and endure him. Mrs. Crump, who never put two and two together, did not dream that this anecdote confirmed Herbert in his suspicion of something coarse and violent in all the women of her blood.

Since the McWhirter house was a sort of inn at which one did not pay anyhow, it was easy enough for Effie McWhirter to invite her niece and grandniece to share its hospitality. They were given a room and their portion of stale bread and beans and vegetables. Doc took a fancy to the precocious child, talked to her, made her accompany him on his foraging expeditions. He hired a melodeon and to Anne's halting performance of two hymn tunes gave mediumistic seances. A medium, a woman of enormous girth, joined the lodgers in the crowded house. Her daughter, an over-developed girl of fifteen, shared Anne's bed and kept the child awake with her violent indulgence in shameless practices. Between Mrs. Farrel and McWhirter there sprang up an open enmity. Doc took coarse liberties with her under his pretense of polarization and she slapped his face. In consequence the mother and daughter would occasionally take temporary refuge with the Anthony Bronsons. But that household was lodged in three small rooms in an alley. Lydia Bronson took in washing, one of the few facts in all her stories that Mrs. Crump spoke of with harsh contempt and open shame. Lou, four years older than Anne, was already sneaking out to meet rough boys; Josey, a blonde cherub-faced child of four, ruled the others with her strident whining. Anthony Bronson, perpetually discouraged by his wooden leg, was perpetually in liquor. He would come home late, catch Lou trying to steal back into the house and beat her for her goings-on with evident enjoyment of his horny fist's pounding her young flesh. Then he would turn maudlin. "Sister Anne, I know I ain't no good. I know it. But look at me with this piece o' wood for a leg. An' look at that fool Lydia and her brat. But Sister Anne, I'm going to reform; I'm goin' to be a man. Give me your hand, Sister Anne; give it to me! I want to promise; I want to swear. Gonna be a *man* from now on." After that he would snore.

Aunt Effie would make peace again. McWhirter was both forgetful and placable and the Farrels, mother and daughter, would return to that precarious and uneasy caravansary. They had no alternative. For there was no money and Mrs. Farrel had no skill with which to earn any. She was, in addition, tormented by both neuralgia and hemorrhoids. Mrs. Crump always spoke of her mother's ill-health and practical helplessness as though they were marks of distinction. They pointed at all events, as Herbert Crump used to reflect, to one way out—parasitism on some male creature. The man, John Toohey, turned up in the McWhirter circle. He was twelve years younger than Mrs. Farrel and what attracted him to her must always remain obscure. To have asked Anne Crump would have been worse than useless. To her it was axiomatic that the bestowal of her mother's favors or her own on any man was—despite wrinkles, poverty, inefficiency, hemorrhoids—a gift that in its preciousness transcended discussion or appraisal. Of the favors of all other women, especially the young, the charming and the kind, she spoke with a sour and ugly sneer. Toohey was not, to be sure, overwhelmingly victimized. Mrs. Farrel's legal status would not bear close inspection. Doc McWhirter believed in "free love." So Anne Bronson Farrel and John Toohey went through some sort of a ceremony in the McWhirter parlor, Mrs. Farrel became nominally Mrs. Toohey and she and her daughter were, at least temporarily, provided for.

Toohey was modestly prosperous at this time. He had made an invention on which somebody had given him an advance; the family lived in decent comfort; Anne went to school. But this period was brief. The advance came to an end; the three people moved into two bare rooms. Toohey, with his last few dollars, laid in a huge supply of oatmeal and smoked herrings. On this food they lived for very many weeks. Never again in life could Anne Crump endure the sight or smell of either. So lodged and so nourished she had entered high school in 1874, determined to wrest a better life from the world for both her mother and herself.

4 HERBERT CRUMP, becoming more and more aware in later years of the existence of moral evil, of the reality of the conflict between God and the Devil staged by Persian and Christian in the universe, used to reflect that during her years at high school evil had the least power over Anne Farrel's soul. Her indomitableness was directed toward good ends. She had already eagerly read all printed matter that came her way; she had formed a special devotion for a tattered copy of Bryant's *Library of Poetry and Song* which, unaccountably enough, the half illiterate John Toohey brought into the household. She elected the classical course in high school, struggled determinedly with her Greek and Latin grammars, joined the literary and debating society, began to express the pain of her longings and of her isolation in verse.

Her isolation was largely due to her poverty. John Toohey disappeared and reappeared. His contributions to the family's support became more and more slender and sporadic. Anne and her mother lived in two wretched rooms, cold, draughty, bare. A bed and a few boxes was all their furniture. Mrs. Toohey, tormented by her old ailments, would sit propped up in bed laboriously sewing. Frankfort relations, probably the Roches, sent Anne the cast-off clothes of their somewhat older and much bigger daughters, the grandchildren of

13

Effie McWhirter. Mrs. Toohey would make these garments over so that Anne could present a decent appearance in school. Food was scarce and what there was was coarse, and Anne would be grateful when a neighbor, a Czech woman, invited her in to have a hot sweet apple-dumpling.

This was a severe period for mother and daughter. At last Mrs. Toohey had to sell the few simple gold things that Farrel had given her. For some time Anne went on weekly errands to the pawnshops of Chicago. She went on other and more corrupting errands for her mother. Word would somehow come that Toohey had money again and was staying at the Palmer House. Mrs. Toohey would burst out in unmeasured indignation and send Anne to the man's lodging. Anne, though she shared her mother's sense of wrong, was too astute to show it. She played upon the fact that Toohey was attracted by her slender adolescence; she let him hold her on his lap and pet her and so she wheedled money out of him. "The money is for you," he used to say. "You're a flower on a dunghill." Throughout this episode Anne was strictly loyal to her mother. She despised Toohey. But she found that she could manage men.

What, listening to this part of Mrs. Crump's narrative, Herbert could never quite understand, was the fierce claim upon John Toohey which Anne's mother and Anne herself conceived themselves as possessing. That there had been no legal marriage was, to be sure, a detail meaningless in itself. But that there had been no deep and abiding affection on either side of this loose union—so much was clear enough. Nor had a child been born of it. What, then, had this middle-aged woman, twice married, twice abandoned before, given John Toohey that obliged him either to live with her or to pay her tribute? But this was another of those points that to the mind of Mrs. Crump transcended discussion. She conveyed to Herbert, on the other hand, a picture of Mrs. Toohey sitting up in a soiled bed in that forlorn Chicago room, her long face with that monstrous Bronson forehead prematurely colorless and withered now, cursing John Toohey and with him the whole race of faithless and lecherous men. . . .

Anne, aged fourteen, fifteen, sixteen, trudged to high school through the bitter lake-winds of the Chicago winters. She had made up her mind that she was going to be a writer, establish a reputation and make money and save her mother from the cruelties of a manmade, man-ruled world. She was drawn to a boy in school now and then, but these fleeting attractions meant little to her. Her confidante and best friend then and for years thereafter was Hattie McCune, a small, dark, gay creature who meant to be an actress, who had run away from a stodgy government clerk's home in Washington and had a vast admiration for Anne's literary ability. The two girls would sit in Thompson's restaurant, watch flashy men ogle them and speculate on art and life and love.

The strain of poverty was very great all during this period. But during her last year in high school Anne got a job to serve on afternoons, on evenings and on Saturday in a candyshop. In Chicago in 1879, six dollars a week was a great help. Of course Anne had to buy her own clothes now; the things from Frankfort had long stopped coming; both Effie and Doc McWhirter had died. Mrs. Crump, with one of the few touches of remorse that ever troubled the hard surface of her self-righteousness, would tell how she had once during those far-off Chicago days, although her mother needed both linen and medicine, spent the whole of her weekly wage for a pink satin waist to wear to a dance. She went to the dance with the proprietor of the candyshop. She could have gone oftener and with others. Even the principal of the school made much of her. She could wheedle more and more money out of John Toohey. She discovered that she was more and more attractive to men.

Anne could never have been pretty. The Bronson forehead could be covered, of course. And in her girlhood she had a great quantity of soft blonde hair. But the blunt and too knoblike forepart of her nose, the harsh insensitive jaw could never have been more than softened, even by the bloom of girlhood. But she was slim, quick in her movements and a good dancer. More than that: on her particular social level she was better read, more nimble of mind, more quick of wit than the men with whom she came in contact. Dull gross clerks and businessmen on a small scale saw in her a being superior to themselves. She led them around by the nose. Still unconscious of her own exorbitant passions, she had a strong sexual magnetism for men. Since at this time she was unawakened, she remained unscathed. But the habit of easy dominance over inferior men established at this period hardened her natural vanity and her axiomatic acceptance of the right of the female of the species to a perpetual and merciless parasitism.

It was not, of course, in such terms that Mrs. Crump spoke of her girlhood. According to her she had been amazingly pretty. She would look long and thoughtfully at her daughter Luella and say slowly: "Oh yes, I was as pretty as Luella." And that on her lips meant a great deal. For Herbert never knew her to admit that any woman in the world was pretty except Luella. "Pretty?" Mrs. Crump would say with a heavily judicial air. "No, I wouldn't call her pretty. Nice-looking? Yes. But not pretty. Whom do I consider pretty? My Luella is pretty."

No, it was Herbert who fumblingly putting two and two together figured out the true account of Anne's girlhood. He was or tried to be just in all his ultimate reflections concerning her. There must have been in her in those old days, years before he was born, a flame of aspiration. But only an easy mental and sexual superiority on a low plane of competition could have brought into being an arrogance, a vanity as steely and as unmotivated in any reality as Anne Crump's.

5   THE years between her graduation from high school and her first marriage were always telescoped in Mrs. Crump's reminiscences. Except for the immediate family, those years were in fact not supposed to exist. To all friends and acquaintances of her later years Mrs. Crump declared with a coy confidentialness that she had run away with her first husband at the age of fourteen and that

her son and eldest child, Bronson, had been born when she was fifteen. Only so could the existence and undeniable maturity of her son be reconciled with the statement that she was only nine years older than Herbert. Her marriage to Harrison Vilas must actually have occurred in 1884 and the telescoped years must have numbered about six.

To the life and activities of those years evidence enough slipped out in anecdote and reminiscence. Anne Farrel had not remained long in the candyshop. She had answered advertisements in the Chicago papers and had become a copyholder in the composing-rooms of the Henneberry Press. Her quickness of wit, her wide reading and her sex magnetism had their usual effect on the foreman and she was soon—it was an open shop, of course—advanced to the position of proofreader. She began to write in earnest now and sold a number of sketches and sets of comic verses to an obscure newspaper of those days. For a short time she was engaged to a young man named Fred Slicer. But the two quarrelled at a dance and drifted apart. Anne was, in fact, just then more interested in her ambitions than in men. She caught the fever of the stage from her friend Hattie McCune. The two young women sat night after night in the galleries of the Chicago theaters; they went to vaudeville try-outs and Hattie almost got a chance to "go on" in her Negro monologues; they haunted stage-doors and got the autographed pictures of prominent actors. Anne, if the report is to be believed, was actually offered a small part in the company of Lawrence Barrett by Barrett himself. Instead of taking it, she eloped with Vilas.

Throughout these years she supported her mother, though she saw to it that John Toohey contributed a certain share. The man was now obscurely but definitely in love with her. He had a superstitious dread of making his feeling manifest, except by letting Anne persuade him to kindnesses to her mother and insisting that they were done exclusively for the daughter's sake. Once or twice at this time Anne had brief contacts with the seamier and more terrifying sides of Chicago life. It was when she went out with her cousin, Josey Bronson. Josey was seventeen. The Bronson forehead was modified in her; it had the bulge but not the monstrous height. Her chin was round and soft, her gray eyes were large; she was blonde and white and pink. Since one night in her fifteenth year her father in one of his drunken fits had first beaten her and then tried to attack her, she had refused to go either to school or to work. Some ultimate inner resistance kept her from following her sister Lou into the streets. But she hung around hotel lobbies and let drummers treat her. On one such occasion Anne had been with her, but had drunk less and so escaped in time. Josey had lost consciousness and had awakened at noon next day stripped to the skin in a room in an entirely different hotel. . . .

Perhaps Anne, in spite of her decent employment and her intermittent writing, feared the drag of her environment upon her ever more eager senses. Perhaps it was because John Toohey, who now had a fairly prosperous butter and egg shop, was persuaded to take her mother to live with him again and thus freed her from an unescapable responsibility. Perhaps there were still other reasons lost or forgotten in the turmoil of the years that had made Anne run off so precipitately with Harrison Vilas. For she always declared that she had never truly loved the man, that then as in later life—to use her own words—he had given her the shadow for the substance. "Poor Harry," she used to muse, "there was always something unreal about everything connected with him." Herbert Crump came to suspect one never admitted but commanding motive. Mrs. Crump hated all of the relations of her first husband. Yet she bragged of them incessantly. Old Mr. Vilas had been a superintendent in the fiscal department of New York. Old Mrs. Vilas had been a Miss Dubose of a good French Huguenot family. Harrison's sister was married to the son of a famous philologist. The MacDavid cousins were rich and had their own box at the opera. Yes, Herbert thought he could see Anne trying to climb out of the sordidness of her own family and environment into a fairer, cleaner, richer world. Of course Mrs. Crump would never have thought of admitting this motive. An iron instinct forbade her to admit anything that could be construed as a diminution of her condescension to any member of the male sex. She, if you please, was an Englishwoman and the upstart namby-pambiness of the Vilases and MacDavids and Duboses had always made her literally sick at her stomach and her mother had characterized it as excreting—only that was not the exact word—"through a quill." When Harrison Vilas fell into one of his fits of feeble fastidiousness old Mrs. Toohey had been in the habit of saying: "Well, Anne, he is a sweet-smelling geranium now, isn't he?" In spite of all that, Mrs. Crump went on bragging of "the children's relations."

She insisted on the other hand, partly because she really believed it, partly to bring home to Herbert his lack of personal advantages and hence the measure of her condescension to him, that Harrison Vilas had been very handsome. "Not so handsome as Bronson," she would say, "but still very handsome." She had never told with any exactness how she and Vilas had met. Their meeting had evidently been as sudden as the consequent infatuation was violent. Vilas was ten years older than Anne and was an accountant in the Chicago offices of the Continental Harvester Company. There seemed no good reason for either concealment or haste. But Vilas insisted on both and as he seemed so much more the man of the world, so much better bred and better educated than the other men whom Anne had known, she yielded to his pleading. They took the train for Madison, Wisconsin, where, in a chance parsonage, Anne Bronson Farrel became Mrs. Harrison Dubose Vilas.

What followed immediately Mrs. Crump told once only. A lingering tenderness for Harry Vilas would come over her at many moments, especially after his death. But various allusions and definite consequences bore out the truth of that single confession. The marriage between Anne and Vilas had scarcely been consummated when Vilas told his bride that he had embezzled a sum of money from his employers. He had staked the money "on the ponies" and had lost it. He would have to wire for help to his father before he dared to return to Chicago. In any event, he would naturally be out of a job. Herbert knew Bronson Vilas; he knew this man's son and he could strongly and precisely imagine the confession made in that hotel-room in Madison, Wisconsin: the feeble self-pity and the even feebler braggardism, the falsely lofty assumption that the matter was trivial and the quaking terror, the lowering finally of the smooth, pointed, foxlike head into the lap of the woman who protested a forgiveness which she did not wholly feel. . . .

6   HELP came from the Vilas family as it had often come before at similar crises in Harrison's life. He was not, it seems, addicted to a very gay life; he was not actively dishonest; he was never intemperate. He frequented billiard-rooms a good deal, but as a sober and skilful player. He had a mild but genuine taste for literature, even for poetry; this was one of the things that had drawn him and Anne together. He was a refined person and to all appearances an inoffensive one. Yet these losses of money, his own or other people's, were always happening to him. For a man without a single robust vice, he had just dodged open disaster and dishonor with singular frequency. He had a gift for psychological analysis too. In a comfortable chair, his long bony feet crossed on a near-by couch, a long, thin, good cigar between the sensuous effeminate lips that softened the foxlikeness of his small pointed head, Harrison Vilas could show precisely how, small lucklessness by small lucklessness, his latest misfortune had stolen upon him. He always had an excuse. It was always a good excuse. And he was profoundly sincere in the establishment of these moral alibis. Yet he must have had an obscure fear that, in the two years just preceding his marriage to Anne, his record had been too constantly unhappy for his father's patience. Herbert Crump at least always suspected that the purpose of the hasty marriage had been to use an innocent young wife as both plea and shield.

The couple returned to Chicago where, through the MacDavid connection, another and better position was found for Harrison Vilas.

They moved into an apartment on the North side. Anne soon knew that she would be a mother. Despite that initial shadow of catastrophe, life could not have been all bitterness. Vilas loved Anne and there was much about him that she liked and admired. She embraced, furthermore, with a touch of ethical unction, the task of saving him from his habit of skirting disaster. Yet in the later years Mrs. Crump had little to say of the early days of her first marriage, but expatiated broadly on the turmoil and horror of its subsequent periods. What was always clear to Herbert, though he was silent on this point as on so many others, was that nothing more corrupting than such a beginning to her marriage could have happened to Anne. She never respected Vilas; she had a weapon against him from the start. There was nothing to interfere with her belief in herself, with the iron supremacy of her will. If Vilas opposed her, blamed her, corrected her, she had but to show him by a look in her eyes that he had tricked her into marrying a thief, a fugitive from justice. Though he may have been, on any special occasion, a thousand times in the right, Anne had made herself initially impervious to granting it. And this attitude of hers corrupted Vilas equally. What restraint, what discipline, what belated manliness might have been brought him by the sense of having to protect the girl he had married—all this was likewise lost. But a protective, a shielding attitude toward Anne was always, in truth, an unthinkable thing. You cannot protect an engine. It goes over you or you hide behind it and let it go over others. Vilas, in harmony with his past and his character chose the second alternative. With this result, that Mrs. Crump asserted, without fear of contradiction, that all men were cowards, though they would like immensely to be bullies and that she for her part, in the words of her sainted mother, was not afraid of the face of clay. . . .

In the homeopathic division of the Cook County Hospital Bronson Vilas was born toward the end of the year 1886. It was the first of the many hospital experiences which Mrs. Crump would discuss in great detail and with a kind of bitterish satisfaction. According to her all hospitals were ill-run and all nurses careless and immoral hussies. The point of all her anecdotes was how she, by her charm and wit, had transcended these conditions even from her bed of sickness and had secured the vigilant attention of some visiting physician or, preferably, of some young intern. With a laugh half sly and half coy she would declare always in the same tone: "I do believe he was half in love with me." This announcement, which may once have held a shadow of truth, sat ever more ill upon her as the years made her increasingly harsh of temper and aspect. On that first occasion, at all events, she had "virtually saved the baby's life" by flinging a scalding hot water-bottle, which would inevitably have been Bronson's death, across the ward, and had astonished the entire institution by the fortitude and wisdom of one so young.

It was one of Mrs. Crump's favorite assertions that no woman is sexually awakened until after the birth of her first child. Such, then, must have been her own experience. The results complicated life severely. As the story of these complications leaked out in the course of the later years, during which Mrs. Crump seemed ever more to lose in shame and reticence, Herbert used to be filled with a horror-stricken wonder at fundamental facts in human life which no novelist revealed, which even physicians would not permit themselves to discuss. Harrison Vilas' salary in those Chicago days was about eighteen dollars and fifty cents a week. The purchasing power of money was considerable then. Nevertheless another child and another would have meant catastrophe. Not to a workingman with the same wage perhaps. But Harrison was excessively genteel in his tastes and outlook. He didn't bathe very often, but he made a querulous and endless scene if the napery at dinner wasn't spotless. Anne, who had for the greater part of her life been used to no napery at all was, despite her rancorous protest, impressed by his fastidiousness. Although, moreover, she always succeeded in presenting a good appearance in public, she was an even more inveterate sloven than her husband. Herbert could easily imagine what were the facilities for personal cleanliness in the wretched rented rooms in the Chicago of the seventies and early eighties in which she had passed her adolescence and girlhood. From the habits acquired there she never re-covered.

Dirt, genteel tastes, eighteen dollars and a half a week and power-ful passions! Slowly, in the course of time, the appallingness of the combination came home to Herbert's mind. It was impossible to let all the children be born. Yet there was no knowledge of even the simplest contraceptive methods and Anne was too slovenly and lazy even to get up to wash. Too happy-go-lucky. She had something of a gambler's hardness and freedom from immediate care. Two glasses of beer and to bed. The rest was left to take care of itself. It didn't, in fact. With the inevitable result of a long series of abortions, some brought about by surgical interference and politely called curettages, others effected by a plentiful use of quinine and gin. Nevertheless Luella was born in 1892 and Eileen in 1897. Anne had done her best to prevent the birth of her youngest child. But nature had been stub-born. She was fond for some strange reason of telling how her mother had besought her over and over again to let—these were Mrs. Toohey's exact words—"to let the poor little fœtus alone!"

In her reminiscences Mrs. Crump treated these events and situa-tions as natural, as matters of course. Herbert would tingle with a vicarious shame. She had none. Where, dimly, she perceived the possibility of a reproach, she bragged and gloried and brazened the matter out. She would adopt what Herbert, who was fond of the older English novelists, would call her "Marry, come up!" attitude—the physical attitude behind the typical gesture of the eighteenth cen-tury, the Hogarthian wench: chin thrust forward, hair dishevelled, arms akimbo. "What, darn your socks? I never yet darned socks for any man! Why, Jesus Christ, I don't darn my own stockings. Why don't you make money and hire servants, God damn you!" And Her-bert, having heard all the stories, would wonder whence Anne got her notions of having servants to do all those human and useful and honorable things which, with a contemptuous scowl, she lumped to-gether under the invariable phrase of "dirty work."

7 Soon after Luella's birth, in the year of the Chicago World's Fair, Harrison Vilas either grew restive or was once more guilty of an irregularity toward his employers. He had to make a change. His position had always indeed been precarious. He insisted on "playing the races." Yet not, significantly enough, because he had the gambler's feverish passion. But his weekly wage could not be made to suffice. The family was always in debt to the grocer, the butcher, the furniture installment man, and always in arrears with rent. How many house-owners and real-estate agents and rent collectors did not Anne Vilas wheedle and put off in the course of the years! Always when everything was at its worst, Harrison Vilas would take his week's salary and try his luck with the ponies. Once, years before his marriage, he had "made a haul." It strengthened in him that tenacious hope of a miracle by which pretentious mediocrity expects to escape what it holds to be the injustice of its fate. Herbert Crump had watched the same process in Bronson Vilas a hundred times and understood it. Mrs. Crump attributed all the economic miseries of her first marriage to the fact that "poor Harry Vilas was a gambler." Yet she admitted that he gambled largely out of despair and also that, ordinarily, except for a necessary pittance, he had given her his salary on every Saturday afternoon. It would have been quite useless to have asked Mrs. Crump why she hadn't then made the money suffice? A plan or a budget or the denial of any eager, trivial appetite on the part of the children—such things were inconceivable to her. "The money was spent, wasn't it? I didn't hoard it, you know. It was spent for the family. It wasn't my fault that it wasn't enough. If ever I got a check for a poem, I used to buy the children clothes with the money."

On the precise happenings of 1892 she was not clear. A position was found for Vilas in San Diego, California, whither he proceeded, leaving his family for the time in Chicago. Anne had a pleasant life for some months. John Toohey, steadfast in his old liking for her, took her and little Bronson to the Fair once or twice a week, while her mother looked after the baby. Anne did her best to stabilize the relations between her mother and Toohey, who no longer pretended to

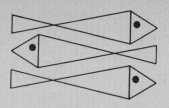

Farrar, Straus & Giroux, Inc.

*takes pleasure
in sending you this copy
for review*
THE CASE OF MR. CRUMP

by
Ludwig Lewisohn

Publication Date: November 20, 1965

Price: $5.50
           $2.25 - paper
           (N 284)

Two clippings of your review will be greatly appreciated

like the woman with whom he had intermittently lived for so long, nor to be true to her. The daughter was at once peacemaker and beneficiary and the World's Fair remained one of the golden spots in her reminiscences. But suddenly Harrison Vilas returned. Mrs. Crump never explained why. He had liked San Diego. The soft climate had suited him. He had picked up a few words of Spanish of which always thereafter he made in a quiet, refined, affected manner a great display. Bronson had later caught this trick from his father and gave himself a little bumptious air of false superiority and refinement of taste by declaring Spanish to be such a beautiful language. *"Buenas noches,"* he would say with a pronunciation entirely peculiar to himself. "Now isn't that beautiful?" And Mrs. Crump would regard this performance with a fond and devoted pride. For Herbert's thorough and exact mastery of several languages she reserved the contemptuous superiority of the "born Englishwoman."

On one feature of Harrison Vilas' return from San Diego Mrs. Crump was harshly, copiously, inveterately specific. He had faced her on their first night together with the confession that he dared not touch her. He had an uncured case of gonorrhea. How characteristic that was of the Vilas men! Harrison hadn't fallen in love with any one; he hadn't even been under the dominance of a powerful physical passion. He had simply lingered too long with indifferent men in a barroom and had drifted thence into a bawdy house. He hadn't meant to be untrue to Anne; he loved no one but her; he was in fact a devoted husband and father. He had been unfortunate. That was all. With the scale of ethical values involved in this presentation of his case Anne seemed, on the whole, to be in agreement. "Well," she said on more than one occasion, "at least poor Harry Vilas never looked at another woman. I will say that much for him. I'm accustomed to being wanted, not to chasing after a mere man." Yet she would in quite the same breath dwell on that old incident with an almost triumphant vindictiveness. "I swore I'd get even with him. And I did. There's something of the Indian in me." She could, in brief, never endure any slight to her naked sex esteem. Her power to command

25

such esteem or to deserve it she never questioned. As a slovenly and withered woman of nearly sixty, beset by some of the ugliest infirmities of age, her ferocity in this matter was as unmeasured as it had been in the days of her youth and her young motherhood.

Chicago and San Diego having both now failed him, the Vilases and MacDavids bestirred themselves once more for "poor Harry." He was made an accountant in the New York offices of the National Cigar Company and funds were found to transport him and his family to New York. Life ought now to have gone better. There was a clear start. The salary was higher. Anne, who had kept up her omnivorous reading and occasional writing, was in a position to meet any of Vilas' relations and their friends on an at least equal footing. But this did not suffice her. A harsh truculence of spirit, which she mistook for sturdy indepedence, made it impossible for her, then or thereafter, to be on cordial terms with any woman she could not patronize, or any man who did not play with her the game of sexual admiration. Of wealth her envy was so bitter and profound that she instinctively and systematically insulted people who had money, without any regard for their human qualities or even for their possible usefulness to herself. Hence the Vilases were as isolated in New York as they had been in Chicago. They attended a Unitarian church but had no social relations with other parishioners. Anne Vilas finally allied herself with certain movements toward the spread of popular culture. But this was not until about 1900 when Eileen, her youngest child, was three years old.

The family's move to New York had one immediate and untoward result. John Toohey definitely and brutally turned Anne's mother into the streets and there was nothing for the Vilases to do but take the old woman in. While her mother's presence in the house was not disagreeable to Anne personally, it was intensely exasperating to Harrison. A guerilla warfare sprang up between these two. He thought Mrs. Toohey downright vulgar with her quaint and drastic vocabulary and her habit of smoking cigar-stumps to ease, as she thought, her neuralgic pains. She thought him a weakling and an affected ass. Each of these two was correct about the other. Anne, of course, sided undeviatingly with her mother. The sense of psychical turmoil in the house did not annoy her. In fact, she rather throve on it. But Harrison had a better excuse than ever for spending his evenings in billiard-rooms and for his periodical flights to the intoxication and promise of the "ponies."

Life settled down into a routine of meanness and disorder. In the eleven years between 1892 and 1903, the Vilases moved nineteen times, usually because they were put out for nonpayment of rent. The children had but one set of winter undergarments each, and Anne had to wash these out every Saturday night and dry them on the radiators of some dim, old-fashioned telescope flat. But nothing could teach this couple prudence or the curbing of certain desires. At Christmas enough money was spent to have normalized the family's finances for months. Occasionally even Anne went to the races. Tradesmen were cheated, rent-collectors were put off. The children were noisy and disobedient. Anne was violently partial to Bronson, Harrison to Luella. When evening came the husband went to a billiard-room, the wife to a gallery-seat in some theater. In the kitchen, on a pile of dirty linen, sucking a cigar-stump, sat Mrs. Toohey, more and more like a huge old bird of ill-omen prophesying doom. . . .

8   ONE incident only broke the clamorous monotony of the years. It was the incident by means of which Anne began to "get even" with Harrison Vilas. As usual there was a doctor in the offing. He had done something to Anne's cervix. She would describe this something at length. On all physiological matters she was and remained knowingly voluble and relentless. Dr. Vogel, a homeopath of course, fell in love with Anne. A time came when Herbert no longer trusted Mrs. Crump's version of this affair. It was too much like an allegory with the moral directed at him. But for a long time he accepted the legend in all its spurious nobility. Dr. Vogel, then,

27

fell in love with Anne Vilas during the period of his attention to her cervix. She also felt herself strongly drawn toward him. And she was world-weary. There had been successive distressments for rent within the past six months; there had been constant recourse to the "ponies." The family's misery was so extreme that Dr. Vogel had taken Bronson out with him and bought him a suit of clothes, so that the growing boy could continue to go to school without open shame. The Vilases were always from time to time the beneficiaries of such charitable acts. Anne was usually ill on such occasions and couldn't help herself; Harrison pretended loftily to be unobservant. Later he would curse the impudence of the benefactor of the moment.

Anne was at home recovering. She had still to lie in bed. Dr. Vogel would drop in daily. One day, except for Mrs. Toohey in the kitchen, they found themselves alone in the flat and succumbed to the temptation of their mutual attraction. At once, according to Mrs. Crump, Dr. Vogel urged her to leave her wretched home and come with him. He would arrange everything; he would be a father to her children. But Anne, though she was so unhappy in her own life and truly cared for the doctor, refused. For had he not a wife and four children of his own? And did not duty come first? Far be it from her to break up another woman's home! Not only did the lovers part forever. But Anne made Dr. Vogel promise to confess to his wife. She herself confessed to Harrison. In what terms she did not relate. But since she had promised herself, at the bidding of the "Indian" within her to "get even" with Harrison, it is not to be supposed that she was a crushed or repentant woman. Harrison sped to the minister of their Unitarian church on lower Fourth Avenue and told his story. But since that dry and precise but not unreasonable cleric had already listened to Anne's version and knew all about the distressments for rent and the "ponies" and had procured free scholarships in a good school for the children, he counselled mutual forgiveness and a new start.

There was, of course, no new start. With the perspective of the years upon these matters, Mrs. Crump would indulge in musings concerning the thanklessness of an ethical attitude in such a world as the present, men being what they were. Harrison did not reform. In her there was—as she called heaven and earth and the very relations-in-law who hated her to witness—no fault or shortcoming to be found. It was her own and her mother's ideal to keep the house "neat as a pin." But what could one do if one was forever moving and had no sense of permanence anywhere? In how many flats had she not settled the family in the hope of better things? In vain. Yes, she believed in children being orderly and obedient, though not in the use of force or of corporal punishment. But what could one do in that demoralized life? Harry was willing to waste money on Luella. But she had to buy Bronson his suits of clothes on the partial payment plan. The boy had no collars and when he suddenly grew tall and could wear his father's, whose pointed head sat jauntily on a very thin neck, there were furious quarrels between father and son. "I had two fresh collars!" Harrison would fairly scream in the morning. "There's only one here now!" Anne would be repressed and taunting. "I suppose Bronson borrowed one to go to school in. You won't buy him any of his own." "And how am I to go to business? I'm a disgrace now with this one suit of clothes to my back! What becomes of the money in this God-damned house is a mystery to me anyhow!" "Oh, is it?" Anne's sneer would become bitter: "Maybe if you made a little more and your beautiful relations would get you a real job and you were man enough to hold it down and if you didn't hang around billiard-rooms and race-tracks—" At this point Harrison would interrupt her with a yell. "Leave my relations alone! Maybe if we didn't have that disgraceful old Toohey woman on our backs—" But here he stopped short in his turn. For Anne's face had a way of hardening that was ominous. Harrison would dart back into the dim depths of the flat, strike Bronson full and brutally across the face, tear the collar from the boy's very throat and stalk out of the house for a good breakfast at a restaurant.

How well Herbert Crump could reconstruct and visualize these scenes from Mrs. Crump's fragmentary but numerous hints and indications and from his knowledge of the people who were concerned in them. And there were two other anecdotes out of the many that she told that seemed to him more and more as time crept on to symbolize and sum up the life of Anne's first marriage, as well as something strange and fatal in the character of Anne herself.

It was a gray day in mid-winter. There had been a scene before breakfast. Luella was at home with a sore throat. She was a large ungainly child of nine and lounged and stumbled disconsolately about the disordered flat. Her hair was down and tangled; she had a rag about her throat. She clamored loudly or wept feebly because she could find no stockings to put on. Eileen, then three, was seriously ill and had been put to bed on the couch in the parlor. Anne was devoting herself exclusively to her youngest who, in another of her favorite phrases, "needed her most." The bell rang and rang again. Then there was a rough knocking at the door. They knew it was the grocer, who had come himself to collect a bill incredibly overdue. They let him ring and knock and finally heard him stamping heavily down the stairs and shouting insults through the hall. Bronson came home from school with a long strident tale of partiality to others and of injustice to himself, into which Anne entered passionately. Mrs. Toohey criticised Bronson's report at some point and Anne turned with sudden ferocity upon her mother. The day grew darker; Luella's throat was sorer; Eileen's temperature rose. It was almost time for Harrison to come home and sniff fastidiously at the flat with its faint sour odor of sickness and slovenliness. Across the floor of the parlor slunk the gray cat which was the children's pet. Suddenly Mrs. Toohey, among whose failings mercilessness to man and beast had no place, darted forward with a gaunt and eerie gesture and caught the cat by the tail. She tore open the door of the flat, rushed into the hall and flung the beast down the dim hard stairs. . . .

That spring Anne and Harrison in a mood of reconciliation were taking a walk on Saturday afternoon. They went into a butcher's shop and bought a large and expensive porterhouse steak for the family dinner that evening. It was an extravagance, but their mood was mild and festive. One the way home a trivial disagreement arose between them. Harrison quoted his sister in his support. Anne answered with a taunt. In a moment the rancid bitterness of the years bubbled up between them. But Anne smiled and kept her voice soft during her biting remarks because they were in the street. Suddenly, as they were passing an empty fenced-in building lot, Harrison turned deadly white, flung the expensive steak across the fence far out into the empty lot, turned and walked away. . . .

Book Two

HERBERT

1   HERBERT's grandfather, Herman Krumpf, had come to Queenshaven in South Carolina in 1865. He had come from the city of
Schwerin at the invitation of the small German Lutheran
church of Queenshaven to be the organist and schoolmaster of its
people. Mecklenburgers and men from Bremerhaven had come in
small numbers to the Carolinian city even before the War between
the States. They settled down as grocers, cotton-factors, dealers in hay
and grain. After the war the little colony grew. But never rapidly.
These people were prudent, careful, slow to leap. A cousin or a
brother or a nephew was not invited to come over until a decent existence for him seemed secure. None of these people were poor; few
were rich. Miserliness rather than prodigality was the vice to which
they leaned. None were illiterate and none were bookish. A Low German paper printed in Chicago, a German Bible and hymnal, odd
volumes of Schiller or Uhland were in every house. These houses
were as scoured and clean and cool and solid and graceless as the
houses in the old country had been. The colony formed a tight community. The people had no thought of entering the society of the
Queenshaven gentry. The slovenly poorer whites of the South they
despised frankly. They were not unkindly to the Negro, but never
got over the feeling of his outlandishness and held aloof. Among
themselves they respected the rich, the pastor and the schoolmaster.

Herman Krumpf was in his middle forties when he settled in Queenshaven. He brought with him his wife, a son of fifteen, a daughter of twelve and a small library of books and music. His father and his grandfather had been like himself organists and schoolmasters. He thought Gellert a fine poet; he had not yet heard even the name of Wagner; he played Bach on the organ with a solid understanding of the master's form and feeling. He taught the children in his classes to repeat:

> *Üb' immer Treu und Redlichkeit*
> *Bis an dein kühles Grab,*
> *Und weiche keinen Fingerbreit*
> *Von Gottes Wegen ab!*

He wore a long beard and a long, greenish frock coat. One evening in every week he drank beer and played skat with Pastor Müller and the cotton factor Rohde. He sought, in all sincerity of heart, to practice the loyalty and honesty of the verses he taught the children in his school and not to deviate by the breadth of a finger from the ways of God as he understood them.

Herbert remembered his grandparents well, although both died somewhat suddenly in his early boyhood. He could always see the parlor in the tiny, red brick house in Anson Street. His grandfather would be sitting with his pipe at the old, black, square piano; the small, neat grandmother with rose-tipped wrinkles as precise as porcelain, a little white cap on her smooth gray hair, would be by the window reading or doing tatting work. They were not very exciting, these old people; they would ask, especially the grandfather, embarrassing questions about a small boy's studies. If the small boy's hands were grimy from playing ball, grandmother would take him into the bedroom and wash them for him. They both spoke German. And that was quite right. But they wanted to be answered in the same language and correctly too. And that was somehow even more embarrassing than questions about lessons. The small boy didn't altogether know why. But it seemed old-fashioned and queer and pretentious all at the same time. The grandfather wanted to know what

33

progress he had made on the piano, for he was to ply the family trade of course. That was not so hard. Herbert would play a Gavotte of Handel or a Rondo of Mozart. The result never varied. Grandfather's beard would seem to lift itself up until it stood out almost horizontally from his face, grandfather's clear blue eyes would seem to have a spark in them. Grandfather would turn to grandmother and say: *"Begabung hat der Junge aber keine Gottesfurcht."* ("The boy has talent but no reverence.")

It was Herbert's father who, quite without wishing it, had gradually caused the family name to be changed to Crump. Three years after the family had settled in America, Herman Krumpf, Jr. had returned to Europe to study. For two years he had worked at the Leipzig Conservatory, for eighteen months at the conservatory in Vienna. When he returned to Queenshaven in the early seventies the *Courier* had played up the story of his studies and accomplishments. Pupils came to him from a few of the old families on or near the Battery who had not been quite impoverished by the war, and even more pupils from among the newly prosperous who were beginning to build their houses in Rutledge Avenue. He was at that time the only professionally trained musician in Queenshaven and Miss Sallie Simon, who had, years ago, studied the harp in Paris and played for Paul Hamilton Hayne and his friends pronounced him excellent. He became a personality in the little city. He became unchangeably "Professor Crump." Old Dr. Manigault, who had studied in Heidelberg, would stop him in Broad Street near the old Post Office and Cotton Exchange and address him correctly and ostentatiously as Herr Kroompf. It did no good. The Americanization of the name had come to stay.

By 1890, when Herman Krumpf Sr. was ready to retire, the little German school had already been swept away in the eddies of American life. The congregation however had grown and thriven and built itself the fine new church on Marion Square with a spire that rivalled the historic one of St. Michael's. Herman Crump became, of course, organist and choirmaster at St. Matthew's German Lutheran Church; he was appointed, equally of course, conductor of the Män-

34

nerchor in the new Turnverein on Meeting Street; the number of his pupils in both American and German-American families increased. He might have been a moderately prosperous man; he was, for years, a very busy one. Herbert always kept a vision, an early one, of his father's tall, spare figure leaning forward and peering on account of his nearsightedness, hurrying with compressed lips and a frown, half of annoyance, half of timidity, from one appointment to another. But as the years went on pupils turned elsewhere; there was a tremendous quarrel in the Turnverein and another conductor was imported from Hannover. Herman Crump had nothing left him at last but his position of organist at St. Matthew's and a few mature pupils who were considered queer because of their fidelity to him.

His was not his father's clear, certain and untroubled spirit. In him the sturdy old tradition of Lutheranism and Bach and simple God-fearing had been broken. In 1881 he had visited Vienna once more and had married the dark, mobile, melancholy and yet joyous Meta Messerschmidt who, to the end of her days, yearned for the blossoming chestnuts of the Prater, who never truly became reconciled either to the soft, fiery beauty of Queenshaven or to the society of Mrs. Rohde, Jr., or Mrs. Claussen or Mrs. Müller, the young pastor's wife. She played Schumann's "Novelette in F Major" in the half-dark parlor, and when she made the great melody of the middle sing and soar, her husband would bite his lips. The romantic movement was in his bones. He hungered for the ineffable and the infinite. He too played the chorals of Bach but, as his father declared, without consecration. Science had cooled his head while romanticism had heated his heart. He had read Büchner and Huxley; he had given up his Christian faith. Art was his religion; his words were often bitter and full of romantic irony. He offended old Pastor Müller; he offended Chris Groth, the leader of the Turnverein. On Easter Sunday he played an offertory that, for obscure reasons, shocked pastor and congregation to their marrow. It made them feel shivering, naked, ashamed. Devil's music. He told Chris Groth that the beer and soldier songs of the Männerchor were trash. Groth shrugged his fat shoulders. He didn't even condescend to reply. Pastor Müller with raised eyebrows wanted to know what that unholy offertory music had been. What? His voice was sharp. A prelude to an opera named *Lohengrin* by a composer of the name of Richard Wagner. Pastor Müller shook his head. "Never again, *Verehrtester!* We are simple people." Herman Crump came home and told these anecdotes to his wife. She threw back her head and laughed. "Idiots! But why do you make your life hard on their account? Give them what they want!" But Herman Crump could not do that. He was, in his humble way, a knight of the spirit.

2   To HERBERT the word home never meant anything else than the house in Calhoun Street into which his parents moved when he was a small boy. Like all the old-fashioned Queenshaven houses it turned its gable end toward the street so that the piazzas, the upstairs and the downstairs, could face the breezes of the south and west. The house stood flush with the street. Behind it, to the very end of the deep yard, stretched a line of tiny, black, two-story cottages inhabited by Negroes. In Herbert's early boyhood Calhoun Street was still paved with half-hewn palmetto logs. Opposite the house on the other side of the street there stood, newly completed except for the steeple which was never built, the large Afro-American Methodist Church. The house next door to the Crumps, which belonged to an Irish family named Delaney, was set far back in a narrow garden, so that from his upper piazza Herbert watched all through his childhood and youth a great clear stretch of the Southern heavens and thus grew up familiar with strong blues and golds, the pomp of sunsets, the grave glitter of crowded constellations.

The visible world intoxicated him from the beginning. More clearly and elementarily the world of sound. He was four years old, as his mother told him later, and had followed his grandfather into the cool, slightly musty church one summer afternoon. He had climbed with the old gentleman into the organ-loft. The sonorous vibrations of sound had made the child tremble and turn pale and the ecstasy had become so insupportable that he had dropped sobbing on the floor and had had to be carried home. Herbert barely remembered this incident. But he remembered clearly, remembered with a quickening of his blood and a tingling of his skin, how music had affected him from his earliest years. At five he himself began to play. He would stop his practice, which seemed an impediment only, to strike chords, simple chords which, by their rich uncomplicated consonance, sufficed to flood him with well-being. Gradually, of course, he became more hardened to the ecstasy of mere sound. But always there recurred moments of its unbelievable poignancy. There were things that for years he could never play through to the end. They broke him. Things by Chopin, such as the "Nocturne in F," quite simple things by Schumann, certain adagios in Beethoven's sonatas. He fled to Handel and Mozart and his father thought that the boy had perhaps inherited his grandfather's sobriety of temper. But Herbert's mother always knew better. For she would sing the *"Möricke Lieder"* of Hugo Wolf and Herbert would sit in a dim corner of the room with tears streaming down his face. *"Lass, O Welt, O lass mich sein . . ."* The boy would grasp his dark, tousled hair; the mother watching him, stopped playing and drew him to her bosom.

There was another world of sound about Herbert, a world to which his father and mother paid little attention. But it thrilled and haunted him and remained forever memorable to him. There were Negroes in the back-yard, as it was called; there was the Negro Church across the street; there were Negroes all around. Herbert would go to Paul Fludd, the butcher, to buy two cents worth of meat for his cat. And the enormous black man would be singing in his vibrant bass voice: "Dee—ee—ee—eep rivah . . ." Hack! The cleaver came down on the meat and the marvelous melody was interrupted. Herbert was too shy to ask Paul to go on and finish his song. So whenever he left the house he would first go a bit eastward toward the Cooper River and listen for the singing of Paul the butcher. But that was not all. He waked up early sometimes in his garret room and would go to the window and see Queenshaven in the dawn like a city carved of mother of pearl under a sky as faintly iridescent as the inner curve of a seashell. He would watch the elderly Negresses coming from the bay. On their red head-kerchiefs they carried large flat wooden platters full of fresh, faintly coral-tinted shrimps to be boiled early and served with hominy at the white folks' breakfast tables. In their rich untutored voices the women would cry their wares: "O you shrimps! O you oysters!" And there was one old Negro man who sang up and down the scale in a dreamy, strange sing-song: "Buy fresh buttermilk . . ." Herbert caught tones and cadences in these Queenshaven street cries of his childhood that many years later puzzled the critics in his works.

Sunday was a great day for the boy. He was permitted to attend church, not in the pew with his mother, but in the organ-loft watching his father play the handsome new triple-manual organ and treading the pedals and desperately but softly keeping the amateur choir in order. These flirtatious young persons wanted to show off; they wanted to sing new and attractive music. They thought the Lutheran Church of their fathers with German song and sermon a little common anyhow. The frowsy, freckled pale-eyed popular soprano had once turned languishingly to the stern choir-master. "Do you know, Professor Crump, what my friend Agnes Bayer sang for offertory at Grace Church last Sunday?" Crump's eyes turned severely on the fluffy, diminutive person. "Well, what?" The girl answered with a pert gesture of the head: "The Intermezzo from *Cavalleria Rusticana.*" Herbert always remembered with a profound pride his father's dry, infinitely decisive: "Good; let her. Not here!" The soprano was the daughter of a very rich pew-holder. But Herman Crump was a righteous man. In his small obscure place in the world he stood firm for the good. He closed his near-sighted eyes after such an episode, leaned forward, played a Fugue of Bach and relented with Beethoven's *"Die Himmel rühmen des Ewigen Ehre . . ."* In that organ-loft Herbert learned both music and morals. Memories of those Sunday mornings came to sustain him in dark and tortured hours of his later years.

Sunday afternoons were drowsy. In the snowless Queenshaven winters they were usually mild and golden. After dinner Herbert would climb up to his attic and dream over a book. Above his dream he listened. In the Afro-American Church with its stump of a tower across the street the Sunday service was an all-day service and people came and went and chanted and "shouted." And now and again the sisters who had "seen Jesus" were carried into the cottages in the Crump back-yard and were prayed and crooned over. And whatever else was going on in the church, even during the early sermon whenever the preacher's voice fell, the congregation chanted a single chant. Sunday after Sunday the congregation chanted that chant, year in year out. All through Herbert's childhood and boyhood and youth he heard that melancholy chant. And he used often to think, as time went on and on and life turned out so strangely for him, that if he could only go alone to visit Queenshaven and walk from Marion Square eastward to Calhoun Street and stand in front of the old house and hear the Negroes chant that chant again, that then the foul ice which fate had made to congeal in his bosom might melt and a miracle happen within him to placate the seemingly implacable powers.

It was a very simple chant that the Negroes across the street so tirelessly chanted. When Herbert was about fifteen it suddenly occurred to him one Sunday afternoon that the chant must not be lost. He wrote it down, jotted it down quite simply without any bass. And in that first simple version of his boyhood it looked like this:

But he knew at once that the notes held neither the great resignation nor the terribly moving aspiration of simple souls that sounded in the endless, dragging, clinging chant. The C natural at the beginning of the sixth measure—did it not create an interval of infinitude? Did not the souls of the overburdened liberate themselves in it for one moment of eternity? Only to return to earth, to be sure, but with a vision and a hope that sounded full and strong and sonorous—for all its undertone of wailing—in the breadth and large peace of the final measure. Herbert, at all events, believed steadily that this chant, interwoven with all the memories of his earlier years, had an extraordinary musical value. It furnished him with the groundwork of the thematic material of the tone-poem "Renunciation" with its motto from Goethe *("Entsagen sollst du, sollst entsagen . . .")* the performance of which by the Society of the Friends of Music came too late to do him any good. Curiously enough, he never, during his boyhood spoke to his parents of the absorption of so many of his hours by the magic of the Negro music. He had an obscure feeling that they might not share his taste. And then, as later, he had an unconquerable aversion from the strain and futility of disagreement and debate.

3   THE earliest years of school were like a dream. But it was school that at last created the division between day and dream. It could be dismissed no longer, but threw its jagged shadow into the home. A little conflict arose which was symbolized in Herbert's memory by one brief colloquy between his father and his mother that took place one Friday afternoon when he had brought home a shockingly bad report of his week's work. His father arose in wrath. He could hear his mother's rich contralto speaking voice and her soft Viennese accent: *"Lass mir den Bub in Ruh, Hermann, seine Begabung liegt halt in einer andern Richtung!"* His father turned to his mother, severe and sorrowful: *"Und die Pflicht, Meta, die Pflicht?"* Then he left the room. The mother turned to the boy. "Papa is quite

right—as always. You simply must do better, darling." But the boy knew that there was no real conviction behind her words. The North German conception of duty for duty's sake, irrespective of temperament or aim, was foreign to her nature. The boy perceived and, of course, passionately embraced his mother's point of view. The day came when he saw that there was much more than he had imagined to be said for his father's too.

The trouble with school, in actual fact, was not the studies. Herbert could have mastered these. It was the teachers, the atmosphere, the boys. It cannot be said that he was pampered at home. He obeyed his parents without question. He was by nature the reverse of forward. But he was, after all, an only child. There was no friction and no corrective rivalry in the home. When the little daughters of his father's sister, Flora and Annabelle Schott, came to visit, he was very gentle and polite. In fact he liked them, especialy Flora, who had a long thick braid of chestnut brown hair and very red lips and liked to play a game with kisses as forfeits. Yet he was always relieved and very tired when the girls went. They were all over the house; they touched things and pulled them out of place in what seemed to him a restless and unreasonable way. It was from his father's side that he must have gotten his innate and almost pedantic love of order. It was a source of quiet amusement to his mother to see Bertie follow the little girls from room to room and with polite unobtrusiveness straighten things out after them.

School was to Herbert a leashed chaos at best, namely in the classroom, an open pandemonium before and between and after classes. The boys' spirit of raising hell for its own sake irritated him obscurely but deeply. He liked some of the teachers and studies no more than they. He would far rather have been at home or playing or walking with Ralph Greene or even with Eddie Bierfischer. But spit-balls and pea-shooters seemed to him, years before he could formulate such feelings in words, stupidly and nastily irrelevant to the situation. Ralph and Eddie more or less shared his attitude. Once in a long while the three boys would simply "play hookey;" they would quietly disappear after the noon recess. But this method wasn't satisfactory either. For the boys, in spite of the quiet bravado with which they didn't quite deceive one another, were all three darkly oppressed by a sense of the consequences of their truancy, especially of the annoyance it might cause their fathers. So they wandered rather forlornly about and ended by planning excuses to be presented at school and at home. Sometimes they envied the "Birdie" Reynolds type who, tall, wiry, sheer muscle and sinew, smote all the other boys hip and thigh surreptitiously in the classroom, openly on the playground and lied to the teachers with an impenetrable impudence on his blue-eyed and angelic countenance. They envied "Birdie;" occasionally they tried to imitate him and always, of course, came to grief. At last one day, in the second year of high school, when Eddie and Herbert were joining in a game of fastening pins, points forward, into your shoes and jabbing the boys in front of you Ralph, the oldest of the three, turned a disgusted face to his friends. "For Christ's sake, quit your foolishness! I want to work!" It was like a liberation to Herbert. He didn't have to pretend any more. He practised for three hours that afternoon and that evening threw his "pony" into the attic closet and found that he could construe his thirty lines of Caesar in just about the same time that it took him to fit the pidgin English of Hinds and Noble's hacks to the Latin on the page before him. School still nauseated him often enough. But the worst was over. By applying his natural methodicalness to his actual circumstances he discovered that he could find time for school, for his music, for his play. He had to sacrifice his great secret occupation—the constant scribbling of music. With a strength of character rare in a boy of thirteen, he deliberately put it off until summer. But vacations were fifteen weeks long and seemed endless in those days.

Sometimes, of course, he broke his resolution. Strange circumstances would arise. Ralph Greene came with a flicker in his eyes that were usually reserved and steady. "Come on, Bert, let's go for a walk." "Where to?" "To Society Street." "Shucks, that isn't much of a walk." Ralph tugged at Herbert's sleeve. There was an urgency and an appeal in his gesture. "Aw, come on!" Suddenly a sense of feverish expectancy communicated itself to Herbert. His throat went hot and dry. "Oh, all right, if you want to." By a common impulse the two boys now hurried along the few blocks down Meeting Street. At the corner of Society Street stood the two Gallagher girls slim, tall for their age, with sweet, identical, oval faces, a few freckles over their tilted noses, large, empty eyes. "How do you do?" they said in a very grown-up way. The boys lifted their caps: "How do you do?" they said in an equally seemly fashion. Ralph paired off with Kate, Herbert with Estelle. A choking silence followed. "Have you ever played circus?" Estelle asked. "No," said Herbert, "but I'd like to if"—a sudden inspiration leaped out of the hot sweetness in his belly—"I'd like to if you're in it!" The girl giggled and looked pleased and let her white sleeve brush Herbert's shoulder.

In the middle of the block they met Hen Hanahan, a boy with a curved mouth that went almost from ear to ear, and a clownlike head, round as an apple. With him was a girl who had fiercely red hair and a slatternly appearance. Estelle turned to Herbert. "Did you ever see the circus? It's in the basement of Hen's house." They were in front of the narrow four-story house. The basement could be entered from the street. Three steps down. It was an ordinary paved cellar strewn with sawdust. The boys and girls went in and sat down on boxes ranged along the wall. The pretence at playing circus was brief and feeble. Hen stood on his head in the middle of the floor. Then he sprang up and slammed and latched the wooden door to the street. Silence and black darkness. Herbert thought that his heart would literally leap into his throat as he felt the head of Estelle on his shoulder and inhaled the fresh odor of the girl's hair. It was she who found his lips and pushed his hands. After that he needed no guidance. There were giggles; there were jokes. All speech was seemly and calculated to fortify the pretence that there was no harm in this game. Nothing fatal and ultimate did in fact happen. But these children of the South had a strong, dumb, ecstatic eroticism—fierce, earnest, almost exalted. The sharp voice of Hen Hanahan came suddenly:

43

"Must be most supper time!" All voices babbled with a cool assumption of naturalness; the door was opened and a calming breeze swept in. The boys and girls wandered out into the dusk and separated casually. Ralph said to Herbert: "Want to come again?" And Herbert answered with the same affected carelessness: "Oh, I guess so." But that night, after the first broken feeling wore off, he covered sheet after sheet of paper with notes and dropped the sheets on the floor. In the early dawn he gathered the sheets and locked them in his little oak desk.

4 WEEKS later, having copied it neatly, he played this composition to his mother. He had hesitated from day to day. But the pride of the artist finally overcame his shyness. She listened carefully and then came over to the piano. "But, Bertie," she said, "I didn't know. Why you're—" She interrupted herself. "Play it to Papa this evening." "You think it's good enough?" He got up; he was as tall as she now. They looked into each others' eyes. "Why, darling, I think it's—no, I won't say. Play it to Papa." He did so that evening after supper. His father sat with one hand over his eyes. Herbert finished and turned around on the piano stool. Herman Crump let his hand fall slowly and turned to look at his son. "A musician's life is a hard one, my son. I had hoped that you might study law or medicine and have an easier time. I suppose I must give up that hope now." Herbert jumped up. "Then you like it?" His father smiled sourly. "It's completely chaotic and what isn't chaos is Wagner. You don't *know* enough. I'll talk to Petersen about giving you a couple of lessons in composition a week." "Why don't you teach the boy yourself, Herman?" his wife asked. He shook his head. "Petersen is fresh from the conservatories and is a good composer. What am I?" In the restrained bitterness of that phrase Herbert heard for the first time the cry of his father's frustrated life, and an ache came into his heart that stilled his brief triumph.

44

All summer he worked with Petersen, the enormous, dark, jovial, half-blind Mecklenburger who had come to America as professor of music in a girls' college, but couldn't stand the sweetishness of the atmosphere and now taught in Queenshaven and gave both organ and piano recitals in the South-Eastern states. Petersen, still in his early thirties, made a companion of Herbert. Together, after lessons, they wandered through the dark, delightful streets of Queenshaven, sat late in Battery Park talking and planning and ended up at a little restaurant or cook-shop, as it was called, on Market Street where Karl Petersen ate six fried eggs and dipped a procession of buttered rolls into incalculable cups of cocoa or coffee and discoursed magnificently on the lives and adventures and works of Liszt and Brahms and Wagner. He had personally known Hans von Bülow and the Bayreuth circle. Some of his anecdotes were drastic, others gorgeous or grotesque. What sank into Herbert's mind was the character of the world that Petersen pictured. A world inconceivably remote from the prim preoccupations and trivial social rivalries of Queenshaven. A world in which art was a supreme and a living thing which men pursued with an unquestioning earnestness. And in that world the forms of life were shaped not according to a received and prescribed pattern, but were molded to serve purposes austere and commanding in themselves. Herbert was far too young to formulate such thoughts in precise language. What he retained from Petersen's talk was the abiding sense of the existence of a world in which perfect freedom was blended with a consecration so genuine that it was beyond the need of solemn gesture or direct expression.

It was during this same summer that the question of Herbert's future arose very practically. His mother, though she dreaded a separation from him, wanted him to be sent to Vienna to study. But there was no money. It was only her husband's instinctive frugality and her own excellent management that kept the family from the open humiliations of poverty. As organist at St. Matthew's, Herman Crump's salary was nine hundred dollars a year. He laboriously increased this to about fourteen hundred. There was no occasion of real need when Meta Crump did not produce an unexpected little hoard. But these sums were small. It was Herbert himself, moreover, who finally opposed the Vienna plan most strongly. He longed for that strange and beautiful world in which so great a part of his imaginative life was spent. But he was almost a child. He was afraid. He did not give this reason; he did not know that even so slight an opportunity would not come to him again; he said he wanted to go to college. This did not displease his father, who often felt his own lack of systematic education, nor Petersen who had studied theology at Erlangen for several semesters before he had given himself wholly to music and who was a formidable quoter of the Latin poets and the Greek Testament. Meta Crump secretly rejoiced at the decision. She could keep her boy for four years more; she would save harder than ever during those four years. She had a dream of herself some day revisiting the delightful city of her birth with Herbert there. She herself would show him the Stefansdom and the adorable old streets clustering about it and in the sunny hills and upland meadows of the Wiener Wald follow with her son the footprints of Beethoven and Schubert. . . .

College. The four years, despite their many intellectual awakenings, were like a mild trance. The boys were all young. There were never more than seventy in the whole college. Existence in Queenshaven was a simple enough thing in those years. There was no extravagance and no harsh poverty. The Spanish war passed like a pleasing legend. None of the bitter problems or conflicts of the world touched those old brown buildings or those sunny trees. Most of the boys expected after graduation either to study medicine at the local medical school or else to read law, either in their father's office or in some other office in Broad Street. There was little or no rivalry in those bare mild classrooms. Those who had a taste for study did well; those who had not, slipped through or quietly dropped out. Ralph Greene, still Herbert's best friend, occasionally protested against this extremity of peacefulness. He had become thin and intense. His small, sharp, hazel eyes behind their glasses snapped, his large, mobile, ugly

46

mouth, showing the irregular teeth, acquired an ironical expression. "I wish to goodness my people had the means to send me to a Northern college. This place is dead; there isn't any incentive. It's all right for you, Bert, with your music. If they don't bother you, you're happy. But I want a political career. This is no preparation. You do nothing; you meet no one!" Ralph tried to start all sorts of movements in the college and Herbert stood by him because he was his best friend. But it all came to nothing and quietly Herbert was just as well pleased. What he did enjoy was the late meetings and walks with Ralph and Walter Ware, a tall, blond, indolent brainy chap who had taken Eddie's place. The three boys would loiter around Colonial Lake with the image of the moon floating in it like a silver balloon and the houses and trees inverted in its dark, star-sprinkled mirror. They would walk around the lake or sit on a bench beside it and discuss politics and literature and sex and the ways of God and man. Ralph was for reforming everything—especially the State. He lived in the burning light of a great future that he had planned for himself. He would be Senator from South Carolina, at least. Maybe more. Walter was more ready to discuss all things than to plan. He was two years older than Ralph, who was one year older than Herbert. He himself knew very well what he really wanted. "Oh, I guess Queenshaven is all right," he would drawl; "I don't like that Northern hustling." He would grin and add a favorite quotation of his father's about *otium cum dignitate*. Ralph would shrug his shoulders. "How about you, Bert?" And Herbert would say shyly: "Well, there really isn't any American composer except MacDowell, is there?" That pleased Ralph. "*There's* an intelligible ambition and a fine one, too." He would assume a slightly oratorical posture. "I don't believe the State ought to do anything for art directly. Paternalism of any kind is un-American. But statesmen should arouse their communities to support artists like you." And Herbert would glow inwardly at being called an artist. Moreover, he had a great faith in Ralph and in Ralph's future.

Before midnight the boys would stroll home through the soft fra-

47

grant air of the night. At the corner of Broad and Meeting Streets they would separate to go in different directions. Perhaps Herbert loved best this last part of the way home which he walked alone. The warmth of debate was still with him, the agreeable sense of community with his friends which was but heightened by a feeling of his essential separateness and superiority in his art. Themes would come to him. He often ran the last few blocks in order to let himself swiftly into the quiet house, hurry silently up the stairs and gain his room. He would light his well-trimmed kerosene lamp and snatch at paper and pencil. It was in such late and silent hours, after walks and debates with his two friends that he wrote his first "Suite on a Southern Theme" and the music for Timrod's "Carolina," both still rather sweetish and oratorical as was inevitable in that Queenshaven atmosphere, and with a kind of false fervor for which he was to blush only a few months later. But Petersen who, though he loved great things, had a child's uncritical heart, liked the Southern Suite and even played it at an organ-recital which he was giving at St. John's Church. This made Herbert's mother very happy. But his father said: *"Um Gottes Willen!* One perpetrates such sins in youth. One doesn't make a show of them." And no sooner had his father spoken than Herbert knew he was right.

5   PLAYING circus had been abandoned long ago. The Gallagher girls were going with older men and affected not to see Herbert or Ralph when they met them on the street. It was rumored that Kate was engaged to a teller in the Southern Trust Company. The two boys and their friend Walter Ware discussed love and marriage theoretically at length. They avoided all concrete allusions nowadays. Some of the seniors bragged about their exploits in a certain street not far from the Unitarian Church and St. John's Church which stood side by side. Herbert and Ralph had neither the courage nor the three dollars. Also, they were sincerely averse to mere ani-

malism and dreamed of a union of passion and love. They dreamed
of these things without much concrete hope or even desire. Ralph, in
his judicial moments declared that he would not marry at all but devote himself exclusively to a great career. He was thoroughly dissatis-
fied with his family's social position in Queenshaven. He never in
those early days put it so crudely. But what he wanted above all to
do was to show Queenshaven—especially that Queenshaven that extended from Broad Street to the Battery—that its essential rejection
of Ralph Douglas Greene would "redound" to its own hurt and
shame. Herbert, more mildly, would agree that he probably wouldn't
marry either. He didn't expect to make a great deal of money. Also
he couldn't bear the thought of anyone coming between his parents
and himself. The three of them were so happy and so united and
Herbert had an instinctive fear, except in the things of art and of the
mind, of the new, the alien, the untried.

For all their brave talk the boys could not quite conceal the fact
from one another that they were constantly troubled and on edge.
Often they suffered profoundly. The sons of families who had been
in Carolina for three or four or even five generations took this situation more lightly and naturally. They had Negro girls. Ralph and
Herbert, children of recent immigrants with the troubled sex conscience of the North of Europe, missed any such adjustment. In their
natures physical needs were easily transformed into moral suffering
and during many limpid nights, especially in spring and summer,
these lads fought devils of alluring shape, and did not always come
off victors. Then followed days of evil dark depression, of harsh
pessimism and a sense of sin. But frankness of discussion was tabooed
by all the impalpable forces of Queenshaven decency. Suffering was
lonely and silent. It was tolerated at the college that a young rogue
should brag how, by transferring silver spoons into her cottage and
threatening to accuse her of theft, he had forced the mulatto cham-
bermaid to do his bidding. But when poor blundering Pat O'Toole
said: "Gee fellows, I'm scared! Did you ever have anything like this
happen to you" and proceeded to describe a common and inevitable

49

physiological phenomenon, he was met with growls. "Shut up, you damn fool!" A Senior deliberately cracked him over the head with a heavy book—a Senior named Washington Fallstone St. Preux—and said: "Disgusting little Mick." Ralph and Herbert, even alone with each other, never dared break through the reserves imposed by this code.

The boys hungered for temptations to which to yield. The temptations, unluckily, were never definite enough. Vague rumors surrounded this girl and that. Who would dare to test the truth of such rumors? A young man of very good family, determined to test such a rumor, had been forced at the end of two revolvers to marry an obviously immoral young slattern. The courts, to be sure, had later annulled this marriage under duress. But the young man was disgraced and his parents were impoverished. Rosie Brierfield had lured Herbert into the glamorous live-oak woods at Otranto on a Sunday School picnic and let him kiss her and had then slipped away. On Meeting Street she walked in front of him in the morning, turned around and smiled and pulled her long yellow braid provocatively and half beckoned him toward her house. He burned and dared not understand. How could one be sure? There was little, pert-looking Irene Allen. She chummed with a notoriously tough girl. Dreadful things were said about her. Suddenly at seventeen she married a very decent chap, bore him twins and became a leader in the Ladies Aid Society of the Citadel Square Baptist Church. With an obscure and piercing shame Herbert looked upon Sarah Wheaton, the daughter of his mother's cook. The young Negress was like a bronze statuette with her small well-poised head, firm, tiny pointed breasts outlined by her single garment, bare, supple knees and legs. Sometimes in the evening Herbert would hear her rough but agreeable contralto as she was driving away the importunate black boys who clustered around her. "Lemme 'lone, niggah! I sho' gonna broke yoh haid!" Sarah would help around the house. She would come up to Herbert's room and touch things there and make a point of brushing him off. And then she would have a humble and gentle look in her

black eyes. But Herbert lacked all spontaneity and animal innocence. He could not imagine himself defiling the home of his parents.
His grandfather, moreover, had been darkly accused by the Southerners of being a "nigger lover" because he had once half-planned to
give lessons to a gifted colored boy. The Crumps, in fact, tacitly dis-
approved of the Queenshaven attitude toward the Negro. Now as
later, in this matter as in others, Herbert found himself caged by
conscience in a world like a moral china shop where he, at least,
could never make a free gesture without the danger of smashing a
hundred apparently precious and necessary things. Did other people
succeed in not smashing those fragile objects? Or did they merely
not see them? Or did those dreadful delicate little idols exist, in fact,
only for him? If he had quenched his longing with Sarah Wheaton
and if there had been consequences, his father would not, like other
Queenshaven fathers, have regarded the matter as an indiscretion
and as the lesser of several possible evils. Herman Crump would have
declared that the very helplessness of the Negro made such guilt not
even expiable. And it was Herbert's worst misfortune that at bottom
he quite agreed with this point of view. That respectable consideration did not, of course, ease the anguish of his blood.

Luckily he was kept busy. He rather surprised himself by the good
work he did during the last two years of his college course. But he
could now choose his own studies and he was constantly more aware
of the close kinship between the arts of music and literature and of
the widespread neglect of this fruitful kinship in the English speaking world. He composed uninterruptedly and with a fervent sense of
continuous inspiration. His mother and Petersen shared his glow.
They adored his two Whitman Suites, his "Prelude to Prometheus
Unbound," his tone-poem—just then Richard Strauss and Shelley
were his twin gods—called "A Poet's Life." Especially did they admire his songs. He poured them out, quietly comparing himself to
Schubert: "Six Songs from the Elizabethan Dramatists," "Four
Songs from Shelley," "Ten Airs to Southern Ditties." Petersen played
his instrumental music at recitals; Queenshaven ladies warbled his

songs from manuscript copies. The local papers spoke of "our young composer." At eighteen Herbert was a bit of a celebrity in his native city. But the music publishers always returned his neat manuscripts. He sent specimens of his work to Richard Strauss. The great man did not answer. His mother was indignant for him.

At breakfast one spring morning with the scent of wisteria in the air a large package came back once more from a publisher. Herbert regarded it somewhat disconsolately across his hominy. "Never mind, my son," said his mother. "All artists have had to struggle for recognition." At that moment Herbert caught the look in his father's dark, honest, near-sighted eyes. "Well, father, what were you going to say?" Herman Crump wiped his lips with his napkin. *"Tja,"* he said gravely; he always spoke German when most in earnest. *"Tja,* what mother says is quite right. But first you must have something with which to struggle. Talent you have—there is no doubt. But all you have been doing, though it is pretty and pleasing, is facile and imitative. You say: 'If they don't want the instrumental stuff, why don't they take the songs?' I will tell you why. Your songs are not popular enough in character to sell and not original enough as art to command attention. You have tried in many of them to add Southern atmosphere to the German tradition as Grieg added Scandinavian atmosphere. But in the first place you are no Grieg and in the second place I believe that America will demand a different musical idiom, *if* she is going to have a music of her own at all." It was the longest speech Herbert had ever heard from his father. He felt small and chilly and forlorn. But he not only knew that every word his father had said was true. He knew that, in his deepest mind, he had known the truth all along, had never, in fact, been deceived or genuinely surprised when his manuscripts came back to him. He had had a delightful time. That time was over. . . .

6 THE thing had to be faced. Many things had to be faced. That was hard in Queenshaven which Petersen called the city of the land of the lotus-eaters. You looked at the mauve and purple islands in the blue bay; you visited the golden sands of Sullivan's Island; you lost yourself in a vision, farther out, of sea-stunted palmettos on the limitless dunes. You wandered about in the quiet streets with their tangled gardens—Church Street, Tradd Street, Legaré Street. It was before the day of business and bustle. Lotus cost nothing; food was cheap. You drifted beautifully from day to day. But in this matter as in others the Crumps were not wholly acclimated. It was two months before Herbert's graduation from college. A decision had to be made. There was no place for another music-teacher in Queenshaven. For the first time Herbert felt a little pang of fear. It was at supper this time, around a large amber lamp splashing into the deep blue night, that the immediate preoccupation of the Crump family rose into words. What was the boy to do?

His mother folded her white well-preserved hands on the table before her and fixed her eyes on her husband. "Herbert must go to Vienna to study. I've saved three hundred and sixty dollars. My sister Eugenie will give him a room. It can be managed." Herman Crump turned and looked questioningly at his son. "Well, Herbert, what do you say to that?" Herbert shook his head. He thought he knew his own mind very well. "But, darling," his mother exclaimed, "what else would you do?" "All right," he said doggedly, "the question is what would I do when I got there. No use going to Leschetizky. I'll never be a piano virtuoso. It isn't in me; it doesn't interest me enough. If I slaved for years more, I'd only be a second-rater." "Well, Bertie," she said slightly irritated, "perhaps you'll tell us what you do want to do!" Herbert looked at his father. "What, of course, I ought to do is to get a doctorate of music in Vienna and go in for conducting," he said slowly. "And that would take years and years. The profession is crowded over there. They don't need an American. So I'd have to come home and look for a job." His father nodded. "I'd rather look for a job now and maybe save some money." Herman Crump leaned

53

forward. "I've been forced to the same conclusion. I foresaw this and that's why I was sorry to see you a musician. It is, of course, my fault that you can't go and prepare yourself more thoroughly." It was, for the first time, one man speaking to another, "I hope, Herbert, that you have more talent for the world, for success, than I have ever had." Meta Crump put her hand on Herbert's sleeve. "What will you do, Bertie?" Herbert got up and put his arm around his mother's shoulder. "I'm going to New York, Mamachen!" He laughed. "I'm going to become rich and famous."

Conferences were held with Petersen who had been everywhere and tried everything. He approved Herbert's plan and promised to give him letters of introduction. He advised gathering the notices of the performance of Herbert's compositions that had appeared in the Queenshaven press. Herbert objected at first. "Ha," Petersen cried. "*Mundus vult decipi.* Furthermore I don't agree with Colleague Crump. He is too hard on your compositions." According to Petersen, Herbert could do any number of things in New York. Musicians with a thorough grasp of both the art and the science were not overplentiful in America. He himself had once, before his eyes had gone back on him, done instrumentation and revision for a music publisher; he had even worked at the simple transposition of songs. In the midst of these discussions an agreeable thing happened. A second-rate music publisher, to whom Herbert had sent some of his older things, accepted his composition of Lanier's "Into the Woods My Master Went." The melody was mellifluous and had a bad touch of the "sacred" in music. Herbert and his parents and even Petersen were quite aware of this and laughed over Herbert's first "opus." Still, it was an acceptance. It was a solid fact in the midst of empty plans.

Next came graduation from college. Herbert had written a "College of Queenshaven March" which Luden's orchestra performed at the graduation exercises in the Academy of Music. Everybody was very warm and festive and exalted. These Southerners had a way of becoming sincerely exalted on the appropriate occasions that was ex traordinarily infectious. After the commencement exercises there was a reception at the president's house on Battery Park. There was punch. The girls were in dresses of dreamy white, and brilliantly lit rooms and dusky verandas and the starry garden melted into each other. Nellie Darrow, tall, slender, dark-eyed, admired by Herbert at a distance for some time, assumed a charming air of grown-up intimacy with him. She took his arm and went out with him through the French window down into the dark blue garden and they stood under a magnolia tree in bloom. Nellie had been in London and Paris. She had met important people and visited studios and salons. She now played the part of a lady of the great world toward a young man of genius and her words and her attitude, utterly new to Herbert in real experience but terribly familiar to his shy dreams and secret longings, tingled to his very feet. Nellie's flecked swarthiness, her too obtrusive collarbone, her thin brown arms with knobby elbows, all seemed magical on that night. Only a deep-seated sobriety inherited from his father's side of the family kept him from tossing his hair. Here was a foretaste of the glory of this world. He saw himself a celebrated conductor. The great orchestra was one and was his. His baton was truly a magician's wand. But he would be restrained and dignified, not mannered and gesticulatory, like too many. He poured out his ambitions to Nellie Darrow who, snobbish, missish and provincial, ended by rather drawing back before the storm she had evoked. He got home late and jumped with nervousness in his deferred and unquiet sleep.

Next morning at breakfast Petersen turned up, tremendous with plans. He ate up everything in sight and drank the coffeepot dry. "Ha!" he cried in the somewhat high, veiled voice that came strangely from his dark enormous bulk. "A letter from my concert-bureau!" He spread out the typed pages before him. "Engagements for organ and piano recitals all next winter. Look! Savannah, Augusta, Atlanta, Montgomery, Shreveport, Mobile, Birmingham. Then later Raleigh, Chapel Hill, Wilmington, Lynchburg, Lexington, Richmond! Ha! Should I stay here and make the organ wheeze at Grace Church?

No, I should say *not!* On the other hand: should I give up a steady job? Not by a damned sight! A job is a job. Therefore I suggest the following." He put his enormous index-finger to the side of his small tilted nose that seemed so inadequate in the expanse of his large, kindly, whimsical face. "I say: let Herbert substitute for me for one year at full salary at *dis*-grace! He's barely nineteen. A year later is plenty time enough for him to go out into the world. He has unfinished compositions. He will have a lot of time to himself and one thousand dollars. Ha!" Herbert laughed. "You old humbug, I play the organ like a butcher!" Petersen waved him aside. "Practice this summer. The folks at Grace Church are no connoisseurs, not by a damned sight!" Herbert's father smiled. "Will they take a Lutheran?" Petersen snorted. "When I applied for my first church position they asked me what I was. I said: 'I am a Lutheran by birth, an Episcopalian by aesthetic instinct, a Presbyterian by adoption, a Unitarian with my head, a Methodist with my heart, a German by descent, an American citizen by choice and so good a musician that the highest salary offered by any church would be exactly half what I'm worth!" "And did you get the position?" Herbert's mother asked. "In twenty-four hours! Beloved friend, just a *leedle* more coffee. *So. Schoen. Tausend Dank. Prosit!"*

It was all arranged with the utmost promptness. The vestry of Grace Church were pleased to have "our promising young composer, the third of a highly respected name to serve a church in this community" become temporarily their organist and choir-master. Herbert was relieved and also saddened. It was delicious to drop back for another year into the soft familiar life of his native city with a position and money of his own. He worked hard at the organ that summer. He destroyed a great many of his older compositions; others he rewrote and tightened. He did new work sparingly and with a watchful critical eye. He avoided the larger forms and deliberately turned to the precise dance forms of the eighteenth century and wrote a gavotte, two minuets, a sarabande in the manner of Handel. He looked forward to the fall when his actual work and salary would begin. He had many final walks and discussions with Ralph, who had borrowed money and was going to the Harvard Law School in October. He had, beneath his busy and pleasant surface life, a feeling as though he were, despite all signs to the contrary, at the beginning of some vague but great defeat. He knew or thought he knew with an obscure yet definite knowledge, that he ought to have gone to New York right away. Was not his remaining here—he brushed the suspicion aside only to have it strike at odd and unexpected moments—was it not somehow the symbol of an instinctive turning from life, of an undue absorption in the things of the inner life, of an inability, perhaps, to see and grasp the world of naked reality at all?

When fall really came this brooding was half forgotten. Nellie Darrow was the alto in his quartet at Grace Church. After choir practice on Friday night she lingered behind with him and he played his new compositions to her and his old ones too. She thought them all equally "beautiful, charming, exquisite, *darling!*" That last epithet made the relation suddenly empty and stale. It opened his eyes to her scrawniness, her incipient moustache, her affectations. The second part of the winter was irradiated by no delusion. Herbert was lonely, restless, bodily and spiritually ill at ease. He began really to hear the choir and the rector's dull, pompous, narrow-minded sermons. What was he doing here? What was this leading to? Whatever the plunge and the pain—he felt that he must be gone. If it had not been for his mother's quiet clinging to him and his obligation toward Petersen, he would not have remained through the season. It dragged to a weary and disappointing end.

7   AT LAST Time which in youth and in Queenshaven had seemed so often to stand still—a golden tower by the edge of a purple sea—shook and crashed. The tower tumbled; the world reeled. Herbert had often heard his father and mother complain how the latter years had sped by them. His mother especially

had moments of somber melancholy. "Before one knows it, one will be at the end." That last spring and summer in Queenshaven Herbert found himself sharing these emotions. Did it not seem as though on one day he was still in his golden tower, safe with the warmth and music of his childhood, and on the next day amid ruins that hurtled down a slope, amid confusion, preparation, amid circumstances that seemed not so much hopeful as fatal? And was it not on some unbelievable third day that he was wandering about the bright October streets of New York, still very warm that year, and hearing the hurdy-gurdies endlessly playing "in the good old summer time, the good old su-u-mmer time," and being already a part of that loose but tenacious institution—the Hasselmeyer house?

Petersen had known the Hasselmeyers for years. When he went to New York at Christmas time for a music debauch, he stayed with the Hasselmeyers. Somehow one always found a place to sleep and a place at table in the brownstone house in 123rd Street facing Morningside Avenue. One did not inquire of Hasselmeyer, the majestic. One didn't see him till dinner when tall, bulky, iron-gray, sardonic he loomed at the head of the table and in his resonant basso profundo poured out his scorn over the universe. Were these boarders at the table? To hear Hasselmeyer one would have said henchmen at worst, pupils at best. No, one asked for Mrs. Hasselmeyer, who seemed colorless and neutral at first. Later one came to know her intelligence, her tolerance of mind, her warmth of heart. Not out of supineness was she the slave of Hasselmeyer and of the house. She loved and admired her grim and ruthless lord. She was of the opinion that life had not dealt justly with him. She knew the storms he had braved and the sufferings he had calmly undergone. Now he was music critic on a German-American daily paper. They could have lived quietly and obscurely in a small flat on his salary. Mrs. Hasselmeyer had deliberately assumed the burden of this establishment to give her imperious husband a sense of amplitude in life, a background and an audience. Herbert, the uninitiated, had asked for Mr. Hasselmeyer on his arrival. Mrs. Hasselmeyer had patted his shoulder with a motherly hand. "Petersen

58

has written, my child. We never bother Papa. There is a nice little hall bedroom on the third floor for you. Yes, I know what you want in a professional way too. I will see what I can do for you."

That evening at dinner Hasselmeyer leaned forward, the cold ironic gray eyes under the bushy eye-brows fixed on Herbert. His bass boomed. "Mamma, is that the youth from Boeotia?" Mrs. Hasselmeyer, who had seated Herbert beside her at the foot of the table, said to him quietly. "Don't mind Papa. You'll discover his good sides too." She nodded to her husband, who spoke again: "Youth from Boeotia, we are told that you compose." He talked like a government or an editorial except for the ironic undercurrent. Herbert found it hard to be self-respecting under this onslaught. "I do," he said. "A song of mine is appearing this month." Hasselmeyer smiled and when he smiled something agreeable and roguish, a late shadow of youth, gleamed on that iron mask. "*Sancta simplicitas,* the song will not sell. If it does, the publisher will steal the royalties." For a minute he addressed himself to his soup. "Are you a good accompanist?" he asked more quietly. "I believe so," Herbert replied. Hasselmeyer feigned extreme horror. "Mama! The devil has sent this youth. Now Gerda can yell and pule in this very house." A heavy-lipped, black-haired sleek young man at the middle of the table spoke in a high, almost falsetto voice. "The devil, so far as I know, Mr. Hasselmeyer, was not active in Boeotia." Hasselmeyer drew himself up. He loomed. He towered. "If we choose to mix up our historical periods and their respective mythologies it is not, as it would be in your case, a result of pretentious ignorance!" He seemed suddenly to grow smaller, to become an old man hunched over his plate. Audibly he mumbled into his thick moustache what Herbert soon came to know as his favorite term of abuse: "*Ekelpadde!* (Horrid toad!)" But nobody seemed to mind—neither the young man so qualified on that first night, nor the quiet Jewish lady, an authoress from Berlin, in her "reform costume," nor Grienauer, the lank shy cellist or his angular wife.

The conversation now became general and Mrs. Hasselmeyer quietly explained to Herbert that Gerda Veröty was the daughter of a very old friend of theirs, a Hungarian scholar who lived in Chicago. For five years the girl had been in Germany to study singing and dancing. The Shuberts had engaged her for their next Winter Garden show. In addition she was planning to give a recital of the chansons of the German Überbrettl or super-vaudeville. And what she had been sighing and yearning and pouting for was a coach and accompanist in the house. "Gerda is late, as usual," Mrs. Hasselmeyer added. "But Papa forgives her. She cheers him."

A moment later the door of the dining-room that faced Herbert opened and unmistakably Gerda Veröty came in. He always afterward remembered that first sight of Gerda as she stood for a moment, her blonde slimness framed in that door. She was lifting one of the straps of her blue evening frock that had slipped down from her slim white shoulder. He knew suddenly what was meant by wheat-blonde, he knew how blue eyes could be, blue as a mountain lake under an autumn sun. He had the impression of something Northern, boyish, of something cool yet burning—of a creature as precise as a snow-crystal yet as haunting as a legend. Gerda came forward swiftly now and then dropped a little wearily into the empty chair beside Hasselmeyer. He growled at her indulgently in German: "So after all our little princess condescends!" She pouted consciously. "Do you require a complete monopoly of bad manners, Papa Hasselmeyer?" "Freches Subjekt!" he trumpeted. But her pertness affected him agreeably. He had the air of a magnificent, ancestral tomcat scratched in the right spot between ear and chin. "Do you want soup, Gerdachen?" Mrs. Hasselmeyer asked. The girl shook her head. "I have no appetite. The weather is so warm. I want to get to work. But I can't rush about in this impossible town and I will not pay a répétiteur ten dollars an hour to come to me." "The gods take care of their favorites," Hasselmeyer declared. He put one hand over Gerda's and pointed with the other. "Without seeming to, you have already observed the interesting looking youth beside Mama." Gerda turned a cool full glance upon Herbert. "This youth," Hasselmeyer went on, "now lives in the house. We are credibly informed that he is a not unaccomplished young per-

60

son who will coach with you daily at"—Hasselmeyer's face became severe and dictatorial—"at three dollars and a half an hour." Herbert, though a bit overwhelmed, opened his lips. Mrs. Hasselmeyer's hand was on his arm. "Let Papa talk. We can arrange all that later." For the first time Gerda Veröty smiled. Her smile was cool but very winning. Almost the smile of a little girl. She looked at Herbert now. "Is that really true?" she asked. "I don't know if it's all true," Herbert said. "But we might try to work together and see how much of it actually is." Mrs. Hasselmeyer nodded. "That's right. Don't let them both bully you."

A few minutes later Herbert followed Gerda into the dim narrow drawing room. He opened the piano and switched on the piano lamp. He was excited, almost drunken. He felt a delicious recklessness. Gerda, looking through music on the piano top, exhaled a breath that brought to Herbert the old, dreamed of world of his desires—a world of freedom and of preoccupation with art. He sat down on the piano stool and looked up at her pale profile. "Well?" he said. "The professional stuff is necessary but rancid. We'd better not begin with that. Let's try this." She opened a piece of music on the rack in front of him. It was a song called "Allerseelen" which was just then very popular in Germany. The song was of no great musical value; it was a trifle obvious in its semi-poetic melancholy. But the verses had an autumnal charm and a real ache in them.

. . . und lass uns wieder von der Liebe reden
wie einst im Mai . . .

"Do you know it?" she asked. "No, but it's simple." He played the accompaniment and Gerda sang. She had a small, rather hard soprano and she tried for neither fluidity nor charm. She sang with the trickiness and false pointedness of the operetta and vaudeville "artiste." She had, however, a highly developed sense of rhythm and a bell-like enunciation and she made her "points" and it was quite clear to Herbert why, if she could dance too, the Shuberts had hired her. All this he knew in some far, shadowy retreat of his brain. Meanwhile his human self was floating in an ineffable and divine ichor that soaked into his marrow. They tried other songs and spoke fewer and fewer words. Gerda, reading the verses over his shoulder, leaned her lithe, uncorseted young body against him. They stopped. He let his hands lie on the keys. She turned to face him with her back pressed against the key-board. The cool, detached look had left her face. There was a faint, pitying tenderness in her eyes—a pity, strangely enough, that embraced them both. She ran her hand with a natural and deliberate gesture through his dark hair. "I like you." He caught her hand and kissed it and bending over leaned his forehead for a second against her thigh. She slipped gently away. He rose and faced her. Taking his cue from her expression he said gravely: "Well?" "Can we work together every morning at eleven?" she asked. "Certainly." "And at three dollars and a half an hour?" A wild gush of feeling blinded Herbert's perceptions. "Oh, don't let's discuss that!" he cried. She flushed. Her eyes hardened. Her tone was harsh. "Don't be a fool and don't be insulting!" She walked out of the room. The shame of the false note he had struck came over Herbert hotly and pursued him cruelly in the dreams of the night.

8   DAILY at eleven they met in the drawing room and worked. They worked conscientiously. Herbert was often tempted to take some flight toward beauty. He would play a few measures of some great song, hoping to entice Gerda. But where her work was concerned she was unbending. She had a hard businesslike patience and pertinacity. Once, tortured by the wretched jingles that had to be gone over and over, by the contrast between Gerda's grace and the trivial content of her ambitions, he had jumped up from the piano in the middle of a measure. "For God's sake, Gerda, how can you stand it?" The eyes he saw were dark and hard and almost old. "I can stand it because I'm going to get a hundred dollars a week for doing it." She clenched her small, strong hands. "Do you suppose I

want to be a music teacher in the backwoods or go home to Chicago and play nurse-maid to my half brothers and sisters—four of them? I hate being poor. I'd do anything to escape the sordidness of it— anything.— I've got the makings of a comic opera star in me. Have I or have I not?" He nodded. "Very well. I want houses, jewels, motor-cars. I want everything I haven't had. Will you go on now or not?" Never before had he met that hunger for the vanities of the world. It shocked and sickened him in Gerda. She seemed to him woven of moonlight; she was the "blue flower" of his ardent and romantic youth. Sullenly he went back to the piano. But his strength seemed to have withered within him. "I can't go on today," he said with a curtness unexpected by himself. She gathered up her music and walked quietly out. At once he wanted her back with a hot and over-whelming hunger. He was willing to do anything—only to have her back. Anything. She was gone. The world was desolate.

He could not sleep that night. The shade of his window had fallen down and a half-moon of burning silver was afloat over Morningside Heights. Despite his sleeplessness a lethargy held him fast in bed. He could not will to get up and hang the green shade back. He listened to the small noises of the nocturnal house—small, unaccountable noises, as though there were a straining restlessness in all things. Faint creakings, tiny sawings, muffled tappings. The noises seemed to make his sense of hearing taut. A sound more rhythmic and soft and human disengaged itself from the ghostly stirrings of the night. He began to shiver as in a desperate fever. Soft, small, slippered feet were on the stairs. The heels of the mules were trying not to click. He knew. He *knew*. And burned more consumingly with that icy heat. Softly his door opened. Gerda came in. Upon her face was the grave earnestness of her desire. She stood still and dropped her kimono in a little silken heap upon the floor. She was like a silver shaft in the moonlight. She whispered. "I'm cold, Herbert." With a sob he stretched out his arms.

When, toward dawn, she left him, his head throbbed with plans. He must get a position. They must be married. His heart grew warm. He had the normal instincts of the young male—to make a home for his woman, to tend the ancient fire, to seek the hearthstone as the center of his life. He thought of his parents. Gerda's loveliness would persuade them. If not, he could not help it. He and Gerda were now one against the world. But at eleven she was waiting for him in the drawing room with her usual hard patience and assiduity. How could she? He wanted to caress her. Rudely she pushed him away. Her voice was harsh. "Don't look at me like a love-sick calf. I'm here to work!" A stinging rage shook him. "What do you mean? What kind of a girl are you?" She laughed and quoted airily:

> For I have forgotten your kisses
> And you have forgotten my name . . .

Then she put her hand on his shoulder. "Dear Herr Professor Crump, let's get to work." Her touch and the pleading in her voice subdued and softened him. He sat down at the piano.

There followed months of atrocious suffering punctuated by rare ecstatic hours. When Herbert had insisted that they must be married, even though the marriage were kept a secret for the present, Gerda had regarded him coolly. "Why, may I ask?" "Isn't it self-evident?" He could not keep the heat out of his voice. "Not to me." She was terse. "We're not the least bit suited to each other. You're a nice boy. But you're a terrible idealist and Philistine. If ever I do marry in eight or ten years, it will have to be a millionaire. As for you—you've got your own career to think of!" He pleaded and stormed. But he knew that his reasoning was bad and that all he succeeded in expressing was his desire to possess her permanently and exclusively. He knew that from his frightful jealousy. Gerda would go out in the afternoons. She went out in the evening with other men. She refused coldly and petulantly to give an accounting of herself. "Herbert, you are to me today what no one else is precisely. That's enough. Don't be sentimental." When he knew her to be safely in the house he could rest from the anguished strain of those other hours—those dry, creeping, burning hours of utter misery and humiliation during which he walked up and down, up and down his little room or hung out of the window in the icy air watching the corner at which she might appear or took apparently careless strolls in the street in front of the house and felt his heart alternately leap like flame and drop like·lead within him. Rarely, very rarely could he persuade her to go out with him in the evening. "You haven't any money to waste, Herbert; neither have I." He wrote a series of songs for her to poems by Arthur Symons that he had recently discovered and that answered all his moods. He copied the manuscript beautifully and dedicated it to her. She took it from him and looked at him with that rare tenderness of hers in which there was always a touch of the death and the passing of things. "You will be a great composer some day and I will have been your first love. How beautiful that is to think about." And she sang to him with strictly curbed emotion her favorite among those songs:

What have I lost in losing you?
Only the savor of all things.
To the same bough the same bird clings;
The same clouds darken in the blue.
Only, all's changed in losing you.

It was winter now, with snow on Morningside Heights and blue shadows on the snow. It was a winter of magic and of pain—a winter from which, in Herbert's memories of later years, the pain faded and only the magic of youth and passion and snow and gold and the aroma of fir trees and the gleam of the white adorable body of Gerda remained. They went together to a meeting and costume ball of one of the great Rhenish Carneval societies. Gerda was a snowmaiden. On her white fur-tipped costume the crystals of the snow sparkled and her eyes were bluer than ever in the midst of the whiteness. But Herbert felt as though a hot iron had been pressed into his entrails and were being slowly turned to sear him thoroughly. For in that brilliant hall she left him almost at once and attached herself to an enormous, dark, middle-aged man with a curving pompadour of almost white hair who had a rather weary splendor in his robes of a medieval dignitary. Mrs. Hasselmeyer, in a simple dark evening-frock, looked at

Herbert with her motherly eyes. "Don't set your heart on Gerda so, my poor boy; she hasn't any." He was beyond concealment or discretion. "I thought you were so fond of her." "I am. But I know her. I've known her all her life. One must take people as they are!" "Who is that man?" he asked chokingly. "Ullman. He's tremendously influential in theatrical circles. Gerda would—" She stopped at the sight of Herbert's sudden pallor. She added thoughtfully: "But she would do it, I believe, detachedly and calculatedly and keep what affection she's capable of for her real friends." Just then Gerda came up to them. She patted Mrs. Hasselmeyer's cheek affectionately. "Don't be glum, Herbert!" It sounded like a command. But her little white-shod foot touched his consciously. She whispered to him, close to his ear, her hair against his cheek: "Later!" Instantly the hall and the people glowed to Herbert's vision and his heart was like a child's heart on Christmas Eve when the candles on the tree are lit and he drank and danced and even flirted with the others. At two o'clock Gerda found him and was quiet and like a tired little girl on the long way home from Brooklyn and went straight to his room with him and slipped out of her white glittering costume and cuddled into his arms. "Hold me tight, Herbert," she whispered. For once she seemed frightened and in need of shelter. But by morning this mood had fled. "Marry you? Let you take care of me? What empty talk! What would it amount to actually? Being poor together, pulling each other down— sordidness, accidents, babies. When you're a great composer and I a second Fritzi Scheff we may talk it over again." "Yes," said Herbert bitterly. "And we'll be middle-aged and tired and corrupt." A sweet gravity came into her face. "True. O how true! That's why we should take what happiness we can now. But you won't let us. You want horribleness, messiness. A wise man in Germany taught me a saying: *haec olim meminisse juvabit,* it will be sweet to remember this some day!" She gathered up her garments and was gone. "How right she is," Herbert thought, "how right!" He sat on the side of his bed in that suddenly stripped and forlorn room, his face in his hands, with every instinct in hot and bitter rebellion against that rightness of hers.

Thaws set in. New York became a pool of slush. It snowed. Then it rained and thawed again. The slush was removed and then the whole dispiriting process started all over again. Gerda missed most of her coaching hours. When she came to them she was harsh, irritable, furtive. She disappeared on many afternoons and evenings. Herbert trained himself to an outward stoicism. He dwelt with dull but often almost insupportable pain. One day Mrs. Hasselmeyer came to him. She sat down slowly. Her rheumatism was bad in this weather. "My boy," she said, "you ought to think of yourself and your good parents. Gerda is trying to get out of her contract with the Shuberts. Ullman is going to get her the leading rôle in a road company. She'll leave in less than a week. She's been rehearsing almost every afternoon and evening." Herbert bit his lips. "And I'll have to ask you too, though it hurts me to the very heart, to get another room. Papa has to go to a sanatorium. The doctors think he has diabetes and we're giving up the house."

It seemed the end. It was chaos. The first warm winds of spring came that week and seemed a horrible irony to Herbert. Gerda disappeared without farewells. She sent for her things. Two days later a post-card came to Herbert from Detroit: "*Haec olim meminisse juvabit. Gerda.*" Mrs. Hasselmeyer sent Herbert to friends of hers who had a room to rent on 124th Street; Hasselmeyer, propped up in pillows, wrapped in shawls, shrivelled, collapsed, but still sardonic and commanding, gave him a letter to a well-known music agency. "Gerda showed us your songs. Perhaps you are not from Boeotia after all. The songs are not bad." He lapsed into complete naturalness at last. "If the damned quacks don't murder me, I'll help you get a decent publisher for them. Regards to Petersen. Goodbye."

Mechanically Herbert moved into his new room; mechanically he tried to write longer letters home. He found that with Gerda so far away, and amid surroundings that he did not know and could not visualize, his misery grew less sharp. He lapsed into an emotional numbness. But his mind was clearer. Since his money was gradually giving out—his mother's savings and his own—he presented Hasselmeyer's letter to the Mosessohn Musical Bureau. A sharp young man at a huge roll-top desk nodded. Hasselmeyer's name had power. The young man went through a card catalog. "There's a very large People's Organization downtown that wants a musical director to organize and lead a chorus for them. They can pay only twenty dollars a week. But it won't take all your time by any means. Just the thing, it seems to me, for some one who wants to go in for composing." Herbert agreed. "That doesn't sound bad." He needed work; he suspected that contact with people might help him. "Very well," said the sharp young man. "Here is the card of the chairman of the committee on cultural activities. Get in touch with her." Herbert took the card and read it. The name engraved above the address on Sixty-first Street was: Mrs. Harrison Dubose Vilas.

Book Three

CATASTROPHE

1   HERBERT took a local on the elevated and got off at Fifty-ninth Street. He had written a note to the chairman of the committee on cultural activities and had received an agreeable reply in a clear, unshaded, extraordinarily firm hand. The lady, who signed herself Anne Bronson Vilas, had asked him to be good enough to meet her at her apartment Wednesday afternoon at three. He was ten minutes early and loitered aimlessly along Sixth Avenue. Slush and mud were still on the ground; the old Empire Hotel looked dingy despite the flaring music hall behind it. The elevated trains, which had but recently abandoned their small locomotive engines, roared and rattled by. A drug shop, a candy shop, an undertaker's establishment. Life seemed to Herbert of an excruciating staleness. He dared not think of Gerda. He dared not think of the Hasselmeyer house nor the brightness of snow. He dared hardly more to think of Queenshaven. It came to him in the guise of that city of mother of pearl, that dawn city seen from the attic window of his boyhood. Remorse blended with nostalgia. He didn't know just why. After all, he was only twenty-two. But his father's earnestness and purposefulness was in his bones, and he seemed to himself, somehow, to have gone to pieces, to have drifted into loose, ineffectual undisciplined ways. He couldn't quite separate the ancestral conscience in him from his own. He stood on the Sixth Avenue curb. Merry chat-

ting girls passed—one with eyes that brushed him lingeringly. His youth rebelled against his cares. Perhaps through this work with the People's Chorus he would find some source of pleasure and forgetfulness.

The house on Sixty-first Street looked shabby. The entrance was a cavern. One felt that the reddish carpets on the stairs were, despite sweeping and brushing, thickened by the mud of a thousand boots, greasy with the effluvia of generations of lodgers, gritty with the dust of many summers. Herbert carefully avoided touching the dark shiny balustrades. On the third landing he found the name he sought on one of three oaken doors. He rang, the door opened, and he found himself immediately in the bright little sitting room and in the presence of Mrs. Vilas. She stood facing him, about his own height. A slim figure in a neat skirt and white shirtwaist. Faintly sallow skin and reddish blonde hair, a little low in the forehead. A chin and nose he didn't like, that gave him at once an indefinable sense of discomfort, but clear gray eyes, speaking, merry, pathetic, younger than anything else about the woman.

"So you are Mr. Crump?"

She gave him a slender, soft, though rather bony hand and beckoned him to an oak rocker. She sat facing him on a couch and between them the afternoon sun streamed in from the two windows.

"It's bright here, isn't it?" she said. "You see," she pointed to the window—her gestures were a little agitated—"you see, the lots across the street aren't built up. At night we see all the lights of Columbus Circle. It's just like fairyland." Her voice was an agreeable alto. She kept it soft. She began to explain about her organization. "They're young people from the East Side and very crude, but, of course, like all Jews, they're musical. They'll be very nice to you personally." Thus she took Herbert into her confidence and ranged him with her, a little aside from and above the people who were to employ him. It was agreeably flattering and at once established a slight intimacy between them.

"You think them good material?" he asked.

70

"Oh, undoubtedly! They all have bright minds." A silence fell. She looked out of the window, then lifted to him eyes full of an indefinable pathos.

"I got into the organization through an old friend of mine, Professor Carey Jones. You must have heard of him." Herbert hadn't, in fact, but he murmured an assent.

"You see," she went on, "I have heart trouble and I need something to take me out of myself." Herbert was about to rise when, from the portières which, falling from grillwork to floor, separated the room from the rest of the flat, there entered a child of five. The little girl had a pale, long face, straight yellow hair, knowing eyes. Diminutive as she was, everything about her was long, especially her forehead and her upper lip. She gave Herbert a hostile look and, after stopping suddenly, trotted up to her mother as though to shield her. Above the child's head, Mrs. Vilas smiled at Herbert.

"This is Eileen, my youngest." Herbert, never very comfortable in the presence of children, said "Oh, yes." Eileen looked at him with her large, knowing eyes. He forced himself deliberately to get up. The child, as if to prevent Mrs. Vilas from doing the same, snuggled into her mother's lap. Mrs. Vilas, with an apologetic smile, told Herbert the day, the hour and the place of the first meeting of her "young people." Their hands then met and clasped over Eileen's head, and Herbert felt the soft texture of the child's hair against his knuckles.

Of the whole scene and meeting he retained an impression of definiteness and brightness. Also an impression of curious intimacy. A little acrid aftertaste came to him from the appearance and actions of the child Eileen. Within the brightness, moreover, danced, like a mote in a jaded sunbeam, something of forlornness. He had a definite knowledge that Mrs. Vilas was stretching out physical tentacles into the world. Not after him particularly, of course. He thought: poor woman, and wondered vaguely what Mr. Vilas was like. The whole matter would naturally have faded promptly enough from his mind if he had not agreed to meet both Mr. and Mrs. Vilas in the vestibule of the People's Club on Sunday afternoon at four.

He found them on that day and hour ready to receive him. Mrs. Vilas in a narrow black hat with the brim turned up in front like a small, inverted shovel (the year was 1903) and a spring coat of black satin, looked both blonder and younger than at home. Behind her stood her husband, tall, thin, suave in manner, his small, pointed, jauntily set head exuding a faint querulousness. Herbert had just glimpsed a deprecatory gesture of the man's bony hands in the shadow when he was caught up in the blitheness, somehow tinged with pathos, of Mrs. Vilas herself.

"Here's our conductor, Harry." Mr. Vilas gave Herbert a suddenly boneless hand. "We'd better go in," he said. "Listen to the noise they're making."

A strong hum of many voices did in fact come from the assembly rooms. They entered and were at once surrounded by a whirling but individually courteous group of young men and women, nearly all black-eyed and swarthy.

"Here's Mrs. Vilas with the conductor," someone called out.

The young men teased Mrs. Vilas about small incidents of the club life that Herbert naturally knew nothing about. She answered with a ready wit. Mr. Vilas looked a little glum and lit a cigar. Herbert was introduced to people somewhat pell-mell and then drawn into a corner with the four young men and women who took the matter of the chorus seriously. With relief he got to the practical questions. Thirty applications for membership in the chorus were already in. They were all poor people, but each member of the chorus would gladly pay a dollar a week. Did he think three evenings of work a week too much? He didn't at all, of course. The arrangement was better than he had hoped for. Tuesday, Thursday and Saturday then. Did he play the piano too? Would he in that case be so sweet and play something right away? A gigantic young woman called for order and silence. A complete hush fell. The young giantess showed Herbert the grand piano in the next room beyond the open folding doors. There was tenseness and intelligent expectation in that hush. Herbert played Liszt, Chopin, Schumann, Brahms. He played for over an hour. It wasn't the applause. His exacting musician's sense told him that these people loved and understood music. Mrs. Vilas came finally, as she said, to rescue him. She laughed her rather trilling laugh, higher than her speaking voice led you to expect.

"Well," she said, "you can certainly make the piano talk." The expression struck him as extraordinarily queer, but people with warm black and brown eyes surged about him. They thanked him intelligently. They begged him not to forget Tuesday night.

He found himself in the dark street, sharply cool to his body, with Mr. and Mrs. Vilas. An inner reaction was suddenly upon him. He thought of Gerda and the corners of his eyes were hot.

"Won't you have dinner with us?" he heard Mr. Vilas say. He hesitated. "We are dining out tonight, anyhow," Mrs. Vilas encouraged him. He dreaded the lonely evening.

"It's awfully nice of you."

They took the elevated uptown, Mrs. Vilas now and then smiling at Herbert amid the roar. She had drawn a black, dotted half-veil to just above her chin, and under the flicker of the electric lights looked almost young. Herbert felt flattered and befriended by her kindness. She had again succeeded in establishing a psychical understanding, a half-merry, half-pathetic conspiratory bond between him and herself which was more definite this time since it excluded her husband.

At a table in a chophouse in the forties oysters were ordered and steaks and beer. Mr. Vilas faintly radiated the impression of one born to better things. He told anecdotes of the great musicians he had heard in New York before his marriage. Mrs. Vilas laughed a bitter little laugh.

"In those days, you see, Harry could afford concerts." Vilas shot a glance at his wife which Herbert resented for her. Then he seemed to feel that he ought to make amends.

"My wife writes, you know." Mrs. Vilas waved that aside. "What chance do I get? About every three months I write something. I had a poem in *The Century* not long ago and *Judge* occasionally buys my comic verses."

73

The beer was heavy, the atmosphere sympathetic. Herbert spoke of his work. He told them something of his compositions. Vilas suggested that some of his wife's lyrics might be suitable for musical setting. A glow of intimacy warmed them all and Herbert, solitary and inexperienced, found himself telling in veiled terms the story of Gerda. And as he told this story, he knew that something in the woman beside him was throbbing toward him. The situation had a morbid profoundly pleasurable tang. He tasted this to the utmost, and on the way home hugged his sophistication. He was twenty-two. He felt like a gentleman in a novel by Bourget. It was delicious.

2   THRICE a week Herbert worked with his singers at the People's Club house downtown. The young men and women were in earnest; not a few of them had good voices; nearly all had sufficient musical sense. A reasonably good chorus was developed. He adored conducting. Had it not always been his dream? They had procured a little platform for him. He stood on it. All eyes hung on his hands. He knew that his hands were strong, shapely and sensitive. A deep-seated shyness and sobriety of spirit kept him from ever admitting to himself that he was proud and fond of his hands, but something within him knew it. With his hands he swayed the always more sonorous masses of his singers. With his hands he could subdue them to sighing *pianissimi*. At beautiful moments the chorus was no longer an aggregation of human voices. It was a single instrument on which he played. Was it because of this intoxication with himself and his activity that he had barely a sense of the existence of the separate members of the chorus, or was it because, though most of them were a little older than himself, they treated him more and more with a grave respect and deference which was sweet to his youth and to his natural humility? Whatever the cause, the fact on which more than once he pondered in the after years remained. He stepped from his platform, answered questions, gave directions to an indis-

tinguishable mass of people and found waiting for him the caressing, half-tarnished brightness of Mrs. Vilas. Her husband did not appear on these weekday evenings. He was, she told Herbert with a touch of resignation, fond of billiards. So she and Herbert used to take a walk together. It was Mrs. Vilas' attitude too that prevented Herbert from staying behind for a while with his singers. She repeated her first remark about them. "They are crude. Of course they are wonderfully ambitious when you consider their origin. They come from the East Side; they are clerks and stenographers and shop girls."

Thus Mrs. Vilas emphasized a cultural and social solidarity between Herbert and herself. The solidarity between them, she seemed to say, went deeper. They were both artists though she, as she let it gradually appear, so baffled and burdened a one. Ah, and she knew too—she looked at Herbert in silent reference to his story of Gerda—how she knew what it was to have a heartache, to give her best and to be unrequited! And in this charming elegiac atmosphere they walked and talked after the high intoxication of conducting. Herbert, who was lonely, and who had many hours of longing and of torment for Gerda's sake had found a friend, a friend such as he had never had. Gently she broke down his reserves and inhibitions; she guided him to pour out his heart; she would heal the wound of his vain love, the hurt of his yet unrealized ambitions. They walked through the night. Soon they came to walk arm in arm. Her voice, eyes, touch were vivid. A fluid seeped into the boy's celibate void. He came home from these walks in a state of elation. He was a conductor now, after all. He had a friend. Ah, in French and German the word had several meanings —*Freundin, amie!* In the stories that came from the European world of art, did it not often happen that the young artist still struggling, still unrecognized, had a friend who was an older woman—a friend, a mistress—who took upon herself for the sake of art, for the sake of life, the ache of the young artist's years of waiting; who then, an exquisite and autumnal figure, faded into the background and gave him over to love and fame? And did not then, after the passing of years, the artist, himself now on the edge of his own autumn, seek out the grave, the ivied grave of that early friend, to lay upon it a white rose of gratitude and compassionate memory?

Herbert could see that scene of his own middle years so vividly that an anticipatory moisture came into his eyes. Would this whole beautiful story happen to him? Ah, he thought so. He did not desire Anne Vilas, but he wanted that story to happen to him. And he was sure that she desired him—his dreams, his ardors, his young body. Thus he walked with head erect and bought himself a few handsome garments and made himself ready for what he conceived of as a delicious adventure.

Twice he dined with the Vilas family. It was disillusioning. There was no maid and the dining room was stuffy. Little wrangles would break out between Mr. Vilas and Bronson, a brown-haired, brown-eyed boy of sixteen or seventeen with his father's small head and querulously argumentative manner, but with his mother's quickness of mind. Mrs. Vilas had already told Herbert that her beautiful little daughter Luella was visiting the Duboses for a while and was, alas, being filled with a spirit of subtle antagonism against herself. But the child Eileen sat at table and in a shrill metallic voice made occasional remarks of a ghastly maturity.

"I like visitors," she piped. "We have nice things to eat and everybody is polite!"

Mrs. Vilas exchanged an intimate and humorous glance with Herbert—the glance of a brave spirit gallantly enduring. It said, "Need I tell you who fails in politeness when the family is alone?" To change courses Mrs. Vilas slipped into the tiny dark hall that led from the dining room to the kitchen. From thence whispered colloquies were heard. Before bringing in the dessert Mrs. Vilas was heard to say. "Do please come in, Mamma." The deep mannish voice of an old woman answered. "Leave me alone, Anne. I'm in dissabilly and I don't want to embarrass Mr. Vilas." Vilas flushed in furious chagrin. Bronson laughed softly to himself. Eileen, with wide eyes on Herbert, shrilled, "Don't Grandma say funny things?" Mrs. Vilas came back with the ice cream. Her eyes were moist. She seemed to Herbert hunted and harassed by all these people. He never knew by what accident, or upon whose impulse their hands found each other for a soft pressure under the tablecloth. That mitigated the disillusion and charged it, in fact, with something subtle and romantic. Of course the autumnal lady in the story had to be tragic; she had to have a difficult fate. From that fate itself came the determination to make her free and beautiful gift to art and life. Psychically she had already given herself to him by this unspoken intimacy, by this silent appeal to him against the rude forces of her existence. Now the echoes of Southern chivalry blended in Herbert's mind with his dream drawn from the fancied lives of continental poets and composers. Now he was, in his imagination, both knight and young poet and elegiac worldling. He lost his last faint contact with the things and facts and characters with which he was confronted.

The following Tuesday night, out in the soft darkness Mrs. Vilas said:

"I must hurry home." He urged her to linger; but she was firm.

"I shall miss our walk," he said. She lifted her eyes to his.

"So shall I." Then she half whispered, "Run in some afternoon—say tomorrow, can't you?"

"Of course I can." She wouldn't let him take her to an elevated station. She left him and faded in a moment into the darkness.

Arriving in his room half an hour later he found Petersen waiting for him.

"Ha, you young scoundrel! Your letters to the folks have been short and *nichtssagend!* I had to run to New York. They told me to look you over."

Herbert had had twinges of conscience enough. But his winter in New York had been both absorbing and also incommunicable in character to his conservative father and mother. He walked up and down.

"I have fairly satisfactory employment. I've written all about that."

"*Ja!* But your mother wants to know something about your health and something about the inner man."

Herbert stopped. "She wouldn't understand. She might be shocked. There's no harm."

Petersen strained his failing vision to scrutinize Herbert. "You are too young to marry."

"Marry!" Herbert was contemptuous in his present mood. Gerda was lost. . . .

"Well, then," cried Petersen. Herbert felt enormously superior.

"From the stories you used to tell me about Chopin and Liszt, it wouldn't appear that marriage particularly enters the question in an artist's life."

Petersen rose to his full enormous height. "Be careful, my boy, be careful! This is America!"

Herbert laughed. "True, but New York isn't Queenshaven, thank heaven. In the meantime, Karl, I know you're hungry and it's only ten o'clock. Let's go somewhere."

"That's what I call an idea." They put on their coats. "What are you working at, Herbert?"

"Not much just now. I'm learning a lot from my conducting, though. But I did a group of songs a few months ago that aren't so bad, I believe."

They went to the West End restaurant on 125th Street and talked till closing time. Petersen had to leave for Baltimore in the morning. He seemed incredibly unsophisticated to Herbert this time. But his old friend's visit quieted his conscience about his parents. Petersen would give a satisfactory account of him in Queenshaven. Thus the deluded boy slept more calmly and happily on that night and freer in his mind for a delightful tomorrow.

3   THE golden-yellow roller shades were pulled down behind the cheap dimity curtains. On the shades burned the afternoon sun and suffused the room with a soft yellowish light. The portières that hung from the grill-work were drawn. The apartment was silent.

The hush was complete. The room was orderly and dustless. Herbert took in all these circumstances. He had not heard the rancorous bickering that had preceded Bronson's taking Eileen to a matinee; he had not seen Mrs. Vilas with broom, dustpan and rag, in a tattered kimono, a towel about her head, the frozen angle of her thick jaw, the unbridled determination in her stone gray eyes. He came with a bunch of early violets, came—the youth of his story—and found her gentle, faintly fragrant in that hushed golden room, still in her hand, as she softly opened the door, the Shelley over which she had been dreaming. The scene and the mood were perfect. Herbert, the half-dulled ache over Gerda in his heart, was attuned to the poetry of loss and disillusion. His songs "Amoris Victima" had been rejected by both Schirmer and Ricordi. Anne Vilas crooned to him a siren song of frustrated poetic ambition and the toils of an unbeautiful marriage and of a renunciation at the core of which there was a spiritual hope. "Still nursing the unconquerable hope," she quoted to him, "still clutching the inviolable shade."

They mingled their disappointments and their aspirations; she read her verses to him and in those verses, which were not much worse than the average of the Stoddards and the Johnsons of that day, there was the routine, imitative sweetness and dignity of sentiment that were supposed to "go" with poetry. Herbert himself preferred a headier vintage and quoted to her the vibrant poems of Arthur Symons that he had set to music. And his quotation of these poems (". . . the music had the heat of blood, a passion that no words can reach . . .") added a note of sensuality to the overflowing gush of their sentiments. They finally found themselves sitting hand in hand when a rattling behind the portières startled them into separating. And this common consciousness as of a guilt already incurred drew them but the closer together and heightened in Herbert the sense of sophisticated adventure. They had both risen. Mrs. Vilas' smile was sorrowful. It seemed to say: "You see I have no respite." She went to the window and let one of the shades fly up. The sun was gone now; the light was sober. Sadly she turned to him, "When are you coming

79

again?" There was a mysterious undertone in her words. "When may I?" "Friday?" she asked in a half-whisper. He nodded. She swayed a little toward him and then drew back. On a chair near the door were his hat and coat. He hurried out. . . .

Desperately, when he came to know that a catastrophe was upon him, still more desperately in the midst of the irretrievable, Herbert Crump tried to recall and reconstruct his state of mind during these crucial days. He had been lonely; he had been disappointed; he had nursed a romantic delusion. True, all true. These explanations did not suffice; they did not include the central fact that he had not desired Anne Vilas. She said that she was thirty-six and he believed her. She did not show herself under the searching light of day. But he definitely disliked her nose and chin; he disliked the too convex semi-circle of her unlovely lower teeth. He had observed, when she had leaned her cheek against an embroidered pillow, how the pattern of the heavy thread had remained for minutes upon a cheek that had long lost the tautness and resilience of youth. When it was too late he shuddered a little at this recollection. But during the days of his downfall all he had known and consciously nursed was that romantic delusion and the impersonal, undiscriminating sex hunger of the young male. That was it—that! Gerda had stung his senses into a vivid life and left him. Why had he not met some other woman, oh, any other woman? Why had he not had the realism of temper to pick up one of the poor bedizened prostitutes who, in those days, wandered nightly about Columbus Circle? Well, Queenshaven had been no school of reality. Herbert, who had known German all his life, took pride in his easy access to French literature. The young artists and adventurers who came to Paris from the provinces always had a mistress who was a married woman. The only thing that Herbert regretted was that he had no little entresol apartment—it always was an entresol in the stories—to which he could invite his friend. Yes, he had been drunk with falseness and with naked sex hunger. Drunk . . .

On Friday he found once more that dim and golden room. He

80

found the lady in a yellow silk kimono. She told him that life had been difficult and had brought on one of her heart attacks. Her heart had not been strong since her early girlhood. It was a functional disorder; there was a regurgitation of both the mitral and the pulmonary valves. This explanation broke his mood irritatingly for a moment, but for a moment only. She drew him gently down beside her on the couch and, taking his hands, she told him how expressive and yet strong they were. She released his right hand, and he put his arm about her and discovered that, under the kimono, there was only one thin soft garment. The curves of her body were directly under his hand; her softly veiled nakedness infected his blood and when, whether accidentally or not, kimono and shift slipped a little from the shoulder nearest to him, and showed a skin still soft and rosy there, the outcome was inevitable and his doom was on him.

There were tears in her eyes when they faced each other afterwards by the window. She suppressed a sob in her throat. She seemed suddenly to have grown smaller and touched the lapels of Herbert's coat and looked up to him as to a master. And this attitude fired him and aroused his maleness and his primitive protective instincts and when she lifted those tear-suffused eyes to his and asked falteringly, in a whisper, almost as a child might ask, "You love me a little, don't you?" he pressed her to him passionately and said, "I do, of course I do." A smile broke through the pathos of her face, a trembling uncertain smile, and she put her hand upon her doubly suffering heart. By a mutual impulse they planned to meet again. It could not be till next Wednesday afternoon. Herbert protested. He had but touched the goblet. He was convinced at that moment that his desire was personal and exclusive. But she protested that there was, alas, no help. Even so, she said, she trembled at every moment. He swore that he would find some better way for them and went out into the sunset city starred with the early electric lights, full of the exhilaration of one whose dream has come true.

He didn't hear from her. When they met at the club they looked at each other across the room which seemed to palpitate with their great secret. But on Saturday night, after the chorus had scattered, he found her lingering behind with Miss Cohen, the tall, dusky, handsome directress. He joined them.

"You just come and have dinner with us Monday," Miss Cohen was saying. "I know it's a long way from Brooklyn. But you can stay all night. Mr. Vilas can amuse himself somehow and your mother can take care of the family."

"Well," Anne Vilas said, "if I don't come, don't wait dinner for me. I'd like to but—!" She made a fatalistic little gesture.

Miss Cohen walked with them to the corner. "I tell you, Mr. Crump, Mrs. Vilas makes a perfect slave of herself over those children. I don't think they appreciate it, or her husband either."

Blithely Mrs. Vilas took a high moral tone. "That doesn't matter. The action must be its own reward."

Alone with Herbert she looked at him wistfully. In a flash he understood. "Why can't you dine with me on Monday night and stay?"

She gave a shocked little laugh. "Oh, Herbert, I daren't." But at twenty-two the rôle of the elegant seducer is sweet upon the tongue. He rose to it.

"There's no danger. Miss Cohen is evidently devoted to you. She's a perfect alibi. Come!"

They walked along in silence for a little while. Long afterward Herbert wondered whether in that silence Anne Vilas came to her decision. For she ended the silence to ask with a quiet deliberateness: "When shall we meet?" He named an hour, a street, a corner. He left her in a glow. He felt that conviction of male triumph which is the certain sign of self-deception and defeat.

They met and dined together at the West End restaurant. They poured out their souls to each other. That is to say, Herbert preened, unconsciously enough, his most seductive psychical feathers and Anne played the gentle, bright, tragic Egeria. All through the meal they drank heavily, beginning with cocktails and ending with green chartreuse. When they got to the Colonial Hotel and registered as Mr. and Mrs. Smith, Herbert walked in a gentle haze. Yet he had noted dimly that Anne was heavily veiled and shrank somewhat from the necessary proceedings. In their room she begged him modestly to turn out the lights. Only by the dim shimmer of a lamp shining in from the street did he catch a glimpse of a pale, slim back. Then he was first uplifted and later oppressed by the pertinacity of her exorbitant passion and noon still found them in a heavy sleep. He stirred and Anne at once covered her face with the bedclothes. She begged him to dress and wait for her down stairs. A sense of both gloom and terror was upon him. But these faded when Anne, in her black frock and pointed hat and little dotted veil, met him in the dining room. Her skin was smoother than usual and agreeably flushed; her walk was elastic; she seemed suddenly rejuvenated. She smiled at him frankly and merrily.

"I feel fresh as a daisy."

They breakfasted and Herbert felt renewed. But now it was her turn to droop.

"I haven't an idea when we can really meet again. Oh, write me just a word, Herbert, just a word. I shall be so desolate!"

At the elevated station she flashed back at him a look of such longing and trust and passionate expectancy that Herbert hurried to his room, wrote a grateful, boyish, thoroughly incriminating letter, rushed out to mail it and returning, dropped in a sudden, leaden weariness upon his bed.

4   ON THE next forenoon he was called to the telephone. Anne's voice gave him at first a small, sharp pang of fright. The pang faded. For a moment she was blithe and clear.

"I thought perhaps you might recognize my voice, Mr. Crump." Then she grew plaintive. "I want to see you, Herbert; I must see you. Can't you drop in this afternoon?" She needed him. Poor little woman. Of course she did. However sophisticated they both were, he reasoned, and however justified she might feel herself to be in

83

embracing this late and transitory happiness, yet the moral shock of her adultery must be severe enough. The least he could do was to stand by her, to help her to regain her poise.

He reached the house on Sixty-first Street a little before three and, flowers in hand, knocked at the now familiar door. He heard a sound as of soft, scurrying feet, then as of a chair being moved, of a blind being pulled down. Then the door was opened by Eileen who gave her hand to Herbert in that grown-up way which made her seem more like a dwarf than like a child, and said: "Mamma will be in in a minute." Herbert sat down, feeling a little embarrassed and foolish under Eileen's clear, knowing gaze. He made a mistake common to people who are themselves very young. He was condescending to the child, who turned up her small freckled nose and looked at once superior and prim. The light was not as soft as usual; a beam came in and in it danced and floated a thousand particles of dust. Chairs, couch, hangings, knick-knacks, books, had an indefinable air of having been slung into a brief order not natural to them. But before Herbert could clarify these impressions to himself, Anne Vilas came in with a swift airy motion. She looked, he thought, a trifle haggard. That was only too natural. She pressed his hand tenderly and smiled consciously.

"I've been flying around all day like a chicken with its head chopped off," she declared with an expression that offended Herbert's image of her in his mind. She dropped into a chair and lifted sad eyes to him. "There is so much to do and so little money to do it on. Harry has been—" she caught herself and turned to Eileen—"run along, baby, to grandma." Eileen looked at her mother imperturbably. "Why?" Then a strange thing happened. Herbert, who did not know he was irascible, felt a wave of violent irritation rise up in him. He wanted to strike that child. He did not know the reason. He knew nothing at this time. But a day was to come on which he was to recall that long-drawn out, cool, unconsciously but immeasurably insolent word of Eileen's—the symbolic word of a family life devoid of order, discipline or love, carried on in alternate moods of base contention and baser indulgence. Immediately it relieved him to see Mrs. Vilas rise,

84

take the child by the shoulders and thrust her into the next room from which arose immediately a dry, shrill, calculated wail of protest. Mrs. Vilas dashed into the next room once more. Herbert heard a hot, hoarse whisper. Eileen was silent. Anne returned and sat down beside her lover.

There was a great sadness about her. "Dear, if you knew what I have to put up with. As I started to tell you, Harry has been playing the races again. Of course he lost virtually his entire week's salary. I don't know how we get along from day to day. The rent is overdue, of course, and all that breeds demoralization. You saw Eileen just now. She's not as sweet as Luella, but she's really a very sweet child and devoted to me. But what can you expect? Last night I naturally reproached Harry with the condition of things. Do you know what he did? He spat full in my face."

Herbert jumped up. She hid her face in her hands. "Good God!" he said. "But that's unheard of. Honestly, that's the first time in my life that I—"

The thing choked him. He thought of his parents, of all the people he had ever known. It was inconceivable to him—the thing he had just heard. Yet he knew it was true, oh, true beyond all doubt. And he had no notion, of course, of how much he was learning on that afternoon. He heard Anne's voice. "Ah, my dear, often and often I think I'll just get a bottle of ether and end it all. I did try once. They found me and pulled me back." What could he do? What would any youth have done but put his arms about her and comfort her and beg her not to think of such things, since there was one in the world who loved and needed and appreciated her? And passion, which could not be satisfied here and now, gave a sharper edge to pity and wrung from Herbert words that he did not count nor weigh nor mean.

They arose from that imperfect and frustrate absorption in each other. But she was gay. He took gaiety for courage and admired her.

"Can't we take a walk?" he asked, "and drop in somewhere for tea?"

"Stay here, dear boy. I'm not dressed to go out. We'll have some tea here. And I want you to know mamma. Poor mamma! You've never even seen her, have you?"

She left him and Herbert had an uncomfortable moment. He wandered uneasily about the room. Then he heard her voice with an overtone of happy irony.

"Won't you come in here, Mr. Crump?"

He followed her into the dim dining room. The table was laid for tea. Eileen was already sitting there. She had a pouting, affronted expression and did not look up from her cocoa. Mrs. Toohey, gaunt, tall, with a long white face emaciated save for a bloodless dewlap, stood up straight in her gray wrapper.

"Well, mamma," said Anne, coaxingly, "here's Mr. Crump." The old woman smiled a kindly smile. They all sat down. They chatted and Herbert was amused by Mrs. Toohey's drastic speech and quaint anecdotes. The two women waited upon him. He was in another man's house. The other man's child sat opposite him. Yet the two women subtly constituted themselves his handmaids. Through little gestures and attentions they called him "master" in an atavistic, immemorial way that women have. Herbert, the stripling, became in his subconsciousness the Old Man of the tribe. . . . Keenest of poisons— this poison that was trickled into him. Precisely because he was an artist who loathed the frictions of the world of matter, who hated to do anything for himself, who forgot to take his meals at proper hours and to send his linen to the laundry—precisely because of this, the poison slowly soaked into him. An old incantation, long grown hypocritical and stale, helped to betray him. A remnant of prudence in him registered a psychical protest when, from the veiled allusions of the two women, he discovered that Mrs. Toohey was privy to the relations between Anne and himself. The old woman ate Vilas' bread and yet Anne had dared to tell her! From this alone a whiff of moral corruption should have reached him. Steeped in his false romance, persuaded by his nobler pity for Anne to find or make excuses, lulled by the harem ceremonial of the hour, he hushed the monitions of his soul. . . .

86

They made another engagement, met in the evening and Anne stayed with him at the Colonial Hotel that night and the next day and another night. He did not ask and did not know how she explained her absence from home. Alone afterwards in his room he felt depressed. The world seemed stale and empty. His inexperience did not tell him that his depression and his sense of anxiety were due to the fact that he did not love Anne, that these many and ardent embraces did not satisfy him. He might have guessed, since Gerda's cooler springtime love had left him with a sense of beauty and serenity. But he did not want to think of Gerda. He did not want to touch that wound. He plunged into the older woman's last sultry edge of summer and in his depression and desolation, when she left him, scribbled her notes which he thought sincere but which expressed nothing but his own confusion, his wretched ignorance of the causes of things.

It was at the end of the fourth or fifth escapade. Anne had left Herbert at noon and he had drowsed uneasily in his room through the afternoon hours. At seven he had suddenly felt ravenous. He went out and ate dinner at a little neighborhood restaurant. When he came back he found Bronson Vilas loitering awkwardly and furtively in front of the house. There was a scared, suspicious look in Bronson Vilas' handsome brown eyes. The look of a small animal that is afraid of being caught and caged. Yes, of a small animal—although the lad was taller than Herbert. To hide his furtiveness and fear Bronson Vilas assumed a deeper voice than he possessed.

"Mamma wants to see you—right away."

Herbert was irritated. He was dog-tired. He suddenly felt the weariness creep into his bones. "Must it be right away?"

Bronson seemed to shake with terror. "Yes, we are afraid mamma is going to do herself some harm."

The cold irritation did not leave Herbert. His instinct spoke to him truly. But his moral nature and his sense of honor rebelled against that instinct. "What a cad I am," he thought. "What a rotten cad." He hurried off with Bronson to the elevated, paid their fare and rode down town. On the way from the station to the house on Sixty-first Street Bronson Vilas almost galloped. Herbert trying to keep up with him suddenly hated the fellow's disjointed, belated hobbledehoy movements. Bronson's limbs seemed to be held to his rump by strings and to be eager to fly off. At the door of the house he disappeared. Herbert found himself climbing the stairs alone. He knocked at the accustomed door. What opened was the rear door of the telescope flat. He entered the short corridor that led from the dining room to the kitchen. At the table in the dining room half crouched Mrs. Toohey. Opposite her with strained face and large gaunt eyes sat Anne. She rose and flew to him.

"Sh—!" she said. "The baby is asleep in the next room."

She drew him to a chair. He sat down and from the air in the room came to him a faint, horrible, penetrating scent. Mrs. Toohey noticed his discomfort. "Ether," she croaked carefully. "But you needn't be afraid. It takes more than a Mr. Harrison Dubose Vilas to do for a Bronson of Frankfort. You can believe the old lady!"

5   HE HAD a moment of both terror and disgust. Anne's melancholy eyes softened him. They were upon him soothingly, full of flattery and adoration. Across the table she took his hand.

"I am so sorry you were dragged here, you poor darling boy; I didn't mean to have you. I just put a few drops on a handkerchief to go to sleep, to forget for a little while. Then Bronson became panic-stricken."

Slowly her eyes filled with tears. Herbert, utterly compassionate, pressed her hand. "What has happened, my dear?"

She controlled her emotion and dried her tears.

"Well, you know how this flat is. There's no place for anything. The children lost the key to my little desk. So I kept a couple of your notes in my stockings—day and night. They're so dear. I can't bear to part with them. This morning, before I got up, Harry was hunting

88

around for something—I don't know what—and grabbed one of my stockings by mistake. The paper crackled in his hands. He thought it was money and found your notes."

Herbert felt as though he had a stone in his bosom. "My God," he said out of a dry throat. Anne's eyes grew more melancholy than ever.

"There's no mistaking the situation from your notes, you know."

"Oh, I am not so sure," he fenced half sincerely. Again her eyes filled with tears.

"If you abandon me, Herbert, there's only one thing for me—only one. But you said you loved me!"

He bowed his head. It was true. He saw it. If he abandoned her there was no way out for her. Not so far as he could see. Her voice rose again softly but with a tragic urgency.

"You did say so, didn't you?"

"Yes, yes, of course I did."

He glanced at Mrs. Toohey and thought he saw an astutely watchful look on her long, white, old face. He pulled himself together.

"Tell me exactly what happened, Anne."

Anne brightened. Something belligerent arose in her.

"Harry raged, of course. He called me every vile name he could think of and you too, naturally. The children heard everything. Never mind that. I gave him a Roland for his Oliver."

Even in his fear and confusion Herbert was struck by another of those grotesque phrases which Anne evidently brought from some world of experience to which he had no key.

"Next he rushed to the office," she continued, "and told the whole story to Mr. Lancy and took a day off. Then he saw Dr. Spicer in his study behind the church and showed him your notes."

Suddenly croaked Mrs. Toohey: "That Spicer's what I'd call a ninny-hammer!"

Anne turned to her mother. "I don't agree with you at all, mamma. I think Dr. Spicer is perfectly splendid. Harry admitted that he spoke most warmly of me. He said he would think it all over and asked Harry and me to meet him in his study tomorrow morning."

Anne's gallantry somehow heartened Herbert. But he recalled the ether and the tears.

"Well, then why were you so depressed?" he asked.

With infinite mournfulness, her eyes smote upon him. "If you love me, Herbert, as you've said and written, everything is all right. But do you? Do you?" She got up and put her arms around his neck and pressed his head against her bosom. "You do, don't you?" He nodded. "You'd better go now, darling. Bronson's on the lookout, but Harry might come along suddenly."

"When will I see you or hear?" he said.

"Tomorrow at one we can meet at our corner; then I'll tell my boy all about everything." She put her bare arms around his head once more and there seemed to be a genuine tenderness in her voice.

It was that tenderness in her voice that stayed with him, that would not let him see the fangs of the trap. A trap consciously set? Deliberately sprung? On this single point Herbert always reserved judgment. Perhaps it was an ultimate vanity in him that forced him to do so, a disinclination to believe that in his twenty-fourth year he was an utter fool. But even though, with the passing of the years, the knowledge of Anne's instinctive duplicity, of her boundless treacherousness, wound its tight serpent coils about his breast, he continued to want and hence to strive to believe that during these early and fatal days she was impelled by a sincere emotion and was the victim, not the mistress of events. He truly believed on this night when, not unlike a criminal, he made his furtive departure from that house, that she loved him with a tender and consuming passion and that honor, kindness, gratitude, affection demanded that he stand by her during this storm that had broken out about them both.

At one o'clock next day the sunlight was brilliant on Eighth Avenue.

The elevated structure threw a black tracery on gold. The colors of the fruits in the open shops had a Southern brilliance and definiteness. From afar Herbert saw Anne coming and the whole situation gave him today a slight thrill of interest and adventure. In a moment her eyes were upon him adoring and intimate, drawing them both into a community of fate that warmed his lonely heart. His greeting showed how he felt. Anne laughed her soft, most youthful laugh.

"You are just a bit glad to see me, aren't you!"

He nodded. "Of course I am."

She pressed his arm.

"From your mood I don't suppose anything very dreadful has happened?"

She grew a little wan. "It wasn't so simple. I denied being your mistress, although your notes—well, you know them. But though Harry raged, Dr. Spicer refused to press that point. It was awfully decent of him, wasn't it?"

Out of his profound relief Herbert answered with enthusiasm. "It certainly was."

"Well," Anne went on more thoughtfully, "you see, Dr. Spicer has known us for years and he knows all about Harry's little weaknesses. He's advised me several times to arrange for a separation."

Herbert had a sudden vision of Anne living alone and of his being able to come and go as he liked. "Why don't you do that?" he asked.

Anne shook her head sadly. "How much money do you suppose I'd get for the children and poor mamma and myself? Harry's whole salary is forty dollars a week."

They had been walking north and now turned west toward the river.

"Shan't we stop first and have some luncheon?" Herbert asked.

She shook her head. "I have no appetite. Let's go on to the Hudson."

A silence fell between them and Herbert knew that she expected something of him. But he in all sincerity didn't know what.

"And the upshot of it all?" he asked finally.

"Dr. Spicer said that Harry had no right to me on account of the way he had treated me and that you had no right to me on account of the way you'd won me, if indeed you had. Therefore, he said, I ought to go away and see neither of you for a while and make up my mind."

91

An icy constriction laid hold of Herbert's entrails. The whole thing wasn't clear to him. But he felt that Anne and her Dr. Spicer were making assumptions of a most staggering kind. The blue river with its black and golden splashes was like a mass of molten turquoise matrix. So clear was the atmosphere that you could pick out the single trees on the palisades. The weather was mild and Anne and Herbert sat down on a bench, surrounded by poplars that faced the river. Herbert kept his eyes carefully away from Anne.

"I've just been drifting," he said slowly. "This work with the chorus is all very well but it leads to nothing. My parents haven't said anything, but I know they're frightfully disappointed in me. And I owe them everything—everything! I've got to get busy and concentrate on my compositions and my career."

He inhaled the tonic air. It had been hard. But surely he had made his position admirably clear. Anne's hand, small, helpless, as though blindly groping, was upon his arm. He turned and saw eyes full of fear—eyes wide with an agony of terror, eyes haunting, clinging, accusing.

"But you said you loved me, Herbert, Herbert! Only yesterday—no longer ago than yesterday you said you loved me. Didn't you say so?" Large, heavy tears trembled upon her lids and did not fall.

"I did."

"And didn't you mean it?"

How could he deny having meant it? How did he know at that moment that his affection for her and his compassion and his physical desire, still unblunted by satiety, did not constitute, at least, a kind of love? He was no "subtle-souled psychologist" in those days. He did not know that Anne's instinct of sex-possessiveness was without shame, and as sure in its operations as an engine of war. He only knew that the confused issue between them had been hopelessly darkened, and that his appeal and explanation had both been vain.

"Where are you going?" he asked, "and when?"

"Do you want to get rid of me?"

There was an infinite melancholy in her pleading for a little love.

He started his habit—he didn't know it was going to be a habit—of agreeable, soothing equivocation.

"The sooner you go, the sooner I'll have you back."

She brightened. "An old friend of mine, Hattie McCune, has a lovely house in Baltimore. She lives alone there with her colored cook. I'm going to her tomorrow—for a month. It'll do me real good to talk to Hattie again. But Herbert, I shall be so lonely for you." That touched and flattered him. "You'll write me, won't you?"

"Of course I will."

"Every day?"

"Every day."

"And you'll miss me, won't you?"

"You know I will."

Now she was blithe again. They went for a belated luncheon. She was, as she could be at her best, an excellent companion. She was victorious and at ease.

It was curious and, had he but known it, significant how promptly her absence diminished his preoccupation with her. With a great zest he went back to his work. On the very day of her departure there came to him the theme and structure of his sonata "Spring Presage," the first of his really mature works. The long passages in the adagio conceived for brasses and so executed years later in the orchestral production express a mood of triumphant liberation; the lovely melody of the andante says a compassionate but resigned farewell. In less than a week he completed these two movements, utterly unconscious himself of their deeper meaning. Daily with a little pang, a strange pang, half of fear, half of physical longing, he scribbled a note to Anne. But toward the end of the week his old friend Ralph Greene suddenly turned up in New York. He had come over from Cambridge in connection with the affairs of the *Harvard Law Review* to the editorial council of which he had just been elected. He was having a brilliant career at Harvard. He didn't say that in so many words, but there was no doubt. He made Herbert feel grimy and of no account.

Herbert felt that he must at once get in touch with people who could appreciate his work, who could help him. Great God, what had he been doing with himself anyhow! He and Ralph went to a few concerts and to a few plays. But he worked all day. And for three successive days he forgot to write to Anne.

6 FOR three days. On the fifth day her voice—a voice full of tears —came to him over the telephone. She could no longer endure the terror, silence, longing, suspense. She loved him so; how could he be so cruel? How? There was nothing she wouldn't do for him. And could he not have spared her five minutes a day to keep her soul at rest? He stammered he hardly knew what replies. He was acutely conscious of the colored boy downstairs, probably listening in, and of his landlady who, having called him to the telephone, had retired to the kitchen but left her door ajar. Shaking with a mixture of fear and rage he asked her where she was, what she expected him to do. She was, it appeared, in the telephone booth of the corner drugstore. Would he come—come right away? He hurried down the stairs; he was ashamed to take the elevator. He ran to the corner. There she stood in her most plangent melancholy. Wasn't he, she asked, a little glad to see her? The sight of her had, in fact touched him a little, but he would not answer. He felt for the first time a desire to be cruel to her—deliberately and revengefully to hurt her.

"How did you explain your sudden return?" he asked finally.

"I am not at home," she said softly. "I've rented a little room on 123rd Street. Across the vacant lots I can see your window from mine. I'm going to send letters to Hattie to mail for me from Baltimore to the house. I was just wild with agony. So the dear girl thought out this plan for me."

"Suppose you're seen here?" he asked.

"Is that all you can think of, Herbert—all? If it weren't for the children, I'd be glad to die with you. And you—!"

She took out a little handkerchief and dabbed her eyes through her veil. He heard a sob bravely suppressed.

She led him insensibly to the house on 123rd Street. There was no elevator here; there were no prying eyes. She opened the door of a flat on the first floor and led him down a dim narrow hall into a tiny, clean, white room with a window that gave on one of those jagged little mountains of rock which still, in those days, existed in upper Manhattan. Herbert sat down on the only chair. Anne, facing him, sat on the bed. It was quiet in the small white room. There was a sense of peace here, a sense of that refuge from the clamor and the demands of life that Herbert always loved and that, by any false semblance of their reality, always betrayed him again. Anne took his hands. Tired, he bent forward and leaned his forehead against her shoulder. Thus they remained for several minutes and Herbert, forgetting that it was she who had caused him the pain and the emotional turmoil which had wearied him, felt a community in this refuge from the hostility of life. He had never ceased to feel a stranger in New York; he had never lost a sense of the great city's menace and indifference. Here in this white room, a woman's hands clasping his own, he felt secure and befriended. Her adoration of him, her clinging to him, took from him not only his loneliness but the sharper feeling of his insignificance in New York, of his vain knocking at its iron gates. What he would have liked was to have gone home and confessed his fears and his failures and be comforted and shielded in his mother's arms. But he was a man and an artist. It was for him to encourage and fortify his parents and to delight them with his strength and his success. He yielded deeply to this vicarious refuge, to this false suspension of the strain of life. And here there was added another element. He and Anne had not been long together in this silence when she drew his head deeper to rest upon her bosom and his pulses began to hammer and soon they reached that situation which was to Anne aim and end, proof of love, excuse for monstrous exactions and sacrifices, ultimate surrender of the male in question, ultimate justification for her to use fraud, chicanery or force to render that subjection of the male permanent and complete. She brightened; she became more youthful; she was playful, consoling, tender. Together they strolled out into the golden and rosy dusk.

He had never had a woman at his beck and call before. Her instinct told her of the power of this situation over his unspoiled youth. She never denied herself to him; she bade him take no precautions. Nor had he been constantly companioned before, especially not by a woman. He had seen girls to long for them in Queenshaven; but when he had sought contact with their minds he had found that they had none. Chaffing and chatting had exhausted him after half an hour and he had retired luxuriously into himself from a society in which any ill-bred and brainless lout counted for far more than he. In Anne's very arms a sudden desperate longing for Gerda would still at times overtake him. That had been his great passion. But it had been almost frustrate. Could he not almost count the hours which Gerda had given him? And how many of those hours had not her ambition and her hardness filled with discords? He let Anne drug him. He met her more than halfway. He wanted to be drugged. He knew fundamentally that in this relation there was neither enchantment nor delight. Even Anne's body, though youthful for her age, bore definite traces of her history. After one of her confinements she must have been inadequately bandaged; she had nursed all her children from the same breast. But the condition of being drugged, of wanting moreover to be drugged, consists precisely in this, that the soul will not receive the message of the senses, that perception is not brought before the tribunal of the mind, that the boundary between dreams and realities is obliterated.

They walked and talked in the fine spring weather. Anne talked well. Neither anecdotage nor repetition had yet attacked her and Herbert had no means of knowing that in her both literary and artistic interests were merely by-products of the sex instinct. Of music she knew little and understood less. But Herbert disliked vague talk about music anyhow. He thought he knew his business, although at this time few would have agreed with him. What puzzled him was life to which, with an obscure dread, he did not feel adequate. He read many books in the hope of finding out something about life. He talked with Anne about things that happened in the world and about men and women and himself and herself. And this absorption in sex and talk was rendered deeper by the knowledge of its precariousness. Anne would disappear for two hours in the afternoon. She would come back wan and torn.

"I can't stand it, Herbert; I just can't stand it. I watched the house. Luella is back home. I saw her and Eileen walking out and I didn't dare let them see me. Luella isn't looking well—not a bit well. I suppose mamma quarrelled with Harry. I can just hear and see it all. Bronson, poor boy, hasn't a penny, I'll be bound! And his father still slaps him. Herbert, what shall I do?"

Herbert looked at her blankly. The best he could do was to keep the annoyance out of his eyes. Bronson was to him merely another man with something slinking and ill-coordinated about him that he disliked. He took no interest in female children. He was, naturally and properly, concerned with his art and with the problems of life. He didn't think he was inhuman. In a still hour of the night he had once had a vision of a little son born to Gerda and himself. Nor was he stupid. He knew that he was in the presence of a genuine sorrow as he saw Anne turn from him and hide her face in the pillow of her bed and shake the very bed with her sobs. But the sorrow was too remote and alien from his age and character to be more than a spectacle, a spectacle that made him a little angry. She had done her utmost by word and action to persuade him that she had become necessary to him. If ever this relation irked him, if he showed signs of restiveness, she had appealed to his chivalry, to the words of love that she wrung from him again and again. Once, a week before, she had employed coarser methods. Suddenly one day she had cloyed him. He had torn himself away. He had gone for a long walk alone—a long walk during which his thoughts had begun to rectify themselves and he had had a glimmering of the desperateness of his situation. He had returned and with a sudden pang of compassion determined to look in

97

on her. He had found her on the bed quite white. There was a bottle, a handkerchief and the fume of ether. He had hurled the bottle out of the window. He had been maddened by rage and fear. What if she killed herself and if he were to be accused of complicity in her death? She had been contrite and gentle and had known how to substitute for a quarrel and an explanation that one action which seems, however falsely, to fuse two into one.

He watched her almost sullenly as her sobbing quieted down. It wasn't part of the bargain that he should be annoyed by the Vilas family. The thought filled him with a disgust so strong that he rose abruptly. Immediately she was up and standing beside him, her naked arms about his throat.

"Herbert, for God's sake, where are you going? You're not going to abandon me too? Because you said you loved me I've left my home and my children and endangered my whole life! You can't, you just can't leave!"

He shook her off. Her plea seemed in truth to be borne out by the facts. Yet he knew it to be a lie, an evil and corrupting lie. Only he did not know how to disentangle that lie from the treacherous facts. The thought that he could not do so maddened him. He flung out of the room. She dared not, half-clothed as she was, follow him beyond the door of the flat. He walked the streets for hours. He went over the history of their relationship. He could not disentangle the threads; he could not say to whom belonged error and guilt and weakness. He could not say. The spirit of his fathers, divorced from creed, became in him a following in action of precepts he hardly ever thought about. He would not and he could not judge. And as he came to this conclusion, unwilling to hold himself guiltless, a pity came over him for the woman who seemed to love him in so tragic a fashion and who, as he thought, now sat broken-hearted in hopeless vigil for a step that did not come. Tired and footsore from his long tramp he hastened back. He found her silent, white, wide-eyed beside her window. Like himself she had neither eaten nor drunk. Soon they sought refuge and forgetfulness in the familiar bed.

7 Toward the end of their lives together, alone once with earth and sky in another part of the land, Herbert Crump meditated upon those early New York days. Though his reason forbade such a conclusion, he could not but regard the coming upon him of his fate as, in the deeper sense, accidental. For that fate seemed to him to have no relation to his character, to its weakness which was no doubt great, to its strength which was small. If Hasselmeyer had been too ill, as he became a day later, to write the letter to the musical agency; if the clerk at the agency had already given Mrs. Vilas' name to some other applicant, or had with his flying fingers skipped the club's call for a director in his card catalog. . . . Trivial enough speculations in one sense, deep in another as the fate of man, worthy of being brought, if there are such councils, before the councils of God. . . . Vain thoughts! Herbert turned his meditations to what the beginnings of his and Anne's story were as given, as incurred. Up to her return from Baltimore she had been, as far as he was concerned, without guilt. She had not given herself those avid senses. If she no longer loved Vilas, she didn't. That was all. If before the definite coming of middle age she craved one more romance, something to remember beside the dying embers of her winter, why in God's name should she not have had it? The bungling and discovery too might have been innocent enough. Guilt came when in the conflict between her late romance and her motherhood it never occurred to her in her mad self-worship to make the one righteous decision—to let him, to let her young lover go. No one expected her to abandon her children. To determine as she did with a determination that nothing could bend or daunt, that stopped at no stealthiness, no falsehood, no coarseness, no open brutality, neither at slander nor at theft, neither at dirt nor at degradation, to keep and hold and possess both him and her children—that was deliberately to devote him to a destruction beside which murder would have been an act of love. He arose from his lonely seat on that far late day. With a solemn and almost religious feeling his feet felt the earth, his eyes sought an early star. Justice would find her out.

At the time in the New York spring, he had not the faintest suspicion that she had determined upon anything. All seemed casual and in fact accidental enough and Herbert did not dream but that all the doors of life were open to him. Her recurrent storms of grief over her absence from her children only cooled and alienated him and there were weeks during which only two factors kept him from quietly drifting away from her. One factor was Anne's tireless, pathetic insistence, not only upon her love for him, but on the verbal pledges of love that he had given and had been forced to reiterate. "Why are you so cold to me, Herbert? Is it because I am older than you? But you always knew I was and yet you said you loved me. You said so only last week. Didn't you mean it?" He didn't know what to answer.

He felt that the appeal was unfair. It was like hitting below the belt. But he seemed unable to clarify the situation between them. Then too he was sorry for her and when he showed that, she took it greedily and emphatically as a new proof of what she wanted to believe and the disharmony ended in the usual way. The other factor that held him was this: he had no employment but the directorship of the club's chorus; he had no money; his sex life with Anne produced an almost pathological lethargy in him. He had no energy with which to look for another way of earning his bread. He knew no one. The relation with Anne had kept him isolated and absorbed. But breaking with Anne and keeping his job—that was unthinkable. She would return in fact then. She would be on the threshold of the club, on his own. She would be wild, she would stop at nothing. So much his instinct told him about Anne already. Only he called this thing in her impulsiveness now and love and attributed it to the exorbitance of a romantic, passionate and devoted nature. Thus he lingered and drifted with the result that things happened which enslaved him the more hopelessly.

In the middle of an afternoon he called for Anne at 123rd Street. They both liked to take long afternoon walks. And their long walks out in the open resulted in their most harmonious moods. Such hours

100

were the only truly pleasant ones that Herbert could recall out of their long companionship, the only ones without a bitter or an acrid aftertaste. They had reached the middle of the block when they heard a clatter of heels behind them. They drew apart a little and looked back. Harrison Vilas, with gangly limbs flying in all directions, precisely like Bronson his son, panting with ineffectual rage, was tumbling rather than running after them. He was upon them, butted feebly into Herbert who, however, had braced himself for a blow and stood firm, raised his hand, dropped it and shouted: "You God-damned son-of-a-bitch!" Anne immediately slipped in between the two men and took each by one arm. Vilas opened his mouth.

"Don't you dare shout, you fool!" Was that Anne's voice—harsh, old, menacing? "We'll walk along quietly," she said. "People are looking."

The two men obeyed her. Luckily there had been only a few people in the street. They had stopped for a moment but now went their way. Across Anne's face, which was tense and drawn but with a light of battle in it, Herbert looked at Vilas. The man, gray and aging despite his slender form and smooth face, might have moved pity. How Herbert wished later on that he had moved his own! But about Harrison Vilas, as about his son Bronson, there was always a moral as well as a physical gangliness, looseness, lack of compactness and co-ordination, that forbade either compassion or respect. Their feeble bumptiousness only revealed more grotesquely their inner supineness. At this most uncomfortable moment Herbert suddenly felt like screaming with laughter at the recollection of Mrs. Toohey's final characterisation of her son-in-law: "Pusillanimous pup!" That is what the Vilases were—pusillanimous, born to be subordinate, to be shoved about, thwacked, cuckolded—pusillanimous, and the more grotesque because they had minds superior to their characters and were always trying to play the part of inner dignity and moral strength. Everything conspired against Herbert, even the character of his adversary. They walked along, these three ill-assorted people, as though they were friends. Vilas talked.

"It's outrageous, a woman like you staying away from your home and children and gallivanting about with a lover!"

Anne glanced significantly at Herbert.

"I'm not Mrs. Vilas' lover. You have no right to insult her."

Poor Herbert. He knew that there was no conviction in his voice. Vilas lunged out feebly across Anne who pushed back his arm.

"Tell that to the marines! I know Anne. This isn't the first time—"

Anne cut him short. "You lie, Harry Vilas, and you know that you lie."

Vilas, accustomed to her lashing tongue, turned sullen. "And this time it's got to be a boy half your age."

Anne flushed. "My God, what a lie!" She turned to Herbert. "I am thirty-seven."

Vilas yelled with weakly ironic laughter. "Forty-three, you mean."

"Thirty-seven," she retorted belligerently.

"Forty-three," Vilas almost shouted. "Thirty-seven." "Forty-three." This went on for minutes and out of this stupid and contentious repetition of numbers there arose a very miasma of bitterness and of the corruption of the relation between two human beings that was like the corruption of some living thing. Anne had the last word. She turned to Herbert.

"Don't believe him; he always was a liar."

Herbert bowed his head.

He never knew how long they wandered about. Their talk was insincere, foolish, rancorous. Anne talked to impress Herbert, Vilas to vent his querulous rage. Once or twice Herbert was dragged in.

"Well, if you two are so innocent," Vilas asked, "why this hanging around together and this concealment?"

Anne's eyes flashed. "Herbert loves me and I love him and I'm not ashamed of that."

Vilas looked at Herbert. "So you love her, do you?"

Herbert's throat went dry. He hesitated. Anne looked at him with her most tragic eyes. "Yes," he said, "I love her."

"You do, do you?" Vilas jeered. "Very well, I'll take up the whole matter with Dr. Spicer tomorrow."

"You'd better do that," Anne said. She seemed certain of her influence with the clergyman.

They fell silent. Suddenly Anne stopped and caught hold of Herbert's arm. "I feel faint. Everything is going black before my eyes."

Herbert didn't know what moved him more—fear of a scene in the street or solicitude for Anne. "There's a restaurant," he said. "Try to get as far as that."

"I will," she murmured from unmoving, pain-touched lips and put her hand over her heart. Vilas half sneered. That sneer fired the chivalrous, foolish boy. "Lean on me, my dear." He was gentle and tender with her. Vilas followed them into the restaurant.

Anne drank a glass of water and recovered.

"I believe I'm hungry," she said.

Herbert begged her to order something. All three acted in a very seemly fashion in the restaurant. Vilas said in a careless, off-hand way, "I believe I'll order something too."

Soon they were drinking beer and eating steaks. Vilas got sentimental. He pitied himself. He appealed to them both.

"I don't believe I've got a great many more years to live. I just want to live those years in peace."

Herbert was touched now. He leaned forward. It was his impulse to assure the man that he had nothing to fear from him. Anne grasped his hand under the tablecloth. Her other hand was once more over her heart. The men were silent. When she recovered herself she said, "I might as well go home with you tonight, Harry. I want to see the children. Go call a taxi."

Vilas got up and fumbled aimlessly in his waistcoat pocket. Then he went out. A waiter hovered about and Herbert paid the bill. "You'll hear from me, Herbert." Anne's lips were at his ear. "Soon, my darling, soon." Vilas returned. He and Anne entered the cab. Herbert stood on the curb confused, worn out in body and in mind. He felt as though these hours had aged and degraded him. All he wanted now was sleep—sleep, forgetfulness, some lustration.

8   WHAT happened between Anne and her husband that night, what in the study of Dr. Spicer at noon next day—these were matters on which Herbert had to rely on Anne's reports. He believed these reports. He trusted Anne. He trusted her in the first place because he had never known a liar. Oh, yes, people fibbed to escape trivial embarrassments or to save others' sensibilities or bragged a little or even stretched their imagination a little to please either themselves or someone else. His father of course would not even do such things. But his father was a bit severe and a bit puritanical in the details of conduct. He had never at all events known anyone who lied coldly, persistently, malignantly in the pursuit of definite and elaborate ends. He honestly thought that such things happened only in detective fiction, in blood and thunder novelettes. Hence, ranging Anne in the order of his ethical experience, he trusted her and believed her words. But that was not all. Anne professed a quite special horror of untruthfulness. She "hated a liar." The root trouble with Harry Vilas was that "you couldn't believe a word he said." Various details confirmed this claim of Anne's warm veneration for the truth: her mother's blunt, unvarnished speech, the tattered copy of Spencer's *Ethics* on her desk, the poem on a great renaissance martyr which she had written with its closing line: "Though the book burn, its soul will not be quenched." Yes, he believed Anne. He believed her for a long time. These early impressions of her, harmonizing with his own instincts and his own experience, went deep.

According to her Vilas had, on that evening, behaved without decency or manhood and had annihilated what lingering pity or affection she might still have entertained for him. In front of the children he had yelled. "A fine mother you've got. I caught her in the street with her lover. It's a wonder I didn't catch them in bed!" He had threatened to put poor Mrs. Toohey out of the house for her complicity. At this point Herbert hesitated inwardly. He saw the justice of this. Anne covered the point with a flood of words. Vilas hated her mother because she had seen through him from the start; he hated her for her frankness and veracity; this was far from the first time that he had threatened to throw her into the street; he grudged her the little food she ate, though without her labor and her economies the family would long ago have gone to smash. A sudden misgiving struck Herbert.

"How did he know where we were?" She wept.

"I haunted the house for a sight of the children. Luella thought she saw me and told her father. Then he watched and followed us."

"And now?" Herbert asked.

Then she related the story of the interview with Dr. Spicer. According to her, he had been profoundly shocked at the account of Vilas' vulgarities. He said that he believed in her virtue because he knew the quality of her motherhood. She had frankly admitted that she and Herbert loved each other. Why not? The tall gray clergyman had shaken his head indulgently. He had advised a separation between her and Vilas who was to give her twenty-six dollars a week. She was to devote herself to the children and to see neither of the two men for at least six months. Herbert felt a wave of relief.

"Then I'd better leave New York for a while?" he said gently.

Slow tears came into her eyes. Sobs followed. Her hand sought her heart.

"I feel so desolate," she sobbed, "so utterly desolate."

"What can I do?" he stammered.

"At least, don't leave New York. Stay for a little. If I could only see you once a week and for a minute, see you even if I don't speak to you, I shall have something to live for." He promised, hated himself for promising, and kept his word.

In an incredibly short time Anne had procured a dingy flat up five flights of stairs in a house on 118th Street near Manhattan Avenue. Thither she transported a couple of mattresses, a couch and a couch cover and some kitchen utensils. There was one chair; there were half a dozen boxes on which one could sit. She delayed bringing the "family" here. She telephoned to Herbert and persuaded him to go upstairs into the flat with her and let him taste of that complete aloneness and isolation with a woman which the natural instinct of man demands. This was no rented room in a strange house where the very transports of passion had to be hushed and careful. "We spend too much money in restaurants," she announced. They went marketing together and brought back food and Anne cooked it well and quickly. She washed the dishes with a song or an apt quotation on her lips. She was buoyant and comradely and gave Herbert a sense of both adventure and home, of both mastery and freedom. She also gave him a sense of their defying stupid people and a stupid world together which was sweet on the tongue of the born artist and rebel. She was witty and merry and devoted. She was free now to go to Sixty-first Street and was no longer griefstricken over her children. They were here; she could fetch them hither at any time. This delightful delay had a familiar cause. Half of Harry's salary was pledged to a usurer for several weeks to come. He had to get straightened out financially before he could give Anne her necessary weekly income. This circumstance was a stroke of good luck for Anne. Before the time had come for the family to be moved uptown she held Herbert by new declarations, fresh promises, a recognition of the comforts, of the ease, which a woman can, if she is willing, bring to a man with whom she lives alone.

This holiday came abruptly to an end. Vilas borrowed money from his relations, who were indignant over Anne's actions and thought Harry well rid of her. The family moved into the flat. Anne announced the fact to Herbert in Morningside Park. She begged him to come upstairs. Dumbly but with a premonition of evil he hung back. She pleaded with him. If he would see a little more of Bronson he would like the poor friendless boy who, though intimidated, had a good mind and real gifts; he could not help liking Luella who was sweet and yielding and unselfish and she thought he already liked poor mamma who had stood by them so bravely and risked the poorhouse for their sakes. Dusk had fallen about them as they were talking. Herbert sat silent on the bench beside Anne. A wave of homesickness came over him, a mingled feeling, a nostalgia for his mother, for Gerda, more deeply still for places he had never seen, a life he had never lived. The pages of his unfinished sonata appeared before him. He had done no work; he had been absorbed in obscure and sordid things. A rage against Anne arose within him and faded just as suddenly. She seemed a momentary refuge from his ills. There was something confused and inextricable about it all—something sad and fatal which he attributed neither to Anne's hard scheming nor to his own youth and unformed character but somehow to the disastrous stars. . . .

He went upstairs with her. Everything seemed orderly and peaceful in the flat. Mrs. Toohey was in the kitchen getting the dinner. Bronson sat reading. The two girls were playing with their dolls in a corner. They were told to get up and shake hands with Mr. Crump. Luella stumbled awkwardly as she did so. She was a large child of twelve with dimples and a winning, uncertain smile. She had an unnaturally tiny, turned up nose. She was pretty. But there was something wrong with her facial angle. Eileen was, as usual, dwarflike and severe. She seemed to regard Herbert with a hostile and suspicious eye. There was no dining table in the flat. Mrs. Toohey brought in the meal, served on plates and so Anne and Herbert sat side by side on the couch and talked softly. Bronson came over and crouched at their feet and talked maturely and sensibly. He had inherited his mother's taste for literature. He wanted to write. But his eyes had been bad; they had always hurt him; he had not been sent to school till he was twelve. He was just finishing high school now. He saw no chance of going to college. He would have to go to work. He asked Herbert's advice and this from someone so little younger than himself flattered Herbert, who said that a fellow so well read and with such definite taste for the things of the mind ought to go to college, and Anne said "He'll go. I'll see to it somehow."

This fair beginning did not last. Anne relaxed her vigilance over the family. Subsequent days and evenings were not so peaceful. Eileen's toneless, dry wail resounded whenever her will was crossed in the least respect. Luella scolded feebly. She had no clothes to wear. She could not go with other girls. Mrs. Toohey said to Herbert: "Some day the old lady's going to get out of this where she can be good to herself." He and Anne fled once more to the Colonial Hotel. Calling for Anne he found that she had scolded the children and accused them of ingratitude and had had a heart attack. From the kitchen came the voice of Mrs. Toohey, raucous and mannish: "I know what's the matter with her. She's got an itching where she can't scratch." She was talking to herself, but being rather deaf she roared. Luella gave a faint scream. Eileen rushed to her mother and climbed on her lap, covering her with her own small body as if to protect her. Bronson in a corner snickered. Anne tore herself away from Eileen who then yelled deliberately and at length. It seemed to Herbert as though the ugly, bare rooms were clouded and poisoned by a sordid fury and confusion. He fled into the outer hall. Anne followed him, slamming the door of the flat behind her. He shook with rage. "Disgusting crew," he muttered. But Anne was at his elbow. "Poor things," she said, "how can you judge them? They've never had a real father or a real home. As for mamma, you know what her life has been. I sometimes think that her mind has been affected by her miseries, I do honestly!" He shrugged his shoulders, though too accessible, as always, to what had but the show of reason and humanity.

"The club season is nearly over anyhow," he said. "It's almost summer and there's no chance to get any work. I'm going home."

"Do you want to kill me, Herbert? For God's sake, Herbert, my whole life is wrapped up in you."

Then for the first time he lied. "Listen, Anne, I'm helpless for the moment. There is nothing here in the summer and I haven't saved a cent and you know it. I'll come back in the early fall and get a better position and help you financially too. You can't get along indefinitely on your twenty-six dollars a week."

"Are you sure, Herbert? Are you quite sure?"

"Of course I'm sure," he said. "Even if I didn't love you—there's no place for a musician outside of New York."

"But you do love me, don't you?"

"Yes, yes."

"And you will come back?"

"Of course I will."

"And you'll write me daily?"

He nodded. In her arms, in the depths of the night, she made him repeat these pledges which he did not mean to keep.

9 How he finally got away was always afterwards something of a riddle to him. There was, of course, the one hard fact that the club and chorus scattered with the coming of warm weather and that he had no means of livelihood. There was also in him a quiet desperation which Anne must have felt. And she dared not yet use the insolence of security. She did her best to enmesh Herbert in soft, strong tentacles, to play upon the physical habit established between them, upon his compassion, upon his sense of honor. She let herself become pregnant, brought on a mild abortion at the end of eight weeks and so, shortly before his departure, appeared white, devoted, gallantly suffering for his sake. The promises and assurances she wrung from him on this occasion she treasured up carefully to confront him with in the days to come.

The beauty of Queenshaven and the peace of his home were both clouded and tarnished to Herbert. After the first day he found himself restless with a faint persistent wretchedness. He didn't know what ailed him. Did he miss his physical contacts with Anne? Did he, despite his parents' love and interest, miss the sense which Anne gave him of being important, the man and master and center of attention? His mother came upon him one morning at the piano.

"There is a shadow between us, my son. What is it?"

He swore that there was none. There couldn't be any, ever. She shook her head and left him. His father questioned him once only.

"You say you could get this chorus work again in the fall? Is it satisfactory to you?"

Herbert shrugged his shoulders. "It leaves me plenty of time." He knew that he sounded depressed and roused himself. "I haven't shown you my songs, 'Amoris Victima' yet, nor the sonata I want to finish."

"No, Herbert, you haven't. You seem to have withdrawn yourself."

"I haven't at all." Herbert felt a strange mixture of irritation and shame.

"Would you rather have a church position here?" his father asked. "St. John's is vacant. I think you could get it."

The words were like sudden balm. He saw the face of Mrs. Toohey; he heard Eileen's shrill wail. His gorge rose at the thought of New York and of that desperate entanglement.

"Yes, father, I'd rather stay. Will you talk to Doctor Scherer for me?"

"With pleasure, my son, of course."

Neither of his parents said much about the songs. Both the verses and the music seemed to their simple solid taste overimpassioned, hectic, morbid, almost sinful. They connected them, however, as Herbert did not know until later, with the small letters addressed to him in a clear, straight, rigid woman's handwriting that came each day.

Those letters! He disliked their coming. Yet if on a given day none came he felt a breath of something ominous. Anne's return from Baltimore had evidently gotten under his skin. He dragged himself to the writing of a few daily lines. He knew it to be a propitiatory gesture. A subtle fear worked in him like a poison, an instinctive, intellectually unrealized perception of Anne's true character. Yet he missed her too, there was no doubt about that. He missed her attention, missed her physically, missed his long uninhibited talks with her. There was no one else in the world with whom he could be so frank, with whom he could so let himself go. The very shadow that she threw between him and his parents, between him and Petersen even, made him miss her the more. His secret, which would have seemed a shameful one to those nearest to him, drew him psychically to its sharer and companion. Yet no force could have dragged him back to New York, to that sordid flat on 118th Street with its swarm-ing, quarrelling, hopelessly alien people.

He dared not write Anne that he would not return. He drifted and drugged his mind and hoped that she would see through his excuses and lies and subterfuges and understand and resign herself. And all the while something within him was certain that was precisely what Anne would never do. He could hear her. In the stillness of the night he could hear her: "If you don't love me, if everything you've said is a lie, why don't you be a man and come out with it?" And he could see, as though she were beside him, the look in her eyes that would accompany her appeal and that would say much plainer than any words: "And if you have deceived me so and upset my whole life with your deceptions, don't be surprised if murder and suicide, dis-grace and disaster follow!" And at the thought of this vicious circle and of these hopeless alternatives cold sweat would cover his body and he was tempted to beg his father to raise a little money with which he could escape and disappear. But he was ashamed, ashamed to do that and as Anne's letters became more tragic and more urgent, he lived almost wholly with fear and disgust and self-disgust and it took him till evening to recover from the shock of the morning's letter and yet dread of the next day's letter kept him sleepless in the night.

Young and inexperienced as he was, his mind was not inactive dur-ing this dull, long-drawn-out crisis. He would sit down at his little desk in the attic room of his boyhood and try dispassionately to think his way through this situation and to think of a way out. He recog-nized that what had actually happened to him could not be told in America. What was he to say? That, being young and passionate, he had wanted a mistress? That Anne had seemed like a ripe fruit to drop into his hands? That, by a tacit understanding, they had entered the relation as lover and mistress but that gradually Anne, taking ad-vantage of that prevalent official morality which, by her very action, by every look and word, she had affected to despise, had imperceptibly shifted her ground and was now stretching out hands toward his very life? Was he to say that? Ah, there were those who would understand.

III

But they would be cold and silent and pretend not to understand. For it would not be profitable in reputation and therefore in dollars and cents to flout the official morality. According to that morality, as it was sincerely and rigidly entertained in Queenshaven by everyone he knew, by his very father and mother, he had entered a man's home and broken up that home and robbed it of its wife and mother. A home! The poor fellow in his study quivered as he considered the relentless sentimentality, the cruel idolatry, cruel to hounding, to lynching, to barbarism and blood—which stood ready to defend that flexible and doubtful notion. He had broken up a home. He could see that headline in the papers. Suppose he plead that Anne was old enough to be his mother. People might quietly laugh at both her and him. Publicly they would brand his declaration as caddish and probably untrue. And if it were true, hadn't he, by God, known it? No one had asked him, you know, to go into that home and defile it and break it up. He could hear voices saying that—stern, self-satisfied, masochistic voices. Anne would be blamed too, less, to be sure, especially in the South where the theory that all women are helpless victims of all men's potential brutality is part of the accepted savage cult that passes for religion. In addition, it would be remembered in her favor that she, at least, seemed willing to mend so far as was possible the social and moral damage that had been done. He did not. His scoundrelism was complete. If such as he were safe, no man's home was any longer inviolable.

Once more he thought of flight. He had no money. There was no place for him. He hadn't the hardihood of mind or toughness of body to brave the existence of the lost and nameless of society—tramps, dish-washers, saloon porters, strummers of pianos in bawdy houses. Nor was he sure that, if he disappeared, his parents would be safe from the echoes of Anne's outcries. She was fond of telling the story of the Mohammedan lady of the time of the Crusades who, abandoned in Egypt by her Christian lover, set out on foot and wandered all over Europe with but one word, his name, the name of Gilbert, on her lips. When Anne told that story she told it with a touch of pathetic humor. But underneath that humor and that pathos were, as Herbert knew clearly in retrospect, hardness, iron determination and an aggressive lack of shame posing as helplessness. No, there was nothing for him to do. Unless she resigned herself he was damned. The world and its official morality put every weapon into her hand. Any rebellion or violence on his part might bring disgrace and ruin not only on him but on his father and his father's honorable name. Thinking upon this whole matter with a sagacity and a clearness sharpened by great danger, considering how he had been tricked and was likely to be ruined in his happiness, peace, hopes, ambitions, Herbert Crump then and there made up his accounting with the official morals of his time and country: a mass of barbarous unveracities, unclean, ungenerous, cowardly, vulgar, to be disregarded, defied, trampled upon by every honorable soul. . . .

His intellectual liberation served only to intensify his emotional dread. He tried to make his letters to Anne more elaborately equivocal. This brought a storm of questions, of pleas for definiteness, of elegiac plaints. He hinted that he might have to defer his return to New York. "And how am I to go on living?" she answered. "I am willing to bear my false and precarious position for a while with you. But without you! For your sake I gave up, after all, the little that I had. Harry still pleads with me to return to him." A hope of reprieve, of liberation came to Herbert. As gently and as delicately as he could, with protestations of sorrow over his youth and helplessness and poverty, he suggested that perhaps it would be better for her to yield to her husband's pleadings and for them both to resign themselves to the inevitable. He waited for an answer. None came. Two days passed without a letter. Three days. Four. Herbert grew sick with anxiety and dread. He leaned out of his attic window in the morning to watch for the postman, to rush down to get the fatal or hopeful letter. On the fifth day he saw, instead of the postman, a slim, slightly jaunty figure in a pointed black hat, a gray skirt and a gray Eton jacket. He thought his heart would stop. It was Anne, of course. . . .

10

IN a moment he faced her—the stairs, the snatching of a hat obliterated from his consciousness. He stood on the doorstep. A little below him she looked small in the luminous Southern air. How well he knew that pathetic humor, not without edge, with which she greeted him.

"You don't seem glad to see me, Mr. Crump."

He was beside himself. "How dared you come here? Haven't you any shame? Good God, I never heard of such a thing! Couldn't you wait till I came back?"

They were walking toward the corner of Meeting Street now. Herbert did not see his mother sorrowfully watching them from the upstairs piazza. He clenched his hands. He could have struck the woman beside him. The situation was utterly unendurable. In this tiny native city of his where everyone, to the last Negro, knew him and his people, where—where . . . His thoughts became confused in their hot, stinging misery. "God, what a shameless creature!" he muttered. "Oh, my God!" Anne's eyes grew wan, but her jaw tightened.

"I won't recriminate," she said, "but I don't believe you had any intention of coming back."

"Then I didn't!" He flung the words at her. "It's none of your business what I do."

"Oh, isn't it though? I wonder what people would say to that. I broke up my home for you; I am living in wretchedness and poverty; you promised in all your letters, all, that you'd come back. I—" she broke off with a sob. "But I don't care about all that. I thought you loved me. Don't you, Herbert, don't you? That's what I want to know."

But he was too terrified for an emotional appeal to reach him.

"When did you come?" he asked. "What do you want?"

Her answer was both businesslike and gentle. "I came on the seven o'clock train this morning. I went to the Sweegan boarding house on Society Street. You told me about it once. I took a room there."

"You've got to leave right away," he said. "You can't stay here—you simply can't."

114

She grew very sad. "I can't do that," she said. "Even to come here I had to stage a burglary, to pretend to the landlord that I'd been robbed. I used the rent money for my fare. I haven't more than a couple of dollars left. I had to leave the family enough to live on."

He stopped and turned to her. "Well, what for God's sake did you expect to do?"

"As I told mamma—poor mamma, she has such faith in you—if you still loved me, everything would be arranged. If you didn't—what did anything matter? I thought I'd get a little room here such as I have at Mrs. Sweegan's. I have all your dear letters with me. I've got a bottle of ether and I could just fall asleep."

A desperate, icy wind seemed to whip his mind clean and clear. The trap was sprung. A strange lady dead at the Sweegan house clasping those letters of his. This in Queenshaven! It meant that his parents would in the long run be driven forth homeless and breadless into a world with which they had no means of coping. It meant disgrace; it meant utter ruin. He looked at Anne with cold eyes. "You damned—! Oh!"

She assumed her jauntiest smile. "I have a revolver, too. I can shoot myself on your father's doorstep, if you prefer."

They had reached the corner of Meeting and Broad Streets. Already several people had greeted Herbert and thrown politely inquisitive glances at the lady with him. He was hopelessly and overwhelmingly caught and defeated.

"I'll do anything you want, Anne; only you must go back to New York. I'll arrange the money for you somehow."

She shook her head sadly. "If you don't love me, I really don't want to go on living. Truly I don't, I'm tired, just tired."

He brought up the words like heavy stones from within. "You know I love you, Anne."

"Then why can't I stay a few days?" she asked plaintively. "It's so lovely and peaceful here. And aren't you going to let me meet your father and mother, Herbert?" He didn't answer. That icy wind blew through his brain once more. "I'm sure I'd like them. Are you ashamed of me, Herbert?"

He could have struck her at that question. He was not ashamed of her as a friend, no, nor as a mistress, had society tolerated the open treatment of such a relationship. But as a woman who pretended to a more lasting claim upon his life he was toweringly and hideously and justly—yes, justly—ashamed of her. Christ! He thought of Mrs. Toohey, of Bronson, Luella, Eileen. Ashamed? The word was feeble. He shook at his own thoughts. Anne saw him turn pale. They had reached Battery Park now and he dropped on a bench. She sat down beside him. Her voice, when she spoke again, was sad and resigned.

"I see you are ashamed of me, Herbert."

He pulled himself together. Only lies could save him. He must gain time. Her knife was at his throat.

"Of course I'm not, Anne. But you can imagine how conventional everybody is around here."

"I see," she said. "Well, just say I'm a friend of yours who is passing through. Can't you do that?"

He nodded. In his wretchedness he was almost grateful to her for this apparently helpful suggestion. "Yes, I could do that."

She caught his arm. "Then you do love me and I won't have to die?"

He softened to her. She did love him; she must love him hopelessly and overwhelmingly. "No, dear Anne, of course I don't want you to die."

"I thought you did, Herbert. Oh, I thought you really did."

He shook his head sadly. The palmettos were rattling softly over their heads; the lustrous bay stretched out toward the blue islands. It seemed to him in his youthful confusion as though they were both caught in the immeasurable sadness of life. The terrible woman beside him seemed helpless to him and pathetic. He promised to do his best. He took her back to the Sweegan House and told Mrs. Sweegan, who had known him almost from his birth, how happy he was to see his friend, Mrs. Vilas. Then, forlornly enough, he started on his way home under the burning sun of noon.

In the cool dusk of the downstairs hall he met his mother. He stopped before her. She put her hands on his shoulders. He noticed suddenly at this moment how much white there was in her dark brown hair. He felt like letting himself go, like weeping aloud. He controlled the impulse. But she saw the deep misery in his eyes.

"If you are in trouble, my son, your father and I are ready to help you. You know that."

He heard himself moaning like a man under a too heavy burden. A fateful, indefinite premonition arose in him. He shook it off. The immediate situation had to be faced.

"I'm not exactly in trouble. But a very dear friend of mine is here for a few days. She's at the Sweegans. You know how people talk. If you would call on her?"

His mother nodded. "The lady with whom you correspond?"

"Yes," he said, and he saw in his mother's eyes her conviction that he must be both passionately and nobly in love with that lady and how could he, at this moment, deny that or explain the confused, sordid, terrifying, inexplicable facts?

"I think," his mother went on, "the best thing would be to have her stay here as my guest. Then nobody can talk."

He felt that same fateful premonition but his lips said, "That's sweet of you, mother; that would be best."

Early in the afternoon his mother accompanied him to the Sweegan House. Anne came down into the shaded parlor in a white skirt and shirtwaist. Her hair was carefully dressed. She had her most melancholy expression in her eyes; she assumed her gentlest air. Herbert's mother, taking for granted that without which the whole thing was inconceivable to her, put her arms around Anne and kissed her and said in her quaint German way which had at times irritated him, but which, at this moment, he found both adorable and somehow tragic:

"Whom my son loves I love too." And at that Anne put her arms

117

about his mother and let her eyes fill with tears and said: "You're very, very sweet and kind, Mrs. Crump." And it seemed to poor Herbert as though Anne was suddenly different and as though a lustration had washed her clean and as though she looked younger than she had ever looked before. . . . Anne had only one small suitcase which was soon packed. The three drove home together and Anne was given a little guest room which had not been used since Herbert's cousins had been in Queenshaven several years before. Anne slept during the remainder of the afternoon. Herbert fought a bitter fight with the flesh. He daren't; he mustn't. It would deliver him wholly into her hands. He fixed his mind on the New York flat, on Mrs. Toohey, Bronson, the girls, and grew calm. . . . At supper, under the soft lamplight, Anne appeared still in white. A breeze blew in and Herbert's mother put over Anne's shoulders a shawl of soft, cream-tinted silk which had belonged to his grandmother. Anne talked well. She didn't talk too much. She spoke of the musical life of New York in careful terms so as not to betray her essential ignorance. Then the talk shifted to books and she played up to Herbert's father who was a great reader and soon they were deep in Dickens and Balzac and Borrow. And Herbert saw it in his parents' attitude and eyes: yes, the lady was of uncertain age, yes . . . but she was cultivated and able and devoted and would probably rob them less definitely of their son than some green girl with the intolerance and selfishness and arrogance of youth. He saw now that they had had a fear of that, of losing him wholly and this perception touched him to the quick and persuaded him to yield to the mood of the hour and to forget New York and Mrs. Toohey and "the family". They all went to bed early and in the middle of the hushed Southern night Anne slipped into his room. . . .

The days passed dreamily. Petersen came, more blind than ever, and liked Anne; Ralph Greene came and she listened to the story of his Harvard triumphs; Mrs. Müller and Mrs. Rohde came and were impressed by Anne's speech and by what they considered her New York air. And one day, with fear leaping up in him like a flame, Herbert discovered that Anne had made a confidant of his father and had played upon his father's unworldliness and compassion and admiration and had told him—quite as though Herbert knew of this plan and had consented to it—that she was going to get a divorce from Vilas. Alone with his father Herbert said surlily: "She can't get one." To which his father replied with a touch of severity: "I don't know anything about such things, but since you placed her in her present situation you should at least wish her to get one." There was nothing to be done—nothing. The truth of the situation, so difficult even for him to disentangle in many hours of thought, was simply impossible to communicate. He could tell his father nothing that would not make him seem a hopeless cad. No, the tragi-comedy had to be played through to the end. In the meantime Herbert enjoyed having Anne there by day, since she was on her very best behavior, also by night. As to the future, he comforted himself with the reflection that if she had trapped him, yet she was trapped no less. How the deuce could she get a divorce in New York state? Vilas would never divorce her on statutory grounds, nor would she wish such a thing to happen. And that wasn't all. Bronson could earn his own living, of course, but Anne could not abandon her penniless old mother or her small daughters. And Herbert, on their walks together and during their nocturnal meetings, had made it definitely clear to her that he intended to remain in Queenshaven, that he had accepted the position of organist at St. John's church at an annual salary of one thousand dollars and that he would never consent to live in Queenshaven anywhere except under the same roof with his parents. To all this she had assented. Hence when, at the end of two weeks, with money borrowed from Petersen, Anne started back to New York Herbert, convinced that the parting was forever, was sorry to see her go. . . .

Her letters from now on were hasty, brief and vague. She spoke of terrible hardships, of anguish and heartache, but gave no specific facts or causes. Frantically she appealed to Herbert for money. He waited a few days and answered that, as she well knew, he had none. Thereafter there was a week's silence. Then came the bolt. An old schoolmate of hers, a lawyer in Chicago, was helping her with advice. Years ago, when she had left Chicago, she had sent an old trunk to the house of her uncle, Joshua Bronson, and the trunk was still there. On this basis she could claim that she had never given up her legal residence in Illinois and could sue Vilas for a divorce on the ground of cruelty. A grizzly terror took hold of Herbert. He wandered about the house praying for courage to tell his parents that it was all a ghastly mistake, that he was being trapped and driven into a horrible bondage and that, if this thing came to pass, he would hate Anne with a deadly and unforgiving hate. He rehearsed long explanations that he might offer. They seemed flat, unconvincing, dishonorable. At the same time Anne wrote sadly and charmingly to his mother and occasionally to his father. Herbert wrote and wired her imploring her not to commit perjury, asking what would become of her poor mother, and of her girls. It was clear that he, at his age—he was just twenty-four now—and with his income could not be committed to any responsibility or even helpfulness. Then Anne wrote to his mother who came to Herbert. "My son," she said, "Anne is taking her mother to relatives in the West; she is leaving her boy and her older girl with their father. You cannot expect her to be without her youngest child. If you expect that, you don't love her. And if you don't, why have you driven her to this?"

Herbert laughed bitterly. "Driven!"

His mother's face grew sad. "I don't understand you, Herbert. But Papa and I have made up our minds not to interfere—only to help. You will never be able to reproach us. If Anne brings the child I shall be good to it."

Herbert wanted to cry out, "You shall not, you must not; I won't even have you touch any of that wretched crew!" He couldn't. The truth of life had been swathed in too many wrappings. He might claw at them until his nails were torn from his living fingers. There would be more, more, more . . . He wired Anne: "Don't dare come unless you come alone." There was no answer, no sign that she had received his message. Her hurried notes took no cognizance of Herbert's written appeals, his condemnations, his deliberate brutalities. Then even these notes stopped coming. There were two weeks of silence. Herbert took hope. Perhaps she had not been able to raise enough money. Perhaps the legal trick had failed. He did not know Anne yet; he did not know yet that Anne never failed. For on the fifteenth day a wire came from Chicago: "Decree granted. On way to Queenshaven." Pale to the very lips Herbert handed the telegram to his father, who first read it and then looked at him.

"What is the matter with you? Do you discover now, now, that you've made a mistake? *Um Gottes Willen!* Boy!"

It seemed to Herbert that by a superhuman effort he forced the blood back into his face. At least he could do the decent thing by his parents; at least he could try to preserve their healing delusions. Why should they be made to suffer? That was his job.

"Nothing of the sort, father. I had a headache and the message was rather sudden."

During the next few days he forced himself to be cheerful. He made all proper and decent arrangements for his marriage to Anne. On the early morning of the third day he was at the train to meet her, pale, grave, erect, flowers in hand. The prompt train stopped. What he saw first was the long, hostile face of Eileen. A porter lifted the child down. Then came Anne. She had on a brown, tailormade fall suit. On her head sat a tall brown hat with waving brown plumes. Herbert stared at her face, unskilfully rouged and powdered after a long night on the sleeper and now exposed to the biting morning light. Something had come into that face which he had never—or never consciously—seen before. It was the face of a woman—old, dour, triumphant and vindictive.

Book Four

EARLY YEARS

1   A MONTH after the marriage of Anne and Herbert the Crumps left Calhoun Street and moved into another house. Herbert's parents had quietly planned this against the event of the marriage taking place. It was an old house on East Bay Street, built of bricks brought from England in the early part of the nineteenth century and covered with plaster, patches of which had grown as iridescent as mother-of-pearl. From the windows of the spacious, square rooms with rococo mantels of white marble there was a view of the bay. The rental was only thirty-five dollars a month. Anne and Herbert were given two large rooms on the top floor as their sleeping and sitting rooms. Herbert's parents contented themselves with the back rooms on the same floor—an initial mistake, Herbert thought afterwards. On the floor below were the common living rooms of the whole family. The furniture was comfortable and in reasonably good taste. Out of one of Herbert's mother's secret little hoards a few good new things and some attractive bric-a-brac had been added. It had been a quiet but constant waking dream of Herbert's boyhood to live within view of the bay, within hearing of the lap and murmur of the lazy tide. That dream had now come true. But it had come true in ways so strange that house and bay and the islands turned to him a mocking or an eerie loveliness. . . .

"It was a hell of an idea that I had to come here to marry you; that you didn't have the manhood to get free of your mother's apron strings to that extent!"

He felt himself blanching with rage. "Does it occur to you that there was no money, that you sprung the whole thing on me anyhow?"

She shifted her ground. Anne always shifted her ground.

"And what's to become of my poor mother? She's down there in Little Rock with Uncle Anthony and without a penny."

Herbert shrugged his shoulders. "I am sorry. I don't know."

"Well, I guess I'll send for her to come here."

He looked at her more calmly. "I think you're crazy, Anne."

"Oh, am I? I guess my mother is as good as yours. The way you and your father jump around after her makes me sick at my stomach."

Herbert clasped his hands which were trembling. "I warn you, Anne, if you don't leave my mother out of these discussions I'll strike you some day."

"Strike! Do you think I'm afraid of you? I thought it was my house as much as hers anyhow."

"Not as long as you shirk all responsibility and all work."

"Oh, I see. Your mother has been complaining to you behind my back. Well, I guess there are niggers in the yard to do the dirty work."

He didn't answer at first. This sort of bitter wrangling could go on forever.

"Since we are living together, Anne, wouldn't it be better to live together in peace?"

"I'm willing, Bertie, but you are doing me an injustice by making me live with your parents. That sort of thing never works out well for either party."

He hardened himself against the superficial truth of this appeal.

"I'd be satisfied with the simplest place. Don't you hear me?"

His lips tightened. Yes, he heard her. But this roof was his only protection. If he left it, that would mean Mrs. Toohey, certainly Luella and perhaps Bronson. And that would mean, here in Queenshaven, where everyone had known him all his life and knew his age to a day, that he would simply perish of the shame and sordidness of it all. He left the room and went downstairs and spoke to his mother who was busy—strong, grave, immaculate—baking a cake and felt, though he could not see, Anne listening stealthily in the hall above. He took his hat and walked out along the side of his beloved bay and wondered for what sin he was being harried in this hell. . . .

There were milder and better days. For the sake of peace both Herbert's parents and himself learned to guard their words and actions. A silent conspiracy to soothe and please Anne arose among them. Herbert was ashamed to have his parents subjected to such an indignity. Anne had begun to tell him the stories of her past and of her family and Herbert, though he believed himself to be democratic in every instinct, was beginning to suspect that blood, training, origin and the resultant habits had much to do with the quality of the soul and with the conduct of life. But he joined in that conspiracy for a reason both flagrant and fundamental. When Anne was in good humor she looked gentler and younger; she laughed that blithe laugh which was the youngest and most engaging thing about her. Her very walk was different—that walk which in her other moods he was beginning to hate. It was a physical characteristic which, to his pained and stricken vision, reeked with moral significance. When Anne walked, especially when she was angry, she held herself perfectly rigid from the waist up with her arms crooked close against her sides. Having tossed her head she left it in that tossed position and seemed with slightly dilated nostrils to be aware of an evil odor proceeding from some unknown source. Only her legs moved and pushed forward her trunk and her tossed head. She was, when she walked thus, an image of bumptiousness affecting elegance, of a virago veiled under a false superciliousness. Herbert dreaded that walk and attitude. He dreaded the tightening of that formidable jaw. He played into his parents' hands. Anything, anything to keep Anne since, God help them, they were married, less old, less harsh. . . .

But days came on which no concessions were effective and all propitiations failed. Herbert, with an artificially enforced serenity, was trying late in the afternoon to work at his sonata. He told himself that personal happiness was, after all, not necessary to the artist. Humbly and reverently he thought of Beethoven, deaf, poor, aging, squabbling over a few groschen with his illiterate cook. . . . Yes, yes. There was one's work. That must suffice. The door opened and Anne came slowly in. She had that fixed and rigid expression which Herbert was beginning to dread. Her eyes at such times lost all light and became like two lumps of gray agate under the bulge of her forehead.

"I must talk to you, Herbert."

"Has it got to be this minute?" he asked.

"Yes, it has."

"Very well." His mood was gone anyhow and his serenity shattered. Anne sat down in the window seat facing him. In those days she still did her hair in the morning and kept her kimono fresh.

"Your mother is taking a great deal upon herself," she announced with harsh emphasis.

He groaned inwardly. "What is it this time, Anne?"

"Without asking me she took Eileen out this morning and bought her a pair of shoes."

Herbert felt bleak and empty. Then he felt like laughing. The situation was evidently going to develop a farcical side.

"I suppose Eileen needed the shoes," he said, taking up a sheet of music paper.

"You seem to forget that I'm Eileen's mother."

He threw down the paper. "Well, what of it?"

"Just this," and her voice was harsher than ever, "that I've got to be consulted."

He grasped his head. "And you break into my work to tell me that? You forced Eileen on me against my will. My mother is good enough to take an interest in her. What more do you want?"

"I'll show you what more I want. If you don't tell your mother that I've got to be consulted first, I will. And you wouldn't like that so well!"

He arose. He walked up and down. He felt literally as though he were losing his mind. "I don't know whether I amount to anything or not, or ever will. But, by God, I'm too good, too good—" he turned and hurled the words forth in his sudden overmastering rage—"to be annoyed about that damned brat's shoes!"

Anne turned jaunty and ironical.

"It's a pity about you." Then she grew dour again. "And I'll tell you another thing. I'm not going to hear Kreisler tonight, if your father and mother go. I'm sick of going in a crowd. I married you, you know. Can't you ever take me out in the evening alone?"

His head sank to his breast. He heard his blood hum in his ears. In the old days in New York she had seemed to be human. Perhaps he could appeal to her humanity, to her reason. "I ask you to remember, Anne, that this is a small town. There are only about five or six good concerts a season. They have naturally gone to them all for many, many years. You can't expect them to stay away now and you can't expect us to leave this house by different routes to arrive at the same place."

He did not realize then that what stung and maddened Anne was that his mother, despite her whitening hair, looked fresher than herself. He only heard what seemed to him an inexplicable raving.

"I'm not going. I can stay home, I suppose. That's so fitting, so kind of you. That's so much better than if they stayed at home. God, I thought I'd married a man this time!"

She tossed her head and dilated her nostrils as though she smelt something offensive. Herbert clenched his hands. A tap sounded at the door. Shyly Herbert's mother opened it halfway. She had a long, narrow cardboard box in her hand. Her smile was sad.

"I have something for you, dear Anne."

Anne stared at the box. "Looks like a syringe," she said. Herbert saw the smile fade from his mother's face, and heard her discouraged voice. "No, it isn't." She laid the box on a table near the door. "Supper will be ready in ten minutes. We can dress for the concert afterward."

She was gone. Herbert stared at the floor. Anne went over and idly opened the box his mother had brought. It contained a dainty little fan, such as Anne had admired in a window display on King Street a few days before.

"Oh," she said, somewhat taken aback, "it's a pity you couldn't have thought to give it to me." She thrust the fan back into the box. "It doesn't matter, I'm not going to the concert."

She went out and he heard her close the door of their bedroom after her. Tears of both rage and grief burned on his lids. Christ, it didn't matter about him. No one but a born fool could have gotten into such a mess. But his parents' lives, in which there were few pleasures enough, must not be broken up. Anne would make no excuses. She knew neither reticence nor shame. She was capable of explaining at supper in the most strident and wounding terms why she was not going. He must prevent that. He must placate Anne and there was still one way of placating Anne—just one. He got up heavily and went into the dim bedroom where Anne was lying on the bed staring at the ceiling. He lay down beside her. He put his hand on her bosom. "Try not to make life so difficult for me, Anne." She did not answer but turned and sought his lips with her own. . . . No sooner had the act of his prostitution been accomplished than Eileen's shrill voice sounded in the hall. "Supper is on the table." Herbert felt as if his bones had been deliberately broken, as though a scalpel had laid bare every nerve of his body. He must, he must master this unmeasured exasperation. Anne, powdering her nose before the mirror, dabbing rouge on her cheeks, was evidently placated. Her dominant instinct was satisfied for the moment and her harshness subdued. At the supper table she said something grudgingly agreeable about the fan. But the Crumps, as Herbert bitterly reflected, had reached the point at which they were grateful to escape open insult. His mother, to soften Anne's mood further, told a quaint anecdote of Herbert's childhood. Anne smiled and nodded.

"Bronson was just like that. I remember when he was three years old—"

Herbert trembled so that the table shook under his hand.

"We want to hear about your childhood, not about that strange man!"

Anne jumped up. "Well, I guess my son Bronson Vilas is as well worth hearing about as anyone around here and a good deal better too, I'd have you know. And now you can go to your God damn concert with your God damn family!"

Herbert sprang up, tossing his arms above his head. Despair, pain, ugly satiety maddened him. "You shameless wretch!" he shouted. He stood in front of Anne. The hard impudence of her expression was indescribably challenging. It robbed him of his last vestige of control. Fully, brutally, with all his force he struck her across the mouth.

2   IT WAS of course the beginning of the end of their stay in Queenshaven. His father came to him quietly:

"That must not be, my son. I cannot tolerate it in our house."

"I know." The words stuck in his throat or filled his mouth like balls of wool. "Only don't think me, bad as it looks, either crazy or criminal."

His father's eyes would not meet his own. "Think, Herbert? I don't think; I mustn't think; it's too late and it troubles me—the feeling that I'm halfway to blame."

Herbert put his hand on his father's shoulder. "For Heaven's sake, of course you're not!"

They stood side by side on a little veranda downstairs that faced the yard. Each wanted to speak to the other; both were striken dumb by a sense of the unnaturalness, the enormity of what had overtaken them. They separated. Herbert felt like beating his forehead and crying out his question: Why, why, into the unanswering universe. He wandered into the kitchen. His mother was busy there with the colored girl, helping her. Mother and son looked at each other. She spoke to him in German so that the maid would not understand.

"Tell me nothing. I know too much already. I'll help you all I can. But go now. She doesn't like us to talk together alone."

He went. Neither then nor later did his parents and he speak out to each other. They were afraid and ashamed of the words that might be spoken; they had not dreamed that life could ever tempt one to speak such words. They said agreeable, meaningless, hopeful, things. Herbert's mother redoubled her devotion to Eileen; his father a gentle courtesy to Anne.

Anne herself, after that first evening on which she had stormed and had threatened to leave in the morning and to return to Harry Vilas and on which Herbert, though deeply shaken by remorse, had prayed to God, hoping that there was a God, that she would make good her threat—Anne had recovered from that terrible blow with amazing rapidity. "Poor Bertie!" she exclaimed. "He's fearfully neurasthenic. He was in New York, you know. I don't believe he's always quite responsible for what he does. If I did, of course I couldn't stay. You have no idea, for instance, how he suffers from insomnia." His parents in fact did not know. He had not told them. The trouble dated from just before his marriage to Anne. It tormented him all through the years. It yielded to no remedy. His productivity during certain subsequent periods, as well as the inequality of his output, must be referred to the fact that his insomnia often forced him to work both day and night. At present Anne would sometimes sit up with him, even read to him and soften him by this gesture. Later she went to bed and snored. Like her mother, whom Herbert had once heard through closed doors on 118th Street, Anne was a mighty and consistent snorer. Already in Queenshaven Herbert's only rest was frequently confined to a few hours on a couch in the sitting room.

Yes, Anne had recovered from the blow. She was in fact slightly more amiable and seemed to feel herself more secure. She felt herself more at home and became more unbridled. Having become pregnant she took her favorite remedies and got very drunk and persisted, under the agonized smile of Herbert's mother, in trying to walk in a straight line across the dining room. This episode satisfactorily over, she declared that she had very few clothes, which was true, and to Herbert's horror started accounts in his own and his father's name at both Read and Company and Louis Cohen and Company on King Street. Herbert begged her not to do this. "I suppose I'm to go naked," she said. "Maybe you want to beat me!" He winced. The bills were not very large. These things are relative. They had as a consequence that Herbert's mother did not feel able to buy herself anything at all. He came upon her in her bedroom turning a frock which he had heard her say was too old to wear and must be discarded. At that moment Herbert knew that Anne's scheme to pry him away from the protection of his home would be successful. He knew too that he would not struggle very hard against her. The shame of the situation was too great. That day when Anne was drunk with gin his mother had expressed a mild surprise. Anne had tossed her head. "Well, upon my word, to hear you talk, one would think you'd never had an abortion. I've had twenty!" And Herbert had seen his mother who, after all, was six or seven years older than Anne and a born Viennese, blush like a girl. He didn't know which was worse—the shame of this or of other simpler, apparently quite natural and human things. Eileen had a habit of over-eating, of stuffing herself to the point of nausea. She would get very sick. Then Anne's face would tighten. "Herbert! Will you just run out and get some oranges and some citrate of magnesia for the baby?" It seemed a very harmless act of human kindness, yet few things so rankled in Herbert as this. He didn't know why then; he was to understand it later. He avoided his parents' eyes and felt as though he were the servant of servants.

He too wanted to get away. When Anne whined or raged: "I must go to New York to see Luella and Bronson. You promised me that, you know," he answered, "I promised it, Anne, provided I could raise the money and your bills on King Street make that seem unlikely. But don't take on," he would add quickly, "your scheme is succeeding. We'll go together, though I don't know what in the world I'm going to do." Then Anne would become human. "We'll get along, Bertie. I'll do anything I can to help you. I don't care how simply we live. Can't you understand how embarrassing it must be for me here where everyone knows your age?" He nodded. He wanted to be just to her. "And another thing," she said. "When I feel free to see Bronson and Luella and see to it that their father does the right thing by them, you'll be much less bothered about them than now. You can see that, can't you?" "Yes," he said. "I can see that too." "Take still another thing," she went on. "Your mother is really a very dear woman. Don't think I don't appreciate that. But when I see how you and your father care for her, and defer to her, I can't help thinking, can I, of my own dear mother, old and forsaken out there and with no one but poor, drunken Anthony Bronson to look after her?" She got up and put her hands on his shoulders with a gesture that recalled the tenderness of old and he hadn't the heart to reply that her mother was forsaken and forlorn and her children far away because she had let nothing persuade her from the wicked scheme of marrying him. She would have answered in her present mood with pathetic, horror-stricken eyes: "But I loved you, Bertie, and I thought you loved me. You certainly made me believe that!" He considered too that pain hurts no worse for being, whether wittingly or unwittingly, self-inflicted. So he granted her her case, made her promise to be more gentle and amiable to his parents, and promised in his turn to see what could be done about their return to New York. Anne kept her promise. Whenever she was clearly triumphant she unbent and was agreeable. She swapped reminiscences of reading with his father; she took long walks with his mother; she curbed Eileen's stubborn wailing. At last Herbert finished his sonata and wrote the first three of his Southern Sketches. Ah, if the days could only have gone on like this. But he knew Anne a little by now. She was counting these days of her good behavior; she was counting every concession she made. She wrote long letters to New York. She was lying in wait; she was merely biding her time.

Herbert took counsel with his father. The two men expressed nothing that deeply affected them. Perilously they clung to the superficial aspects of the situation. A church organist in Queenshaven had no future. At the end of all these many years the older Crump was earning only a little over two thousand dollars a year. Herbert had better strike out for himself. Yes, his father could raise a few hundred dollars for him to start with and even send him a little more later on. Moreover, he and his mother had agreed that Herbert might have the extra furniture which they would not need now and his own piano. With eyes turned from each other they chatted on in hollow cheerfulness. It was better so—better. With his mother Herbert had no intimate talk at all. Anne watched him. If they approached each other she was there. With a grating harshness she had announced during the earliest days in Queenshaven that she "did not propose to have herself talked about—especially not in a foreign language!" But Herbert did not try very assiduously to have a conference with his mother. He was afraid that she would not observe so strict a reticence as his father had done. He did not want to hear the truth from other lips. He knew it. He knew that Anne was forty-four; he knew that he had been trapped and tricked; he knew that Anne, despite her superficial culture, which after all amounted to no more than an unreflective acquaintance with a good deal of English fiction and verse, had a vulgar soul. All this he knew. And as his knowledge deepened his shame mounted. Never, never—how well he understood this in the course of time—would he be able to communicate his story and his pain. For this shame, eating into his soul, originally tender and reticent, resulted in a constant terror lest others know concerning the farcical sordidness of his fate. Not once did he speak ill of Anne to his father and mother. To the end he let them believe that the songs of his cycle "Amoris Victima" were inspired by her. He told his acquaintances in Queenshaven that he must go to New York to find a broader field of activity. He emphasized his wife's intelligence and helpfulness. The more devoid of shame Anne grew, the more shame lashed him into concealing her want of it. . . .

All he hoped for the moment was that his being dragged to New York would take place in seemliness and peace. Even this hope was not fulfilled. At dinner one day his father quietly said to him:

"We can manage to start you with four hundred dollars."

Herbert looked into his father's eyes and nodded gratefully. He knew what economies, even privations, that would mean. Then he glanced at Anne, hoping she would say something at least gracious. Her eyebrows were raised, her chin thrust belligerently forward. Her voice was at its harshest.

"Oh, is that all?"

Eileen, who had a habit of parroting her mother's remarks, piped metallically, "Is that all?"

Clatteringly Herbert threw down his knife and fork. He was choking. His mother raised a beseeching hand. He turned his eyes, which he knew to be full of hatred, upon Anne.

"In addition there are, you know, the debts you ran up on King Street."

"Huh," Anne snorted. "Expect me to do without anything, did you?"

For the only time his father spoke out. "Mother and I have done our best, Anne. You seem to forget how, on your first visit to our home, you appealed to me to help my son make you an honest woman."

Eileen threw her arms violently about her mother as though she feared an attack on her. Anne got up.

"Is that so? Well, I don't know that I'll stay here to be insulted by anyone. Come, baby!"

With Eileen clinging to her she walked out of the room. The three left at that table were silent. They didn't even pretend to eat. Without looking up, Herbert's mother spoke:

"Go to your wife, my son. Otherwise she will think we are conspiring against her."

Tears burned in his eyes and his voice trembled. "Mother . . ."

"Yes, we understand, papa and I, but go."

Coldly and deliberately he placated her. There were only a few days left now before he must leave his father's house perhaps forever. He wanted those days to be at least outwardly serene. Anne rather staggered him at first by asking whether his father was willing to apologize. He got around that point by hypocritically remarking on

133

the respect and forbearance due to the older generation. This to Anne! Having cooled off, he almost laughed in her face. But rage shook him again when she seriously complained that Eileen's feelings too had been hurt. He gave the child a quarter. By supper time a polite truce had been established which Anne embellished with plentiful anecdotes of the beauty of Luella, the delicacy of health and brilliancy of mind of Bronson, and of her own gifts, conquests and excellences. Being listened to with an outward show of interest and having gained every point, she became quite agreeable, kissed Herbert's mother good-night, asked him to take a late stroll with her under the palmettos by the bay, spoke of the magic of the moonlit scene and swore that she would always remember Queenshaven with profound delight. . . .

The last night came. Herbert and Anne and Eileen were to leave on the early morning train. Herbert's mother was a little pale. But if anyone had come upon the scene he would have found an apparently very united family, held together, despite the discrepancy between the ages of the son and his wife, by firm bonds of affection and mutual understanding. Such scenes soothed Herbert and allayed the burning of his shame. Later he paid for that falseness. In the middle of that very night he dreamed that he saw his mother utterly pallid, her back against a stone wall, her hands stretched out in front of her to where a pack of wolfish, slavering hounds were snapping at her, their fangs nearer and nearer to her bosom. . . . He woke up with a toneless cry. Anne snored. He could not sleep again.

3   BRONSON VILAS had procured a furnished room for them in a comfortable rooming house on Morningside Avenue. A vague discomfort filled Herbert at the thought. Anne at once heightened this discomfort which, left alone, might have faded, into active distaste. No one ever accused Anne of having a light touch. She expatiated loudly on the convenience of having Bronson willing, useful,

intelligent, kind, on the spot. Of course Bronson was happy to do all that he could. He admired and liked Herbert so much. He, like poor mamma, had been on their side from the start.

"My only boy!" Anne exclaimed. "He's never been appreciated. His father seemed actually to dislike him."

Appealingly she looked at Herbert who laughed. "Maybe you want me to be a father to him."

Anne looked hurt at Herbert's levity. "No," she said quite seriously, "but you can take an interest in him and advise him. You seemed to be glad enough to do that at one time."

The implication that he had "curried favor"—another phrase that Anne loved—with Bronson in order to win her was one more of those retroactive falsifications that Anne was beginning to indulge in at this time. Free of Queenshaven and so of the incontrovertible evidence of her pursuit of Herbert and of her trapping him into marriage, Anne began immediately to build up a legend of their relations and adventures which, in an incredibly short time, had lost all contact with the facts of life. In this legend she believed, or feigned to believe, with a deep and romantic ardor. Any doubt thrown upon its exactness she treated as a foul affront.

Bronson of course spent that first evening in New York with them. Herbert sat there depressed and forlorn while mother and son discoursed at length on the income, disbursements, habits and shortcomings of Harrison Vilas.

"You're sure he pays Luella's fees at boarding school promptly?"

"Yes," Bronson declared, "I believe he does; in fact I'm sure. But he won't do a thing for me."

Anne turned to Herbert. "Do you know what Bronson is doing?" Herbert shook his head. "He's working as a packer in one of the storehouses of the National Cigar Company—as a packer!"

Herbert didn't know what to answer. It really didn't interest him whether this man worked at this job or some other man at another. He didn't doubt that Bronson was worthy of something better. But Anne's aggressive eagerness irritated him.

135

"Well, you don't care," she said bitterly. "But Bronson means as much to me as you to your mother. We'll see about this. It takes me to tell Harry Vilas what I think. That's what I'll do!"

Herbert jumped up. "Oh, no, you won't!"

"Oh, won't I, though? I'd just like to see you stop me! Jealous, eh?" She smiled. She glowed. She was delighted. This was a situation that suited her, that fed her sex vanity.

Herbert threw up his hands. "For Heaven's sake, no, I'm not jealous!"

Anne was arch. "Well, what would you call it, Mr. Crump?"

He shook his head. He hadn't thought it out yet. He couldn't quite formulate it. He didn't want to tell her that he felt like a man forced to feed on another's leavings, on things stale and mildewed and fly-specked. He simply didn't want that other to come back and once more paw over those rejected leavings. That was all. But he couldn't say that. Only he didn't want to hear any more. He went out for a walk leaving Anne and Bronson together.

The first thing to do of course was to get a flat. They had only a little over four hundred dollars in the world and the money had to be made to go as far as possible. Their few possessions too were being promptly shipped from Queenshaven. Herbert did not feel quite alive without a piano. Hence on their very first morning in New York they started out. They took the subway up to Washington Heights where there were plenty of apartments both new and cheap. This was a cheerful expedition. Anne, much experienced in such matters, liked the task. Herbert was betrayed then, as he was to be again, by his apparently indomitable bourgeois instinct. He never could acquire any of that bohemianism of the artist which, from afar, he both admired and envied. The notion of stretching his legs out under his own table, of working at his own piano in his own study, in seclusion from the world with his own music and books and quiet thoughts—this notion had an attractiveness for him to which he succumbed again and again. On this first occasion the pleasure of choosing a home of his own made him determine that, outrageous in origin and character as his marriage was, he would do his share toward rendering it tolerable if only Anne would do hers.

After some searching they found a little apartment in a new house on 173rd Street which Anne declared to be satisfactory in every way. It had three windows toward the street, a bright kitchen and a good bathroom. There were two living rooms and two tiny bedrooms. The arrangement of the rooms was better, of course, than in the older type of New York flat. And not far away were beautiful, woody neighborhoods. High Bridge and the Speedway and the small parks sloping down the banks of the Harlem River were only a few blocks up Amsterdam Avenue. Herbert dreamed of himself, after evenings of quiet work, strolling in that direction through the mild night. The apartment in addition cost only twenty-four dollars a month and the janitor seemed a kindly and obliging person. Luckily the things from Queenshaven arrived almost at once. It was found that Herbert's mother had added dishes and cooking utensils—enough for a start anyhow—as she had already given Anne some of her quaint, beautiful, old silver. For two or three days Herbert and Anne worked hard to get settled. Bronson came up in the evening to help. But even this irritation did not wholly spoil Herbert's pleasure. So soon as the routine of life was established he would guard his personal privacy. Anne could do as she liked. She couldn't here as in Queenshaven wound and curb him through his parents. He intended at the very least not to be annoyed.

Next and most pressing was the question of work and money. It was amazing how much of their little sum had melted away in the few days during which they had been here. Herbert was afraid to look at the stubs on his checkbook. But he was not unhopeful. He determined to do anything that would leave him some leisure and peace of mind for his creative work. Weeks ago he had sent the often rejected "Amoris Victima" to one of the smaller music houses. He took his sonata and his "Southern Sketches" and went to the offices of the firm. He was admitted into the rather dim private room of Mr. Nathaniel Joffe, the owner of the house. A tall Jew, indefinably elegant, a little cynical and deprecatory, the soft eyes of a dreamer behind his spectacles. A smile that had no intention of being wistful and yet was so.

"So you're Mr. Herbert Crump. Well, I meant to write you; but you told me when you sent your manuscript that you were coming here."

Herbert nodded. "The songs have been rejected by three or four houses," he said. "I suppose you'll do the same, but I thought I'd like to find out personally just why."

Joffe leaned back in his swivel chair. "Uh-huh. By the way, what were you doing in Queenshaven?" he asked.

"Why I was born and brought up there."

"Good God!" Joffe exclaimed. "Have you got anything besides the songs?"

"I've got a sonata and something for piano or piano and cello."

Joffe stretched out his hand and Herbert gave him the manuscripts. The publisher turned the pages slowly, stopped, whistled a bar or two out of the "Adagio of Spring Presage," laid down the manuscript and turned to Herbert.

"There's no money in this business unless you publish trash. I haven't done that so far and in consequence I've got a certain reputation among musicians and musical critics, which doesn't keep me from being as hard up as hell." He stopped and his soft level gaze took Herbert in more searchingly. "I don't suppose you've got any money."

Herbert grinned. "No."

"Got a job."

"Nor a job."

"Jesus!" Joffe smiled that unintentionally wistful smile. "Look here," he said. "Let me keep all this stuff of yours. I'll undertake to bring out the songs. The rest I'll have to think over. I might be able to get an orchestral performance of the sonata from manuscript and so create a demand for it."

Herbert glowed. "That would be wonderful."

138

"That is to say," Joffe added, "if you can write all the instrumental parts."

"Of course I can."

Joffe sighed. "All right. We'll see. Slim chance, at that." He got up. "Need money?"

Herbert felt a singular freedom with this man. "I'll need it badly soon."

Joffe slipped off his coat and took a fresh one that matched his waistcoat and trousers from the stand beside him.

"I'll send you duplicate letters tomorrow confirming these agreements. When you return your copy signed, I'll try to scratch up an advance of a hundred dollars for you." He gave a little groan and waved aside Herbert's thanks. "If you've got nothing better to do, come out and let's eat some luncheon."

He took his hat and cane, stopped in the outer office to give some directions and then guided Herbert to the Albemarle Hotel across the street where they ate together. The two men understood each other immediately. Joffe, some eight or nine years older than Herbert, had started out in life as a concert violinist. He had come to the conclusion that he would never be a great artist and thinking that there were enough second-rate fiddlers in the world, had made up his mind that there ought to be a place in America for a music publisher of decent ideals and an open mind for new men and their idioms. It was all uphill work. But he had a few moneyed friends who believed in him and his efforts and was, in addition, a bachelor who lived modestly with his mother and sister. Necessarily in the course of their talk there came out both Herbert's age and the fact that he was married. At this information Joffe sucked in the air through his teeth as though he were in sudden pain. Herbert, visualizing Anne, Eileen, Bronson, stung by that terrible shame, threw out defensively, "My wife is a writer." "What name?" Joffe asked with curiously withdrawn eyes. "She uses her maiden name, Anne Bronson Farrel." Joffe shook his head. "Never heard of her." His tone was blunt.

4 HERBERT was happy. He had the impulse to telegraph his mother: "Songs accepted." He restrained the impulse. He ought not to spend the money and a telegram might frighten her. He left the uptown subway several stations before his own. He wanted to take a walk, to be alone with himself and the taste of his good fortune upon his tongue. The hard invisible walls of the great world had yielded just a little. He was no more amid the hopeless or noisy or overeager clamorers without. Joffe had not said much about the quality of his work but the publisher's actions and his attitude had more than sufficed. The hundred dollars too would help wonderfully. Herbert felt sure that other agreeable things would happen. He didn't after all want so much. Gradual recognition, a decent living. And how he would work. Now with a little encouragement he would carry out his plans. There were notes for dozens of songs; there were, above all, the notes for his great orchestral suite, "Concerning America" which had come to him irresistibly as he had read and pondered the American poem that appealed to him then as the greatest of its age, William Vaughn Moody's "Ode in a Time of Hesitation." Furthermore he meant in this suite to solve what he thought even then, in 1907, the problem of modern music: the complete blending of cerebral quality with tonal beauty. Yes, he would work, and he was happy. And as happiness begets kindness, he felt more warmly toward Anne than he had done for a long time and hurried the last few blocks on his way home. . . .

His key slipped into the Yale lock but the door did not yield. The night latch had been turned. He rang the bell; he knocked; he waited. At last he heard stealthy, slippered feet along the hall. A voice— Anne's voice deliberately disguised—asked, "Who is it, please?" For one mad moment there flared up in Herbert's brain the thought: "There's a man inside. She's deceiving me. I'll be free. . ." With weary irritation, all the happiness and hope stone dead within him, he dismissed the thought. No such luck. "It's I, Anne. What the devil—?" "Sh-sh-sh!" The door was opened just enough to admit him. Anne's face was set in harsh lines of fear. The bones under the sallow skin looked blunt and belligerent. Her matted hair was bunched grotesquely above the enormous forehead. Gray strands hung limp from the temples. Herbert stared at her. God, she was letting herself go! This is what he had to come home to. There must be a way out! He turned upon her roughly. "What is the matter?" "Do you have to yell like that?" she whispered with vicious emphasis and her breath was hot and foul in his face. "Bronson's asleep in there on the couch. He's worn out and ill. He's in trouble. We must get him away. He thinks the police are after him."

They had reached the rear sitting room where Herbert's desk and piano stood. Eileen was crouched in a corner solemnly playing with paper dolls. From the front room Herbert could hear the heavy breathing of a man. He dropped into a chair. The scene and atmosphere were too ugly and alien for words. What was he doing here? What were these people to him? They had fastened themselves on him like a disease. He hid his face in his hands. He could not help hearing Anne's hot whisper. She was telling him the story. A fire had broken out in a picture frame factory next to the tobacco house in which Bronson worked. The fire had lasted only a few hours but it had been devastating. One could walk from the tobacco warehouse into the gutted factory next door. Bronson and several other young clerks and packers had celebrated the fire by drinking a lot of whisky. The liquor had put them in a larky mood. They had wandered into the gutted factory. They had come upon a pile of handsome frames with good pictures in them. Before they realized the nature of the action each had picked up a picture to take home. But as they had come out, the stern eye of a fireman watching from afar and the distant sound of a shrill police whistle had sobered, frightened and confused them. They had fled. Bronson was sure the police were bent on hunting them down. Looting is a penitentiary offence. Bronson must be gotten out of town immediately—this very night. He could visit the Bronsons in Chicago. Herbert looked up. He was calm now. But bitterness and cold disgust flooded him. How did this coil of sordidness concern him?

141

Glancing toward the corner he caught Eileen's sullen hostile look upon him. He got up wearily. "I think I'll take a walk and eat a little dinner out."

Then Anne broke down. Large tears trickled unrestrainedly down her cheeks.

"Don't be so cold and cruel, Bertie! Haven't you a little love or even pity left for me?"

Eileen came out of her corner weeping. She clung to Herbert.

"Please help poor Bronson. I'll break my little bank. There's nearly two dollars in it."

Poor Herbert. He was twenty-five at this time—a musician, a dreamer, sensitive and emotional. His heart had no defence against such assaults. He hesitated and was lost. Anne gently pushed him back into his seat.

"Think of your own dear mother," she said softly to him. "It isn't much I ask."

He gnawed his lip. Something in his mind told him that he ought not to be moved, that any weakening would be destructive to himself. But he was too deeply committed now. Anne's pleading eyes would not let him go.

"What do you want?" he asked.

Her whole being tightened again. "I've telephoned for information to the Penn Station. There's a train for Chicago at nine." She stopped a moment. Then she added with an unaccustomed humbleness which somehow tore at Herbert's feelings. "No Pullman, you understand, just day-coaches. He'll have to sit up all night. The fare is seventeen dollars and eighty-five cents. Then if you'll just add ten dollars so that he doesn't arrive quite penniless."

"You know how little we have in the world, Anne."

She nodded. "Of course, but he'll have to go to work in Chicago and pay you back. I've told him that."

"Very well," Herbert said, and turned with the emotional resilience of his years to the hopeful aspects of the situation. He would get the hundred dollars from Joffe; he would be rid of Bronson. Anne put her arms about him. "You're awfully good, Bertie." He frowned. He considered his last thought that it was cheap to get rid of Bronson at the price. "Please don't say anything about it," he insisted. But he was not to get off so easily. Anne went into the other room and came back holding Bronson by the arm. She pushed him a little forward and with a grotesque blending of hangdog self-abasement and jovial man-to-man heartiness, of cringing and bumptiousness, Bronson grasped Herbert's hand and shook it vigorously up and down. "It's mighty good of you, Herbert; I certainly am grateful to you." Herbert felt his cheeks literally tingling with vicarious shame. "It's nothing," he said. "Please." "Well, I don't know about that," said Anne. And Eileen, who was a good pupil at school and knew her third reader almost by heart, piped at her shrillest and most solemn: "A friend in need is a friend indeed." Herbert threw himself into a chair shrieking with laughter. The unconscious irony of the last touch was irresistible. But Anne, who was never shy in the presence of platitudes, smiled benignly. "The baby is quite right. Well, I'll just run in and get some dinner." She went into the kitchen followed by Bronson and Eileen.

In the half-dark room Herbert sat down at the piano and began to play softly. But soon he broke off in the middle of a measure. The discords in this dwelling and in his heart were too profound for music. He had come to this place which he was forced to call home in a mood that belonged to him, that was the natural outcome of his temperament, his origin and his age. This mood he had wanted to share with the woman whose husband, at least according to the law, he was. But the mood had been swept away by alien clamors, needs, fears, by things proceeding from sources of character and action with which he had nothing to do and could have nothing to do. What was to become of his life and what of him if this substitution of the alien and the repulsive for the inherent and the natural were to go on? It could not and it must not. He touched his piano and the backs of his books as though to reestablish his own identity to himself. Then he heard

Anne's voice. "Oh, Herbert!" She appeared in the door. "Well?" he asked. "Poor Bronson is naturally nervous and he's accustomed to having a bottle of Bass's ale with his dinner. Have you got a quarter?" Herbert remembered that he had hesitated to spend a small sum for a telegram to his mother, but he was in a mood beyond contention now. He took out a quarter and flung it somewhat contemptuously down on the desk. Anne gave him an ugly look. "I'm not a dog, you know." He shrugged his shoulders. He noticed, however, that she picked up the coin and that, during the rather silent and embarrassed meal that followed, Bronson drank his ale.

Immediately after dinner Anne came to Herbert for the money for her son which he now gave her and which she took in silence. Immediately thereafter she and Bronson and Eileen started for the station. Herbert felt an infinite relief in the emptiness of the flat. At least that man was not coming back to it. And for two hours his soul was his own. He took out the notes for his American Suite and worked absorbedly until he heard Anne's key in the door. She came in followed by Eileen who was sleepy and went to her bedroom at once. Anne sat down, took off her hat, slipped what was then called a "rat" out of her coiffure and let her thin hair tumble down. "Well," she said, sighing with relief, "Bronson is safe." She seemed to ruminate for awhile. Then she resumed. "Tell me, Herbert, what did you do downtown today?" Briefly and objectively he told his story. "That's fine," she said. "Fine. But if you're going to get that money and knew you were going to get it, why did you act that way about the few dollars for Bronson?"

Herbert flared up. "What has that fellow to do with my poor earnings?" She looked at him with that gesture which resembled the perception of an evil odor. "You knew I had the children, didn't you, when you came around making love to me?" Herbert controlled himself, but the effect was severe. "Don't drive me too far, Anne," he warned her. "Drive you? What in hell do you call driving? What do you think you are, anyhow? You love your money, don't you? There

144

must have been a pawnbroker among your ancestors." She stood before him ugly in her jeering malevolence and for the second and last time in his life he struck her full in the face.

5 PROFOUNDLY he regretted his stupid blunder. He knew that it was inexcusable. If anyone had told him only a year ago that he was capable of such an action he would of course not have believed it for an instant. The action in fact was so out of character that he seemed to himself to be living in a phantasmal world in which all ordinary laws were suspended. And this impression of the fantastic was deepened by Anne's reaction to his brutality. He heard her say to Eileen: "Don't annoy him. He's nervous, madly nervous. I don't want him to lose his mind, you know." Hearing this he felt that hot stifling impulse toward violence arise once more within him. She exasperated him to the quick; she falsified all life and insulted him and jeered at him. Then she called him a madman. He watched himself carefully. He avoided dangerous discussions. He would give her no further grounds for her slander.

Perhaps it was because of this self-watchfulness of his; perhaps it was because there was no strong and immediate cause for irritation. At all events, some quiet months set in. Joffe did not succeed in getting an orchestral performance for the sonata. But a well-known conductor's opinion of it fortified his own. He came to believe that Herbert had a future and determined to help him toward that future out of his own meager resources. There was editorial work of one sort or another to be done; there was the reading of manuscript music for the firm. Herbert edited for Joffe a volume of the more recently discovered German folk songs. The German editions were all written for the lute and to arrange the songs for the piano was a considerable and not unpleasant task. Next at Joffe's suggestion Herbert wrote a series of simple études for beginners on American themes. These, when seen by experts, were pronounced to be charming and sure of

145

success, and Herbert got an advance royalty of two hundred dollars. His total earnings did not average over a hundred and twenty-five dollars a month. But this sufficed. Anne, after her brief spurt of extravagance used as sabotage in Queenshaven, settled down to her accustomed level of economic life. With this difference: that in her new marriage narrow means did not issue in disorder. The rent was paid promptly; no one gambled; an occasional garment could be bought. Herbert's personal habits were frugal to the point of severity. But this involved no hardship for him. He took no interest in money or in things. He got concert tickets for nothing. The excitement of his work sufficed him. He could not help making this observation, however, that, though Anne would frequently discourse on the horrors of her life with Vilas, she was careful never to admit that she had bettered herself in any respect and Herbert came to suspect that the ups and downs, even the danger and sordidness of a gambler's conduct of life, suited her better than security and order. But this suspicion mattered very little to him at the time. He was glad that there were no ugly scenes, that Anne, without understanding it, took a sympathetic attitude toward his work. She was more careful of her personal appearance again, too. She ran her little household cheerfully. She ran it badly, to be sure. She had an inveterate habit of leaving soiled dishes stacked on the washtubs in the kitchen and of forgetting platefuls of left-overs in an iceless ice-box. In consequence a plague of cockroaches set in and mice could be heard scrabbling and squeaking in the night. Anne, magnificently innocent as usual, declared herself disappointed in the house. It was evidently an older house than she had been given to understand. The other families were obviously dirty. She upbraided the janitor on the landing. The janitor scratched his head. "Maybe so, missus, but none of the other tenants don't complain, I notice." Anne laughed ironically. "You can tell that to your grandmother, Mr. Rouse. I wasn't born yesterday, you know." She had left the door of the flat open and Herbert, overhearing this conversation, grinned sardonically to himself. He was hardening a little. On all non-essential matters he pretended to agree

146

with Anne. He wanted to enjoy the blue and russet autumn; he wanted calm for his work; once a week he had a conference with Joffe and luncheon with him. That sufficed him for the present as a contact with the world.

The peace of life was, to be sure, not uninterrupted. Every Saturday afternoon and evening Anne and Eileen went out to spend the time with Luella, whom her father would not permit to visit the Crump apartment. This was a blessed circumstance for Herbert. The afternoon and evening constituted his real Sabbath and day of rest. He used the time first to write home—to write while there were no prying eyes on him, no atmosphere subtly hostile to this task about him. Next he would sit still in the healing silence, in the calm from which for a short time the hot and ruthless throbbing of Anne's will was absent. And from this Sabbath mood of quiet, ideas and motifs and melodies would arise, and when, near midnight after the theatre, her key clicked in the door, he would sigh resignedly and quote to himself those verses of Matthew Arnold which came to be a great stay to him:

> Tasks in hours of insight willed
> May be in hours of gloom fulfilled.

(These lines, it will be remembered, are the motto of his tone poem, "The Thinker," op. 14, in which in an idiom that blends the realistic with the metaphysical he expresses the dying down of the discords of the world and the consequent liberation of the creative will.)

With Anne's return on Saturday night however there returned not only her tenseness and overeagerness, her general discordance, but those specific cares of hers that broke again and again the comparative quiet of his fall and winter. Seeing Luella naturally fixed her mind more strongly on the other members of her family. The Chicago Bronsons, daughters and sons-in-law of the late Joshua Bronson, had received Bronson Vilas kindly enough, but they had not known what to do with him and had had their own theories as to the reasons

147

for his sudden unannounced and equivocal visit. Since he was pale and anaemic and they knew of nothing he could do in Chicago, they had shipped him off to a farm owned by some relations of theirs near South Bend, Indiana. From this place Bronson wrote long whines to his mother: he had to get up at five o'clock in the morning; he had to work like a common farmhand; the people were so puritanical they wouldn't even let him smoke. What was going to become of him anyhow? Sitting there late Saturday night, taking her hair down as usual, next eating an onion sandwich, her desirous, demanding eyes fixed on Herbert, Anne would discourse on the injustice which life was inflicting on her handsome and gifted son. But she had a sharper care than that, a care that really gnawed at her vitals. Her old mother whom, in her wild pursuit of Herbert, she had so casually dropped on the Chicago Bronsons and who had been bundled off by them to Anthony Bronson in Little Rock, Arkansas, wrote letters very different in tone from those of her grandson. There was a strain of stoicism in Mrs. Toohey. Anthony worked at sign-painting when he was sober and was good to her. So was Mrs. Bailey, the woman with whom the two old people had lodgings. But she had no money, of course. Would Anne appeal to Herbert for a little cash for her? She had made herself a nightgown out of some material that she had, but she would like to have one other. She had a decent black skirt; if she had a black waist she would be able to take a walk once in a while. But these things, she wrote, could well wait. What she begged for right away was a box of a certain kind of suppositories that always eased the dreadful pain of her old trouble. The bleak and hopeless pathos of these appeals reached Herbert's heart. He always gave Anne all he could possibly spare for her mother. But she sometimes delayed writing or delayed sending the money orders. At other times he believed that in her besottedness she actually diverted some of this money to Bronson or used it for gifts with which to bribe Luella whom the Duboses had influenced against her. Once, at all events, Mrs. Toohey complained. She did so with a touch of irony, even of sternness. But her gallantry flagged in the end. "It is hard," she

148

wrote, "it is hard to be old and poor and sick." This was too much for Anne. "I can't stand it, I can't stand it," she whimpered. "We've got to bring mamma on right away, right away, right away." And as she repeated these words she struck her hands in a childlike fury strange in a woman of her years against the desk beside her. Herbert, horrorstruck, got up and paced the small room. "It's impossible," he said. "I'll send your mother money every week; I'll send it myself. But in this tiny flat! It's impossible; I should go mad." But Anne either did not hear or feigned not to hear. She screamed: "Right away, right away, right away!" She ran into the bedroom dragging her corset which she had unhooked behind her and for many minutes Herbert heard her wild exclamations and her rending sobs. On the next afternoon she came to him calm, white, reasonable.

"There's a little rear flat on the floor above that rents for eighteen dollars a month. I'll bring Bronson on here. He can get a job that will pay the rent and his board. Then I'll bring mamma on and she and he can stay up there. You won't be bothered; all it will cost you is the price of a little food for mamma. Are you willing?"

He laid his hand on her arm. Heaven forbid that he should stand in the way of the succor of anyone. "Certainly. What bothers me, Anne, is the problem of the railroad fares."

She drew herself up. "I'll raise some of the money somehow or die in the attempt. Will you try to raise some too?"

"I'll do my best," he said.

She put her arms about him. "You're awfully good, Bertie—sometimes."

He closed his eyes. He did not want the added shame of her thanks. He loathed and dreaded the whole business. Only he was human and helpless and willing to pay money to escape having forced upon him a share in an alien guilt.

6   THE plan was not carried out in quite its original form. Anne's plans never were. She had the excuse furnished her by the natural exigencies of life and this excuse was a good one. Here now, she told Herbert, was the twentieth of the month. Those little eighteen dollar flats were in great demand. Only one was vacant. But the janitor had promised to show it to no one and to let her have it, if she would pay the next month's rental now. Herbert looked at her coolly.

"Aha, this is the way Bronson is to pay the rent of the flat, precisely as he paid back his fare to Chicago. Furthermore, this scheme obliges us to raise the railroad fares by a certain date."

She interrupted him harshly. "You promised me this, Herbert Crump!"

"I promised you something entirely different."

"Why, what a liar you are!"

"I, a liar?" Herbert jumped up. "How dare you?"

"Hell, come off your high horse. Jesus, I wouldn't be such a piker for anything you could give me."

He pulled himself together. "No," he said, "you're never a piker, as you call it, with any few pennies that I may happen to have. But you're a cheat in this as in everything else. However, I'll give you the eighteen dollars tomorrow if you'll only shut up. That's all I ask."

"Well, upon my word of honor—" she began, but he heard no more. He left first the room and then the flat.

He wanted just now to buy her off, to keep her from nagging, even to keep her if possible in good humor. New elements were faintly beginning to color his professional life and he had a premonition, though as yet no clear perception, of the complications to which these would lead. The thing had started at one of his luncheons with Joffe. His friend's melancholy brown eyes had rested on him.

"Don't have any babies yet to tie you down. There's got to be a personal element in a career like yours."

Herbert felt himself getting pale with that old shame over the monstrousness of his situation. Oh, if there had not been that alien brood he could have answered calmly enough, "My wife is somewhat older than I and we'll be careful." But the extent of the abnormality and sordidness of his situation kept him from revealing any part of it. After the luncheon he called himself a coward and a fool. The fact remained that he could not speak, that he could not above all, blur and confuse this man's interest in him as an artist by throwing into the situation at its very beginning a problem so bitter and bizarre. The misjudgment of which on this, as on later similar occasions, he was guilty, was, of course, his failure to take into account the perceptiveness of people as well as his own ill-success as a deceiver. Wherever he went, now or later, it was perfectly clear to everyone almost at once that there must be something dreadfully wrong about his marriage. Anne was dimly aware of his involuntarily creating this impression and this awareness made her the more rancorously eager to be on the spot, on all occasions, in order to counteract it. What she never knew and, being Anne, could never be made faintly to suspect, was that she had only to be on the spot to elucidate to all beholders the real dreadfulness of Herbert's predicament and to throw on his side the sympathy of men and even of women. Side by side these two people walked, each in another and a separate darkness. . . .

It was not long thereafter when Joffe explained to Herbert what he meant by the personal element in a career.

"Look here, Crump," he said, "I've been thinking about you. You've got to make a more practical start."

"Easily said, but how?"

"Well, I've got an old friend, awfully good sort, who is one of the really generous and sincere patrons of music in New York. I want to bring you together with Mrs. Goldstein. I've showed her your stuff and she thinks highly of it. If you two hit it off personally she'll arrange to have you give a recital of your own music at her house."

Herbert laughed. "Too damned good to be true."

Joffe looked steadily at him. "Look here, what's crushed you so?

Pump up a little vanity, man; the seventh-raters are all bursting with it."

Herbert shook his head. "Quite true. It's just not in my line."

"Well, anyhow," Joffe went on, "Jennie Goldstein's music room holds two hundred people. She'll soak 'em five dollars per. A few will come because they really want to. The rest—and they're the people who'll rave loudest and make you known—will come because they like to say that they've been at a musical at Mrs. Goldstein's at number so and so Fifth Avenue. The main point is, of course, that you'll get the proceeds."

Herbert laid down his knife and fork. "Don't tell me a thing like that, Joffe. I've never seen that much money."

He had gone home that afternoon, eager to tell Anne of his possible good fortune, but on the way the impulse had weakened. On his arrival it had died. Eileen had a sore throat, Anne had announced to him at the very door. Would he look at the baby's throat? It might, you know, be diphtheria. You never could tell. In addition the janitor had been insolent to her and she wanted him, Herbert, to give the fellow a piece of his mind. Herbert agreed casually but determined to do nothing of the sort. He knew by this time that in her disputes with people, especially with those whom in her moods of asperity she called "servants," she was always so grotesquely in the wrong that any reference to the controversy would only make him look like a fool. As he went, depressed and irritated, into the bedroom to change his clothes, an idea and a vision came to him that seemed to pour a heavenly and intoxicating ichor into his blood. He could keep a part of his life all to himself. It was his anyhow. Anne had no share in it. None. If ever, and how rare that was, she had done a kind or helpful thing, she had immediately destroyed its effect by the enormity of her subsequent exactions. Nothing that was his was hers of right. For any wrong he had done in the romantic folly of his youth, he had already paid in suffering and humiliation. He would give her money for her family. That was what she most wanted anyhow—that, and the exercise of one function of his body. Since he could not leave her

152

—at least not now—and destroy his career before it was well begun and also shame his parents by the inevitable and sordid scandal that Anne would create—he could at least keep the better part of his life to himself and pass through the misery and ugliness to which he was condemned with some beautiful secret to console and fortify him hidden in his heart.

Thus, pleading, under Anne's watchful eye, an extra conference with Joffe, he had started downtown on a certain Wednesday noon. Anne had indeed said: "Well, you're dressing up a whole lot, aren't you?" But he had succeeded in preserving a light touch. "Some fellows from one of the big publishing houses will be there. They all dress well." And he had not seen Anne's face, drawn in a wild suspiciousness watching him from the window as he went. Calm yet with a tingle of elation he rode downtown and went, for the first time in his life, to have his nails professionally manicured. The manicurist had fantastically made-up eyes and peroxided hair. But the hands with which she touched Herbert's were smooth and young and living and he was a little ashamed of the pleasure he took in the soft curve that ran from her chin into the V-shaped opening of her white silk shirtwaist. He had almost forgotten the texture and the scent of youth. Even this faint and formal contact with it uplifted him. He walked, as though he were free, a few blocks down Fifth Avenue to the appointed meeting place in the lobby of the Waldorf Astoria. Here in a very few minutes he was joined by Joffe and a black-eyed, black-haired lady in her middle thirties who reminded him at once, especially on account of her small but distinctly Jewish nose, of a handsome, glossy, dark bird, and the quick abrupt graceful movements of whose head were birdlike too. Her husky speaking voice recalled Gerda's.

"How do you do?" she said to him quickly. Then she turned again to Joffe. "Come on, Nat, I'm hungry. Let's get a good table."

The headwaiter evidently knew Mrs. Goldstein and gave them a table by the window.

"Order something, Nat. The mixed grill is good here sometimes.

153

Order cocktails." Then she turned to Herbert. She acted as though she didn't have a minute to spare. "I think music is so wonderful. I adore your songs. But I think your instrumental music is more original. I always say, we ought to do all we can for music. Don't you think so?"

Herbert grinned. "I'm an interested party," he said. "My opinion is no good."

She pulled Joffe's sleeve. "Did you hear that, Nat? I like that."

Joffe nodded. "Crump's the most modest of living artists."

"How perfectly wonderful!" she cried. "Where are the cocktails? I have an appointment at three. You must play at my house, Mr. Crump. Nat, do you know, Mr. Crump must play at my house?"

She pattered on, but it was apparent to Herbert, as Joffe had told him, that under her patter there was both a good mind and a good heart. She could be relied on. Ten minutes before it was time for her to leave she suddenly plunged into the practical. She fixed a date three weeks later for Herbert's recital at her house. He would hear from her directly and also through Joffe. She paid the bill, snatched up her sable coat and rushed out. Joffe too had to get back to his office. Herbert, alone on the sun-flooded avenue, felt very lonely. People had a definite world in which they moved. He was extraordinarily isolated. He was ashamed to think how much he owed Joffe. Would he ever have friends, appointments, meetings? Would he ever, in that concrete sense, belong anywhere? As he walked along rather aimlessly this preoccupation yielded to another and a sharper one. He would have to practice for the next three weeks. He would have to make certain preparations. Then too Mrs. Goldstein had asked for his address and would no doubt communicate with him. This business of keeping the better part of his life a secret didn't work out so smoothly after all. He would have to tell Anne. It was a depressing thought.

7   THIS depression, this hesitancy, the inner determination to
    keep as much for himself of what small good life might bring
    to him—all these elements perhaps gave both his speech and
bearing a factitious air.

"You say you are going to give a recital of your music at a private
house on Fifth Avenue?"

She eyed him with a mixture of genuine alarm and assumed contempt. He strove after firmness and naturalness.

"Exactly. It's quite the usual thing."

"Well, I never heard of it."

He shrugged his shoulders. "There's a good deal you've never
heard of."

She snorted and unconscious of the irony said: "You teach your
grandmother how to milk ducks! What's the woman's name?"

"Mrs. Alfred Goldstein."

She tossed her head sideways and dilated her nostrils.

"So you have to curry favor with rich Jews to get on. I see myself
doing a thing like that."

He turned on her. "Do you realize that Joffe has been my best
friend and is trying to help me through his friends and that he's given
us our very chance to live?"

"That doesn't give him the right to insult me," she bridled.

Herbert looked blank. "For Heaven's sake, how has Nat Joffe insulted you? What has he to do with you?"

She was rancorously ironical. "Well, I've always been taught that
there are certain social courtesies due to a man's wife."

He grasped his forehead. "I don't know what you're talking about."

"Oh, you don't, don't you? Well, let me tell you one thing right
now. I'm not going to be insulted. If this Mrs. Goldstein or whatever
her name is doesn't acknowledge my existence and doesn't invite me,
I'll go downtown and tell both her and that Nat Joffe exactly what I
think of them."

Herbert stared at her. She had plaited her scanty hair in half a
dozen stringlike pigtails which were pinned tight to her head. She

155

no longer concealed her forehead from him. She had put on flesh in the last years. Her jowls were beginning to get heavy which, in such moods as these, gave the lower part of her face an added fierceness. Curious how at this moment a half-forgotten quotation stole into Herbert's mind: "Gentleness is an excellent thing in a woman." And after that a word that was no word at all formed itself in his thought —pestiferocity. And next he felt like crying. But that passed too in a moment and next, still staring at her, he heard something saying inside of him: "Yes. This creature can ruin you. And she will before all is over. She will. No use struggling." And then suddenly he heard Anne's voice alarmed, pathetic, her other former voice, her softer young voice which she now so rarely used.

"Bertie, don't, don't look at me as if you loathed me! You don't, do you?"

Resignedly he shook his head. "No, no, Anne, but I'm tired. Let's say no more." And then to his own astonishment he heard himself cry out again: "No more!" Anne looked at him as though she feared for his reason.

He wrote a good deal at odd moments. He worked up his piano technique. Anne said nothing about the concert until a note came from Mrs. Goldstein, a note on very heavy, very expensive paper, written in an enormous squarish hand. All preparations had been made; the sale of the tickets was going well; Herbert was to take good care of himself. The note was kind, energetic, sensible. Gingerly Anne picked it up from Herbert's desk.

"Quite a flirtatious tone your friend takes. Doesn't mention her husband or me. Does she think you're a bachelor?"

It was morning and Herbert was in a calm mood. Moreover, living with Anne had trained his argumentative faculties. Not that it ever did any good to catch Anne tripping or to worst her in an argument. Since she didn't know that she was worsted, since it was inconceivable to her that she could be wrong on any point, one got, of course, no satisfaction. In later years Herbert often contented himself with grinning and saying: "Mrs. God has spoken." But today he still had faith that reason could prevail with her.

"I don't understand your sudden emphasis on little conventional details," he said. "You used to be a liberal-minded woman. Look, you lived with me before we were married—"

"You're a nice one to throw that up to me," she broke in.

He held up his hands. "I don't, not at all. That was all right. But you will admit that you did exactly as you liked, irrespective of convention. Your attitude has changed strangely."

She became pompous. She seemed actually to swell up. Like the frog in the fable, Herbert thought.

"I don't see any connection between the two things," she said. "I loved you and you said you loved me, but this woman's actions aren't decent and I'll see whether she's going to get the better of me."

Herbert yielded to an impish temptation. "There was also that little matter with Dr. Vogel that you told me about."

Anne bounded from her seat and clutched Herbert's thick hair with both hands. She pulled rather viciously but the incident brought Herbert an illuminating perception: how much more satisfying it was morally to be the attacked than the attacker. Anne retired weeping to the bedroom and Herbert knew that he would never commit the sin and silliness of violence again.

There was another scene every time a note came from Mrs. Goldstein and every time that Herbert answered one. Concealment or privacy was out of the question in the little flat. And Anne's vigilance was far more energetic than Herbert's feeble and fitful defense of himself. The result of these contentions was that any anticipatory pleasure or pride that Herbert might have taken in the recital were harried out of him long before the appointed day. He felt limp and stale and disgusted with the world and with himself. He saw one thing clearly: if he were to go on living with Anne, and for the time being he saw no alternative, some method of life would sooner or later have to be devised in which he could have a measure of privacy and detachment. Things dear to his heart must be kept from her unless they were to be stained and violated and thus perish and decay under his very eyes.

Three days before the recital Mrs. Goldstein sent four tickets "for Mrs. Crump and anyone else you may care to invite." Anne's comment was: "Pretty damned high and mighty. The man isn't born that I'll just go trailing along with." But she began to make certain preparations and was, Herbert saw, secretly pleased and would be quite ready later, provided she could reduce his significance to a subsidiary one, to brag of her triumphs, conquests and repartees in a Fifth Avenue "mansion". On the appointed day she rose early—the recital was to be at eleven in the forenoon—got breakfast promptly, which was rare, and then retired quietly to dress. Herbert had had a fair night's rest and hoped he would get through the thing at least creditably. He had begged Anne to be ready at ten-thirty sharp since waiting and delay chafed him and made him nervous. She had promised. He had taken his things into the sitting room so as not to interfere with her and was shaved and dressed at ten. He looked at indifferent things, played a few measures on the piano, walked up and down. At ten twenty-five he looked into the bedroom. Anne saw his image in the mirror of the bureau before which she was standing. "Don't make me nervous, Bertie, now. I'm doing my hair." With a conciliatory touch of humor he said: "Five minutes more." "All right, all right, only don't look at me." He went back to the sitting room. He began to suffer acutely. But he couldn't afford to provoke a scene at this moment. Since he was both the artist and the breadwinner she had him at her mercy. A mad world, he reflected, a moral topsyturvydom. At ten thirty-eight he could contain himself no longer. "Please, Anne," he called out, "please." "Right away," she answered. Watch in hand he saw the unendurable minutes drag. At ten forty-one she appeared. He looked at her. Well, at least she had done a good job. Her make-up was skilful. To his unpractised eye, at least, she looked well-groomed and assuredly some years—not nearly as many of course as she fancied—younger than her forty-six. "All right, Anne," he said, "let's hurry now." "Did you see my white

158

gloves?" she asked. He shook his head. "Well, I carefully laid them on the desk here this very morning." "If you had they'd be there." "Well, I did just the same." "Don't argue now, Anne," he pleaded. "Look for them, or take your black pair." She dashed into the bedroom; she pulled out drawer after drawer. The contents of the drawers were in inconceivable disorder. At ten-fifty, pulling a drawer completely out of the bureau, Anne found the gloves which had fallen out lying on the floor behind. "Well," she said, "I could have taken my oath I had put them on that desk." At eleven they managed to get a taxi on Amsterdam Avenue. To Herbert the whole occasion seemed ruined. With the rooted instincts of all his ancestors he hated disorder and unpunctuality. It worked in him like poison. In the cab Anne patted his knee. "I know my boy will do booful." He nodded. Better this than contention. At eleven-sixteen having been delayed by crosstown traffic they reached the house facing the park. A very blond apple-headed footman admitted them. Upstairs Mrs. Goldstein swept them both with a rapid, penetrating glance. "Glad you're here at last." There was a distinct reproof in her voice. Anne's scarcely perceptible bridling did not escape that dark eye. Mrs. Goldstein pointed to great doors slightly ajar. "In there, Mrs. Crump, you'll find a place reserved for you." Anne hesitated, half opened her lips and then disappeared. Jennie Goldstein took Herbert's arm. "Do you want a glass of port?" Herbert shook his head. "No, but can I have just two minutes before I start?" "Come." She took him into a little smoking-room and left him. He sat down and closed his lids. What, in the eternal world of art, did this woman matter who had her claws in his flesh and nerves? She must not be permitted to have power upon his soul. He would play for the honor of art which, as his grandfather used to say, is the honor of God. Jennie Goldstein reappeared. "Ready?" He smiled into her eyes. "Quite." "Good man." She took him through several rooms and thrust him gently into a low door. He found himself facing the audience—well-groomed, expensively-dressed women, a very few elderly men. The concert grand was at his left. Applause, polite but friendly, cheered him. He bowed and took his seat. He began with three of his "Southern Sketches" which were fluent and poetical, easy to grasp, somewhat in the manner of MacDowell's "New England Idylls" but, he secretly thought, more original and massive in execution, more virile and significant in thematic material, less polite. In the third wailed the forlornness of swamp and rice field, throbbed the anguish of the Negroes under the broiling sun. The applause was obviously genuine. From now on he lost himself in the thrilling act of artistic communication. He played "Spring Presage"; he played the two completed movements of his suite "Concerning America," he ended with two early gavottes, light, cool, lovely, exact traceries of pure music. He got up; he scarcely heard the clapping; an inner glow told him that his work had reached his hearers. Mrs. Goldstein came and took him by the hand. "Brauer of the *Standard* is here. He wants to talk to you." Herbert had to look up at the gray haired giant who growled, "So far you're a German composer. Just like MacDowell. But you seem to have more brains and more guts. How old are you?" "Twenty-six." "Uh-huh, not so bad. More power to you, as the Irish say. Good-bye." Then Herbert was introduced to a great many rather heavy ladies who said pleasant things, but whose names he didn't catch. He was in a delightful haze from which he was suddenly startled by the sight of Anne's face in the background. Her eyes were fixed, her features rigid as though frozen. What was it now, he asked himself. In a flash he knew. Anne was envious of Mrs. Goldstein with her beautiful house; she was envious of those other women. Worse and more sinister, she grudged him his success. She was envious of him partly for herself, much more for her son Bronson who was working as a farmhand in Indiana. She hated this house and these people. And for the moment she hated him.

Mrs. Goldstein rescued him from a group of ladies. "Stay. We'll have a bite of luncheon. Just your wife and you and Nat and I." She squeezed his arm encouragingly. The audience drifted out. Soon those four were seated at table in the breakfast room. Anne had pulled herself together. She took a flirtatious attitude toward Joffe.

"I was beginning to think you were a myth. I heard so much about you and never saw you." Joffe laughed off the implied reproach. Mrs. Goldstein was talking to Herbert. He could only half hear the others but he heard enough. He heard Anne. "Oh, yes, Herbert composes well . . . Why not? . . . Never did anything else . . . But suppose you never have a chance? . . . I have a son . . . Marvelously gifted . . . Eileen is a born musician . . . He won't even teach her . . . Oh, I've had poetry in all the leading magazines . . ." Mrs. Goldstein raised her voice a little. "Nat, what was that you said about Brahms to Mr. Crump that day we all had luncheon together?" Joffe laughed. "My good remarks don't recur, Jennie. Record them on the spot or they are lost." Anne turned a rigid, agate-eyed face that suddenly seemed slightly swollen upon Jennie Goldstein. "So you had luncheon with my husband! Well, this is the first I've been told of it." Herbert felt faintly nauseated with shame. Mrs. Goldstein turned cold eyes on Anne. She made no direct reply. She said, "I'm sorry that we must hurry; I have an engagement." After several strained minutes she gave the signal for rising. Then she touched a bell. The footman appeared. She bowed distantly to Anne. She squeezed Herbert's arm. "You'll hear from me." The footman held open the door; he guided them downstairs. In a moment they were on the street slowly walking uptown. "Well," Anne said, "I didn't know you were such a liar. So you had luncheon with that vulgar woman. Maybe she'd like to go to bed with you. I didn't see her husband anywhere around. Maybe that Joffe sleeps with her too. I've always been told that Jews are vulgar. But they seem to suit you. Why don't you go and live with them? Couldn't she squeeze your arm a little oftener and paw you around a little more? I call it disgusting, that's what I call it. A hell of a lot of good it does to have those fat, ignorant women listen to you. I should think you'd have more self-respect, more common decency. I'd die before I'd curry favour with them. But why did you lie to me? Tell me that—why are you such a rotten liar—" He turned. He walked off in the opposite direction. He almost ran.

There flashed into his mind the anecdote of Harrison Vilas throwing the steak over the fence and running away. Poor devil! He probably had had good reason to run. God, what a woman . . . What a world. . . .

8   IT WAS all very well to keep on walking. He got tired. He had no place to go. He had only a few dollars in his pocket and his checkbook was in the desk at home. He knew perfectly that there was a type of man who under such circumstances as these would go on a spree, would seek a brief forgetfulness in some intoxication. The iron habit of forethought held him back. If he did such a thing his last state would only be worse than his first. He wanted not more darkness but more light. He walked into the park and sat down wearily on a bench. Suppose he left Anne. How? All he possessed in the world, all his heart clung to—his music, his books, his piano, his family photographs—were in that flat. Anne would shriek in the streets and denounce him as a madman if he were to try to take what was his. Well, suppose he escaped with all he had some Saturday afternoon? Anne would raise a terrific outcry; she would sue him for alimony. He would have to flee. Where to? And what was he to do? His mind seemed to cloud. Maybe some other man would find a way out. Maybe he was, as he had feared long ago, not adequate to life. Perhaps the artist, held by that profound initial preoccupation, had not enough ingenuity and energy left to cope with intricate problems in the outer world. Perhaps . . . It began to rain softly. A tiny patter on the branches of the trees, on the gravel at his feet. How tired he was. He must go home and rest.

The flat was quiet. There was a whiff of valerian in the air. Anne's puffing and snoring could be heard from the bedroom. Herbert lay down on the couch and rested. The shadows fell and crept into the room. By and by he heard Anne stirring. He closed his eyes and pretended to be asleep. She came in, saw him and stopped. "Poor boy," she half whispered to herself. Then she went into the kitchen to broil the chops for dinner. "How strange," Herbert thought. "She has a real tenderness for me, but the aliveness of that feeling is dependent on my being here—her object, her thing, slave, prisoner, merged with her family, serving her interests; it depends on the exclusion of my parents, of my art except as an impersonal means of winning bread, of friends, interests, occupations beyond these walls. She operates with the most primitive instincts of the wife and mother animal toward its mate. If she were young and the mother of my children that would be bad enough and irksome enough and crushing enough. Considering her age and Bronson and Luella and Eileen Vilas, it is grotesque, a ribald caricature. . . ." Then he wondered what the end of it would be, but he was too tired to wonder. Soon Anne called him to dinner. They ate together in a not unkindly silence. Herbert spent the evening over a book. He went to bed early, marvelling vaguely at the inextricable intricacies in the relationship of any two human beings whom life, however violently and accidentally and abnormally, had once thrown together.

First Mrs. Goldstein sent a check for six hundred and ten dollars; then one for one hundred and five. It meant clothes, Herbert thought, and more than that it meant three months of no editing but of quiet creative work. Joffe had advised him to spend the money on a public recital in a regular concert hall. Herbert hadn't the courage for that. His life robbed him of the initiative and resilience proper to his years. He would have been glad enough to have gambled on his career if he could then have gone for a while to his father's house. But fate had practically closed that door to him. Anyhow, as he realized in a very few days, what was the use of his engaging in fine speculations? Anne faced him.

"Well, Bertie, now we can send for mamma and Bronson."

His heart sank. He spoke without looking at her. "You said you were going to raise some of the money."

"Now what chance have I had? And you, with all that money! Honestly, Bertie, I didn't think you were stingy."

"Am I stingy?" he said thoughtfully. "I don't think so. But you abused me on account of the way I made the money and insulted my friends who helped me make it. Now you want me to give you a lot of it to—to create circumstances that will make life simply unbearable."

She was too astute to argue. "I can see your point, Bertie. But my position is a hard one. Poor mamma will die out there. I can't let that happen."

He sighed. "No, you can't."

"Very well," she went on. "And I swear to you I am bringing Bronson on solely so that you won't feel the added burden. He loves his grandmother and he'll be glad to help provide for her."

"Very well. How much will it take?"

Anne looked at a slip of paper covered with figures. "A hundred dollars will do it all."

He got up. He was relieved. He patted her shoulder. "All right. That won't break us as things are at present."

"Then please, Bertie, please give me the check now. Then my mind will be at rest and I won't have to annoy you any more."

He went to his desk and made out the check. Thank Heaven it would still leave him a balance of over six hundred dollars. Anne thanked him with tears in her eyes. That shamed him. "Don't, Anne. It's only money." They seemed to be very united in this hour. Yet in truth they were not. For Anne never succeeded in confusing Herbert's mind. All that she had said and plead and to which his predicament had made him assent was true and pertinent only on the assumption that he had loved her and sought her in marriage. But this assumption was false as hell. And hence her pleas and reasons were equally false. He would not have been stingy if he had denied her the money nor hard of heart if he had told her to send her mother to the poorhouse. For she and hers had no inner relation to him and no claim on him, because they had come upon him like an assault, a violation, a disease. . . . He shook off these thoughts. What was the use? To her last gasp Anne would fight for her legend that they had fallen overwhelmingly in love with each other and consciously planned—both of them and from the first—to be permanently united. He had no means of disproving that legend which grew more and more to be her strong shield and her effectual defense. The best thing for him to do was to quit thinking and to go to work.

Four days later in the middle of the night a little sled that Eileen possessed and that stood securely propped against the wall toppled over without apparent cause and clattered noisily on the wood of the floor. Anne leaped from her bed and threw on a kimono. She had a great faith in the reality of occult phenomena. She was fond of telling of how once, years ago in Chicago, her mother in a dream had seen her with a hole in her throat and, hastening to her, had found her coming down with diphtheria. She was sure now that the falling over of the sled was a message from her mother, a call for help, a warning. She had not yet sent the money to Little Rock which Herbert had given her. Terror held her as in a vise. She could sleep no more. As early as possible in the morning she hurried off and sent money to her mother by telegram. She came home feeling relieved. But her respite was brief. Late on that very afternoon came a wire from Mrs. Bailey in Little Rock: "Your mother terrible sick. Come immediately." Anne held herself erect through sheer inner force. She knew that she needed to be strong for the frightful trip ahead of her. But her suffering was terrible in its very rigidity. She could not cry. Herbert was very tender with her. He dismissed all considerations of her responsibility; remorse made her grief only the harder to bear. He went out for her and wired to Little Rock and drew another hundred dollars from the bank and bought her ticket and gave her the rest of the money and sternly crushed his irritation over the moral dilemma into which he had been unwillingly thrust. That dilemma was an ugly one. Action can be mastered, not thought and impulse. He could not help secretly hoping that Mrs. Toohey would not recover. He hated himself for that secret hope. But the notion of the greater part of his small earnings being wiped out by Anne's staying through her mother's convalescence in Arkansas and by her bringing her mother to New York and his having then to shoulder the added responsibility—that notion was too crushing. Hardly less crushing was the idea of funeral expenses and heaven knows what more. Then there was Bronson. If her mother died far away from her Anne would move heaven and earth to have Bronson with her. Herbert gagged at his thoughts. He was out on some errand and stopped short in the middle of the street. Was he a callous brute? He hoped not; he would rather err on the side of kindness. No, the simple fact was that Mrs. Toohey's son-in-law and Bronson's stepfather should have been a man of fifty-five. Well, he was twenty-six. The situation with its demands was something hopelessly wrenched out of the natural order of things. It was an outrage done to fundamental instincts. It would revenge itself some day.

Anne left that night. Herbert was kind to Eileen who was gentler and more childlike whenever her mother was not present. She helped to keep house in a quaint little fashion and invented a pet name for Herbert out of her story books and a friendship sprang up unexpectedly and shyly between the young man and the little girl. They took a walk together and Eileen, her hand in Herbert's, said: "Your father and mother were awfully good to me. Mayn't I visit them sometime?" And Herbert, greatly won over, promised the child that she should have her wish. On the third day after Anne's departure the peace of these strange companions was broken. Anne wired that she had found her mother dead and must have two hundred dollars more by telegraph at once. Herbert went out and dispatched the money in a fatalistic mood. He almost felt like sending her all he had. But the rent was due and Eileen and he had to live. Four days later Anne wired for another hundred and two days later still for an extra fifty from Chicago. On the day before her last telegram was received Bronson Vilas walked into the flat on 173rd Street. Herbert put his hand to his throat. He was getting used to this sensation of choking and anxiety and horror. "How did you—?" "Mamma wired me my fare from Little Rock. Do you know what she's doing? She had poor Grandma Toohey embalmed in Little Rock and shipped to Chicago for services and cremation. She'll be here in a day or two." He got up. From the kitchen he brought in, scraping and clattering, an old wooden rocker. He put it down next to the piano and sat down and rocked.

9 MONTHS of dim days scarcely distinguishable one from another. Anne came back from Chicago older, grimmer, more implacable. She came bearing in her arms the ashes of her mother in a box of tin. Life had defeated her; death had beaten her to a goal. Her mother had been in her seventy-second year and not sorry perhaps to lay down the burden of her harsh and futile days. Anne refused to entertain any reflections that might have softened or reconciled her heart. Remorse gnawed at her vitals. She woke up in the middle of the night from some disastrous dream crying out those words of her mother: "It is hard to be old and sick and poor." Over and over she told the tale of her desperate western trip. In an unpainted shanty, on a sere street, the wooden-legged old uncle and the woman of the house, cringing at first because they thought she had money, insolent and callous later on, had shown Anne the hard, dirty bed on which, near a window overlooking a neglected graveyard, her mother had died the night before. "Pneumonia? Yes." "What doctor?" "Aw, doctors ain't no good and expensive too. We give her Squibbs' Mixture." Anne would cry out "Squibbs' Mixture!" and beat against her temples with her small, dry hands. She had found what was left of her mother at a greasy, shabby undertaker's house. There were abrasions and discolorations on forehead, lips and arms. Had the old man with the wooden leg gotten drunk and beaten his sister? Anne dared not ask or think. She had waited for the money from New York, her mother's body in pawn meanwhile to the unctuous undertaker. Chicago, the crematory, the Bronsons, had seemed mild and kind and human by comparison. But she rebelled against this stroke of fate with a blind and bitter rebellion. It was the first time she had

been defeated; she would be defeated no more. "Bronson must go to college," she announced. "How?" Herbert asked. "He is going. Mamma might have been alive except for you. My only boy shall not be ruined." So Bronson sat week in and week out in the little flat upstairs preparing for college entrance examinations and Herbert was the only breadwinner in the family. It rather amazed him that, when an invitation came from his mother, Anne permitted Eileen to go to Queenshaven for a visit. But she wanted to spend more time with Luella whose health gave her cause for anxiety. These arrangements left him many free hours, for which he was grateful. Yet he produced very little. Strength and elasticity had gone out of him. He speculated vaguely about the future. He tried to talk things over with Anne. She would appear to be listening carefuly and then in answer would fill his ears with clamor about Bronson's future, Luella's health, Harry Vilas' failure to do his duty by his children.

Joffe was still his only friend and employer. Mrs. Goldstein had left New York soon after the recital to spend the winter on her estate in Alabama. She was not heard from again and Joffe did not mention her. The publisher frankly told Herbert that his affairs were not going very well. Highbrow stuff didn't sell. Other publishers had the established classics. They sat together at lunch. Herbert in an access of what his father would have called "gallows-humor" said:

"Listen, Nat, I think I could do some popular sentimental songs. We could both assume false names for the purpose. What I don't know, but what you ought to know, is how such things are introduced."

Joffe sucked at his cigar. "Humph. Oh, they're introduced from the vaudeville stage by popular song and dance people."

"Well," Herbert asked, "how about it?"

"I know where I could get in touch with two or three. But I don't believe your songs will be rotten enough."

"Oh, don't you? I know more about the popular heart than you do."

He remembered coming home one day unexpectedly. A woman

who lived on the same floor of the house had dropped in. She sat at his piano playing. Anne, Eileen and Bronson were grouped about her singing with fatuous conviction. He had stood quietly in the hall and listened. First they had sung "My Bonnie Lies Over the Ocean," then "Jingle Bells, Jingle Bells," next "Juanita" and "In Old Mobile" and this meretricious romanticism about a South of which they knew nothing had seemed to touch their shallow and facile emotions most strongly. Then the neighbor had sung a recent popular hit.

> Oh, honey just stay in your own backyard,
> Don't mind what the white folks do.

Herbert had listened to the comments. Inconceivable strangers to him—these people with whom he lived. There had been a scattering and embarrassment at his sudden entrance. But the scene had been instructive to him. As he told Joffe: he thought he knew.

The thing happened quickly now—happened over night. Herbert went to work astutely. He knew the chords that stir the Vilas heart. He knew the spurious, melodic emphasis and fluidity that were needed. He manufactured three songs—words and music. Without explaining his purpose or attitude he played them to Anne and Bronson. For the first time they were sincerely enthusiastic over anything he had written. They joined in the chorus. They applauded. They admired him. Herbert thought of his father and grandfather, but sternly he quelled the anguish that threatened to flood him. He was more or less damned anyhow. He might as well be damned thoroughly and make some money out of it besides. He took the songs down to Joffe and performed them for his friend at the old piano in the outer office. Joffe's eyes grew large and round.

"God, what garbage! Are there really people who—"

Herbert laughed. "You chamber music hound, much you know! Not only in the great open spaces but right here in New York. This is what touches the common heart. Isn't everything here—home, mother, country, Dixieland, cottonfields, the wicked city, the dear old front porch and even the little sister who went astray?"

He turned around and Joffe, hunched in his chair, suddenly looked aloof and at least a thousand years old. "God of Israel!" he muttered. Then he became his natural self.

"I can't publish the stuff, old man. I wouldn't do it with conviction, but I know someone who will. He'll drive a hard bargain though."

"Let him," Herbert said. "I only spent about five days on the things. Get me a little cash."

On the way home the false exhilaration oozed out of him. Anne was upstairs with Bronson. The flat was empty. Herbert sat down at his piano and played the blessed and immortal airs of Hugo Wolff.

> *Lass, O Welt, O lass mich sein!*
> *Locket nicht mit Liebesgaben.*
> *Lasst dies Herz alleine haben*
> *Seine Wonne, seine Pein!* . . .

Tears streamed down his face.

Less than a week later Joffe sent him a check for $750 from Abraham Stolzenberg and Sons. Across the enormous check was printed in scarlet letters: "Is the song a hit? Sure! Then it's a Stolzenberg!" Over the telephone Herbert begged Joffe to accept a commission. Joffe refused and added: "Go to see Stolzenberg. He wants more songs. If one in ten is a hit he makes big money. So he can afford to buy them outright at $250 a piece." The whole episode and what he considered the ill-gotten gains filled Herbert with an unwonted recklessness. He loaned—this was the polite term always employed—Bronson some money; he gave Anne a hundred dollars for clothes; he bought himself a much needed suit. Anne was pleased. She wanted to make a good appearance. Her cousin, Josie Bronson, was coming on a visit to New York. "It's my private opinion," she confided to Herbert, "that Josie was never married to that Fred Clarkson with whom she ran around for years. According to the papers there was a scandal in Florida some years ago. Clarkson's wife, or ex-wife, accused him of squandering all his money on jewels for Josie. I bet you dollars to doughnuts that she's got the jewels. Anyhow, she's married now to a doctor named Steven Barnes, and she signs herself Josie B. Barnes. I'd like to put her up. She can have Eileen's room." At dinner, in the kitchen, Anne told Herbert and Bronson old and new anecdotes and details of the early Chicago years, of the horrible household of the Anthony Bronsons, of the observed and suspected adventures of Josie. What she did not know was that the picture she drew stirred the imagination and touched and troubled the senses of both of the men to whom she was talking. Bronson's eyes darkened and fled from Herbert's even more furtively than usual. Herbert, struck by the strange shamefulness of the situation, tried to master his thoughts. In vain. He had to be satisfied with Anne. Anne's son with whom he was burdened was old enough to desire a more desirable woman and free—at his cost—to pursue the object of his desire. In this house for which he paid, in this house of his slavery and defeat, it was to come to pass that he, relegated as the husband of this man's mother to middle-aged quiescence, lying beside the woman of whom he was weary to death—was to watch, was to hear others— those—at the dance of youth and life denied to him. No. No. With successful hypocrisy he spoke. "All right. You can invite your cousin. We'll celebrate a bit. We've been too humdrum anyhow."

In the middle of a brilliant day Josie Barnes blew in, charmingly gowned, dripping with diamonds, empty-eyed, slim and smooth-skinned as a girl. "Oh, how lovely to see you again, Cousin Anne! Why, Bronson's a big man. Did you ever?" Then archly to Herbert: "Oh, what I know about you, Mr. Crump!" They had luncheon. "How well you're looking, Cousin Anne! Stay? Stay in little old New York. S'long as Stevie sends me the dough or I can touch some other man for it. Is Stevie jealous? That's no name for it. But listen, dearie, he's busy with his patients all day and you ought to see the burg of eight thousand that we hang out in. Well, he wanted his mother to visit him. All right, I said. Nix while I'm here. But you go ahead. And me for Chicago and points east." In the front room, after luncheon, she was left alone for a few minutes with Herbert. "Gee, it's getting warm. How about the beaches? Say I'd like to go in bathing with you." She eyed him with frank, direct approval. Herbert tingled. Anne came in and proposed that they should all take dinner out. The question arose where. "Oh, take me to Little Hungary," Josie begged. "Oh, boy, them slumber-punches!" She was delighted at her own wit, but its feebleness did not grate on Herbert. His wearied satiated nerves and senses fed on her physical presence as on a balm. . . .

The afterglow was still pink in the sky when Bronson and Josie, Anne and Herbert entered Little Hungary and took a table not far from the Gypsy orchestra. Herbert ordered cocktails. Josie and he were unaffected by them. Anne became talkative, Bronson swagger. A heady Hungarian wine came with the dinner. Rapidly the restaurant had filled up almost to suffocation. Blue smoke clouded the lights. The conversation merged into a single mass of clamor. The wine affected Herbert too, so that the lights danced and the rhythmic arm of the chief of the Hungarian fiddlers seemed strangely humorous to him in its affectation of abandon and he laughed aloud. But something at the core of him watched both himself and the others. Anne, laughing her old, most trilling laugh, was flirting with a blond, large businessman at the next table. Bronson was trying to kiss Josie behind her fan. The slumber-punches came—blue, thin, flickering flags of fire over the scarlet liquor. The women shrieked but drank. Bronson, affecting a deep and manly voice, croaked tonelessly: "Honey boy, I hate to see you leaving." Herbert ordered slivovitz all around. "They're strong," the waiter said. Herbert leaned nearer to the man. *Schadet nichts.* He himself was drunk, but he knew that he must guide events this night. If that old woman's son and that sleek cocotte under his very eyes . . . he'd cut his throat. He didn't know why. He was sure. . . . Anne no longer knew what she was doing. The blond businessman stood up. "Who th' hell go'an vote f'r me f'r pres'dent?" Anne lurched heavily to her feet. "Me." "Shake." They shook hands nearly weeping. Anne sank back into her chair with a snore. Her hat was grotesquely awry. She looked crumpled and funny. Bronson hummed tonelessly. The eyes of Herbert and Josie met in understanding. . . . Herbert paid the bill and somehow—he didn't know how—they were in the subway. "Sit with your mother, you fool," he said to Bronson. He and Josie snuggled into a seat side by side. Presently Anne leaned forward, frightfully sick. The guard came in disgusted. Herbert slipped him a dollar bill. Dawn was on the horizon's edge when they got out. Josie and Herbert drew in the air of morning. Sullenly Bronson supported Anne. On the stairs of the house Anne was overcome by the weight of her clothes. She stopped to undo her corsets. "Take that rat out," she cried. "Take that mouse out!" Bronson started to enter the flat with them. Herbert gave him a shove. "Go where you belong." By a common impulse Herbert and Josie helped Anne to undress and got her to bed. She dropped and snored. Josie slipped into Eileen's room. Herbert stood beside his piano and waited. Then he looked. The door of Eileen's room was wide open. He went in. . . .

10   LIFE ran down like a clockwork. Like a cheap clockwork in a mechanical toy. In his childhood Herbert had had such a toy. A little man of tin in a blue workingman's blouse drawing a tiny delivery wagon behind him. You wound the clockwork in the wagon and the thin, stiff, tin legs under the blue blouse would quaintly walk. But always more stiffly and slowly. And then one day something snapped and the little legs would move no more. Herbert kept thinking of the little tin man. He kept waiting for that final snap.

The morning after the party in Little Hungary he had gone downtown early. When he returned Josie was gone. Anne met him with a look of unbelievable vengefulness and rage. "You God damn son-of-a-bitch." He thrust a clenched fist close to her face. She hated him with her eyes. He went out again and came back later in the afternoon. This time she was full of fear. "Bronson's gone after that damned whore. He's in love with her." Herbert shrugged his shoulders. A fantastic week set in. Bronson found Josie at a hotel. He stayed with her night after night. What little character Bronson had deliquesced. He regaled his mother and Herbert with physical details. Anne, though hating Josie, endured this in order to let a sense of his defeat sink into Herbert. "Proud of yourself, weren't you? That free-for-all!" Then Josie disappeared and white, desperate, drunken with jealousy and frustrate passion, Bronson wandered about New York for days and nights. Anne's terror grew and grew. She telephoned police headquarters. But in a few hours Bronson came quietly in and went into the bathroom and with a Gillette razor blade sawed at one of his wrists and then got frightened and came running in splashed with blood and whimpering for help. And Herbert had to run for the doctor. There was no use, he told himself, trying to get the better of Anne. He was no match for the Vilases. They melted about one and sucked one into the putrid acid of their own corruption.

Life ran down. Long futile weeks and months. Joffe's health was poor; his ventures were not succeeding. Herbert wrote five more popular songs for Stolzenberg who said they were not as good as the first three. He took them all for seven hundred dollars flat but said he wanted no more for a year. Luckily the transaction was unknown to Anne. She was away from the flat several times a week. Something was wrong with Luella. She either did not know what or would not say. She insisted on Eileen's return from Queenshaven in order that the sisters might be together more. It was wicked, she said, for them to become estranged. Eileen would do Luella good. Eileen came, much softened by her stay in Queenshaven, less shrill and impertinent. She had tender little messages for Herbert and clung to him and was more childlike. It didn't last. Anne had long, whispered conferences with her from which the child emerged taut, hostile, insolent.

Chapters seemed to be closing during these dim months. Harrison Vilas had long suffered from intestinal ulcers. One day his condition became acute and he was hurried to a hospital for a hopeless, last-minute operation. He sent for Anne and died holding her hand. Anne came home from that death bed with triumph in her eyes. In the presence of his mother and sister Vilas had declared that he still loved her and that she had always been an excellent wife and mother. Herbert quite believed that. She had no doubt played skilfully upon the enfeebled mind and confused emotions of the dying man. As for himself, he felt a slight discomfort and dismay at the thought that Harrison Vilas was no more. Now there was no one left in the world but himself who really knew Anne; now nothing could temper or restrain her legends concerning her past, her character, concerning the undivided guilt of Vilas in the failure of her first marriage. Also there was no one left now to whom to send Bronson for help and no one who must take care of Luella. Herbert could not imagine what the future would be like. But he felt tired and dispirited at this time and years and years older than his age. At least the problem was not immediate. To Anne's voluble indignation the Duboses proposed to keep Luella. "I'd like to see them!" Anne exclaimed. "I'll start habeas corpus proceedings. She's my child, isn't she?" "You'd better be glad they're willing to take care of her," Herbert warned her. "You think so, do you? Well, of course, I did think I had a husband in you. As long as Harry Vilas was alive you valued me. Now I'm an old shoe. I suppose, however, that I can go out and earn a living for Luella." Herbert knew, of course, why Anne was so brash. Vilas had left Luella one thousand dollar's worth of life insurance. To Anne that seemed a great deal of money.

The brashness did not last long. A hunted look came into Anne's eyes—a look of unbearable strain. She moaned in her sleep. For once she was not talkative on the cause of her distress and Herbert felt sorry for her. She whispered to him. Something was wrong with Luella. What was it? What had caused it? An adolescence delayed beyond her sixteenth year? Or was it because at a crucial period her father and mother, especially her mother, had seemed—oh, only seemed, Anne cried out wildly—to have abandoned the girl? Whatever the cause, Luella's condition could be disregarded no longer. She could not sleep; she talked incessantly and lost the thread of her speech and babbled rhymes by the hour and was suspicious and had moments of violence. It could not be, could not, must not. . . . Anne's lips froze on the unspeakable word. A week later, having gone to see Luella she telephoned home that she was needed, that they must not expect her. She stayed away two days and nights. She came back haggard and worn out. She had had no sleep in all that time. It had been necessary to remove Luella to the Hospital for Nervous Diseases. What was it? The specialists hadn't decided yet. Manic-depressive insanity, or, or—dementia praecox. And that, the second, was hopeless. "Oh, God!" Anne cried. "It can't be that! It mustn't be that!" Erect she stood and seemed to challenge fate. Then she broke down. "Bertie, have a little pity. Show me a little love. Think!" He forced himself to be sympathetic, to be tender. He could not help thinking how sorely he himself needed someone to give him a little life and sympathy and free affection. These people tugged at him, rifled his soul, drained dry his heart. Yet what was he to say or what to do? At a mere look of withdrawal in his eyes Anne had stood before him, a tragic figure. "Did I ask my mother to die? Did I ask Bronson to attempt suicide? Did I even want poor Harry Vilas to die? Did I—I—" she broke into wild sobs—"did I want this thing to happen to my child? Why, what sort of a monster are you?" He lowered his eyes; his mind was confused. Was he a selfish brute to be irked? Would not, in fact, these tragic disasters wring any heart? He redoubled his self-discipline; he did his best. He even went with Anne to the Hospital for Nervous Diseases, and saw the eerie horror there.

Deep within him Herbert knew that he was almost at the end of his endurance. His world was being smashed, his soul stamped out. Anne talked of nothing but Luella. Would she get well? And how soon? And what then? She was like a monomaniac herself. It went on for hours, days, weeks. Time stood still. The mad girl sucked up the universe. Herbert fled to Joffe and confided in him. Joffe's eyes grew stern.

"Flee to Europe."

Herbert shook his head. "I can't abandon Anne in the midst of her misfortunes. It would be too cruel."

Joffe nodded. "Very honorable and thoroughly stupid. That's not my business, however. But maybe this would help you. There's a school of expression and college of music in Central City, Ohio. They want a professor of theory and composition. Two thousand a year and easy work. My brother lives in Ohio and they consulted him. They want an American and a college graduate, spotless character and, since nine-tenths of the students are young women, preferably a married man." He grinned. "You fill the bill. How about it?"

Herbert reflected. "Are houses cheap there?"

"Very."

"What do you think, Nat?"

"I'd take it. Compose all you can. Your best chance, as I see it, is to break through gradually by the sheer mass of your productive work. At present you're wasting time."

Herbert agreed. Joffe wired to Ohio. The appointment, to take effect in October, came at the end of ten days.

Anne scarcely listened to him. Luella was worse. She didn't care where she lived. Luella must get better. She didn't object when Herbert said he had not seen his parents in over three years and must visit Queenshaven before going to Central City in the fall. Of course she said, "That's right, abandon me when I need you most!" But she did not really mean it. She looked at the appointment letter of the college, took all the available money that Herbert gave her and agreed, provided Luella had recovered, to meet him in Central City ten weeks later.

Even on the train Herbert felt like a man who had been through a long and weary illness. How clean and fresh it was to be alone. How cool and pure and wonderfully peaceful. How green the trees were and how washed the sky looked. How good food tasted. How strong

177

and young his body was. Foolish to have been as hopeless as he had been. Life would relent to him. As his grandfather used to say, God is good. Soon he would press his father's hand and feel his mother's kiss and stretch himself out between the sheets of lavendered linen and hear the tide plash and gurgle among the rocks of the bay.

Book Five

CHRONICLE

1   It was early in September, 1911, when Herbert Crump set out on his journey from Queenshaven to Central City, Ohio. Many thoughts and many emotions, various and contradictory in character, were equally vivid within him. There is, he knew it well enough, no such thing as a pure stream of thought or an emotional state of complete oneness. If by a miracle one were to achieve either, the bond between the inner and the outer world would snap. For nothing could make the outer world of experience and appearances anything but madly intricate, contradictory and untamed. The artist and thinker, impelled by his nature to strive after inner harmony, was by this very fact perhaps divorced from that naïve acceptance of the chaos of things through which one can be at home and successful in the world. Reflecting thus Herbert suddenly became objective toward himself and was amused at his tendency to ally his small troubles to the eternal nature of things and to drag the universe into his tiny conflicts. Yet were not those troubles and conflicts, by the mere virtue of his being a man, in very fact symbols of all the enduring dilemmas of that ultimate consciousness at which the trend of things had labored for so many ages? True. But riding in the smoker of a Pullman car, dressed in a suit of Kuppenheimer clothes, on one's way to a job at two thousand dollars per annum, it is hard for a man of any

humor or modesty to conceive of himself as the protagonist of an action in which he is about to incur that partial and necessary guilt which turns the action into tragedy and marks him for disaster. One's tendency is to try, out of sheer lack of arrogance and solemnity about oneself, to muddle through. Yet Herbert was not without a premonition that by dutifully taking this trip and thus affirming once more, and God only knew how definitely, the lie of his life with Anne, he was shouldering his portion of guilt. What was the use of pressing his breast against the dagger of that thought? Miserable, undignified modern that he was, in breeches, leather belt and Arrow collar, he was as truly being driven by the gods, the dark uncontrollable forces, as that King Œdipus of old.

He had been away from home for three years and he had taken it for granted that these three years would touch his parents as lightly as, let us say, the previous three years had done. And on the first evening of his visit he had in fact noted no more than that his mother was a trifle grayer and his father a trifle balder. Nor could he, as the days went on, add up enough concrete things to account for the sum of his unescapable impressions. A touch of moroseness in his father, of querulousness in his mother sufficed to explain little. But he found that they hardly saw even their few old friends, that they went nowhere, that both had acquired a habit of mere empty brooding. And one day when, as he had often done in the earlier years, he teased his father about the strictness of the latter's musical ideas, his mother turned to him with a smile that seemed to him one of abstract pain: "You're the same dear boy as ever. But—" here she drooped and let her mouth go in a slack and bitter fold—"but what good does it do us? Others have you." His father frowned. "Be still, Meta." Herbert, extraordinarily shaken, protested. "Mother darling, no one 'has' me— no one. If I haven't been home in so long it's because I've been poor. The situation is much improved now. I'll come often. And not only that. You must come to Central City." His mother grew ironical, ironical out of a bitter resignation. "Yes, I'll come to Central City, just the way you and I were to go to Vienna, Bertie." And then his father nodded. It was unheard of. Silence spread through the room, silence like a thick cloud. Through the open door Herbert heard the tick of the old clock in the hall. It ticked: too late . . . too late . . . too late. They had clung to him more than they had known—his father and his mother—or than he had known; they had substituted his life, work, plans, ambitions, for their own. They had lost him. They were drained. They had given up the will to live. They had crossed a hilltop and the downward slope was swift. . . .

What was he to do? One does and must, after all, go on living. There are perceptions, sudden torches in the indistinct gloom of life, which are literally unbearable. The eye must be averted from that fatal glow. Had Herbert permitted himself to prolong in all the swiftness of its fiery terror his perception of that moment in which the old hall clock said: too late, too late, he would have gone mad. No, not as a figure of speech. His mind would have withdrawn itself from a world and a fate too overwhelming, even as the eyes close under the too intense blaze of the sun. He fled to duty, old palliative, gray, murmuring nurse who lets us see life bleed to death with a good conscience. His first inner gesture was this: his duty to himself as a man and an artist would have been of course to break the false, muddy, accidental molds of his personal life, to forfeit his position in Central City and to refuse to return to Anne. What power the habits of consent and suffering and the thousand involuntary en-chainments of life had left him of translating this decision into action —that was a problem which he chose to dismiss. What he needed, what he got, was the consolation of the notion that he must be guided as he was, in fact, being guided, not by his duty to himself but by his duty to his parents whom he honored as human beings and whom he loved with a great and now compassionate love. What was his duty to them? Not, evidently, rebellion, vagabondage and voluntary pov-erty. He had a salary of two thousand dollars now. He could increase that salary considerably by additional work. It was his business to establish a house to which his father and his mother could come, to have money with which to add to their comforts or to save against their declining years, to consolidate as rapidly as possible such a position in ordinary human society—conquests in the world of art being far and uncertain anyhow—as would mitigate their sense of loss and failure.

He was enormously consoled and cheered by his conclusion. It introduced motives of reason and goodness into his wretched life with Anne and seemed to lend that wretchedness the dignity of his resignation and his purpose. He would no longer let her irritate him so. He would take a cooler view of the whole situation. There would be a house in Central City. In that house there must be two things: a study for himself, if only an attic, and a guest room. He would live as detachedly as possible, as much absorbed in his work as possible and earn and save as much as possible. He forgot how young he still was and thought that he could definitely substitute peace and a good conscience for both ambition and happiness. Distance, time and reflection on her misfortunes, also softened his memories of Anne. She wrote rather gently and pitifully out of her great anxiety. The physicians assured her that Luella's case was one of manic-depressive insanity and therefore curable. But the cure would take many months. The charges at the Hospital for Nervous Diseases were high. Yet Luella's thousand dollars must not be quite used up. Hence, though with a heavy heart, she would take Luella to Central City and place her there as a paying patient in a proper hospital. Herbert read this letter to his mother who felt sincerely sorry for Anne and warned him as a matter of common humanity and good sense, not to judge Anne by her behavior during these rapid and unheard-of crises in the life of her family. From these quiet talks with his mother, from the mild radiance of his own plans for the future, there came a measure of contentment into Herbert's heart. At last he completed his suite "Concerning America" and wrote nearly the whole of his tone poem "The Thinker." Joffe informed him that the business had been mildly subsidized and that "Spring Presage" would be published at last and at an early date. Thus a shadowy sweetness spread over the last weeks of Herbert's stay in Queenshaven and in a mood as near happiness as he had known for years he started on his journey north.

On the train doubts began to attack and harass him. His carefully woven psychical fabric showed rents and frays. The image of Anne in her dour and indomitable mood arose before him. He thrust it from his consciousness. Nonsense, she was no more evil than other people. Because he and she were ill-suited to each other he must not let antiquated moral myths scare him. We're all miserable sinners; the moral color of the world is neither white nor black but a prevalently dirty gray. There came to him more searingly that moment in his parents' house when the old clock had said: too late. Nonsense and nerves, he told himself again. Exaggeration. Of course his parents were aging. The common human fate. And he was doing his best, unselfishly, to help, to cheer, to provide against contingencies. What more could anyone do? Let us be sensible. The notion that he was affirming and so truly incurring his share of guilt by returning to Anne, that he was thrust or seemed to be thrust into that guilt by his duty to his parents, and that therefore tragic disaster must end this story of his—good Lord, that notion was sheer literary reminiscence. Literary reminiscence and nerves. He had better use his common sense and come down to earth.

He went into the dining car and ate luncheon and felt better. In the smoking car after that a man told him that this Queen and Crescent road was one of the most beautiful in the whole world. All day tomorrow they would ride through the mountains of North Carolina and Tennessee and Kentucky. Herbert was thrilled by the thought. He had never seen mountains. And all the next day, on the platform of the observation car, he watched those eternal masses which both stand and soar, saw pine trees fronting a far sky on ultimate peaks, the orange flash of cattle on high meadows and at last the stars clustering about the heights. He repeated to himself: The hills from whence cometh my help, and heard with his inner ear the motif of what was to become the first of his later moderately well-known string quartettes (opus 15 and 16).

Central City on the forenoon of Herbert's arrival seemed to him both bright and placid. Soft coal smoke in the air tempered the sunlight. Anne met him in the Union Station. She had grown thinner and was slightly pale. She wore a neat little hat and one of her dotted veils that came to the chin. All circumstances seemed to soften her; she clung to him with a momentary drooping of her body, with tears as of old in her eyes. She wanted to know how he had left his parents and even listened to his brief account. Then she said:

"Luella is improving. I've seen her daily, of course, and she has a special nurse. In a month or six weeks she'll be out. But the strain has been almost too much for me. I feel nauseated after every meal. The doctor says I have colitis."

"What's that?" Herbert asked.

"Inflammation of the colon or big intestine."

"That's a shame," Herbert commented.

He felt his comment to be inadequate but he could do no better. Anne was always slightly afflicted in body.

"Well," he changed the subject, "you've found a house, haven't you?"

They were in the taxi now.

"You'll like it, Bertie. Nine rooms and bath and only forty dollars a month. Everything's here too and I've done my best—fixed up a study for you in the big front attic with your desk and piano where you'll be away from everyone and everything. There's even a tree against your window."

He put his hand on her arm. "That does sound delightful."

"Of course," she said, and her face tightened a little. "I couldn't have brought Luella on or attended to the house or anything else alone. I would just have broken down. Bronson has done all the real work."

"Bronson?" Herbert asked, all the old misery and shame flooding him.

"Be reasonable, Bertie." She took his hand. "Bronson is entering the state university here. He'll work hard and complete the course

184

in three years. He'll take a job in the summer and in the winter he'll run the furnace for us and help in other ways. When he has a college education he can earn a decent salary and help with Luella and even with Eileen's education. And he ought to, too. I know the burden of it all is heavy for you, Bertie. But tell me yourself, isn't this a rational plan?"

He bit his lip. Yes, the plan seemed rational enough, granting the circumstances, granting the unbelievable circumstances. How he could endure Bronson for three years was dark to him. Still, he would not be quite thirty-two even then. For the sake of his own plans, remembering his own resolutions, he must accept these years as a sort of penitential period.

They reached the house, the half of a so-called double, standing behind a tiny, very green lawn which, Anne informed Herbert, Bronson had mowed so nicely. The house was built of red brick with white woodwork and was neat, friendly, homelike. The street was quiet and full of greenery. Eileen flew toward Herbert and kissed him. Bronson came out, shook hands in a painfully humble fashion, took Herbert's bags from him and disappeared into the house. Standing on the little front porch Anne turned to Herbert.

"You do like it, don't you?"

He nodded. Perhaps in spite of the strangers in it he could make a home here and carry out his plans. They entered. There was a good Anglo-Persian rug on the floor; there were mahogany-veneered chairs and tables of Colonial design. In the back parlor were their old things, but the dining-room was new and in the front bedroom upstairs, Anne's and Herbert's, there was a gleaming new white enameled "set." He sat down on a dainty rocker and observed the neat curtains.

"But Anne, how did you manage?"

"Well, Bertie, we couldn't live in an empty house, could we?"

"Where did you get the money though?"

"I didn't get any. How could I? As it is I've had to use three hundred dollars of Luella's money just for running expenses and extras. I bought everything on open account. But don't begin worrying

185

again. I told the people we'd have to have plenty of time to make payments."

Herbert leaned forward and folded his hands between his knees.

"I thought I'd have a little peace here, Anne."

"So you will. But people can't live in an empty house."

He wanted to say contemptuously: "People!" He caught himself. He too wanted a house for reasons, so deep and burning, of his own. He followed her to the large, bright attic where were his books and his music, his old desk and piano. He sat down in his battered Morris chair.

"Now isn't it nice, Bertie?"

He nodded with conviction.

"Look at the trees, right outside your window. You always said you loved trees looking in that way."

"I do," he said, "I do. I can work here, I'm sure of that."

"Well, then!" Anne spoke as to a naughty child who had just promised to be good. "Now I'm going to run along and see about the luncheon."

"All right."

He tried to put the bills out of his mind, he tried to put Luella and Bronson out of his mind. He would work hard at his composing. He might get additional work in the city. His salary was for eight months' work. He could utilize the summer. Weren't there summer courses for music teachers? He had heard of such things. He would pull through somehow. He loved this room. Things might not work out so badly. Anne always accused him of looking initially on the dark side of things and of thus inviting trouble. He would not do so now. He would give life every chance.

The boughs of trees tapping at wall and window soothed him to sleep that night. Early in the morning, breakfast having been promptly ready, he walked down High Street to the Central City School of Music and Expression. Gold letters on black announced the housing of the school in a large, bulging, frame structure. The building must have been erected in the early nineties. Its bulk seemed somehow flabby; unmotivated little turrets projected here and there from the roof; atrociously carved balconies stuck out in front. Herbert had to pass group after group of young women who were loitering in front of the house and who stared at him with eyes bold through their very innocence. On entering he saw at once the glass door of the president's office to the right, went in, gave his name and was immediately ushered into the presence of Doctor Gauch. Large, black, sleek and obese, Doctor Sebastian Gauch pulled himself up like a mountain behind his desk and stretched out a short, thick, moist hand. He used his clear high-pitched voice with great restraint as though he were afraid of suddenly singing or shouting.

"We welcome you in our midst, Doctor Crump. We bid you welcome from the heart."

Herbert murmured something polite. He discovered later on that Gauch called all the members of his faculty doctor. It sounded well. Gauch sat down again and on the great frontal curve of him lay thick, golden insignia of the Masonic and of other orders. "I needn't ask you," he went on, "whether you're comfortably settled. Mrs. Crump dropped in the other day and told me of the comfortable house she had found and how she was preparing the home for your coming."

Herbert grew chill in the region of his bowels. So Anne had been here. And had tacitly conspired with this man in his unctuous drivel about the home.

"I was distressed on the other hand"—Gauch's voice became a confidential whisper—"to hear about the misfortune in your family."

"My family!" Herbert almost started out of his chair. "Ah, yes, yes, of course," he corrected himself.

Anne had been very careful on this occasion. She had been on the scene first. There was a family: he, she, and the—Heaven help him—the children. He felt limp. Doctor Gauch arose once more.

"I must take you to meet your colleagues and show you the scene of your future activities. I trust you will be very happy in our midst."

They left the office together. Considering his three hundred pounds

187

Gauch was light on his feet. Herbert saw classrooms, rooms with pianos, a fairly large combined chapel and concert hall with organ pipes painted in a depressing blue and lightless silver. Everywhere he and Gauch met clusters of girls in more or less filmy garments who drew aside respectfully at their approach. On the third floor they came upon the faculty—minus a few assistants—in a group.

"Here we are," said Gauch. "Ladies and gentlemen, this is Doctor Crump. I hope you will give him every assistance in your power. May I introduce: Mrs. Ingram, voice; Miss Sterling, elocution; Doctor Andrew Black, violin; Doctor Hans Breitner, piano. You will now excuse me, Doctor Crump. Other duties call."

Benevolently he waved his hand and strode down the hall. Herbert had shaken hands with a squat, dark woman, an emaciated, sparrow-like spinster with pale overeager eyes; with Black, a thick, dark, handsome, muscular young man with a pouting mouth and an extraordinarily clear, honest gaze, and with Breitner, a frail, delicately-built German of about his own age, wheat-blond, ironical, with exquisitely sensitive musician's fingers. Miss Sterling asked Herbert how he liked Central City. Mrs. Ingram said that he would like Central City because it was a city of homes. Black's clear eyes grew roguish.

"And we're here to fill the homes with melody, eh?"

"*Mister* Black," Mrs. Ingram said rebukingly.

Then the two ladies disappeared in different directions. Breitner turned to Herbert.

"You don't speak German, do you?"

"Oh, yes," Herbert said. "My parents are German."

"Beautiful. Andy Black studied in Leipzig for four years. It's our secret language."

"Secret?" Herbert asked. "How about the president?"

Breitner laughed: "*Der* Gauch!"

That pun was evidently a standing jest. Black grew serious. "Gauch started out as a Baptist minister somewhere in southeastern Ohio. He's as ignorant as the beasts that perish. He found one day that he had a throaty, sentimental tenor and became choir leader on the staff of a notorious evangelist. He saved up money and started this school. Sebastian is a thundering hypocrite. But he has his advantages. He doesn't know enough to interfere with our work and he pays salaries promptly."

Herbert felt very much at home with these two men. They were evidently his own kind. Both, moreover, had seen his songs and liked them and Breitner had used his "Études on American Themes" with pupils. Hence he seemed not quite unknown to them and a confidential, comradely relation was established at once. They initiated him in the clerical technique of his new job, got him his schedule from the secretary, found which cubbyhole of an office was to be his own and even, passing through the halls, introduced him to a few of the advanced students.

"You don't have to bother to come back to this temple of the muses till registration day, which is day after tomorrow," Black told him finally. "Don't start the grind till you bally well have to."

Alone once more in High Street there came to Herbert a definite vision of Anne's conference with the Reverend Doctor Sebastian Gauch. He could see Anne making her pathetic eyes, "enlisting" as she herself was fond of saying, the reverend gentleman's sympathy. He could hear the swollen verbiage of those two. There was an element of irony in it; there was also an element of danger. Still, he reflected, the danger was not so great, since partly by force, partly for reasons of his own, he was accepting the present situation in regard to the family. He determined not to lose his head, not to let his deep sense of being wronged rush him into headlong speech. He must counteract Anne's machinations quietly. He waited therefore not only until he was home but until luncheon was nicely over before he spoke.

"So you went to see Gauch?"

Anne, scenting the subtle implication, turned belligerent. She instinctively understood the inadequacy of defensive tactics.

"I certainly did. What else was I to do?"

189

"What do you mean by that exactly?"

"Mean? Did you think I could furnish a house on what you gave me? Well, the Buckeye Furniture Company didn't know me from Adam, but Doctor Gauch was good enough to telephone them and they gave us credit. Now do you see?"

Yes, he saw. It sounded reasonable, despite the aggressiveness of Anne's tone and manner. There was no way of accusing Anne—and how futile it would have been—of using a more or less legitimate errand to Gauch for the purpose of establishing at once the legend of his own consent to all her plans and of his voluntary responsibility for the family. He could not restrain himself, however, from a mild revenge.

"Did you, in addition to the rest, tell Sebastian your little story about running away at fifteen and having Bronson at sixteen?"

She got up. "It's none of your damned business what I told him. This is a fine how-do-ye-do. You should have married a Dutch cook!"

He fled to his calm attic room with the trees looking in—trees now with bronze and yellow leaves. There was no use bandying words with Anne. He had work to do; he had his courses to plan. He had found that he was to teach Practical Harmony and Counterpoint, Advanced Composition, the History of Musical Forms, and, worst of all, the Aims and Methods of Music Teaching in Grade and High Schools. About the last subject he knew nothing and cared less. Luckily there were plenty of books. It might be more amusing than he feared.

3 A ROUTINE of existence was established that had its superficial advantages. Bronson entered the state university, Eileen the seventh grade of a public school. Herbert found it to be a great blessing that he had a regular occupation which kept him away from home for five or six hours a day. But gradually, as the weeks passed on, there arose a new tangle of mortal difficulties which Herbert, in

his varied and profound preoccupations, had not foreseen. They were difficulties, moreover, which he hated to face. He had come here to find peace and to establish a foundation in life on which he could hope to fulfil his duty to his parents. Were these good ends, for the sake of which he endured the Vilases and was patient with Anne, to be frustrated by that ungovernable wildness at the core of life to which in hours of thought he was bound to attribute all his original misfortunes? He stood in his classrooms or sat in his office or walked through the narrow halls of the Central City College of Music and Expression. And everywhere he was surrounded, as in a cloud, by the clear eyes, smooth throats, soft arms, the rustle and the fragrance of girlhood. These middle-western girls of 1911 were, in addition, subtly and adorably different from the repressed and burning misses of his Southern boyhood. They were frank and natural. They were less afraid of themselves and therefore bolder. They seemed to like him, their young professor, even as they liked Black and Breitner. Within flexible but reasonable limits they were not afraid of showing this liking. A few came into Herbert's classroom early or lingered when the work was over and chatted with him or strolled into his little office to consult him about their work, about their future, about little musical events in which they were interested. Herbert, trying to deaden or destroy the mild state of delightful intoxication in which he walked, watched his colleagues and wondered about them. Soon he knew. Andrew Black was engaged to an American girl whom he had met when they were both studying in Leipzig. He showed her picture, a lovely, intelligent head, a very pure outline, a great mass of smooth, blonde hair. Breitner had been married less than a year. His first child was on the way. Yes, these two men both had that which protected them. Even so, Herbert observed, with the acuteness which his suffering brought him, that Black habitually played tennis until he almost dropped and on off days ran half a mile before dinner. He noticed in addition that the girls, knowing him and Breitner to be married men, were on easier and more familiar terms with them than with the unmarried Black. The situation was delicious and terrible, tempting and shameful. How much of the inwardness of his situation the instinct of the girls told them Herbert did not know, or had Anne been pointed out to them on porch or street? Or was it all his imagination that smooth hands were always brushing his own and the scent of hair was always in his nostrils and that even more heady and desperate preceptions were always being thrust upon his defenceless heart and his defenceless senses? Defenceless! For the staleness of his relation with Anne was not the ordinary staleness of an average marriage in which the rite of passion and of love turns into a more or less satisfactory habit. Anne, with Bronson beside her and Luella within reach and Vilas dead and Herbert safely locked into the social and economic order of a provincial town, Anne, quite safe in her own acute estimation at last, threw off the last rags of caution, seemliness and restraint. Not in public, to be sure. Before strangers she still appeared well made-up, well groomed, in order to sustain the legend of her elopement at fifteen and of her nine years' seniority to Herbert. At home she let herself go with an unheard of abandon. She never combed her hair until night; soiled underwear showed beneath her dingy kimono; she scratched her head and then cleaned her fingernails with a toothpick. Remonstrance, even supposing that Herbert had had the courage of such an indelicacy, would have been useless. Anne would have stigmatized him as an unfeeling brute. Her health was poor. One heard little now of the old poetic and protective heart trouble. The long months of agonized strain over Luella had really wrecked her digestive system. She suffered from hyperacidity and was annoyed by a constant slight feeling of nausea. A dozen times a day she would draw up and wrinkle her face in an expression of disgust which, in her case, had an indefinable tang of contemptuousness and say: "I feel exactly like vomiting." That was not the worst. The colitis accentuated strongly a tendency to her mother's old trouble which Anne had either inherited or acquired and when she did not announce that she felt like vomiting, she would declare with an almost proud defiance: "I've just bled like a stuck pig." The evidences of this ailment were on towels, on bedlinen, on the very floor. Anne seemed to triumph in the exhibition of her infirmities and was guilty of practices from which Herbert averted his eyes in unendurable shame. Morally she had, as always, right on her side. Who would not sympathize with a mother's health broken by the tragic illness of her child? What husband would not be most tender to his wife when, in Anne's favorite phrase, she needed him most? The test of love, she said, was solicitude. She hated fair-weather friends. No sir, give her the tried and true! In spite of her physical wretchedness she was keeping house too—an easy enough matter for so and so and so and so who had always been "horses" anyhow. But for a "delicate woman"—she always spoke these two words mincingly but with a stern eye on Herbert—for a "delicate woman" it was no light task. No, no one could blame her. If ever a woman was doing her best, she was the woman. . . .

Such was the discourse that Anne held to Andrew Black and to the Breitners when they came to call; such were the ideas which, more plaintively, she communicated over the telephone—having called him up upon a trivial pretext—to the Reverend Doctor Sebastian Gauch. And Black and the Breitners and Gauch agreed conventionally to her obvious truisms and this agreement was, Herbert knew, a moral bludgeon poised above him in case he were to criticize, to be impatient, to rebel at any point. Under the cover of her private and public rightness she became more and more slovenly and flaunted more and more sickeningly before him the evidences of her dirt and her disease. Why, Herbert asked himself, why? Did she hate him? He could not believe it. For not a week passed during which she did not return at least once to her old, clinging, pathetic, appealing mood and, with the large eyes of other years, say: "It can't be, Bertie, that you don't love me any more. I'd die if I thought that." And before strangers she hinted broadly how she and Herbert had been swept away by a great passion and had braved difficulties and dangers, horrors and heartbreak and were now at last in the secure harbor of home and love. . . . And all the while, triumphant in her moral rightness and wifely devotion she went about filthy, vomiting, bleeding and with a subterranean glee crucifying his manhood and his youth. If she had been in the wrong, in conscious need of forgiveness at any point, the situation would have been more endurable. But Anne was as always, righteous and invulnerable. She had let every one know it too. She had taken care that Herbert's position should be unmistakably defined. A man who has gone through a great and defiant romance to win his wife does not flirt about or abuse or neglect her when she is in delicate health. Not in a decent American community anyhow. The community itself, on which he was dependent for his bread, would see to that! So Herbert walked the rounds of husbandly dutifulness, often burying his nails in his palms at the college, propitiating Anne at home.

Such were the conditions of life when Luella Vilas, restored to health and reason, returned to the bosom of her family. Anne, surreptitiously getting Herbert deeper into debt, fitted up the quiet rear attic for the reception of her daughter. The physicians at the hospital had prescribed calm and care; they had prescribed above all, according to Anne, that Luella's will meet with no obstacles; her mind would be in a state of unstable equilibrium for some time; relapses were always possible in these cases. Herbert, returning from college found Luella present at the luncheon table. She had now, in her twentieth year, attained her full growth and was very tall. Her movements and gestures had their old touch of awkwardness and lack of coordination. She talked very much and very loud and laughed unmotivatedly. Herbert saw that Anne trembled inwardly, fearing at every moment a pathological increase in Luella's excitement. It seemed to him, on the contrary, that the girl was merely overeager to show at last that she was well and sane and cheerful. Thus in a kindly mood he answered her when she addressed him as, curiously enough, she did constantly. But black looks came from Anne to both him and Eileen, who were trying to treat the situation simply and naturally. They understood her looks. They must agree with Luella, laugh when she laughed, not interrupt or contradict her. They exchanged glances; Luella caught the glance and fell silent; Anne's face assumed its swollen look of rage. She came into Herbert's study an hour later.

"Do you want to drive Luella mad again?"

He explained his attitude quietly. "Isn't it better to treat her naturally than to grovel and by that very act to communicate one's fears to her?"

Anne's face swelled again. "Oh, you know all about it, do you? You and Eileen! Maybe you're in love with Eileen. You act as if you were. Well, let me tell you it's I who have gone through Luella's illness with her and have been in consultation with the doctors. Everybody in this house will do about her as I think best."

"In other words," he said, "we're all to regulate our actions according to Luella's whims."

She was beside herself. "You damned fool! If you drive Luella mad again I'll murder you. It's not enough that you killed my mother—"

He took her by the shoulders, pushed her out of his study and locked the door. He sat down with his head in his hands. His thoughts drifted to Queenshaven, to Joffe and Mrs. Goldstein, to Andrew Black and Hans Breitner. Thank God, there were sane and kind and just and charming people in the world. Perhaps he too would not be condemned forever to this. . . .

In spite of Anne's protestations he observed that she gradually shifted the care of the household more and more to Luella. The doctors had said that a little light housework would not be a bad thing for her at present; it would give the girl a normal interest in life. So Luella ordered the meat and the groceries by telephone and Luella cooked. With this result, that the hours and the quality of food became a wild gamble. Meats, potatoes, and even fish were served half raw. Anne praised everything loudly.

"Well," she said over some particularly unwholesome mess, "Luella is a born cook, isn't she?"

Disagreement she would have interpreted as "tantamount to driving Luella mad again." When Herbert protested to her in private she adopted another line of argument.

"Of course it's too much for Luella. But I notice that when your beautiful Eileen refuses to wash the dishes you have nothing to say."

He shrugged his shoulders. "Eileen is doing double work at school and good work. Why don't you help any more?"

"Because I'm a sick woman, that's why."

"Lazy, you mean," he retorted.

"There isn't a lazy bone in my body. I'm sick, I tell you, man. Why don't you hire niggers to do your dirty work?"

"Good God!" he said, "My work! Is it I who require this establishment or the Vilas family?"

"That's right," she answered with a bitter look. "Taunt me, mock me!" . . .

Dirt and disorder grew. Herbert quietly begged Eileen to dust his desk and piano occasionally. She nodded in reply. They were afraid to speak to each other. For herself and for Luella, Anne was jealous of the fact that Eileen's youth—she at least might have been his little sister—her affection for his parents, the clearness of her awakening mind, made her seem to Herbert the most natural, kindly, and human being in that house of his shame and despair. If Eileen consulted Herbert about her studies, Anne frowned. When he offered, as she had once so urged, to give the child piano lessons, she indulged in the foulest innuendo. Thus she forced Herbert and Eileen into a tacit confederacy with which she taunted them, which she took as an excuse to lavish all her attention and care on Bronson and Luella. Oh, yes, poor Bronson has to shovel coal in the furnace room and Luella was good enough to be Mr. Crump's cook. Eileen was exempt. How had she managed so to ingratiate herself? Well, Herbert needn't think that such conditions would go unnoticed. The neighbors were beginning to talk. Mrs. Henry had asked her only the other day why Luella wasn't sent to college. Was that lovely and brilliant girl to be nothing but a household drudge? Of course, Anne had tried to cover the situation. But she would not always be able to do so. To use her exact words, it stank to high heaven!

4 FROM these oblique attacks, from the disorder and uncleanliness in the house, Herbert could withdraw himself for hours and even days. He was slowly learning not to listen, not to let his emotions become engaged and thus measurably to guard the independence and continuity of his inner life. But with the coming of winter he had to sustain attacks from other quarters and to these he found it impossible to shut his mind. The Buckeye Furniture Company politely but firmly suggested that the time for the payment of at least one hundred dollars had come; the Anderson Company pointed out that their open accounts presupposed settlement in full within sixty days and that nearly four months had now elapsed; the B. and F. Levy Drygoods Company declared that they would be forced, though much to their regret, to stop extending credit to Mr. Crump and his family unless the current bills were settled immediately. Totally unaccustomed to such things Herbert studied the bills that accompanied these letters. The bills of the furniture and carpet companies were fairly brief and clear. That of the drygoods house was long and detailed and consisted of dozens of items of female wearing apparel: dresses, veiling, hose, ribbons, corsets, hose, combinations, hose. His eyes swam. He laughed bitterly. It looked as though he were supporting a harem. Hose! That meant stockings. Ah, yes. He was providing three women with stockings. Three. And he was starved for love and had no child and couldn't afford to give his mother a present. He counted just for fun; nineteen pairs of hose. They were all silk, he noticed. He, of course, wore lisle socks. A couple of pairs of black silk socks for evening usually lasted him for a year. He felt a pressure on the top of his head as though a weight of stone had been suddenly but softly slid on the top of his skull. He got up and opened his study window and drew in the icy winter air. He felt better. The thing to do was to add up the bills and see. They came in all to $1438.98 —nearly two-thirds of a year's salary. He determined to be calm. Excitement would not mend matters. He called Anne upstairs and quietly showed her the letters and the bills. She was indignant.

197

"Well, if that doesn't take the rag off the bush!" she said. "Why, all these people promised to give us plenty of time. And Mr. Johnson at Levy's promised me personally the other day that he wouldn't annoy you with bills."

Herbert walked up and down. "I don't know what I'm going to do. I get two hundred dollars ten times a year. Forty goes for rent; you get one hundred for the house. That leave a margin of six hundred dollars to provide for the two unsalaried months and for everything else. It's an impossible situation."

"But you led me to believe that you'd increase your salary by outside work."

He could not help being bitter. "Not for nineteen pairs of silk hose."

Anne took the war path. "Well, I'd like to know why not? Luella tore up all the stockings she had in her spells at the hospital. She can't go with bare legs."

"Wouldn't lisle have been good enough?" he asked.

Her face grew red and swelled. She shook with rage. "No, damn you, no! All the other girls have silk stockings."

He felt icy within. Anne seemed so grotesque and old and horrible with her red, swollen face fighting for silk stockings for Luella. She seemed no longer a woman to him at all but a weird ancestress. He noticed that she had forgotten to cut off the two hairs that grew from a mole in her chin. He walked toward the door and saw her eyes following him.

"The other girls," he said, "are probably not dependent on the charity of a stranger and a poor man. As for these bills—they were incurred by you for the benefit of the Vilas family. Do as you like about them. If these companies sue and disgrace me and I lose my job—the Vilas family will have a chance to be parasites on someone else."

He went out. He thought he heard her broken voice crying, "Bertie!" Her late appeal had lost all power to move him. In the sitting room through which he had to pass to leave the house sat Luella in

198

a neat, very short dress, thrusting forward her long, shapely legs in their glossy silk hose. . . .

A week later Herbert was summoned to the office of the Reverend Sebastian Gauch. The coarse, dark eyes regarded him with a wooden curiosity.

"Your wife was in here the other day, Professor, and she and I had a heart to heart talk."

Herbert did not answer.

"Now there is no objection," Gauch went on, "to incurring debts for proper purposes. What businessmen want is a right attitude to those debts. Why haven't you written to your various creditors courteously asking for more time and promising partial payments however small?"

"Because it would have been a useless lie. I have no margin for any payments. My wife knew that when she incurred the debts without my knowledge."

Gauch waved a fat and extremely disapproving hand. "According to the precepts of both our religion and our law man and wife are one. But I have given your case some thought. I happen to be a director on the board of the Central City Banking and Trust Company. I think it will be best for you to take up a loan large enough to cover all your liabilities. For six months you could pay only the interest which is eight per cent in this state. Thereafter small payments on the principal would be expected. Does that suit you?"

Herbert reflected. It was another trap. The Vilases were selling him to Gauch. He would have to give his note to the bank. His personal honor would then be definitely involved. Honor and Anne. Funny thought. He smiled at it. But anything for peace and a respite. Gauch answered the smile.

"I think you'll find, Professor, that this arrangement will be satisfactory to everyone. I'll get in touch with the bank and notify you promptly."

Gauch kept his word. Herbert faced a hard-eyed, florid man at a gleaming mahogany desk, signed several papers and was given a deposit slip for $1470, the bank having deducted the current quarter's interest from the fifteen hundred dollars loaned him. It happened to be likewise pay day at the college and Herbert stopped to get his salary check. At the door of the Treasurer's office stood a thick, dark man in a greasy, dirty hat with a dead cigar hanging out of the corner of his mouth. A blunt, black nail tapped Herbert's arm and he both heard and smelt a beery whisper.

"Say, I don't want to give you no trouble, Professor, but I got a bill here that's got to be paid."

Herbert moved away from that finger. "I know nothing of any bills." The man grinned the shadow of a heavily ironic grin. "Aw, I guess you do all right. I represent the Busy Bee Baking and Catering Company. I guess you used the goods we furnished and you know we ain't been paid in seven weeks."

Herbert turned and fled. He had seen Black approaching. Students might pass at any moment. He reached High Street and ran past the shop of the St. Louis Cash Grocer at his own corner, for he suddenly remembered having seen the baggy old man in serious conference with Anne on the day before. He turned the corner and saw a youth in the cap of the University Dairy Company leaving the house with a grin and a shake of the head. He waited until the man had jumped into his wagon and had clattered off. Then slowly he went up to the house and opened the door and immediately heard Anne's voice from the rear sitting room. "I've never been so insulted in my life. I'm going to dress right away and see the president of the company. If Herbert were half a man he'd—" She saw Herbert's white face and stopped.

"If you'd pay your bills instead of stealing the house money—"

She put her fingers in her ears and began to hum "After the Ball Was Over" as loudly as she could. He took up a heavy metal lamp with a large shade of green glass, lifted it high and smashed it thunderously on the floor. The house shook. Eileen, to whom Anne had been talking, cringed and wept. Down the stairs could be heard the awkward, uncoordinated clatter of Luella's heels. Anne rushed to the door and closed it. Her soiled kimono flapped behind her like the plumage of a disreputable bird. She turned and hissed.

"I'll murder you if you excite Luella!"

"You shiftless slut!" he shouted. "Show me your accounts!" He remembered the small tan notebook in which, in his mother's dainty hand, the items of expenditure had been recorded. Anne sat down pompously.

"When you address me as a lady is accustomed to being addressed by a gentleman."

"Show me your accounts!"

He raised his fist.

"Oh, please, mamma," Eileen wailed.

Anne drew herself up jauntily. "Don't worry, Eileen. I'm not afraid of the face of clay. But I'll tell you this, Mr. Crump, that I've got something better to do than to keep accounts."

"You will from now on and you'll do all the ordering yourself. I won't be dependent on the whims of that girl!"

Anne flew at him, her hands in his hair. He beat her off. He stood above her.

"What have you done with the money with which the bills should have been paid?"

"Money," she laughed hysterically. "Money is all you think about. Well, I haven't got any. There isn't enough to go around. There are a thousand expenses you never think of. Do you imagine I can let Luella do all the work for nothing? Do you think that Bronson has no extra expenses at the university?"

"I am going to leave," he said. "I'll simply disappear. You and your brats can go to hell."

He went up into his study. He laid his head on the desk before him. Fool that he was, to make a threat he could not carry out. His father had written recently that he was not at all satisfied with his mother's health, but that she had a morbid fear of seeing a physician. Herbert moaned at the miserable thoughts that thronged his aching head. Then he heard the door open and presently Anne stood beside him and her hand was on his shoulder.

"Poor Bertie," she said. "Has he got just too many troubles for words, poor boy?"

An intuition that he could have sworn to told him that Eileen has pleaded his cause. He raised himself up.

"The Busy Bee collectors pursued me to the treasurer's office," he said. "Can't you even pay the bill for bread?"

She sat down in the Morris chair and faced him.

"I wonder, Bertie, if you know how hard my situation is?"

"I'm willing to listen."

"Luella has the morbid notion that she was taken sick because I left to marry you. I dare not argue or fight with her. So she wants this and that and the other thing. See? Then Eileen sees her advantage in the situation and joins in with her. Other girls have this, other girls have that. Why can't we? They want to go to dancing school; they want a piano downstairs; they want to give parties for their girl friends. If they go to parties they have to give one occasionally. Bronson is different. He's always been accustomed to doing without things. He's got one suit of clothes and he cleans and presses it himself, but he can't go to college without all sorts of extra fees and contributions and obligations. Naturally, he comes to me. I'm between the upper and the nether millstone. I try to keep things from you, not to bother you; I want your love. But I have the children. What shall I do? What can I do?"

There was a silence broken only by a suppressed sob or two from Anne. Herbert stared at the wall in front of him.

"You've made out a good case for yourself, Anne, as usual. But that doesn't help us. You have those children. But you forget that I'm barely thirty."

"You promised to help me with them."

"Yes, in a spirit of co-operation. Bronson and Luella are adults. I'm trying to pull them through but there must be no debts; there must be the most stringent frugality. If this thing can be done only on oatmeal and dry bread—very well. Then I'll share that and have nothing better myself. But debts—that's unforgivable!"

"And what am I to tell Luella?"

"Just what I have said."

"And if she goes mad?"

He got up. "That's monstrous, trying to enslave me to that consideration. Luella is completely accidental in my life. She was born when I was ten years old. If I am forced—forced, mind you—to extend an unwilling charity to her it must be on terms that stop short of ruining me."

"Charity," Anne wailed. "Oh, God, charity, he says."

"Yes, and unwilling charity. And that applies to Bronson too, of course."

She stood up too. Her eyes were the large, helpless, pathetic eyes of other days.

"Bertie," she cried, "for God's sake! Don't you love me any longer?"

"No," he said coldly. "And I never did."

She threw herself on the floor and sobbed and writhed and beat the boards with her small, dry, shrivelled hands. Herbert watched her detachedly. She had neglected to apply henna to her hair and it looked dead and the color of decaying straw and there were flecks of dirt and blood on her kimono.

5   THEY both grew calm and patched up the economic situation. By not paying their big bills quite in full they saved out enough money from the bank's loan to start even once more with the butcher, baker, grocer and dairyman. Anne promised to have a serious talk with the children and to keep an account book. She actually bought a small notebook and Bronson, an adept at all small, trivial tasks, spent an afternoon at sharpening pencils beautifully. Anne reported to Herbert that the children were fully aware of their obligation to him, at which he winced; that they would do their best to co-

operate, but that there was one difficulty left. No one could manage without any expenditures at all. If they came running to her again for the change for unavoidable trifles, the house money would be broken into and nibbled away. There must be allowances for the children, however exceedingly modest. There was no gainsaying the justness of this argument. It was agreed that the children were to have a dollar a week apiece. Herbert thought of his debts—they seemed like a mountain the shadow of which chilled him—and of the fact that his precious margin, precious and absurd at once, of sixty dollars a month would now be reduced to thirty-seven dollars. But there was no way out. And so—why Anne insisted on this was a mystery to him—on every Friday afternoon from then on, the three Vilases appeared in Herbert's study for their dollar apiece. Whom did Anne wish to humiliate? Or was the humiliation of these others only a fact of his wounded consciousness? Surely not. Bronson would try to be offhand and mannish and Luella, reasonably restored now and a handsome enough young woman, would first laugh flirtatiously and then toss her head in imitation of her mother and Eileen, on more natural terms with Herbert, would slightly overemphasize this naturalness at the expense of the others and thus render the scene a trifle more grotesque and painful still. The profound impression made on Herbert by this weekly scene, the insight that it gave him into the dark, uncharted mysteries of the acts of giving and taking appears in his afterwards famous musical grotesque "The Mendicants." The extraordinary vividness of the three brief movements to be played as one will be present to many minds: the shuffling and moaning and trepidation and the snatches of wild, forlorn singing of the first movement called "Without the Door"; the false strutting of those inimitable march measures, the affectedly careless warbling which breaks suddenly into a cringing moan (the moment of the gift), the resumption of the march pattern as the mendicants troop out, of the second movement called "Within"; the cries, the imprecations, the bitter rattle of flung coins, the moral chaos of the brief third movement called "Without Once More." . . . Herbert wrote the

204

entire composition over a single week end of this period and sent it to Joffe, who was stirred and impressed by the concreteness, the metaphysical implications, the tonal beauty of this new idiom and promised early publication.

They patched up the economic situation with a lie. They patched up the emotional situation with a lie of darker cast. Anne came to Herbert in her most tragic mood.

"You didn't mean what you said about not loving me, did you, Bertie?"

He sat like a stone. No words would come to him. Yet he saw, clear-minded here too, that this conversation could have but one result. For if he stuck to the cold truth that he did not love Anne and had, in fact, never loved her, the grotesqueness and unnaturalness of their present situation, from which neither could escape, would assume ghastly shapes, shapes unbelievable and unendurable—shapes that meant madness or crime. The fiction that he loved her had become necessary—more necessary than ever through her infirmities, the burden of the family, the wretched tangle of debts, of social contacts, of all their relations to the world. Before Black, before the Breitners, before anyone they might know, before any chance visitor of this strange household, the implication of love between him and Anne was necessary in exact proportion to the unnaturalness of the situation. It was shield, defence, explanation, shameful in itself and yet a substitute for a still deeper and wilder shame. If he had not at least once loved Anne, what sort of a feeble imbecile must he seem? And he could not go about the world telling his story. It was a difficult enough story to make clear to himself; it had to be thought out and thought through again and again in quiet hours. From his own grasp the truth glided at moments—the incredible truth that at the core of him and from the beginning he had never done other than dislike Anne. Not only had she never had any magic for him or inspired in him an exclusive passion. Definite physical and moral characteristics in her had irritated and disgusted him always. Today? He hoped he didn't hate her. Who would believe this inner truth? No one. Not his own father and mother. Hence on this day and on other days, in order to have peace in the house, in order to rationalize his position before the minds of friends and associates and neighbors, he yielded to Anne's soft, persistent emotional pounding and agreed with her that his great love of her was not dead but numbed— numbed for a brief, sad, clouded space of time—by the cruel friction and pressure of untoward circumstance. The lie troubled his conscience. It troubled him on account of the other lies of speech and action to which it committed him. She besought him for a sign; on her knees, with uplifted tearstained face she begged him for the sake of her soul's peace, to give her an outward and visible sign. Worn out by her importunities he consented to dedicate to her the immediately forthcoming edition of his suite "Concerning America." He added the dedication in proof. It happened that this was the first of his works to have at once a small but definite public success. Anne glowed. She emphasized the dedication in and out of season. When the first copies came she handed one triumphantly to Breitner who had dropped in. Breitner treated her with an ironic sweetness which she liked because she did not quite understand it. She pointed out the dedication to him too. He gave Herbert a quiet look.

"Delightful," he said. "Charming. I wish I could do something like that for Ellen. She's been in a naggy mood lately."

Anne wasn't sure of her ground. She said rather blankly: "Well, if that's the only reason. I've a good mind to tell her what you said."

Breitner and Herbert left the house together. Breitner nudged him: "*Ach, die Weiber, die Weiber!*—women, women," he said with a sad gaiety. Ellen Breitner made no particular appeal to Herbert. But she was of one age with her husband; she was the mother of his little son. Herbert was grateful to his friend's gesture of including him in the freemasonry of the normal fate of men.

The unveracities of action and speech with which they patched up their affairs produced, of course, only very imperfect results. The big shops soon began demanding payments on their balances; the quarterly interest had to be paid at the bank; the little account book that Anne had bought dangled soiled and empty after the first three pages from its nail in the kitchen. Luella continued to order the supplies for the house by telephone. "She becomes disturbed when I interfere," Anne plead with Herbert in a tone of wild anxiety. "The ability to run the house has become to her the symbol of her sanity." He did not answer. It was futile. There were worse things. Bronson bought thirty dollars worth of books at the college book store in Herbert's name. Before even a part of the debt could be paid Bronson resold the books to the second hand department of the store and lost the money betting on a football game. Anne admitted that this was very, very wrong. Yes, she would give Bronson a good talking to. Oh, yes! Then, with an elderly confidentialness which, from her to him, seemed to Herbert a last indignity, she said: "I can't be too hard on Bronson, though. After all, he is his father's son, isn't he?" Only the modest sums of royalty or advance royalty that came from Joffe saved the situation from open disaster. But it was a weary task: month in and month out to stop one hole of debt here only to have another instantly gaping yonder. When Saturday noon came Herbert drifted into a delicious melancholy sense of ease. Till Monday morning at least he could not be called to the telephone and hear some hard, polite, vulgar voice: "We've got a little account against you here, Professor Crump. Now you promised to make a payment this week and naturally we took your word. We don't want to make any trouble for you, but we've got to meet our obligations and we expect our customers to meet theirs. Get me?"

On Monday morning he consciously shouldered the burden—the whole burden of this life. Resistance was not only useless. It involved him in the griminess of sordid details and still more sordid squabbles. Once when he had again to pay an accumulated balance at the grocer he had asked to see the month's bills. He was no judge of what it took to feed five people. But his attention was caught by the constant recurrence of three items: salad dressing, marshmallow cream and cocoa. Eighteen large bottles of salad dressing, ten cans of marshmallow cream and seven large cans of cocoa had been consumed in the course of the month. Mildly enough he asked Anne whether that wasn't excessive. Judiciously she put her head on one side. No, she said, she didn't think you could call it so. Luella liked spreading salad dressing on bread and butter. The dear girl ran the house; she was getting no educational advantages. She had few friends. How could one deny her a simple pleasure like that? Herbert might have the face to do so; she, for her part, simply hadn't. She couldn't be as small as that if she tried. In her childhood in Kentucky there had always been all that anyone wanted to eat without question; as her dear mother used to say: Don't give me any pie at all, unless you give me—pie! The marshmallow cream, Anne explained, was used on cocoa and to make candy, the cocoa itself was largely consumed in the form of fudge. If the two girls, who never had clothes enough or anything else enough and could hardly afford the movies, were to have any sort of bearable life, were to have any friends at all, these things were indispensable. Herbert didn't answer. He was routed as usual. Anne was right, also as usual. He begged Joffe for editorial work again; he gave some private lessons in Central City; he applied for a chance to teach in the summer school of the college; he limited his time for creative and hence financially speculative work to Saturday afternoon and Sunday. He took it for granted that he would constantly have to pay additional bills. For many weeks sometimes, he had to abandon his art entirely in order to provide, among other things, silk hose which were never mended, salad dressing and fudge. He did not permit himself to get angry very often nowadays. That would have added an unnecessary "expense of spirit in a waste of shame." (He was rereading Shakespeare's sonnets a good deal at this period, studying the old airs of Campion and Dowland against the sketching of his "Five Romances on Shakespearean Themes," opus 19). No, he carried himself calmly enough, and Anne had no conception that an indignation beyond speech or strife, a sense of justice so wounded that the stars would fall and the earth shrivel like a cinder if this wrong were not some day to be righted, was irresistibly stealing into Herbert's breast. This emotion and the conviction based

208

upon it became so fundamental and sacred to Herbert that he could afford to joke about it. He and Breitner would meet just before bedtime to drink a glass of beer in a neighboring barroom. Breitner complained gently that his wife was pregnant again.

"Salaries don't increase, Crump, and Ellen says that she's going to take all the babies that God sends her."

"I'd like to swap with you," Herbert answered. "You at least know what you're working for. I abandon fugues for fudge. And for silk hose—elegant and expensive—glossy hose on the legs of virgins. They don't mind showing me their legs either—hosed or unhosed—for do I not stand *in loco parentis* to them? I also pay for silk combinations and I am permitted to see them too. Luella especially who is twenty-one now and has a beautiful young body, I assure you, doesn't mind me a bit. Am I a man? I am the spouse of the ancestress. Why should anyone mind me?"

"For God's sake, Crump, why don't you get a divorce then?"

Herbert drank another glass of beer.

"On what grounds? Anne is in frail health and the most devoted wife in sight. She's told Gauch how she adores me and I her. Luella cooks; Bronson tends furnace. Can anything be more sweet and touching? But if I could scare up some trumpery grounds in this state, do you see the Reverend Sebastian not firing me instantly? Hell!" He paid for his beer. "Give my love to Ellen and the boy and thank God for them and for the child that's coming."

They met thus almost every night. Herbert had found that a few glasses of beer just before bedtime eased his tormenting insomnia a little. He used to order a case of beer and drink a bottle at home before going to bed. But he had found that too expensive. Bronson had drunk up the beer on the sly. Then he had denied doing so. Anne's comment had been: "Whatever else my son is, he's not a liar!" So Herbert Crump and Hans Breitner foregathered nightly in a barroom to their great physical comfort and spiritual refreshment, but hardly to the advantage of their reputations as gentlemen and artists in Central City. When the world war came it was pointed out and remembered against them that they had always had the disgusting proclivities of the Boche.

6   THERE was a late, harsh winter that year and then a spring so sudden that it was like a miracle. In the two last weeks of April the world turned warm and blue and golden. Central City was full of trees and vines and shrubbery and the trembling of all the young leaves in the mild breezes made Herbert's heart tremble too and made him feel, as he had felt it long ago, the very flowing of his blood. He had a touch of gray at the temples now but he was not yet thirty-one and, standing by the open window of his study, looking into the sunny greenery of the trees, he felt the warmth of youth and life, the call to adventure on open seas or in distant cities and imagined himself far away, and walking in the streets or in the woodlands of which he had read and dreamed. And beside him, in these visions, walked a girl with deep blue, slumberous eyes and a high, firm bosom and heavy, dark blonde hair and kind, competent hands. She had on high boots and walked with an ease and vigor equal to his own. Ah, the health and sweetness of her. When Anne took a walk she dragged and dawdled and crept and yet tried to be jaunty and laugh off or brazen out her age and stiffness and declared that she had never been fond of racing and had not come out to run and that a gentleman—if Herbert by any chance knew what that was —didn't quarrel or strain forward but adjusted himself to the pace of the lady with whom he was taking a walk. But Herbert at his window was not thinking of Anne at all, though, questioned or self-questioned, he would have known at once by virtue of what contrast he delighted to see the girl of his vision stride forward with so much elasticity and vigor. And he could have told too who she was. No wraith nor vision merely, but a very tangible young woman who, as his class records told him, was twenty-two and came from Cleveland

where she had completed the Junior year of an arts college before coming to Central City to specialize in music. In class he called her "Miss Blair" and acted as pedagogically detached as is conceivable, too much so in fact. But there at his window or even in bed, kept sleepless by Anne's snoring, he called her Frances. Anne's presence didn't in the least deter him from his fancies or from calling the girl Frances in his mind. He could do this because his experience had not made him cynical at heart, whatever, in intimate and desperate moments, he might say. Deep within him he believed in love and even in marriage with an almost adolescent faith. He himself, he reasoned, had never been married. He had been trapped and ruined and was being tortured in this cage in which the stupidity of social custom permitted Anne to keep him. But of that mutual magic of flesh and spirit, that inner grace which makes marriage and of which laws and ceremonies can be but an external confirmation—of that experience he knew nothing. And so great were his longing and his faith that if, by some miracle, he could have exchanged his cruel bondage for marriage to a healthy, intelligent woman, he would have done so without the slightest hesitation. Much more so, naturally, if the young woman could have been Frances Blair. In theoretical discussions on sex, which Anne loved, she had accused him of championing the polygamous instincts of the barbarous male. But on self-examination he could find no such instincts in himself. Anne, suspecting him of vague longings and outgoings and disquietudes of blood, fancied that he wanted another woman in addition to herself. She either could not imagine anyone not wanting her or else she astutely worked with this assumption in order to stamp as polygamous lechery or, another of her favorite expressions, mere promiscuity, any dream or longing that Herbert might entertain. He, in fact, wished her a thousand miles away or, in his brutally frank moments, dead. She was always sickly, always running up bills with one homeopathic quack after another, yet never sick enough not to rant, interfere, mismanage, strut or whine. He bore her as one bears a disease. In his dreams of love and healing she had no part.

He didn't know how long ago it was when first those slumberous and yet clear blue eyes and that heavy mass of hair and that cuplike chin and that air of deep, beautiful, inner quietude had definitely detached themselves to his vision from the other dark and bright heads, from the other girlish forms in his classes. How soon had he, though actually seeming to avoid looking at Frances, spoken only for and to her? How long ago was it that he felt the strangely sweet, the stinging and secure conviction that what was going on in him was not without echo or answer in that high, lovely bosom? He did not know. It was certainly weeks; perhaps it was months. He only knew that as long ago as Christmas she had, before going home to Cleveland for her vacation, slipped into his little office to say goodbye to him. She had spoken only the most conventional words. But they had both repeated these rather foolishly in order to linger yet a moment and then she had put her smooth strong hand into his and in that tiny cubbyhole of an office had come so close to him that the faint fragrance of her had made his head swim. Then she had gone. But this moment and the ever-present memory of it had sustained him through the dreadful farce of Christmas in this house that he called his own. Anne insisted on a tree which Bronson trimmed and on a homey, old-fashioned, Tiny Tim Christmas atmosphere, and on taking comfort and giving extravagant gifts, especially to Luella. The gifts were bought on credit or by using up the month's house money and paying no bills. So near the tree with its candles lit, in the bosom of the Vilas family which burst with Christmas spirit and feeble witticism and discordant song and rancid sentimentality, sat Herbert Crump, wrenching his face into a smile, forcing himself to speak and answer, aching at the core of his heart amid these strangers for his father and mother alone and far away. And then the repulsive moment of the unwrapping of the presents came and Luella yelled or Bronson, assuming a voice deeper than he had, growled the never varying formula: "Oh, thank you. That's just what I wanted!" And Anne, fatuously ancestral, beamed on her family and Herbert considered within him what he would have to pay in weary and unproductive work and humiliation for the trash which these people had always wanted. At that most ghastly moment of the year the scene with Frances Blair in his office stole like a beam of healing into his heart. Let the Vilases howl. He was not utterly abandoned by God and man. At last he had something that neither they nor Anne could soil or take away.

And since? Since then there had been many, very many incidents between Frances Blair and himself—incidents delicate and evanescent and no more gross or palpable than the swaying of a flower on its stalk: sudden belated meetings in the halls of the college or at its gate in the early dusk of winter and the exchange of casual words. But speech could not, in the nature of the case, be their method of communication. A married professor and a student, a young girl, in a mid-western American city! One unconventional word might, like the word of an evil and powerful sorcerer, have opened abysses at their feet. Their eyes spoke for them; fleeting gestures spoke; a greeting unseen by others, a feathery contact of hand and hand. Once at dusk they had walked along High Street together for a few blocks. They had walked as close together as they dared and their arms had touched. Then she had taken a streetcar and Herbert had helped her on and felt her round, firm arm for one enchanting moment in his light grasp. Out of such moments and contacts he built a world of dreams into which he escaped and it was during these months that he wrote the lovely and romantic but later too hackneyed "A Melody of Spring in Winter" for violin and piano. When Andrew Black came to the Crump house with his fiddle to try it over, even Anne looked up and for a moment was conquered by the piercing quality —Schubertian yet with a modern tang—of its melody. Then her face became dour and red and swollen and when Andrew left she said with a contemptuous sniff: "Sounds positively lovesick." Herbert had laughed harshly, "You're no admirer of my work, I know; and I know why, too. It is funny." A furious quarrel had recently arisen because Herbert had refused to become enthusiastic over some painfully conventional verses, the verbiage of a hundred poetasters, which

Bronson had written and which a decrepit dunderhead on the university faculty had praised. Now Anne was bitter and disdainful about her husband's work.

All this had happened in the winter and now seemed very long ago. Spring brought its immemorial urgency. After classes one day, Herbert had gone into the chapel and climbed up into the little organ loft and played his "Melody of Spring in Winter" and had poured all of himself into the playing. He had finished and sat for a moment amid the tall shadows bent over the manuals. Desolate and for some reason unknown to himself suddenly disappointed to the edge of bleakness, he had climbed down and walked the length of the chapel with bowed head and had then at an unforgettable moment seen Frances. She was leaning against the wall beside the closed door of the chapel. Her head with that great mass of soft hair was lifted up and thrown back a little. Her eyes, dark in this light, her half-opened lips, her lovely chin and throat, all seemed to aspire, to yearn forward. Herbert stopped. He lifted his hand to touch her and dared not. He moistened his lips. "I wrote that piece," he said, "thinking of you." He saw her flush and her hands hide her face. Then he fled.

Now he tormented himself day and night and told himself he was a fool to add this torment to his others and yet hugged it to him and gloried in it. Frances had stayed away from his class on the day following their meeting in the chapel and he had found it difficult to speak at all out of his profound discouragement. The next day she had returned and at the end of the period of instruction had loitered with several other girls around Herbert's desk and had then left at the same time with a little wistful lowering of her head. He remembered that gesture and others like it and treasured them up within and had marvelous hours alone in his study when he tasted all the glow and triumph of his sureness of Frances' feeling. Beautiful hours and yet sad. There was nothing to hope for, nothing at all. The slightest indiscretion would precipitate an ugly scandal. If it broke loose, Frances and he would be smothered in the slime spawned by the envy of suppression, satiety, impotence. If, as he strongly suspected in moments of calm calculation, Anne and Gauch would in such a case hush up the scandal for her sake and the sake of her innocent children —yes, they would say: innocent children—why then Frances would be sent home with a stain on her character and he would be more abominably and loathsomely enslaved than ever. The best that he could hope for was what he had—the moral support of the girl's feelings toward him, the assurance through them that he was not, in some strange dim way, a freak, a *lusus naturae,* an outcast, a repulsive ape. He needed that assurance. Far were the days of his youth, far as a legend lost in time, the white and golden days of Gerda. And, as the proverbial drop of water does, in sober fact, produce a hollow in the hardest stone, so had the thousand sly and poisonous suggestions of Anne worked upon a nature not hard nor given to pride or vanity, too stripped perhaps of the forces that arise from a just self-esteem. For weeks Herbert had often dwelt in a state of self-abasement that had made his fate seem in harmony with his qualities and his deserts. Anne's silent or insidiously suggested or even outspoken point was that she loved Herbert so because she had the wisdom and experience to look below the surface and beyond what meets the eye. Harry Vilas had been attractive, almost as attractive at one period as Bronson. Bronson was an exception, of course. By and large she was through with handsome men. Give her the qualities of mind and heart! In this respect she was, of course, very exceptional. Most women of any age and all young women—not that she was so old herself—wanted a good-looking man, one of whom they could be proud. She supposed it was natural, after all. She just happened to be different. Josie, she intimately informed Herbert on Bronson's authority, had never been interested in him. That had been an accident of drunken stupor. She had been after Bronson naturally all the time. More than one friend and finally the other day Luella herself had wondered how a nice-looking woman like herself—pretty she didn't pretend to be—could have married Herbert. She had answered, of course, that she knew her business best and that all is not gold that glitters.

To such discourse on the part of Anne there was no possible reply. Agreement was out of the question; disagreement would have meant a kind of self-assertion of which Herbert was wholly incapable. He received these speeches in silence. In the course of the years their substance soaked into his consciousness. Subtler than Anne's speech were certain actions of hers. If she and Herbert were in a streetcar and other passengers, above all young girls, laughed or giggled without apparent motive, Anne would toss her head and look disdainful and her gestures and her looks said as plainly as words: Laugh if you like, I know my business best. And very strangely it did not occur to Herbert until years later, that what people may in fact occasionally have laughed at were her airs and graces, her obvious age under her veil and rouge, coupled with the superannuated kittenishness of her public demeanor toward himself. Later too he knew her retorts concerning Josie and Bronson and the friends and Luella to have been downright lies. In the early years in Central City he still held Anne to be, whatever her other vices, reasonably truthful. Ah, yes, it helped him to live to believe in the soft glances and the wistfulness of Frances Blair. It helped him to work. And when Anne let herself go and was particularly slovenly and repulsive and then called him to come and see how fresh and charming Luella and Eileen looked in new frocks earned by his sweat and never dreamed—or did she?—that she was stamping his manhood into the very dust, he closed his eyes and thought of Frances Blair's uplifted face on that winter afternoon. Did she know or didn't she? That was one of the mysteries about Anne that was never solved. Was she coarsely stupid or poisonously malevolent? Later, much later, Herbert reflected on this point again. In the May of this year all thought was driven out of his mind by a crash that shook the foundations.

He was summoned home by a letter from his father. His mother's health was worse than he had been permitted to know. An operation was imperative. He had better come as soon as he could. When he had opened and read the letter Anne had said: "Don't tremble so, Bertie." He controlled himself and withdrew into himself. There was no one in this house with whom he wanted to share his desperate grief. In his hollow skull boomed a brazen bell: too late . . . too late . . . He went to the college and in a dry, hard voice told Gauch who was all oily, external sympathy and assured Herbert that he could absent himself quite as long as he thought fit under the circumstances. He went unseeing through the halls of the building to his tiny office and sat down at the battered old brown desk. He leaned his head on his hands, resting for a moment. The door opened and shut again and Frances Blair stood beside him. He looked up at her and pointed to his father's short, grave letter which lay on the desk beside him. Leaning over his shoulder she read it and bending lower slipped an arm about Herbert's neck. He turned to her and their eyes met and then for one fleeting moment their lips: "You must hope for the best—you must." He nodded and got up. He could not trust himself to speak. They shook hands hastily, her left hand already apologetically on the doorknob. Then she was gone.

7   It is said that grief and the accidents of mortality soften the heart. They may also harden the mind by liberating it from hope and illusion. When Herbert came from his mother's grave and from the house of his father who, though lonely and bowed, was self-sustaining, he found himself stronger because he had nothing more to fear in the world or in the universe. His mother was safe from pain, hope, disappointment, with the innumerable generations of the dead. Therein, Herbert perceived, in that immortal freedom from all mortal fever, resides the majesty and the fulfilment of death. He to whom this perception has once come can never again wholly lose the power of detaching himself from the too fervid flux of things. . . . Already in his father's house during the ten days following the laying to rest of his mother there had arisen in Herbert from these emotions and reflections the thematic material and the crucial moments, such as the famous, austere massing of the brasses while the

sensuous, mortal strings die away in the distance—of his first symphony which was, immediately upon production, acknowledged to be the finest orchestral work yet produced by an American.

These inner experiences created by his mother's death were not wholly unperceived by Anne. She declared repeatedly in the course of the years that she profoundly regretted the untimely passing of her mother-in-law, not only for the dear woman's own sake, but because that loss often seemed to her to have robbed Herbert of the last vestige of both human feeling and of common decency. At the time, to be sure, she behaved characteristically enough. Up to the moment of the funeral she wrote Herbert affectionate and consoling letters. On the day following he received a telegram saying that she was very ill. Since he did not answer that message another came, ironically worded: "Very ill. But just stay with others." To this also Herbert paid no attention. When, at the end of ten days, he felt assured that his father could spare him, he wired to Central City the hour of his arrival, grimly aware that an appropriate scene would be staged for the minute of his return. The scene turned out very much as expected —a little uglier and coarser perhaps, but that effect may have been due to the purging of his eyes by absence. The lower rooms of the house were empty. Herbert set down his valise in the hall and went upstairs. He heard confused noises from the front bedroom. He entered. Propped up in bed sat Anne, struggling for breath. Her hair was tightly rolled up in curlers made of toilet paper; her soiled nightgown was half torn off; Bronson was anxiously rubbing an ointment into her flaccid bosom. Herbert sat down.

"Don't exert yourselves any more," he said. "I see."

Bronson stopped and looked scared and sheepish. Anne bounded up with a cry of rage and horror.

"I've nearly smothered to death, I'd have you know! I've had a hemorrhage from the rectum and that affected my heart."

Herbert got up.

"You know I have a hemorrhagic diathesis, Bertie!"

He went up to his study. Later he was called to dinner. Anne ate

218

a magnificent meal. Bronson, Luella and Eileen dined hurriedly and then rushed upstairs. Presently they reappeared in their Sunday clothes. Anne turned to Herbert with a deliberate, challenging impudence.

"The children are going to dancing school. They're young, you know."

He shrugged his shoulders. He went out into the soft night of early summer. He barely heard Anne's: "Bertie, you know I'm scared in the house all by myself."

He tried to hear her as little and as superficially as possible thereafter. He worked on his symphony. He completed his year's teaching. Frances Blair was gone. A conventional little note of thanks for his interest in her and of sympathy for his loss awaited him. But across the bottom of the page she had scrawled: "Goodbye, my dear, goodbye." He kept the note in his pocketbook. Those scrawled lines were a lasting source of comfort to him. He did not reply. No use involving the girl in the bitter confusions of his present life. Let her forget him. But as his mother's death had freed him from fear and allied him consciously to the larger life of his kind, so this woman's written words allied him to that life and its recurrent hopes in still another fashion. However slowly, however painfully, he would fight his way to freedom. On some far day—blessed rather than happy—he would, like other men, like the meanest and lowliest among them, marry a woman and beget a child. And when this child called him father, then—and not until then—would the sacred frustrate shade of his mother be appeased. Whence or how this conviction came to him, he did not know. But he dwelt in it securely to the end. We should go mad at our mortality without the constant miracle of renewed life, of life, beautiful in the sunshine but doomed to the same issue as our own so that our parents, our children and ourselves, ageless and of one age, commingled dust or spirit, may dwell together in an eternal world. . . .

Herbert knew, of course, that it would be futile, now or later, to plead with Anne the fact of his tragic disinheritance through her. She had become befuddled, like so many loose and inferior minds, by a romantic pseudo-liberalism devoid of reason and out of contact with the nature of things. Housework she considered degrading. Oh, that she had been brought up to some recognized profession and were not so very delicate! She would then scorn to be dependent on any man. Herbert, to see how she would take it, declared that a woman who ran her house wisely and bore healthy children was the least dependent of human beings, since her services were literally of unique and inestimable worth. To which Anne replied jauntily that any peasant wench could do as much, that in her experience children came between a man and a woman more often than they served to unite them and that, as she had often said, Herbert ought to have married a Dutch cook, not an American lady. Anyhow, and here her jauntiness gave way to a reproachful pathos, anyhow, she had been "like with child" for Herbert several times in past years and he had never shown any particular eagerness to have the children born. This point Herbert had to grant. He was worsted in the argument. Anne was in her early fifties now and had passed her climacteric several years before. The danger of his having a child with the Bronson-Farrel blood in its veins, allied forever by that blood and by early associations with the Vilas family—that danger, thank God, lay in the distant past. He was silent on this point thereafter. Sometimes he would steal away early in the evening to the little house of his friend Breitner on Indianola Avenue—a poor, bare, little house, for Hans and Ellen saved what they could and incurred no debts—and watch the little boy being put to bed. Witnessing this scene kept his purpose true and strengthened his resolve.

He completed his symphony, received an unexpected check for two hundred dollars from Joffe who was issuing his earlier works in rapid succession now, found that there were still two weeks till the summer session and determined to take a trip to New York. Anne raised a strident clamor. Had she no right to a change? Did anyone ever see such selfishness? Did he leave her behind because he wanted to find a woman to sleep with in New York? A man was usually supposed to take his wife with him. Moreover she wanted and had long wanted to consult a New York specialist about her troubles. What, she wanted to know, did she get out of life? The house, Herbert answered, and the support of her children. In brief, she got what she wanted most. It was he who, rightly looked upon, got nothing that he wanted, nothing that he needed. The quarrel went on and on, downstairs and upstairs. Herbert fled to his study, but she followed him. She alternated reproaches and appeals. She promised not to bother him in New York nor to interfere with his engagements. She plead once more that life was terribly difficult for her too. She was, so to speak, between the devil and the deep blue sea. The children pulled at her. If she refused Luella anything the girl asked why she had left her father and abandoned her. And there was no reply, since Luella would not tolerate any reflections on her father's character. But if she acceded to Luella's demands, there were more debts, there was more trouble, and she was in danger of losing the one thing that mattered to her in all the world—her husband's love. No wonder that, ground between these forces, she seemed stale and worn to Herbert. Would he not then have pity on her and grant her this chance of being alone with him once more and of readjustment and refreshment for both their sakes? Didn't he remember the dear old days in New York and their long walks and talks and plans and the deep spiritual community that had seemed, oh seemed, at least, to exist between them? It was two o'clock in the morning when she made this final appeal and into Herbert's mind stole the past with its accustomed pathos. It seemed to him, indeed, as though those now distant days could not have been so evil. Hope was still measureless. Nothing had yet been lost. His mother was still alive. "Then,"—the verse ran through his head—"then, in the deathless days, before she died." God, how weary he was and how stricken now compared to then. Tears came into his eyes. Anne who was crouching before him drew his head upon her shoulder. She had won her game. . . .

On the journey she was blithe and companionable. In New York she had a heart attack. Since Herbert took this lightly, she subsided into a pathological melancholy and could not rise from her bed. But however ill she was, she always revived in time for dinner and for the theater or a concert. She consulted a physician who, according to her, said that what she really needed was a major operation on the rectum and that since her heart could stand neither the anaesthetic nor the surgical shock, her condition was very precarious indeed. She managed, in brief, to suck the hours and days into herself, her needs and ailments and wrongs. All that Herbert succeeded in getting for himself were a few long luncheons and conferences with Joffe. The result of these he kept strictly to himself. It was quite evident that slowly but steadily he was building up a reputation. There were, after all, not so many composers of even his aims or the quality of his ambitions in America. There was, too, an increasing sentiment that the works of native artists had been neglected. Several of the great orchestral organizations had Herbert's works under consideration. Joffe thought that he could promise Herbert one or even two productions during the coming winter. Over the symphony he grew grave with enthusiasm. He undertook to publish it and assured Herbert that, sooner or later, he would have a chance at conducting it himself. In all this there was unluckily not much immediate money and for some time to come Herbert had better hang on to his job. Herbert on his way back to the hotel calculated out of his uplifted but patient heart that Bronson would graduate from the university in 1914. The fellow must then go to work and support his sister Luella. By that time—he himself would still be a very young man— all things would ripen, ripen perhaps to the ultimate goal of freedom —freedom from Anne. And that thought and hope filled him at the same time with an inexpressible sweetness and with a detached, grave pity for Anne. His imagination saw her defeated, her long stranglehold broken at last. Poor Anne! She was doomed after all to a sorry fate. He must be a little kind to her. . . .

8 AFTER this trip to New York life seemed to have fewer varia-
tions and hence the days melted into each other and the weeks
and months flew by. The annoyance and embarrassment of
debts continued. But Herbert, though he never became hardened to
this torment, yet became accustomed to it. He was in addition better
able to fulfill his promises to tradesmen, since checks from Joffe came
a little oftener and were a little larger. His pleasures were few. Walks
and talks with Andrew Black or Hans Breitner who had both become his steady friends and understood much without speech; small
escapes and easements to which he learned to look forward in the
routine of daily living. After the last meal, for instance, winter or
summer, he would take half an hour's walk before going to his study
for the evening. At that hour the neighborhood was very quiet and
peaceful. No vehicles disturbed the streets; the occasional distant tap
of the heels of some late homecomer only accentuated the quietude.
Herbert usually walked to a group of very old and beautiful trees
that had been left standing in the middle of Indianola Avenue. He
would lean against one of the great trunks and if the sky was clear
look up at the stars and think of his mother who was part now of that
world in which there is neither variableness nor shadow of turning
and thus he would purge his eyes and cleanse his soul from the glare
and heat of those raging egotisms with which it was his fate to dwell.

By watching the Vilases he conceived a lower opinion of human
nature than he had entertained before and began to understand quite
well the moral symbolism of the doctrine of original sin. That sin
was evidently the primordial failure to make any selection among
one's desires, the failure to face the consequences of one's actions, the
quite unreflective exertion of the unleashed will. Luella, the early fear
of a relapse gone, boomed and buzzed about the house like a great
handsome insect with a broken wing. She laughed loudly and talked
much and offered her opinion on every subject and since Anne
listened to everything that Luella sputtered with a quiet fatuous and
besotted respect, rational conversation was impossible in the house.
Two favorite sayings of Anne were repeated by her children and

223

became both motto and guide of conduct. One was: "Well, I guess I've got as good a right to my opinion as anybody else has to theirs!" The other was: "I want what I want when I want it!" From these two sayings on the lips of the Vilases, Herbert often thought, one could deduce, however fallaciously, the Catholic doctrines of the denial of the right of private judgment and of the saving power of poverty and obedience. Luckily the world was not peopled by Vilases. Everyone else he knew or had ever known had a conscience that was reasonably enlightened and sensitive. Sometimes this conscience, as in Gerda's case, had highly original and personal reactions. That did not matter. It served to shape life; it gave life form. Anne and her two older children had no shaping force within. Their moral world was a moral chaos. Luella, to be sure, was often restrained by a facile good nature and Bronson by a deep-seated cowardice. But these restraints were, from their very character, fluctuating and accidental. Periods set in during which no restraints functioned. Luella would boom and buzz quite wildly. She wanted to travel; she wanted clothes and more clothes; she wanted the house different; she wanted to invite "fellows." The conception of a relation between worth and fulfillment, between desert and reward, had been omitted from the Vilas temperament. That temperament was a maw. Bronson would become unbridled under the pressure of the urge of sex. Whenever he was chasing a girl he would exchange his slinking and cringing for a barnyard strut. He would try to act the man of the world, deepen his voice, drink whisky, smoke cigars and read innumerable newspapers which he would drop, hit or miss, all over the house. Anne admired her son inordinately at such times. If some adventure of his came to a successful issue, she wanted to know the exact details and smiled at Herbert in knowing lecherous and vicarious triumph. Ordinarily Bronson compensated for the feebleness of his will by harboring a sense of being wronged. Intrigue had kept him from making a fraternity, the enmity of a professor from being elected to the editorial board of a college paper; he had been excluded from Phi Beta Kappa by a stupid and unjust technicality. These tales of his wrongs were, in some strange way, delicious to Anne's ears. They proved to her the excellence of herself and of her offspring and the vileness of a stupid and unappreciative world. Thus, in one manner or another, the house resounded with the crying and striving of these untempered wills and appetites. Except Eileen's. Though of the same blood and origin as the others, she represented that saving factor in the biological process known as a spontaneous variation. Rendered hysterical and morose in turn by the pangs of a long and difficult adolescence, she yet displayed more and more unmistakably a mind that could think clearly and justly, a heart accessible to the appeals of goodness and the needs of human co-operation. In Anne, of course, the primordial will to her desires gathered power from success and harshness from the lengthening years. She thought that both Bronson and Luella had too many hesitations and made too many concessions. It took her, by God, to stand up for their rights as well as her own. It made her sick to see how, at times, they would "positively truckle" to Herbert. Upon her word! She had actually come in one day and found Luella sewing on a button for Herbert. You could have knocked her down with a feather! There were no servants in this house, so far as she knew. . . .

How well Herbert got to understand them all. He could, if that had been in his line, have written a treatise on the development of ethical perceptions. Instead he wrote, in such hours of detachment as he could conquer for himself in the course of many months, his second symphony, the most purely beautiful, the most concentratedly musical, of his later works. But those hours were few after all. Twice a day he sat at table with the Vilases. In addition Anne talked. Then there were the recurrent holiday seasons during which both custom and the closing of the college building kept him more at home. How could he not have learned to understand these people? He understood their cohesion. He also understood their internal wars. He always remembered one great quarrel and rebellion that took place late in the winter of 1913. In spite of sickening and desperate bills at several drygoods shops the girls found themselves with little or nothing to wear. They had a few dresses. They had no underwear, no night-gowns, no stockings. They had gone to Anne who had declared that she could get no more credit till the present bills were paid and that she herself had only two torn nightgowns and as many combinations in the world. Then Luella, inspired but not egged on by Eileen, had spoken out. Her eyes snapped as always when she was eager or excited. She knew very well, she said, why Eileen and she never had anything. Oh, no, it wasn't poverty. Some of the girls they knew were much poorer and had never in all their lives had a ready made frock from B. F. Levy's or the Fashion Company. No, but they had mothers, those other girls, mothers who took care of them, who ran a sewing machine and got in a seamstress by the day to help. And that didn't cost so much. Yet those other girls always had everything they wanted and were never, like Eileen and herself, in rags. Yes, in rags! She gave Anne a wildly bitter look out of her handsome, unnaturally distended eyes. Oh and that wasn't all. Oh, no. She and Eileen watched other girls and their mothers in many ways. And that made them feel that they had no mother at all. They didn't feel free, for instance, ever to bring young men to the house. Other mothers prepared refreshments and withdrew. What happened in their case? They had to rush around and do everything themselves and wear themselves out. Then their mother would come in and start a highbrow conversation about herself and of course no boy ever came back a second time. She broke down and wept and Eileen looked curiously and fatalistically at Anne, knowing perfectly well that, however in the right she or her sister might be, they were no match for their mother. Anne, in fact, had long drawn herself up for battle. She had tried once or twice—this scene took place in the dining room—to exchange tauntingly ironic glances with Herbert. But he eluded her eyes. Now she looked dour and swollen. This, she declared, was the worst she had ever heard. Of all the rank ingratitude this certainly did take the cake. Other mothers, forsooth! What other mother, she would like to know, had fought for her children as she had or—significantly she glanced at Luella—gone through unheard of crises with them and battled, almost to their own undoing, for their very lives? And now they wanted her to wait on them, to be their servant! How dared they compare her to ignorant illiterate women like Mrs. Holt and Mrs. O'Brien and Mrs. Derflinger—good, honest creatures enough, but with nothing else to do except sew and wash and cook? Ha! Who had put them up to this anyhow? Who? She turned upon Eileen: Who? Eileen spoke in a small discouraged voice.

"If you mean me, mamma, no; I told Luella it would be no use. I told her you'd talk about big things like visiting her every day in the hospital and wouldn't admit that the little things count too."

"Well, upon my word!" Anne started.

Eileen got up. Her little figure was tense. "You're all right in crises, mamma, as a heroic mother when you can impress teachers or doctors with your culture and your cleverness and we can't argue with you. But we know what we mean just the same."

She walked out, straight, prim, quaintly grave as a marionette. Luella followed her stumblingly.

"I haven't heard such a thing since the day I was born," Anne exclaimed. She swung around to Herbert who was standing by the window. "Bertie, do you understand?"

The girls had touched him so, poor things, but he could not help grinning at Anne. "Yes, I understand. The girls feel lonely for a real motherly mother—a sweet, gentle homebody about fifty-three, not pretending to be less either, neat gray hair parted in the middle. No make-up. The sweet motherly mother sits by the window or by a lamp sewing for her pretty daughters. Plain things will do for her. She——"

Anne jumped up. "I think you're the most cruel beast in the whole world! You ought to be beaten, as my mother used to say, with many stripes!"

Herbert laughed. "I am," he said. "Don't worry, I am. But just now I was simply delineating for you the girls' ideal."

Anne regarded him with concentrated viciousness. "You go to hell!" she said.

9 IN JUNE 1914 Bronson graduated from the state university; in July Luella entered its summer school as a special student; in August the great war broke out. Anne passionately embraced the cause of the allies; so did Bronson. Herbert entertained a natural though moderate sympathy for the land of his fathers and of his art. He was not displeased at this cleavage in his household. If Anne seemed to lean toward any view that was dear to him he at once began to distrust the reasonableness of that view; it at once became smudged in his consciousness. He had the comfort, moreover, of finding not only Breitner—that was a foregone conclusion—but Andrew Black, a Scotch-American of long native descent, a man of the most just and generous mind, in substantial agreement with him on the universal guilt of the nations and of the undiminished value of the German contribution to the lasting goods of mankind. Thus the war became, in a strange way, a sort of benefit to him. The mighty and epic preoccupation with its implications involving all the issues of life and thought, helped his mind to withdraw itself from the grotesque and sordid miseries amid which he lived. Annoying things happened, to be sure. It was Luella, of all people, who, feebly violent, attacked him at his own table with the rancid commonplaces of the daily press. Herbert forbade the discussion. Anne asked him whether he thought he was the Kaiser and reiterated the family maxim that Luella had as good a right to her opinion as anybody else had to theirs. Herbert contented himself with the obvious remark that Luella had, in fact, no opinion at all, but was merely making an imitative noise. Then he left the table. He had to leave several times—once or twice in the middle of a meal—before the stubborn babble died down.

That fall Bronson obtained a position as assistant in English in a college in northern Ohio. The salary was very small. He could be expected to do no more than support himself. Unluckily he didn't even do that. On a dozen occasions Anne found it necessary mysteriously to remind Herbert that Bronson was, after all, his father's son. Bronson didn't gamble or bet on the ponies; Bronson was above that.

He drank. He didn't drink a great deal—less, in fact, than his friends and colleagues. He was unfortunate in the inimitable Vilas fashion. After four glasses of beer or two drinks of whiskey he grew very pale and his handsome eyes began to roll—one actually turned in and gave him a cross-eyed appearance—and he grew amorous and made a noise which long expertness could recognize as the tune of "Juanita." If he reached this point he was lost. He no longer knew what happened to him. The consequence was that he wired from Cleveland, utterly ignorant of how he had gotten there, for the railroad fare to return to his position in time for his Monday morning classes. Or he would suddenly appear in Central City because he just had to have an alibi. Or Anne would rush wildly to him in order to persuade his landlady not to report the poor boy's behavior after an evening of harder drinking than usual to the college authorities. Yet all these annoyances and expenses had to be borne not only during this year but during several successive ones because the alternative was Bronson's losing his job and being helpless on one's hands again. One couldn't blame him either, as Anne said; it wasn't as if the poor boy were well. His eyes always ached. His digestive system gave him such misery that he was forced constantly to dope himself with paregoric. He had never, from the beginning, had a fair chance or a square deal. How true all that was, Herbert reflected. How the Vilases always trapped one hopelessly and defenselessly with their misfortunes and their innocence! Superficially he agreed with Anne's commonplaces. Privately he came to the conclusion that, under given conditions, guilt and misfortune are strictly inseparable and that the most dangerous criminals are not those whose overt acts and lack of alibis, moral and physical, give society the chance to exert its restraining force.

Christmas came and Herbert hoped that it would be mitigated by a visit which his father had long promised and had long delayed. For a few days, too, there was a certain blessedness in having his father in that house in Central City. The brawling caravanserai almost became a home. Both Bronson, back for the holidays, and Luella behaved very circumspectly and agreeably; Eileen, now in her eighteenth year, a brilliant student at the university, full of her own thoughts concerning the entire situation, treated the elder Crump with a sincere and tender affection. Anne professed a great pleasure at welcoming her father-in-law. But on one pretext or another she prevented the two men from being alone together, discouraged Herbert from pressing the point by private threats of an open and vulgar quarrel, resented the attachment between Eileen and Mr. Crump and insisted on regaling the latter with endless discourses concerning the perfections of poor Bronson, a man of nearly twenty-nine now, and of dear, sweet Luella. She wanted her father-in-law to take off the little skull cap of black silk which he wore to protect his head from draughts; when Breitner called, she harshly and insultingly resented the use of German in her house; knowing that Herbert would do anything and bear anything to spare his father the sight and hurt of loud, coarse dissension, she tortured him through the power this knowledge gave her in every subtle and treacherous way. She reached the climax of her performances when she quietly informed Herbert that an extra mouth to feed would make no small difference in the month's budget and, while Luella was industriously spreading salad dressing on bread, deliberately drew a dish of marmalade beyond Mr. Crump's reach. Eileen gave a little cry of horror and got an evil look. Next Anne announced that they were too poor to serve both fruit and oatmeal for breakfast and asked her father-in-law which he would take hereafter. Herbert ceased urging his father to stay. With an unbearable feeling of grief, shame and defeat he drove him to the station and said a quiet farewell. Back in the house he watched Anne rouging and powdering herself for an evening party. Calmly, dispassionately, as he was putting his studs in his dress shirt, he said: "Anne, I honestly believe you're the most black-hearted bitch in the whole world." She didn't want to have a scene or to disturb her make-up. So she tossed her head and dilated her nostrils as at an evil odor, smiled ironically and said: "Thank you for the compliment, Mr. Crump. Be sure I'll remember it."

The war seemed to hurl time down the torrent of its years. One got up in the morning and read the papers: one waited a few flying hours for the afternoon extras; then suddenly it was morning again. Overshadowing and disastrous things blotted out the neutral hours. Days, weeks, months, were telescoped. Especially in retrospect his last two years in Central City seemed to Herbert to have passed like a vision, like a dream. Yet he had solid results to show for them. He wrote his third symphony (opus 23) and, on Joffe's advice, set to music a number of lyrics by the new American poets who had come up since 1912. This volume, "Ten American Songs," (opus 24) was extremely well received. Especially one of them, the setting of Ridgely Torrence's "The Son," became almost unpleasantly popular and was soon heard from every concert platform in the land. It was an ironical circumstance too that, as the wave of anti-German feeling rose and any German music later than Beethoven was felt to be charged with militarism and disloyalty, the distracted conductors of orchestras turned more and more to Herbert's works, as to those of a simon-pure native-born American whose descent they didn't, after all, have to advertise. Joffe, a confirmed pacifist and philosophical radical, played up Herbert's Americanism with his tongue in his cheek. In addition Herbert won a prize offered by the National Federation of Women's Music Clubs. All these circumstances eased his financial situation. Not that he could ever hold or save a penny. The earnings of his mild successes went into lost years, went toward paying the debt at the bank which, in spite of many payments had, through enforced new borrowings, risen to over two thousand dollars, went, in other words, to pay for the education and past and present necessities of the Vilas family. Due to the hopeless disorganization of the household and to the gradual rise in prices and to both Luella's and Eileen's attending the state university, these expenses had reached such proportions that, though Herbert trebled the amount of his salary, a year's end found him with just deficit enough to rob him of all peace and satisfaction. . . .

The disorganization of the household was an unbelievable thing.

Before rushing off to classes Luella telephoned for what she thought she might like. At noon something was hastily scrambled into shape. Very commonly Luella forgot what she had ordered. Someone—who had it been—had taken the things from the grocer or butcher and stuck them away. What was uppermost was prepared. Then horrible stenches arose from obscure places and were tracked down and the decayed or mildewed food was discovered and thrown away with many exclamations of surprise and disgust. Anne could be counted upon for very little. Both her heart and her colon required the minimum of confinement to the house, required the systematic cultivation of her higher interests. So she too attended lectures and classes at the university and soon discovered that at least one professor was, she could not help believing, "more than half in love with her." For the cleaning of the house there was no systematic provision. Although Anne's housekeeping allowance had been raised again and again and was now large out of all proportion to Herbert's fixed and certain income, she never had a penny. A colored student from the university would come in to wash the dishes for his board. Dust and dirt prevailed. Once in many weeks Anne would put on an old kimono, tie a towel about her head, take broom, dustpan and scrubbing brush and in her unvarying description of these rare occasions "go through the house like a dose of salts." After such unwonted activity she would more than ever "bleed like a stuck pig" and thus for many weeks enjoy the double pleasure of martyrdom and of a justified liberation from "dirty work." Laundering was also a mighty gamble. Since there was no fixed place for soiled linen of any kind and it was therefore stuck away in drawers and receptacles from attic to basement, loud and quarrelsome hunting parties for it were undertaken when at the end of a month or six weeks, a family washing became hopelessly imperative. Not all of it was ever found at one time so that the stock of table and bed linen and towels had constantly to be replenished. Anne, loudly declaring that, as everyone knew, she was the soul of order and neatness, wondered eloquently at these mysterious losses and speculated as to the honesty of the colored student whom, at the same time, to show how liberal she was, she treated with an insultingly condescending familiarity. A good deal of soiled linen was also, from time to time, tracked down by its smell. Considerable quantities were not recovered till the household was broken up. In order not to become submerged in the surrounding dirt, Herbert carefully took charge of his personal linen and of six bath towels. Every week he carried these things to the laundry and called for them himself. No mending or darning for himself or others was ever dreamed of. He lived the life of a bachelor in an unclean and distracted boarding and lodging house and for this privilege he had to support the entire establishment.

A trivial incident, amusing in spite of the desperate annoyance it caused him, became to Herbert Crump later on the symbol of that house during these confused and hastening years. It assumed in his imagination the character and the concreteness of a myth. He knew from it how myths arise and how, their human origin and background obliterated by time, they may come to seem the mere weavings of a wayward fancy. For who, without an intimate knowledge of Anne Crump and of the Vilases, could have interpreted the story of Tiddles and her progeny? Tiddles was a white kitten which Eileen brought into the house. In a few months Tiddles had become a full grown cat, long and lean but of an engaging individuality. There was something preoccupied and careworn, something at once virginal and maternal about the animal. Of her leaning toward maternity there was soon proof enough. But though Anne and her daughters almost smothered Tiddles with their affection, no basket or warm corner was prepared and the cat had her kittens on the hearthrug in the dining room. Eileen named the black and white kittens Pretty-Face, Funny-Face and the Count. Herbert mildly suggested drowning the little creatures at once. There was a loud chorus of protest. Kill those cunning darlings. Why they were too cute for anything! Anyone would be glad to have them in just a few weeks. Faintly but definitely the house began to smell of cat. The little animals scampered upstairs and down, excreted in every corner, were found daintily curled up on tables, in drawers, in beds. They were too many to be housebroken; no one had the time anyhow. When they were weaned they mewed with hunger. One day they were gorged, three days they were forgotten. Luella fed them occasionally and even cleaned up after them when the faint odor became a massive stench. Then she stopped and declared loudly that the cats were Eileen's cats anyhow. Yet Herbert protested in vain. The cats were darlings. Everybody in the neighborhood wanted one, only it was so hard to part with them. The weeks drifted by; the weeks became months. Herbert had to lock his study to keep it free of cats. Since winter no one had gone into the basement. Now no one dared to go. And now Pretty-Face who seemed hardly to have attained her full growth and whom Anne described as the most virginal cat she had ever seen, presented the world with Fuzzy and Wuzzy and Tom. Oh, how cunning the new kittens were and how touching it had been, Herbert was told, to watch Tiddles as, earnest and careworn as ever, she was trying to assist Pretty-Face in her first accouchement. He was begged to wait. All the cats would be given away together quite soon now, all except Tiddles and maybe Pretty-Face and well—Bronson, home for the holidays, had taken such a shine to Tom. The feline generations flourished; the house stank; a pest of flies rose from the basement. The cats were all intelligent and clinging cats. Whenever Herbert went out he had to turn back at the corner to drive homeward a procession of cats and kittens who, bright of eye and erect of tail, were bent on following him. Such was the situation when, in an unobtrusive manner, Tiddles gave birth to two more kittens. These were almost unnoticed by the family. Interest in kittens had waned. The drove of cats remained unfed, untended but protected by sporadic outbursts of violent affection and of ecstasy over their cunningness. Herbert tore himself away from an absorbing piece of work. There was a huge new wash boiler in the house. It had been bought in a fit of theoretical economising and never used. He stuffed his nostrils with cotton dipped in perfume and quietly corralled the cats in the basement. Then he hung wads of cotton soaked in chloroform

234

into the wash boiler, added Tiddles, Pretty-Face, Funny-Face, the Count, Fuzzy, Wuzzy, Tom and the two nameless latest born of Tiddles and clapped on the heavy lid. He went upstairs and telephoned the city department of public health to call for nine dead cats. Luella avoided him for days; even Eileen looked hurt and disappointed; Anne wept. Her looks and gestures declared more loudly than words that he had again betrayed that streak of native brutality—probably Prussian in its origin—under which she and her children had suffered more than she cared to say. . . .

10 By the late spring of 1916 it was apparent to Herbert Crump that his position in Central City would soon become untenable. The fashionables of the city murmured against the College of Music and Expression. It was quite too obviously a hotbed of Prussianism. Professors Breitner and Crump had publicly assisted at the German-American charity bazaars and had actually signed an appeal for East Prussian relief. Even Professor Black was definitely under suspicion. Gauch was known to have characterized the Germans as the enemies not only of mankind but of the religion of Christ in his own chapel. Still his name too was—Gauch. As for the curriculum of the college, that seemed to be Hunnish to the core. On this point Gauch sounded out his faculty. Herbert, speaking for Black, Breitner and himself, regretted that they could not retroactively change the history of music in this year of grace. Gauch waved his fat hand. "Then, gentlemen, if the registration collapses and a reorganization of the faculty becomes necessary, I trust you will not lay the blame at my door." They said they would not and knew they were fired. They soon heard that three gentlemen named Gozzi, Monteverde and Petrosini had been engaged to take their places in the fall. Andrew Black laughingly but definitely pretended to know that, until a year ago, Gozzi had been named Goetz and Monteverde Greenberg. But he could never quite establish his point. Herbert,

235

with an unaccountable lifting of the heart, wrote to Joffe who replied at once. He was not to worry; his works and his name were quietly making their way. There was a vacant associate conductorship on the staff of the Manhattan Musical Society. The trustees were at their wits' end as to whom to appoint, since very eminent German conductors had been driven out on trumped-up charges from both Boston and Cincinnati. Herbert would probably be their man. Moderate salary but enormous prestige. In addition a committee headed by Mrs. Goldstein planned for next Christmas a great performance in Carnegie Hall of a requiem for all the soldiers who had fallen on all sides. Herbert might very well keep that in mind.

Anne informed of the situation said: "I'd love to go back to New York. I never really liked this place."

"How about the girls?" Herbert asked.

"They'll stay," she replied. "And of course we'll have to send them enough money to live on. Eileen will graduate next year; Luella has found out that if she makes sixty points of college credit beyond what is required for graduation they'll accept that in place of entrance requirements and let her take a degree."

Herbert consented. This abominable household would be a thing of the past. Anne came close to him.

"We'll take a little apartment, Bertie, and be alone together and have a real honeymoon. We never had one, you know."

He looked at her. She had aged markedly in the last few years. Deep crowsfeet grooved the corners of her eyes. Her skin sagged; her neck was frankly that of an old woman. Great pores showed on the bulbous forepart of her nose; one could see that the stubborn chin would be rough to the touch.

"Isn't it a little late for such notions?" he asked.

"Not for me, Bertie. I feel that I'm just beginning to live."

He looked away from her as he said quietly: "At fifty-three?"

She flared up. "Forty-one, you mean."

"Fifty-three," he reiterated.

"Forty-one," she screamed.

236

He bit his lip. He remembered that far day when she and Vilas had rancorously flung numbers at each other. How things had a habit of recurring where Anne was concerned. And how neither years nor sorrows nor disease robbed her or these occurrences of vigor and emphasis. She had the indomitableness of a force of nature. . . .

They did not get away from Central City easily. The summer was a lurid and protracted nightmare. Bronson, home for the holidays, collapsed with dreadful pains one afternoon. He took whiskey and paregoric. The pains grew worse. A physician who was called in pronounced Bronson's appendix to be in a very angry state. Only an immediate operation could save his life. Anne became heroic and magnificent. The operation was performed at the most expensive hospital in the city. Bronson had a private room. Anne, according to her reports, ran the hospital from the chief surgeon to the youngest nurse for the benefit of her son. Herbert paid the bills. She upbraided him for not paying a certain week's bill until the succeeding Monday.

"I didn't have that much cash," he said calmly enough. "Anyhow, since Bronson had no money of his own, wouldn't it have been more honest for him to have gone into a ward?"

She flared up. "Not while I live!"

"You mean: not while I can be robbed!"

She tossed her head. "You and your dirty money!"

He didn't reply. This was their last chance. The elephants, as he grimly called the Vilases in his mind, would not be able to trample on him quite so freely in New York. It was almost farcical that five weeks later Luella came down with appendicitis and the whole depressing and infuriating process had to be gone through again. With this difference, that whereas Anne had clamorously declared it to be mere common decency for her husband to support her with his presence during the ordeal of her son's operation, she harshly told him that he was not wanted around Luella. She did not want him to have a glimpse of youth and bodily favor even on the operating table. Sad and grotesque acknowledgment he reflected, of all she spent her life in denying. . . .

237

Two scenes from these last days in Central City stamped themselves on his mind. The house was being dismantled, the house from
which he had once hoped so much, to which he had come with honest
resignation and with firm resolves. He was glad to see that accursed
house breaking up. His mother had never seen it; his father had been
driven forth from it. He had suffered in it every pain, every humiliation, every deprivation of body and of soul. The loud confusion of
these days seemed to him a more fitting expression of the house's life
than the veiled chaos of the past. Anne's strident generalship alternated with the quarrelling of Luella and Eileen. What here belonged
to whom? That was the savage and recurring question. Anne decided, usually, in favour of Luella. One day Herbert was coming
down the upstairs hall at the end of which a bedroom was situated.
He could hear the querulous voices of Luella and Eileen from downstairs. The bedroom door was wide open. Anne, her hair done up in
curl papers, her dirty kimono open, her stockings bunched at her
ankles, was smearing rouge on her gray cheeks. Her heavy jowls
drooped forward; her harsh voice rose: "Jesus Christ! Can't I even
take time off to make myself presentable? You shut your mouth,
Eileen! Mr. Crump, I'd thank you not to stare at me!"

Herbert hurried downstairs. This creature wanted a second honeymoon.

The last day came. Creditors had been reassured; funds had been
provided for the immediate needs of Luella and Eileen; the packing
had been done. It frightened Herbert to think how little actual cash
he had for the moment, considering that, after all, he had to continue
to support all these people. But a letter had duly come from the Manhattan Musical Society giving him the appointment as associate conductor at five thousand dollars a year and speaking of his work in
ponderous but flattering terms. Anne was buoyant. They were leaving by the morning train. The day had been frightfully busy but
thanks to her skill as a packer, she said, every thing was in apple-pie
order. She was resting at the dining room table, her united family
about her, and refreshing herself with an onion sandwich and a glass

238

of beer. "Well," she said, "things are certainly looking up. Who would ever have thought it? Fancy Bertie's being a famous composer and getting a position like that. I'll say this for myself though, that I've stood by you, Bertie, through all these lean years, and never complained and you can't deny that I was always good to your poor mother and your father. Come to think of it, by the way, it was I who gave you your very first chance with the People's Chorus in New York. Well, well, well! They do say though that your own always comes to you in the end. I'll be able to take a little real comfort now as the wife of the distinguished Mr. Crump."

Book Six

CRISIS

1 NEW YORK once more in the brilliancy of its autumn. An apartment, this time on the very peak of Washington Heights with a view of turquoise river and sky and the bronze palisades from every window. Herbert found Fifth Avenue especially thrilling. The well-groomed women, the silks and antiques and glowing pictures in the shop windows, the very jewels. He didn't think he was worldly or desirous of worldly things. But the avenue at once stimulated and also soothed his starved and fevered senses. He loitered about here. His office in the rooms of the Manhattan Musical Society was quite near. Except once or twice a week he was under no present obligation to be in the office. But a marvellous thought had come to him in time. He could be vague about the extent and definiteness of his obligations. Anne need not know. His old dream of keeping the better part of life free of the stain of her consciousness of it might now come true. He could make luncheon engagements; he could make tea engagements. He could meet men and women and perhaps. . . . He didn't finish the thought. A delicious shiver went through him and the skin of his whole body tingled. The vista of life was suddenly magical and he was content to linger at the gate. . . . He loved the streets; he loved the very subway. In Central City you could almost label the passers-by according to their denominations. What varieties

240

of temperament and experience were there not in these crowds that came from the ends of the earth? O enchanted city, he thought; I have but to stay and wait. I am still young and some day that will come to me which will lift from me the burden of my ache and loneliness and disinheritance and disgust. And in this mood he wrote his "Poème Musicale," obviously charming, brilliant, accessible to every taste, on which his father, who was quietly proud of the symphonies, withheld all comment, but which was the striking success of the society's second concert that season. The directors were immensely pleased with their appointment and promised Herbert an increase of salary for the following year.

Anne did not grasp either Herbert's mood or the probable implications of the whole situation. She was too ignorant and too self-centered. Nevertheless, an instinct spoke within her and impelled her, on the one hand, to be cleaner, more presentable, more regularly attentive to the dyeing of her hair and the skill of her make-up and, on the other hand, to indulge pretty steadily in the process which she called "taking people down a peg or two." "You think you're damned grand now, don't you?" she would say. "Well, do you suppose those old hags who sent you flowers after the concert have any real appreciation of your work. You told me yourself, by the way, that you considered the "Poème Musicale" flashy. My God, what a hypocrite you are—talking all these years about the austerity of art and refusing to compromise and keeping us all poor and now trying to turn yourself into a matinee idol." She measured him with a contemptuous look and dilated her nostrils. She gazed critically at his legs which, she had always declared, were too short for the size of his trunk and so gave him an undersized look. "Well, take it from me," she said, "you're not cut out for the part."

Sometimes he didn't answer her. Sometimes he flared up and in foolish and uncertain ways strove to defend the new and yet tender confidence in himself that he was winning. Long futile quarrels arose. These quarrels had no substance but their own bitterness. Anne tried her best to undermine Herbert's belief in himself, in the sincerity of those who appeared to like or admire him, in his personal implication with his career. Herbert, stung by this on account of the insecurity and newness of his emergence from obscurity and from enslavement to the Vilases, would characterize the past, strip Anne of her pretensions, stigmatize her history, person, family. "God, you're a disgusting cad!" Anne would shriek. "You didn't talk that way I notice when you came gum-sucking around me on Sixty-first street. Harry Vilas wanted me to the day of his death. I was no discarded wife and I'll never be one, let me tell you right now. You just try your matinee idol tricks with some filthy slut who ogles you when you're conducting. I'll disgrace her and you from one end of the country to the other, if I don't fill you chuck full of lead first!"

Icy and with that old feeling as though his insides were gone, Herbert would let his words hammer down on her. "You trapped me when I was a boy. You stole my youth. You robbed my father and mother of hope and life. Then you made me the servant of that Vilas brood. I hate and despise you so that I sicken all over."

They weren't pretty things, these latest quarrels, Herbert reflected. They didn't give one a very high idea of the dignity of human nature. When Anne came to him afterward, as she regularly did, and said pleadingly: "You didn't mean everything you said, did you, Bertie?" he was able, as the result of his reflections, to reply: "We're beyond that point. You say things that no one should ever say. And then you force me to speak the unspeakable." But Anne didn't understand that. She shook her head dubiously and sorrowfully and Herbert saw that he should have remembered that she really and sincerely did not understand either the notion or the feeling called shame.

The quarrels were never quite allayed any more. Rancor hovered between Anne and Herbert like a tangible thing. The old, old resolution of quarrels between a man and a woman had long been failing them. It was years since Herbert had sought Anne spontaneously. Moral and physical inhibitions had become more and more active. If, at the end of many days, or even weeks, Anne wooed him persistently and his mere physical mechanism functioned, he was beset by bodily uneasiness and profound moral depression. In Central City, knowing Herbert to be safely imprisoned and being herself preoccupied with her family, Anne had not emphasized this fundamental circumstance. Now terror of the possibilities of New York and of Herbert's new situation slowly filtered into her mind. That terror became pivot and center of life. She was, as Herbert had often observed, a monomaniac with a shifting mania. In Central City that mania had been the glutting of her children. From now on it became the question of Herbert's fidelity to herself and of her own sex needs. He watched her with amazement, pity, utter weariness, intolerable disgust. This woman in her fifty-fourth year, gray-haired and wrinkled, mother of a man of thirty who had just taken him a wife, mother of two grown daughters—this woman began deliberately and steadily to act like a creature obsessed. When this phrase first slipped into Herbert's mind he told himself that, of course, his vision was blurred and his judgment perverted by his long years of suffering. Then at the end of an evening's work, Anne came into his study in a fresh kimono, with her hair, though well-dyed, loose in a tangled bunch on one side of her head, and spoke with eager, angry, frightened eyes.

"What's to become of me, Herbert Crump?"

He looked his counter question.

"What I mean? You haven't touched me in three weeks and a half. "I suffer! I tell you, I suffer!"

He put his hand over his eyes. "If one hasn't the impulse? Can one discuss that?"

"It all depends! Why haven't you the impulse? I'll tell you why. You've deliberately let yourself go and cultivated a feeling against me and nursed a low lust for other women. That's why. What's the matter with me? I'm a woman; my desires are as powerful as ever— and a damned sight more so. I ask you again: what's to become of me?"

He took his hand down. He now felt cold and hard. "Take a lover," he said. "That's what you used to do."

She leaped up like a creature wounded. Then suddenly a new thought petrified her. Eyes like two gray pebbles confronted him.

"Have you a mistress, Herbert?"

Something in him gave way. "I have nothing," he cried, "nothing! I have never had anything, God help me, except terror and misery and shame and dirt! All I ask you to do is to leave me alone!"

A light, now of irony, came back into her eyes. "Of course," she said, "if I am dealing with a madman, there's no use."

She began, to use a phrase of her own, to keep tab on him, to time his comings and goings and engagements.

"You left the house at a quarter to eleven this morning. You say you went to the office and then had luncheon with Doctor Markowski. But you didn't come home till six."

"I went back to the office."

"Well, you weren't there at five, I noticed, because I called up."

"I wasn't in my own office but in Markowski's."

"Oh, were you? Well, the girl at the switchboard said that she hadn't seen you since morning."

"She may not have seen me. I don't report to her, after all."

"I didn't say you did. But you can't get into your office or to Markowski's without passing through the outer office."

"Yes, there's a back way."

"So you sneak in and out by the back way? A likely story!"

"True, just the same. But it's none of your business."

"Oh, isn't it, though? Well, we'll see about that! I won't be lied to!"

"That's impossible. If there's something I don't want to tell you, that's my right and has nothing to do with lying."

"God, what rotten sophistication! So there is something?"

"In your sense there is nothing; in mine there are a thousand things. I will neither be spied on nor give an accounting of every hour. You act as though you were my mother. Well——" he had a sudden access of cruelty—"you're old enough to be."

"You God-damned cad, you!" she shrieked.

"The perfect Xanthippe," he said.

244

Concentrated fury spoke from her. "I'll show you. The man isn't born who will get the better of me!"

He sat down. His head ached. "Listen, Anne, let's reason together. What you're afraid of is my having relations with another woman, isn't it?"

"I didn't say so, but go on."

"Well, if that were true—it doesn't happen to be—but if it were true and you discovered it, would you divorce me?"

"I'd see you in hell first."

"I thought so," he said. "I'm doomed and I know it. But if that is your attitude, of what interest are my movements to you? I should think you would rather not know. You can be under no particular illusions in regard to our relations to each other. Life has somehow tied us together. Let us make the best of our wretchedness. Let us have peace."

She turned to him the head of a Medusa—cold, stony, vengeful with an undying rancor. Her voice grated like the voice of an old man. "You fool! You think I don't see through you? You want a chance to carry on with your sluts and whore-masters while I sit at home being talked about as the old wife of the brilliant young composer, being made into a laughing stock—a laughing stock! You think you're going to get away with that? Try it! Just you try it! I'll hound you till you drop!"

2   As OF old he sat, trying to unravel the tangled strands of thought and motive. Anne had been in her way quite right. Not only on the day of their last quarrel but on many days he had lied to her about his movements. He had done so both instinctively and deliberately. An outsider might have called these lies almost perverse and certainly gratuitous. For Herbert had done nothing that needed to be concealed from anybody. Occasionally, in fact, when rehearsals were not as heavy as usual, he had merely taken

long walks. But pondering in his study. Herbert shook his head. No outsider could judge. No one could understand the defensive operation of his wounded will. If Anne had ever been defeated, had ever known the grace of the vanquished, there might have been a margin for doubt and for discussion. But from that day, now ten years ago, on which she trapped him into marrying her, to this day, to this hour, Anne had prevailed. At every point her will, being without scruple, had been victorious. He had not in all these years done a single important thing that he wanted to do or left undone what he hated and loathed. And now Anne thought that through her vigilance and through her imputation of lies to him, she would continue in these new circumstances to exert her evil mastery over his life and being. Never! She was quite right. He lied to her. The extent of her rightness was the measure of her damnation. Why did he not simply answer her prying questions by saying that it was none of her business? Because then, having no other refuge, he would on many days have been able neither to rest nor to work in the place he called his home. For Anne gave no quarter; Anne never grew weary. A quarrel once started meant a hectic evening, a lurid night and therefore a broken next day. Anne had to be placated with lies and these lies of his Herbert solemnly and with profound conviction added to the burden of her guilt. . . .

Anne was right also as to the deeper issues and as to the substance of Herbert's unconquerable hope. He wanted not only a margin of freedom from her; he wanted that freedom for a definite end. He wanted a woman. He laughed grimly when he thought how the great part of his American world would look upon that frank and strong desire. For that whole world had something of Anne's private lechery and public primness and would approve even the foul and unwilling prostitution of such a marriage as his own. Once he had said to her: "Granting our biological make-up, the rightness of the act of love can be estimated only by the power and persistence of mutual impulse and delight. Where that impulse and that delight are absent, prostitution begins." Anne had astutely answered: "I dare you to proclaim that opinion openly." He was aware of the fact that, in the event of an open conflict, she would have all the active forces of society and all the machinery of the law on her side. He understood her implication thoroughly. Guile, so far as he was able to use it, was his only weapon. Absurd to tell him to resign himself. To resign oneself to such evil wholly was to become a participant of it. Morever Anne was now fifty-four, he thirty-four. She might live twenty years longer and neither age nor infirmity would change her. She would be capable at seventy of running up and down the streets of New York to guard his marital fidelity. With him it was soon or never. The shocking spectacle of Anne made him doubly sensitive to the dignity, both physical and spiritual, that should attend our later years. He must have what he so deeply sought within the next few; else, despite his music and his work, he would pass out of the sunlight into the shadows more disinherited and defeated than the meanest among men. Had he then quite given up his hope of a complete liberation from Anne? He could never give it up in his heart. There it surged up again and again and stabbed him with a strange unearthly sweetness. But for the present he was, alas, again a semi-public character. Not that the directors of the Manhattan Musical Society were very conventional people. A quiet separation, a seemly Parisian divorce, these they all considered as proper and natural things. But he knew Anne. The scandal she would create would have all her own foulness, treacherousness and ferocity. And those were boundless. What then did he hope to find? An agreeable, emancipated young woman who would accept his talent and his devotion in place of more worldly advantages and with whom he could establish a bond that would heal him in body and in mind. He needed both.

His insomnia wore on him; an acute anxiety neurosis darkened his morning hours. But that was not all. Tenaciously his mind clung to the moral issue. Anne had to be defeated. She had to be defeated at the core and center of her will. Otherwise life was not worth living and the universe a dunghill. When would she be defeated? When a young and intelligent and agreeable woman whom he desired and loved, desired and loved him in return freely and generously —chaffering neither over money nor legality but giving him, who had never been given anything, the most precious of gifts. . . .

Was it a romantic hope? It seemed at all events in no danger of being realized. The only definite thing that his lies to Anne had hitherto concealed was an occasional tea with the Stephen Halliwells. Not that these afternoons were not important to him. They came soon indeed to be of an overshadowing importance. But they had only an indirect and negative bearing upon his ultimate desires and hopes. Stephen Halliwell was the most active of the directors of the Manhattan Musical Society, a small, dark, compact handsome man in his early fifties. He was a very astute and enormously successful financier. But his heart was really in music and literature—he himself wrote very agreeable verses—and it was through him that Joffe had succeeded in getting Herbert appointed to his position. After one of Herbert's earliest rehearsals with the orchestra Halliwell, who had quietly looked in, had invited him home for a cup of tea. Thus Herbert had first entered the Haliwell house and had first seen Mrs. Halliwell. The house was a rich man's house. Italian primitives glowed golden in the otherwise somber drawing rooms. The serving of tea was an elaborate ceremonial. Yet Herbert felt as much at ease and at home as he had done in Breitner's barren little house on Indianola Avenue. He was among friends here in a world in which material inequalities were considered external and accidental. Gloria Halliwell had the reputation of being beautiful as well as wilful and imperious. She told him in the course of time how it saddened her that all but a very few women disliked her. He visualized Anne in contact with Gloria and from this extreme example understood all the rest. Gloria, a tall and rather stately dark blonde was then in her forty-fifth year. Herbert never thought her beautiful despite the blue of her eyes, the girlish freshness of her lips. Her nose was too much like an eagle's and her mouth too large. But beauty streamed from her—a beauty beyond the accidents of time or space. She could part her hair in the middle and look almost girlish. She could say: "Dear friends, I was born in 1872 and in a year or two I shall be a grand-mother. Let me do as I like." And still beauty abode where she was. She could dispense with all the trickeries and small deceits and sly concealments and vague suppressions and subtle affectations of her sex and yet her presence blotted out all but such quiet loveliness and serene grace as matched hers in another fashion. Hence the average artificial woman hated her on sight. Her secret was a boundless vital-ity, a firm and penetrating mind, an unblunt freshness of joy. A pagan joy and so, like the joy of a Roman poet, not untouched but deepened by a sense of the passing of things and of their drifting to-ward an eternal winter. She saw at a glance that Herbert was un-happy; she perceived that his bearing was out of harmony with his talents, his prospects, his personality. She poured life into him out of her own abundance. Two restrained words sufficed for her to grasp the essence of his situation. If he composed anything he played it to her and Halliwell and these friends steadied and uplifted him by their quiet assumption, which did not exclude criticism, that he counted definitely in the permanent world of art. Gloria moreover was a poet. Her verse had edge of diction and depth of music. It was far less important than her personality. But Herbert, partly in genu-ine admiration, but more out of personal devotion to his friends, set some of her lyrics to music. This required conferences and discus-sions and since there were usually other people present at teatime and Herbert dared not and could not come in the evening, Gloria and he would occasionally have luncheon together. He never forgot the first time. He had called for her at the Halliwell house and stopped for a moment to chat with Stephen. They had taken the Fifth Avenue bus and Gloria had turned to him: "Does Anne know of this adulterous expedition?" "God forbid." And he had laughed with her as full-throatedly as he had not done since his boyhood. By what she was she crushed and swept out of existence the meanness and possessiveness and ugliness and hatred of the common fictions of sex. His world, contaminated and poisoned since his earliest manhood by the stuffiest form of femaleness was clean, fresh and blossoming.

Gloria Halliwell, resented by her own sex, gave him back faith in life, hope for the future, tenderness for the race of women. . . .

Anne was the skeleton at all their innocent feasts.

"She has to be invited," Gloria declared. "I'll be supremely nice to her. But unless we have her, you can never come to dinner or in the evening."

Herbert shook his head gloomily. "Your intentions are as adorable as you are. But I'm scared."

Stephen looked solemn. "She can't be so dreadful."

Gloria's expression had a noble wistfulness. "Women can be very dreadful, Stephen darling, when they let their instincts grow rotten and won't use their minds. Poor things, poor things!"

She turned to Herbert. "Let's try a tea to start with. Thursday. I'll write her the sweetest kind of a note. Stephen, you be nice to her and Herbert, you act distant toward me."

Herbert, when he left that day, kissed Gloria's hand. He had a premonition. . . . He knew Anne. . . . When, on the following day, Gloria Halliwell's note came Anne said: "Well, they've certainly taken their time about inviting me. Did you ever see her? Oh, you have, have you? This is the first you've told me about it. Damned funny, I call it. You say you think I'll like her. Well, I don't know about that. Did you ever see such an unformed hand as she writes? Pretty illiterate, I guess. You say she writes poetry? You seem to know a hell of a lot about her. What am I to wear anyhow? I won't have these rich women lording it over me. I remember that Goldstein woman. God, she was vulgar! From all I can tell, this one isn't much better. I'll go though just to see what they're like!"

3   THE tea at the Halliwell's was not gay. Herbert, coming from a rehearsal, had preceded Anne. He was standing beside the fireplace talking to Madame de Kraye, a thin vivacious woman of fifty, stylized to look like a Greuze portrait, when Anne was ushered

in. He saw at once from the way she held her head in a tossed position and pushed her trunk forward that her mood was one of determined hostility. Her face was set and had its slightly swollen air. Gloria melted into her most winning ways. They might, Herbert thought, have temporarily placated a Moloch. Anne seemed in fact to soften. From the sofa where she sat beside Gloria he heard her voice. He had acquired in the course of the years the strange faculty of always hearing her voice despite the voices of others. What he heard was not encouraging. "What would you do, Mrs. Halliwell, if you were a very passionate woman and your husband neglected you?" Anne was now half elegiac but belligerency smoldered about the edge of her sadness. Herbert knew that was giving Mrs. Halliwell a chance to become her confederate. He also knew that Gloria was stiffening inwardly, saw her evade an answer with a gracious jest, saw her arise quite soon and send her husband to take her place beside Anne. Stephen, a man of singularly unspoiled nature, despite his experience and his knowledge of affairs, showed by an expression in his dark limpid eyes that he did not relish the situation. He was gravely polite but almost silent. Anne's eyes sucked in the room. Madame de Kraye was teasing Herbert about the extreme severity of some of his interpretations; Blei, the round little concert master of a rival organization, began to grow technically argumentative. Gloria, having come up to them, impulsively put her arm through Herbert's and squeezed his hand. "Stop abusing Herbert. Of course he holds himself in. But you feel the glow under the stringency." Abruptly she dropped his arm and whispered: "Dear, I'm afraid I've done it now." She had. Over her shoulder Herbert caught sight of a pair of eyes like agate and of the tightening of an increasingly swollen jaw. . . .

To his surprise and relief Anne said little. He had expected harsh and fluent diatribes. Instead she admitted that Mrs. Halliwell could be very charming. "But why shouldn't she be? She's never had anything to do except cultivate her talents and her personality. Do you suppose she's ever put her hand in cold water in her life?" In spite of Herbert's private conviction that if Gloria Halliwell had been poor

251

she would have put her hand into cold water a good deal oftener and more effectually than Anne had ever done, he agreed to this observation. He agreed to a number of other less flattering ones concerning his friends because they lacked the virulent ferocity he had expected. Perhaps, he thought and prayed that he was right, the years were bringing Anne a shadow of good judgment and moderation. Then he let the whole matter slip from his mind in the absorbingly busy and agreeable months that followed. Doctor Markowski, threatened with pneumonia was ordered to Florida until spring. The other associate conductor of the society was Herbert's senior both in years and service. But he was an unambitious man, satisfied with a routine repertory. Stephen Halliwell and Herbert put their heads together and planned a concert at which Herbert was to conduct his own second symphony and Gustav Mahler's Ninth. The rehearsals were constant and an enormous strain. But Herbert was both inspired and sustained by the Halliwells who had been close friends of Mahler during his New York period, afterwards to his untimely death and were in constant touch with his gifted widow in Vienna. Stephen would drop in at the rehearsals and drive Herbert to his house for rest and refreshment and discussion. Once a week in addition Herbert would have luncheon with Gloria alone. She taught him to be merry and to treat life with a lighter touch; he talked well with her and was conscious of it. She took his arm or laid a hand on his shoulder and made him feel that her affectionate friendship extended beyond the musician to the man. She made him dream that he might yet recover a part of the youth that had been stolen from him; she kept him from seeking other and more dangerous contacts. He knew that in the long run even this beautiful friendship, tinged though it was by a slight inevitable eroticism, would not suffice him. Gloria was ten years his senior. She was undividedly devoted to her husband and her children. She was, despite her flawless talent for comradeship, a great lady. But for the hour, the day, the week, the month he was happier, serener, more gratefully conscious of his powers and qualities than he had ever been before. So long and many

252

were the necessary rehearsals and conferences that he left home early and returned late and saw less of Anne than he had done at any other period of their lives together. And he observed with an intimate relief that Anne, instead of sitting at home and waiting for him in dour reproachfulness, also went out a good deal during his absence. She was not exactly agreeable. Abrupt, harsh taunts concerning his probable occupations during his many hours away from home came from her and she made constant demands for money for special unforeseen needs of Luella and Eileen. But Herbert, since he had the money now and needed little for himself, gave it to her gladly and without detailed inquiry. It was the cheapest way of buying peace. He was tired from his thrilling but absorbing work—too tired to observe how often Anne's treacherous eyes rested upon him in a cold vindictiveness that was biding its time.

The concert came and went and left Herbert rather limp and in a deeper sense rather ashamed. Critics and audience accepted him but were cool to Mahler. How far this was due to the war psychosis could not be told. His position was more secure than ever but he could not help being more concerned for art than for his own art. For several days after the great event which Anne had watched with a cold yet burning eye, Herbert stayed at home to rest and to reflect. On the fourth of these days she came to him at breakfast with a drawn face.

"Will you please look at this, Bertie?"

She handed him a typed sheet of cheap paper and the stamped and postmarked envelope in which it had arrived. It was the first anonymous letter that Herbert had ever seen. But its character was unmistakable. The writer who signed in the traditional fashion a Wellwisher warned Mrs. Crump, if she valued her marital happiness, to pay more attention to her husband's movements. In public restaurants and other places he had been seen constantly in the company of Gloria Halliwell, a dangerous and notorious vamp who had the habit, without ever soiling her own skirts, of robbing wives of their husbands' admiration and affection. Mrs. Crump was bidden to take active measures while there was still time. Herbert threw down the sheet.

253

"How vile but also how silly. Affection and admiration aren't articles that can be stolen like rings or hairbrushes. They're inner states that either exist or don't. Some fool woman of course who envies Gloria Halliwell."

"Or whom she's injured," Anne said quickly. "Don't you try to be high-falutin'. As a matter of fact, the woman is a disgusting vamp. She has nothing to do but make herself attractive and she's subtle and shameless and does her best to make other women look dingy. Don't try to teach me to know her. But you haven't told me yet—is it true?"

"Is what true?"

"That you've been openly running about with her?"

Herbert tried to keep cool. "We've had luncheon together occasionally."

"And who's paid for the luncheons?"

"I have, naturally."

"So you can waste your money on that rich woman! Well, by God."

"Don't!" Herbert raised his voice. "When I consider what you wring from me for your family I don't think that my little expenditures can be questioned!"

"Is that so?" Anne said. "So you expect me to sit still under that? You make yourself the talk of the town with that vile and dangerous woman and you think I'm going to do nothing about it?"

He threw down the paper he had been trying to read. "I expect you as usual to try to do everything that's disgusting and calculated to hurt me. But there's one thing you may not know. If you break up my friendship with the Halliwells you'll be very sorry for it in the end."

"I don't believe that at all. And anyhow I'm hardly the one to be threatened and browbeaten in this instance, Mr. Crump."

He found the Halliwells at home alone the next afternoon. He told his wretched story. They were not surprised. Stephen had also received an anonymous letter warning him to restrain his wife from her dangerous and disgusting activities, the latest object of which was Herbert Crump. Gloria was nervous. She felt as though a grimy and

254

contaminating and yet ghostlike hand had been laid upon her. Stephen looked glum. Then he brightened in his somber way.

"You needn't either of you take it to heart," he said. "In my opinion, Anne wrote both letters herself."

"Even Anne isn't capable of such infamy," Herbert said.

Stephen looked at him. "*Capable de tout,* as you ought to know."

"No doubt. But she's not really clever. Where did she get her exact information?"

Stephen seemed unwilling to tell all this thoughts. "You may find out some day. I advise you and Gloria to have your conferences here for a while."

They dropped the subject. A shadow and a stain remained. For a while Gloria and Herbert took Stephen's advice. But now and then as spring came on and as the young leaves began to twinkle they grew reckless and if they couldn't find Stephen they would take a walk together and then get hungry and drop in somewhere for luncheon. Every now and then Gloria invited Anne who was stiff and watchful and as dour as she dared be and kept on talking about the anonymous letters and about what she called her own sex starvation. "Ah, my dear," Gloria said to Herbert one day, "I'm afraid Anne will succeed in breaking up our friendship." It was a warm afternoon and Herbert had run in on a chance. Gloria in tea-gown and mules was resting on a couch. Herbert was sitting on a low chair beside her. Stephen had sent word from his study that he would join them for tea when his secretary left. Herbert leaned forward and took Gloria's hand for a moment. "I don't know what I'll do if she does," he said. "I shall be the more desolate for having known what it is not to be." The door flew open. The scared face of the maid appeared for a second and was then grotesquely whisked back under the obvious impact of a push or thump. Anne stood beside them, purple of face, with nostrils widely dilated, with arms akimbo, visibly dripping with sweat in her murderous fury. "Closeted with my husband again and half naked this time!" she screamed. "I'll show you!" She came a step nearer. But Gloria arose and succeeded in sweeping rather beautifully to the

255

door. "Stephen," she called. But Stephen had heard and met her. "I'm afraid," she said, "you'll have to order that dreadful woman out of the house." She turned back. "Goodbye, dear Herbert," she said. "My heart aches for you." She went out. Stephen addressed Anne. "You've never acted in a becoming fashion, Mrs. Crump. We cannot receive you any more and if you write anonymous letters again I'll have you arrested for misuse of the mails." Gravely he turned to Herbert. "I needn't tell you that our friendship for you remains unchanged." "So you stand there, Herbert Crump, and let me be thrown out of this damned house!" Anne yelled. "Must I call the servants?" Stephen asked. With a grotesque assumption of wounded dignity she pushed herself forward to the door. With a sob in his throat Herbert fled down those homelike and familiar stairs, picked up his hat in the hall and walked out into the mocking sunlight. In a moment Anne was beside him. "Bertie!" she cried pleadingly. He took a deep breath. He opened his lips. Words? Words were meant to reach a mind that could consider, a heart that could feel—a human fellow creature. Silently he walked away.

4 THE concert season being over he had time enough for reflection in the days that followed. He knew that the crisis had come. And from this piece of knowledge he derived two others: that crisis is a matter not of outer but of inner event and that it does not issue in immediate action. Anne had in fact done things to him that were far more cruel than breaking up his friendship with the Halliwells. From her treatment of his father, for instance, one could almost arrive at the necessity of punishment in a future life. The trouble with historical Christianity was, of course, its absurd identification of nature and freedom with evil. But when one came in contact with the only really evil thing in the world, that is to say, a thoroughly bad heart, the Christian symbols seemed to meet the case. Anne's jealousy of him he could dimly understand. What he could

not understand was Anne's failure to ask herself whether she had the right, jealous or not, to rob him of every refuge and of every comfort. He asked her whether she had, in fact, ever put that question to herself. She looked blank. "But why do you need a refuge?" she asked. "Why can't you be comfortable with me?" Impenetrable as she seemed to be, an instinct apparently told her that there was danger in Herbert's very quietness. She tried to be both cleaner and better-tempered and more appreciative of his work. The impression which these efforts made on Herbert was to him an ultimate test of the situation. They struck him as not even mildly pathetic but as funny to the point of ribaldry. The eleventh hour lay so many years in the past. . . . What he, absurdly scrupulous but impelled to that scrupulousness by something in his blood—what he was concerned with was the economic situation. He must provide for Anne in the case of his leaving her and he must not be penniless himself. Since she knew definitely of nothing but his salary and since the expenses of Luella and Eileen had been measurably calculable and not just wildly arbitrary this year, he had been able to save some money. These savings Stephen Halliwell had increased for him through little Wall Street manipulations. Hence Herbert had several thousand dollars in bank of which Anne knew nothing. He determined to buy a house or an apartment—rents were rising appallingly during those years—in which she could live and to allow her in addition one third of his salary which had been fixed at six thousand for the following season. Out of the rest of his salary, plus his increasing additional earnings he would be able to meet the future payments on the house or apartment which would after all be his upon Anne's death, and also be able to live in comfort. He knew at the core of him that he was substituting these plans and calculations for an immediate and liberating act. The inner protest was obscure and intricate. Does hate bind as well as love? No, he thought, not in his case. Or else he didn't in that sense hate Anne. He didn't want to be revenged on her; he didn't want to punish her. He couldn't help going back to his old image. One doesn't want to be revenged on a disease that had fastened itself upon one. One wants to be rid of it, forget it, never be conscious of it again. . . .

He proposed to begin with, since the girls were coming home for the summer holidays, that he go to the country alone. Anne wailed. "It's natural for me to want to see my children. And yet, on that account, my husband proposes to leave me. Was ever a woman more unfortunately placed?" He insisted that he would not live in that small apartment with a crowd of people. Anne's face grew rigid. "Are you planning to meet some woman somewhere?" He began systematically—it was the middle of May—to look for a convenient place to go to when he met Gabrielle Bénard. . . . She walked into his office. She had heard that Beethoven's *Ninth Symphony* might be performed next season. She wanted a place in the chorus. It seemed to Herbert that she was quite the most beautiful creature he had ever seen. Her eyes were as blue as Gerda's had been. Her hair as much like wheat. There was a strength and a distinction in the features. There was a glow through her fairness that one associates with the darker women of the South. She said that she was French Canadian and spoke with a strong British accent. She knew Herbert's works well and discussed them with a penetrating personal enthusiasm. He watched her. Was she girl or woman? Virgin or adventuress? One could not tell. And that uncertainty had a troubling charm. Not for the heart, but for the nerves and senses. She was sophisticated, at all events, for she saw that she had made an impression on him. She asked him to hold her bag while she drew on her gloves. They went out together and went to luncheon at a hotel off the Avenue. Herbert who had never, in spite of every effort, been able to master being ashamed of Anne in public, bathed in the gratefulness of Gabrielle Bénard's companionship. He had been proud of being seen with Gloria Halliwell too. But she was so obviously a great lady and he her younger friend. The relations between Gabrielle and himself might have been anything. After luncheon they went into the park. Gabrielle said she had heard that he was unhappy and that she had also heard people remark on the contrast between his public success and his private misery. Of herself she said little. An incandescence began to burn in Herbert's brain. For the first time in his life he felt as though his self-control was slipping away. Gabrielle was the type of woman over whom a man might go to pieces. He didn't care. Better to be destroyed by a beautiful adventuress if she was one, than to decay with Anne. . . .

He plunged. He met Gabrielle daily for a week. She told him that she had been married at nineteen and divorced a year ago. He was horrified. Other men without his special experience might regard such a circumstance as harmless. Not he. But his nerves and senses were wretchedly involved. He spoke frankly with Gabrielle. She had a certain elegant detachment. "What you need is fresh air and young animals," she said with her enigmatic smile. "I'm afraid I'm mad about you."—"You had better get over it, dear friend. I'm not the right sort for you. You need a nice girl and babies."

He came home with burning viscera and a confused head. He did not at once observe Anne's bitter sneer.

"So you're in love, are you?"

He spoke out of a deep preoccupation with his own feelings. "Yes," he said slowly, "in a way." Then he turned to her. "Love? I've heard that word bandied about too much. You use it. At least I want this woman. I'm sure of that. If I suffer I shall be suffering for a reality."

Anne laughed a contemptuous laugh. "You fool! In the first place she's got a child. In the second, it's my belief that she's being kept by some rich man. She's just leading you on and using you."

He awoke. He sprang up. "How do you know? What do you know?"

She was jaunty. "All that I need to. There are ways and ways of finding out. But I'm going after that woman and get back the notes you wrote her. She shan't be able to brag with them!"

He looked at her. "I believe you lie."

"Do I? Well, tell me this, why did Gabrielle Bénard"—triumphantly she brought out the name—"never ask you to her apartment? She has one, you know."

259

He turned away and walked in his study. It was true that Gabrielle had never asked him to visit her. All that Anne said might be true. And that was bad enough. But what was worse was this: He was evidently imprisoned in Anne's consciousness. Oh, no, his mind was sane and clear. He attributed to her no more than tireless vigilance and inexhaustible energy and complete treachery in her pursuit of the aim of keeping him—object, thing, chattel, slave—to herself. His will, needs, agony, rebellion; his writhing in pain and disgust; his perception of something like decay eating into his brain and soul, contaminating his whole universe, making leprous the face of man and of nature—all these things were as nothing to that old woman with the brutal jaws. So far as he was concerned she had identified herself with fate, with God. . . . The thought daunted him in time and place. Under the aspect of eternity it heartened him. It was not likely that such a thing should prevail. . . .

He couldn't reach Gabrielle the next day. On the day following she came to him.

"We mustn't meet any more." She held his hand. "I have a little girl; I have a mother. I'm not conventional and I love your fine spirit. But I can't let myself be subjected to the rancor of that fury."

He avoided her eyes. "You've seen her?"

"She came to me and she plead with me not to rob her of her husban. Oh, she was very pathetic, but I'm a woman. I know. If I hadn't promised, she would have threatened scandal and violence. If I don't keep my promise, she'll throw vitriol in my face."

"Nonsense," he said. "She's taken you in. She's a coward except with her slanderous tongue."

Gabrielle shook her head. "If I were quite free and if you really loved me. . . ." She held up her face and he kissed her. They parted. . . . He went home late and wearily. He had called up the real estate agent. He would buy the house in Greenwich Village. He must begin to carry out his plan. When he reached the apartment he heard unfamiliar and ominous noises. Visitors had arrived from the west: Bronson, and his sickly wife and their tiny newborn baby. . . .

5   HE WAS stunned. The visitation had been threatened. He had told Anne that if it came to pass he would go. She now slipped into the hall to meet him.

"Listen to me, Bertie; please listen, won't you? Just for a minute!"

Carefully, so as not to touch her, he passed her in the hall and went into his study for his Boston bag. She followed him.

"Bertie, for God's sake! What could I do? They haven't a cent. Poor Bronson has been unfortunate; Bertha runs a temperature: it's my private opinion she's got t. b. And there's that poor, little, sick baby."

He didn't answer her. He found his bag, brushed the dust of many weeks from it and took it into their bedroom. She kept at his elbow.

"It's just for a few days, Bertie. They'll get a room in the neighborhood; Bronson is looking in the evening papers for a job this minute."

Herbert took pajamas and shirts, socks and collars out of a drawer and threw them into the bag.

"Bertie," Anne whispered hotly. "Say something. Anything! It isn't my fault. What am I to do? You knew I had the children."

He was ready to go now. He hadn't taken off his hat at all. She barred his way. He didn't want to touch her. She looked more unclean than usual and there was a smell of diapers in the air. He stood there numb and disgusted. With an effort he raised his hand and flung her out of his way and passed into the hall. He reached the outer door and opened it. She leaped behind him and hung herself with a frantic clutch into his arm. She let herself drop so that he dragged her behind him across the landing. She was heavy to drag; sweat started out all over him. God, she was heavy. . . . At the head of the stairs he tried to free his arm. But her grapple was like that of a drowning creature. He lifted a foot for the descent. She bounded suddenly and threw herself in front of him diagonally across the concrete stairs. She grasped two rungs of the balustrade with her hands. Her body covered seven or eight steps. It was too far to jump. He couldn't tread her under. She would probably trip him anyhow and hurl them both down the stairs. He heard horrified whispers and exclamations behind him. In the door stood Bronson with the scared eyes of a small animal, like so long ago. Beside him, dark, sallow, slatternly, stood his young wife. Herbert glanced at those two; he glanced at the prostrate form in the dirty kimono with straggling, greasy grayish hair in front of him. Was this purgatory? Was this a madhouse? He felt his limbs trembling from the effort of dragging Anne. It seemed to him that he was unclean in a limbo of uncleanness. He went back into the flat and locked himself into his study. Before lying down on the couch there for the night he sat at his desk and reflected. In any natural and human conflict Anne would always remain victorious because she passed beyond the limits of the natural and the human and plunged herself and others into an uncharted moral chaos where thought and action was paralyzed. To go on living in a world that held her one must fight her with her own weapons. One must use concealment and treachery. He had not wit enough to think of a scheme by which to escape her. But others might have. There were tricky lawyers in the world. . . . He was too weary to think further. . . .

In the morning Anne and the Vilases acted as though he were an ogre that must be placated. They brought Anne's grandchild and dandled it before him. Herbert, always touched by little children, could not help answering the baby's feeble, winning smile. Bertha, at a glance from Anne, inclined the child toward Herbert. The little creature stretched out its thin arms and inconceivably tiny hands. Before he knew it the child was in his arms, snuggling against his chest, its soft little fingers on his cheek. He held it tenderly despite himself; he smiled down at it. A chorus came to his ears: Wasn't it remarkable how the baby had taken to his Uncle Bertie right away? Wasn't he the wisest baby anyone had ever seen? And he was so frail, poor little thing. Bertha had been forbidden to nurse him and even the Walker Gordon milk didn't entirely agree with him. The baby sucked Herbert's finger. Gently Bertha relieved him of it. "Breakfast is ready, Bertie," Anne announced. He started up as out of a dream. How wise the Vilases were. How they conquered one. He couldn't put the poor,

262

sick, little baby that he had held in his arms out into the cold world. . . . He laughed inwardly. To a detached observer the thing would have had its quite farcical side. Into the arms that he had wanted to put about Gabrielle, Anne had slipped her grandchild. . . . Immediately after breakfast she announced that Herbert seemed to have forgotten their invitation to Doctor Markowski's birthday party that night. He had indeed forgotten. He supposed he would have to go. And Anne would put on her war paint and go too, and act coy and possessive toward him before others. And this after last night. What ribaldry! He laughed. "All right," he said, "we'll go." . . .

The party had a glamour for him. Drinking began before the sun had quite set and crimson clouds seemed to burn on the western windows of Markowski's house in a little downtown street. The rooms were crowded with people. They all knew one another and there arose gradually a mood of psychical abandon. Men and women began suddenly to tell their secret thoughts. Anne resisted the prevalent mood without understanding it. She adopted a conventionally flirtatious attitude toward the men; she acted as though this were the feeble chaffing of grocery clerks at an Elks' ball. Rachel Cohn, the violinist, dark, tiny, long-nosed, emaciated, a world of suffering in her large, intelligent, brown eyes, put her arm through Herbert's.

"Dear master," she whispered, "isn't Anne funny?"

"Ghastly," he said. "She's quite out of her own world and she's never even touched mine. But how did you know?" Rachel snuggled up close to him. "I've been going through your work; I have eyes. So have others. By the way, do you imagine it isn't known?"

"I haven't gone about telling my troubles."

"No, you're a self-respecting sort of darling. But Anne has a loose tongue. In ten minutes she told me this evening that she was a terribly passionate woman, that she had just saved you from the toils of a designing adventuress, that you were a very sick man, and that your sickness had taken the form of a sexual inhibition against her."

"Impossible!" Herbert exclaimed.

263

"Innocent! She goes up and down the earth with that line of patter. You mean to say you didn't know?"

He shook his head. "How do you explain it?" he asked.

"Can't tell you tonight. I'm too tipsy. But listen."

"Yes."

"I adore you strangely."

He put his arm about her frail shoulders. "How sweet of you!"

"I know I'm not your type," she went on. "It doesn't matter. I accept life as essentially tragic, anyhow. But look how Anne is glowering. I think it would discipline her if you kissed me."

He sat down on a chair that stood behind him. Rachel snuggled into his lap. He bent down and kissed her and she clung passionately to his lips. Anne strode up to them. Her face was swollen to bursting. "Well, of all the indecent and disgusting performances, I call this the——"

Rachel raised her head. "But why, Anne? Do you even know? I think that in another incarnation Herbert and I were brother and sister. His kisses have the unbearable sweetness of incest." She got up. "Oh, what a fool you are, Anne!" She reached up to Herbert's ear. "I'm at the Brevoort." Herbert got up and faced Anne. "You'd think this was a bawdy house," she said. "Will you take me home?" He shrugged his shoulders. It was late. Other guests must have left. They were almost alone in the smoking-room. "Yes, we can go," he said. . . .

He thought a good deal about Rachel in the next few days. When he thought about her he felt less lonely and dejected. He had to have some psychical refuge. Eileen had arrived with her fiancé, a blond, watery-eyed, good-hearted, stupid, middle-western country boy. Luella had arrived, larger and more buzzing than ever. Bronson and his family had taken a furnished room in the neighborhood. But the whole clan spent its day in the Crump apartment. When Herbert was not locked in his study he had to get away from that alien tumult. So he called up Rachel and they had luncheon and spent the afternoon together. She was enormously intelligent. He felt so at home with

264

her. How spiritual, in the strictest meaning of the term, human relationships seemed to be. He had known the Vilases for twelve years. Except for Eileen in certain moods they were complete strangers to him. There was no common meeting ground; there were no common perceptions. He was immensely grateful for Rachel's friendship. They were at luncheon one day in the Westminster Hotel, sitting on a little sofa in a niche, side by side and hand in hand. They looked up at the urge of a sudden common impulse. Anne tood in front of them. A desperate, helpless rage shook Herbert. "How dare you follow me about, you disgraceful creature?"

Rachel smiled subtly. "Sit down, Anne," she said. "Don't mind Herbert's irritation. None of us wants a scene here."

Anne sat down. She bridled and dilated her nostrils in the old way. "Well," she said, "have you two slept together? Have I grounds for a divorce?"

"Not yet," Rachel answered, "but we can manage that quite easily, if you like."

"Such shamelessness!" Anne cried.

Herbert put his hands to his head. "She lies." He spoke in a toneless, tired voice. "She always lies. It isn't a question of divorce or even of a legal separation. She'd fight both to the limit. Can't she at least leave me alone? She knows perfectly well how I fear and hate and despise her."

Anne wept. "Can a woman be blamed for wanting to keep her own husband?"

"No," Rachel said, gently, "if he really is her husband. At all events, what does she get by outraging his feelings?"

"But does he have to run about with women?" Anne asked.

Rachel looked at her steadily. "I'm afraid, Anne, that you're stupid. Your secret is that you have none. If you're not careful, Herbert, she'll shoot you some day."

Herbert laughed. "No such luck. If she killed me nothing would matter; if she only wounded me I'd be rid of her at last."

265

Tears made furrows down the heavy rouge on Anne's cheeks. "You don't hate me as much as that, do you, Bertie?"

Herbert summoned a waiter and paid the bill. All three left the dining room. "I'm going to my office," Herbert said. Walking away he saw the two women taking a conventional leave of each other. . . .

A few days later he made an engagement with Rachel to call for her at the Brevoort. Walking slowly down lower Fifth Avenue he had the impulse to look behind him. A tallish figure in a gray raincoat with a rigid trunk, holding a newspaper before her face was following him. The newspaper was lowered for a moment. Pursuer and pursued looked into each other's eyes. He took a taxi and gave his office address. He had a vision of the end of Anne's story and his own and closed his eyes to shut that vision out. . . .

6   ONCE or twice more he met Rachel. She asked him whether she should take an apartment in New York in the fall. He shook his head.

"What I have to offer you isn't good enough for you."

She looked at him with her melancholy, intelligent, brown eyes. "I'm not concerned over what I get but over what I want to give."

"Dear friend," he cried, "I too want to give. I'm freezing up inside."

So they parted. Each time they had been together Anne had known of it. She sat at home like a spider holding the world in her web. She knew when Rachel left the city and congratulated herself and Herbert on the disappearance of that "hideous little kike" . . .

Herbert bought the house in Greenwich Village. The Conrads, charming and gifted and wholesome people, who were on the directorate of the Manhattan Musical Society, offered him a large bungalow on Long Island Sound for the summer for next to nothing. It would do, he thought, for Anne and the Vilases; it was three hours from New York. He had a dim notion that he would establish Anne in the house and not return to it till summer was over. The house was big enough to hold Bronson and his family, Luella, Eileen and the youth whom she had suddenly married. Anne was always worrying about her family. She had hectic visions of people maltreating Luella in her absence or after her death. Herbert thought that by providing a home for them all which it was in his power to take away again, he was laying hold of a fairly solid weapon in his fight for freedom. Perhaps he could barter with Anne. Perhaps he could promise to settle the house on her and on Luella after her if she would pledge herself to leave him alone. That was all, it seemed to him, that he wanted now. Just to be left alone. He would have been happy in a bare room in a lodging house, if only Anne and the Vilases were not there. Was that so much to ask? He let Anne buy furniture and rugs and hangings for the house. He loaned—they still amusingly enough called it so—several hundred dollars to Bronson. He loaned money to Eileen and to Elmer Troutman, her husband. Anne spent as much money as possible. She wanted to keep Herbert poor and therefore helpless. Coolly he watched her. Luckily he had funds in reserve. . . .

By the end of June they were settled in the house downtown. In a week or two they planned to go to Long Island. Then Herbert's father had a stroke of paralysis and he hurried for the last time to Queenshaven. He knew from the first that he would not see his father alive any more. He was not sorry. What could they have said to each other? His father had now known thoroughly for years of Herbert's immense personal wretchedness. He had recently taken much quiet comfort in the publication of his son's works and in the printed comments on them which Herbert had always promptly sent him. But the shadow of Anne lay between them. Since she had come into their lives so many years ago now father and son had been cut off from veracious communication with each other. They did not somehow dare to touch upon that dreadful open secret. The elder Crump, so simple and so honorable, had shrunk from the moral corruption in which, surely not wholly faultless himself, his son dwelt. Why Herbert should have been so overwhelmingly punished for a common

267

sin of youth—that was a mystery which it would have been futile to discuss. . . .

Herbert sat beside his dead father and casual beholders might have thought that he showed little feeling. But he was considering with an immeasurable pain within, a pain that reached out after and questioned fate itself, how different, how really sweet and mellow life could have been for his father and mother if he married an ordinarily suitable, ordinarily good woman, kind, helpful, mother of children of his own. Herbert thought of his friends in the world of art and of the intellect who scoffed at the Philistine virtues and who said that to understand everything was to forgive it too. Ah, he knew better. Those friends of his possessed the fundamental virtues— veracity, mercy, unselfishness—and were therefore entitled to research and experiment in the moral world. But he had insight into a region where those virtues had not yet been reached. And that region, from which Anne had arisen, was one of chaos and of spiritual death. Foul, unimaginable shapes could curl up like wraiths from that world. Goodness and honor—those were the names of salvation. He knelt beside his father who had been both good and honorable, knelt there long and arose and kissed that icy forehead. . . . Petersen, who was quite blind now, played the Adagio of Beethoven's "Sonata Pathétique" at the funeral services of his old friend and on the way back from the fresh grave laid his hand on Herbert's knee.

"Your father was very proud of you, Herbert. But in the last year or two, just as you were getting to be more and more successful, he always said: 'My poor boy.' Why was that?"

At last tears came into Herbert's eyes. "Because, Karl, one may have talent and reputation and even make a little money and yet be dreadfully poor."

The blind man shook his head sorrowfully. "You're only thirty-five, Herbert."

"True," Herbert answered, "better days may yet come."

Next day he took a walk to Calhoun Street and for the last time saw the home of his boyhood and youth and gazed long at the upstairs piazza from which his mother had watched him and Anne on that day of doom and had said to herself in her wise mother's heart that she, at least,—oh, the measureless irony of it!—would not make the mistake of former generations who wanted to rule and curb their children, but would help her son toward his heart's desire. . . .

In the New York house Eileen met Herbert.

"Everybody's in the bungalow. Mamma is wretchedly ill. You ought to go out to her right away."

Herbert looked at Eileen steadily. "Really ill?"

She reflected. "Yes, I believe so. She's certainly in great pain."

Herbert walked to the window and looked out upon the dusty street. "She'll survive us all," he said.

He heard Eileen's voice, still high and cool but touched by feeling and experience now. "She loves you terribly."

"So does the tiger love the sheep. When the sheep is in the tiger's stomach and the powerful acids of the tiger have destroyed the sheep —then love has reached its completeness."

"But what would there be in life for her without you?"

"That's for her to settle with her own soul. How about you and Bronson and Luella? She's never hesitated to sacrifice me to the family."

"I know," Eileen said slowly, "she's got that very strong maternal instinct and yet she gets no happiness through us. She has no life but in you."

He shook his head. "Do you understand, Eileen?"

"Not entirely. Because I can't imagine myself never stopping to think. But you'll come, won't you?"

"I suppose so."

He went to his office for mail. He was asked for on the telephone but when he spoke no one was on the wire to answer. The same thing happened twice within the following hour. Then Frank Conrad came in—half-Lincoln in figure and aspect, half-dandy—strong and inexhaustibly full of both warmth and light.

"Run down with me this afternoon, Crump. We'll go a-fishing and we'll forget the world, the flesh and the devil."

"I hear that Anne's ill," Herbert said.

"Yeh, I believe I heard my wife say something of that sort. Never mind, old top, I guess it's no killing matter. You and I'll go out into the middle of the Sound and smoke and fish and interview eternity. Never mind the pulings of the so-called fair sex."

Herbert agreed. He always felt alive and sane with both Frank and Agnes Conrad. Not because they were uncomplicated people. Conrad's novels had both power and subtlety. Both Frank and Agnes had had their storms. But they both radiated the final conquest of reason and goodness. Anne, plunging always at once into a bitterish and provocative intimacy, had asked Agnes Conrad the second time they had ever met: "What would you do if your husband left you?" Agnes, elegant and neat, an unaffected touch of the eternal Gretchen still tinging her competent forties, had answered calmly: "If he wanted to go, I suppose he would have to go. I should still have such things as music and nature and friendship." Anne had later characterized this answer as that of an affected old fool and had speculated at length and slanderously on Frank Conrad's frequent trips to New York while Agnes stayed on their estate on Long Island. . . .

By nightfall Herbert reached the bungalow on the Sound. Anne was upstairs. She looked dilapidated and tried to be angry and pathetic at the same time. She had dreadful pains in her loins and back. Cloths had continually to be dipped in hot water and applied to her. Luella complained loudly that she had thought it would be "lotsoffun" to come out here. Now she was cook, dish-washer and sick nurse. Herbert asked Anne why she didn't have a servant. Her allowance was large enough. "Don't bother me," Anne screamed. "I'm in pain! God, what a brute!" She complained and kept everyone busy during the greater part of the night. Next morning she announced feebly that she was a little better. If Herbert had the heart to leave her to go fishing he was welcome. He wouldn't have done so some years ago.

But since he had been mauled about by all those vile women! Well, she supposed she could stay and suffer alone. . . .

Herbert paid as little attention to the chaos in the bungalow as possible. Eileen returned and she and her young husband mitigated the confusion. Anne insisted on putting on a girlish, frilly bathing-suit. She learned to float and was coy and eloquent over her accomplishments in the water. Luella with a somber hostility in her face declared that, if her mother had not abandoned her when she was a child and if she had had a proper bringing up and proper education she would not have to be afraid of being nearer and nearer thirty. . . . Herbert spent many hours with Conrad in a boat out on the Sound or walking on the wild, hauntingly primeval dunes at the very end of the island. From these scenes there came to him the large serenity of the "Elegy" (opus 27) dedicated to his father's memory which was to be for so long the last of his works. He finished it rapidly, scribbling in the shadow of one of the great rocks that dotted the beach and declared one morning at breakfast that he would run in to town to see Joffe. Anne, suddenly wild-eyed, said that she must go too to consult her doctor. She must telephone for an appointment. She hurried to a neighbor's house to telephone. She had made desperate scenes when she had discovered that there was no telephone in the bungalow, but Herbert, instinctively resisting her for once, had refused to make what seemed to him a wholly unnecessary expenditure. She had a commutation card of her own and announced that though, curiously enough, her own husband didn't seem to relish her society, all hell couldn't prevent her from going too. At the Long Island station Herbert left her. In his own office, in Joffe's office later, at Joffe's club where they had luncheon, regularly every thirty minutes Herbert was summoned to the telephone. And as regularly when he spoke there was silence. Joffe's dark eyes rested on him broodingly.

"Look here, old man, what crime have you committed? You're being watched."

"Impossible," Herbert said. "Mere coincidence, of course."

But in his heart arose a wild and eerie dread, a dread like the night fear of a fevered child on whom familiar things suddenly turn the pallid masks of demons. He felt as though the whole world were going mad about him. In the evening he returned to his house. Anne sat there gaunt, taut, sinister.

"Did you see the doctor?" he asked.

"No. I felt too wretched and lonely and deserted."

7 THE city was hot and dusty. Everyone he knew was away. Joffe too was leaving at once. The dust swept into the house and everything one touched was gritty. Anne sat brooding in the drawing room; Herbert walked up and down in his study above. That wild and eerie dread would not leave him. He had felt touches of it before in the course of the years. It had been like a beast in ambush in the jungle of the subconscious. Now the beast had sprung. He tried to define the feeling that dominated him to himself, to be clear about it in his own mind, not to yield to it to the point of madness. The world of reality had receded from him. All familiar scenes were like drop curtains in the theater of a nightmare. Portentous shadows swept through that theater. He stood amid those shadows from which appeared, multiplied a hundredfold, appeared again and again, Anne's frozen mask. . . . He dropped his face into his hands. Was he losing his mind? No. Still that mind of his stood secure above the terrors and eerie visions of the depth; still it analysed, still it knew. Years and years ago he had been trapped and imprisoned with creatures of whom his soul had no knowledge; they had tried to wrench him away from himself, his instincts, his appetences, his true life and make him melt into their miasma. . . . But pillars had stood to uphold his own world, the spiritual universe into which he had been born—his mother, his father. The pillars had fallen. He was alone. As the body can be poisoned by noxious fumes, so can the soul. . . . Suddenly a nostalgia came over him for the strong, cleansing waves of the sea. And the Conrads were there too. Anywhere from this

empty, dusty house with that evil brooding woman down stairs. . . .

He told Anne in the morning that he was going back to Long Island. She brightened up immediately. By the sheer force of her will and her temperament she could suddenly look younger than her years. This was, as Herbert remembered later, almost the last of those moments in which, at the price of his freedom and his peace of mind, she pumped a shadowy and histrionic vitality into herself.

"All right, Bertie. But I'd better stay over another day. The house wants looking after and I've got some errands. I really should see the doctor, you know. Those pains in my loins are liable to came back any minute. What train are you taking?"

"The eleven—ten."

"Fine! I've got to go up town this morning. I'll see you to the station." He didn't protest. He rather welcomed this confirmation of the strictness of the imprisonment in which she meant to keep him. No wonder that he was filled with a prison dread. He also welcomed the prospect of taking the three-hour trip alone. Perhaps he could shake off this horror within; perhaps he could re-establish a contact with the world of reality.

He got to the bungalow in the midst of preparations for a party. . . . Loudly and excitedly Luella informed him that she never had any fun, that parties were lots of fun, that he was always serious and her mother always sick and that other girls had parties and fellows and fun. She was giving a party that night for the young people of the summer colony and she hoped that he would, if he pleased, not interfere. The dread, the sense of unreality swept through him again as he watched Luella. He felt a gentle tugging at his sleeve. He turned a little. It was Eileen who beckoned him to join her on the veranda.

"I'm scared," she said softly. "Luella doesn't act natural. It started just that way the other time."

"Have you told your mother?"

"Of course. But you know how mamma is. She won't believe anything she doesn't want to believe."

273

He nodded. "True. She'll lie to her own soul until it overwhelms her."

"Anyhow," Eileen said, "I'm afraid to oppose Luella. If anything happens mamma would blame me."

"I'm afraid she would," he agreed.

"So," Eileen went on, "if you'll spend the evening with the Conrads, I'll see to it that the house is fit to live in by morning."

Herbert looked at Eileen.

"Have you told Elmer?"

Sorrowfully she shook her careworn little head.

"No. I hate it so for him. He's not brilliant, as you know. But he's sane and normal and kind and truthful."

Herbert suddenly understood Eileen's marriage. She had fled from her family. Better kind and decent mediocrity than moral corruption and cultural pretentiousness. He put his hand on her shoulder.

"You're a good kid, Eileen. Don't make it too hard for yourself. I'll manage somehow."

The Conrads were glad to have him with them. For a few hours his dread left him. It returned in the hushed bungalow in the middle of the night. It returned more intensely when Anne arrived on the next forenoon. He overheard the end of a whispered conference between her and Eileen soon after her arrival.

"I'd thank you to shut your damned mouth, Eileen! Luella is quite right. Of course she'd like to marry. And I don't see why such a beautiful girl doesn't find the right man."

"Perhaps men notice something abnormal," Eileen said thoughtfully. Herbert heard Anne jump up and heard her voice grow harsh.

"You get out of here and don't you let me hear you say such a thing again. Luella has as good a mind as anyone I know. I guess you're jealous of her looks."

Anne was defying fate. She was defying fate in this matter as in every other matter with lies. When, he wondered, would fate find her out?

He withdrew into himself. There were fields and roads for him to be alone on. There was the rock-strewn beach on which he could sit for hours and hear the pounding, splashing, gurgling, lapping, the bright sudden hiss, the long thunderous moan of the waves and let these sounds weave themselves for him into musical patterns which he was not to record. Only at such hours did that eerie dread leave him. It rose about him like a cloud that shut him out from the kindly world of both man and nature, at the sight of Anne's face and at the sound of her voice. He watched her across the table at luncheon and dinner. He had never gotten accustomed to her. He had never been able to summon, hard and often as he had tried, a mood of sincere resignation. His nerves instead of becoming calloused had grown more sensitive and raw. Her nose, her jaws, her imperfectly hennad hair, her coyness and her wrath, her moods of retrospective fatuousness or bridling defiance, or self-pitying pathos, her intonation and her shopworn phrases—all, all stung him like whips, like scorpions. She seemed bitterly ugly to him and inconceivably old. He knew that neither impression squared with the facts. But what he saw with the insight of the woe of the long years was not Anne as strangers might have seen her. He saw Anne's moral nature shaping the outer and visible Anne into an image of itself.

Absurd and dimly liberating what happened next. Agnes Conrad, anxious and concerned for him came to him on the porch. The evening paper, just in from New York, had bad news for him, she said. The storage warehouse on his street, on his very block, had caught fire through an inner explosion. There had resulted one of the worst fires in years. The whole street was involved. He took the paper and read the account in which his house was specifically mentioned.

"Well, dear Agnes, the house is insured. There's nothing I can really do. So I might as well wait and see."

In his mind's eye he saw tall orange and scarlet sheets of flame closing in upon that house; he could see it totter; he could hear it crash. And that inner vision excited him joyously. But he was careful not to show his feelings. Anne and Luella came out and heard the news. Luella began to babble wildly about her clothes and letters and trinkets.

"Well, Herbert," Anne said. "Are you just going to sit there like a bump on a stump and do nothing?"

He shrugged his shoulders. "What is there to do? One of the warehouse walls is tottering. The police have closed the entire street." Anne looked contemptuous. "Well, I like that," she said. "I'm going in in the morning, of course. I guess they'll let me through."

Luella babbled more and more wildly. . . .

Anne stayed in town for two days. Agnes Conrad felt that there was something strange and pitiful about Luella and thought it was fright and anxiety over the fire. She and Frank took her to bathe and swim with them and to meals at their house. Herbert felt almost human and natural alone in the bungalow with Eileen and Elmer. Then Anne came back and bragged. The house had not been touched by flames. It had sustained only water damage. By her skill and charm and eloquence she had persuaded the lieutenant of police in charge—tottering wall or no tottering wall—to let her get to the house. Men and boys, fired by a woman's dash and gallantry, had swarmed to help her. She had rented a suite of rooms in a lodging house on Greenwich Avenue and the men and boys had helped her to carry thither all the contents of the house except a few rugs and some magazine files that had been hopelessly soaked. Everyone had congratulated her. The town rang with her exploits. Ha, it took a woman to do things! Herbert felt depressed. Not even cleansing flames. . . . Luella, unconsoled over the possible loss or misplacing of some of her things, babbled more incessantly than ever. . . .

8   IN A week the terrible fact could no longer be hidden. Luella raved. She wrote a long, incoherent letter to Frank Conrad which was a confession of love. She believed that he loved her. She had the hallucination that he had given her unmistakable signs

276

of his passion. She went about the summer colony telling the story, telling too that Herbert had taken undue liberties with her. But her madness and its strong erotic tinge were both self-evident. Her extremities were like ice. Her head swam in a searing fever. The pupils of her eyes were so dilated as to give her a wild and unnatural splendor of aspect. She hated her mother with a cold, concentrated fury. Agnes, infinitely compassionate, took the poor distracted girl to her house and sending Frank out of the way put ice bags on her head and played soothing music to her in the hope of having her fall asleep. Anne stalked about the house, gaunt and desperate. A physician was needed and a nurse. Luella threatened hourly to walk into the Sound. Once already she had nearly overpowered Agnes Conrad. If Anne came near her she raved uncontrollably. Both the physician and the nurse had been telephoned for to New York. Both delayed coming. In Herbert's breast the chords of pity, so far as the Vilases were concerned, had been scraped to the snapping point long years ago. He told Anne that he would pay both doctor and nurse as well as the later charges at the hospital. But his life and inner peace must be his own thereafter. If ever he had owed a debt to her or hers he had now paid that debt a thousandfold. He was going to the city in the morning; he would send doctor and nurse. He would not return.

Anne arose. Her stony eyes stared with a prophetic fixity into space; her thick face was gray; her lips curled up from her strong teeth in a cruel contemptuousness. She had always known, she shouted, that he was an inhuman cur. But this piece of treachery was too foul for words. She was tied down by the frightful illness of her child. And so he thought that he could go unmolested to the city and sleep with some strumpet and make her, Anne, a laughing stock to all men and thus drive her to murder and suicide and by that very fact condemn Luella, lacking her care, to hopeless and perpetual madness. Judas! she shrieked and her voice rang out over the utter stillness of field and beach and sea. And again: Judas! But let him not think that she could be so easily betrayed and beaten even in the hour of her utmost need. If he went to the city in the morning she would go too and neither God

277

nor devil could keep her back. . . . Ominous heavy silence. Through the open door Frank Conrad stepped in from the piazza.

"Forgive me, Crump," he said. "I was coming over to get some more ice for Luella. Ours has given out. I couldn't help overhearing. Do forgive me, but that woman is crazy." He turned to Anne. "You're certainly not going in to town in the morning nor until a trained nurse has arrived. My wife is taking care of Luella out of the kindness of her heart. But the responsibility is yours. The moment you leave we'll leave too."

"And you stand there, Herbert Crump," Anne cried, "and let that man insult me?"

The two men looked at each other and burst out into uncontrollably bitter laughter.

"That man, of all men, who drove Luella mad by his insidious lechery!"

Conrad grew pale but he kept his tone quite level. "Guard that slanderous tongue of yours, woman. I'm afraid Herbert doesn't see through you even yet. But others know you for what you are—liar, nymphomaniac, thief!"

Anne tossed her head as Conrad walked out into the darkness. She stalked to the window and stared into the night. Minutes passed. She turned back to the room.

"I'm going just the same. I won't, won't, won't be trapped—not while I can crawl after you, Herbert Crump, on my hands and knees!"

Again minutes passed and then a lighter tread was heard on the veranda. Agnes stepped in. There was a hurt, shocked look in her kind, brown eyes.

"What's this I hear about your going to town, Anne?"

"I'm going." The hard jaws were set.

Agnes came close to her. "You're not going. I love my husband, God knows, but if any child of mine were in such desperate need and desperate danger I wouldn't be able to think of such a thing as his physical fidelity to me. You're not a mother at all. You've got the soul

278

of a prostitute. But you'll assume a decency you haven't got this time and stay."

And for the first time since Herbert had known her Anne's insolence found no words.

He left by a train almost at dawn. As on that day, many years ago, when he had gone from New York on what was to be his last visit to his mother and father, only in a harder and more conscious fashion now, he felt that departure to be like recovery from a noisome and crippling illness, like passing from a world of smoke and stench and decay into the kindly sunshine of the clean earth. To be within reach of his music and books he rented a room, a plain, humble, furnished room, on Greenwich Avenue; and that ugly room seemed to him triumph and refuge and convalescence and youth. From this room he could see the street on which, dirty and without windowpanes, like a blind forsaken monster, stood his house. A naked jagged wall of that warehouse was still standing, threatening every moment to fall and the street was closed to traffic. For two days he avoided that sordid desolateness. Then he thought that books or music might have been forgotten. He told the policeman at the corner who he was and showed his keys and was permitted to pass on the understanding that it was at his own risk.

It seemed infinitely natural to him that the stone steps were crumbling and the old-fashioned cast iron balustrade bent into a wildly grotesque shape and that there came to him, when he entered the hall of the house, an odor like the odor of corruption. He went up the stairs and heard the sound of his footsteps on the boards echo through that hollow shell of a dwelling. He had never known, he had never imagined how clean flame is and how repulsive destruction by water can be. Fire touches with that cleanness even the ashes left. It is swift, terrible, pure; water penetrates with a slothful, surly movement; it distends and contorts and produces forms of life that are like the dreadful accretions of diseased tissue. Mildew spread its spidery fibers over the dank walls; were those noisome fungi in dim corners? Boards were waterswollen like the limbs of poor suffering creatures;

masses of paper that had once been periodicals were great pulpy wads like tumors. The foulness of disorder was in this place, of nature perverted and malignant. But, alas, the structure stood. The water had come in sickly streams, in stealthy trickles, in vagrant spilth. It had come in no thunderous flood and the foundations of this ghastly house were still firm. Therefore the law, Herbert knew, would compel him to repair and rebuild. He shook his head with an earnest and final gesture. Let men bring sun-dried wood and fresh paint with its healthy, savorous odor of turpentine and snow-white plaster and spotless paper for these walls. He would always know that house as it was in this hour and remember it thus . . . thus and not otherwise . . . thus forever . . .

He heard ponderous steps coming up the stairs, turned to look and saw the broad, towering form of a police sergeant. In a moment the officer had joined him and loomed above him in an unmistakably kindly fashion.

"This sure is a hell of a mess. But you'll never know it when it's done over."

He tapped the wall with a beefy, expert finger. Then he turned back to Herbert.

"Look here, mister, I think there's something you ought to be told. You're being followed."

He turned to the window and looked out with a vague glance. One huge hand was behind him curved and cupped. Herbert wadded up a five dollar bill and slipped it into that hand which closed and became a fist and was raised aloft in righteous indignation.

"No, sir, it ain't right! Your wife's havin' you followed by one of Ratburger's men. Will you come here, sir?"

Herbert joined the officer by the window. In front of the house was standing a lank, blond, depressed-looking, pimply-faced youth. The officer pointed with his thumb. "That's him." Herbert looked up. "You've done me a real favor, sergeant." The officer nodded. His eyes met Herbert's in a look of honest masculine fellowship.

"There can't be any doubt about it?"

The big man grinned. "Naw! Try it on. Watch that guy shadow you."

Herbert went downstairs and out into the street. A curious bitter little chuckle rose from the depths of him. So this was Anne's vulgar trick; this was the cheap secret of her knowledge of his movements as well as of the dirt in which they lived. She stole his money and spent it on detectives. He went up to the pimply-faced youth in front of the house. He spoke quietly.

"You're following me, you damned scoundrel!"

The watery eyes shifted. "No, sir, not at all, sir. You're mistaken, sir."

Herbert laughed. He walked rapidly to the next street, turned west, swung suddenly around and saw the fellow run with assumed carelessness up the stoop of a house. Again he laughed. He strode back to Greenwich Avenue, hailed a passing taxi and saw the pimply-faced lout jump into another. He grinned at his driver. "See that taxi behind us? It's going to try to follow us. Lose it, will you?" A mad amusing race through the streets. Both taxi drivers seemed to be in a sporting mood. They turned sharp corners almost on two wheels. The touch of danger exhilarated Herbert. At Thirty-third Street and Eighth Avenue his driver managed to slip through just as the traffic officer raised his white-gloved warning hand. Herbert looked back and saw the detective gesticulating with lank arms and legs like a spider caught in its own web. It was enough. He paid and tipped his man. He walked over to Forty-fourth Street and late luncheon. There was peace in his heart. He had found Anne out at last. . . .

He was sitting in his simple room that evening when the door opened and Anne came in. He sprang up; he shrank into the farthest corner of the room. He knew that he had gone white as paper. He saw Anne's eyes grow large and wretched.

"My God, Bertie, are you afraid of me?"

He clenched his hands; he nodded; he was himself amazed at his profound horror.

"Bertie!" she cried, and came a step nearer.

281

He almost huddled in his corner.

"What's the matter, Bertie?"

He forced himself to speak though he hated it—hated the desolate old futility of addressing words to Anne.

"I caught Ratburger's man shadowing me today."

She put her head on one side; she looked at him with a coolly searching glance. "Ratburger? You're sure you're quite sane, Herbert? What is Ratburger?"

His horror deepened. But at the sight of her trickery of mind and gesture, seen for the ten thousandth time, a bottomless weariness overcame him and he could hardly drag the sounds from his throat.

"You're caught this time. Does that fact penetrate your mind? I have proof."

She gave him one last wild questioning look. Then with a histrionic gesture she flung herself at his feet. "Bertie, Bertie, can I help it if I love you so? The thought that you'd touch any other woman is enough to kill me. I have to know. I must know. Of course this is the wrong way. And I won't ever do it again—ever! Only don't abandon me, only go on living under the same roof with me! You can do anything you like—anything! Only stay with me, won't you? For God's sake, for your dear dead mother's sake, don't leave me!"

She crept nearer to him on her knees and dropped her head on the floor.

"I don't know what I'll do yet," he said dully. "But one thing I do know. I'm not your slave. You haven't bought me. If ever again you know anything about me that I haven't told you I'll kill you."

"But Bertie, I might find out by accident; friends might come and tell me."

"You heard what I said."

Slowly he came out of his corner.

She arose; she drew herself up; she adjusted her hat. "Hmm," she said. "It's very well for you to talk. But what right have you to keep me in a torment of jealous fear? That's slavery too. Why can't you behave yourself? You think you're tired of me. What you need is a psychiatrist. A wife has some right to protect herself, you know."

She drew on her gloves. "I've got to go back to the hospital now to see Luella. Your lovely friend Conrad ought to be made to pay her bills. But I'll see to it that people know about him. And I'm not so sure but what you had something to do with her breakdown too. The nurse told me that in her opinion two men must certainly have made improper advances to Luella. If a woman's own daughter is not safe from her husband, she must have some recourse."

He held the door open for her. "Won't you go?" he asked. "I'm tired."

"Very well," she said. "I'll go now, but you needn't think you're going to trample on me just because I've tried to protect myself as best I could. You happen to be my husband and both the law and society have something to say about it all!"

She tossed her head and dilated her nostrils. Proudly she walked out. Herbert dropped into a chair. Nothing could daunt that forehead of brass, that soul of leather, that heart of steel. . . .

Book Seven

JUSTICE

1   TALL headlines blared in the New York newspapers. They were black and stiff. In one paper they were scarlet and stretched across the entire front page. Wick was the name that sprang at one in fat, impudent letters—Thomas Thorpe Wick. Herbert visualized clearly the tall, grave, elegant figure with sad eyes far younger than the graying hair. He had met the brilliant and urbane scholar, critic and teacher several times during the past winter. He had a vision, hallucinatory in its clearness, of Dr. Wick reading the headlines with an unbearable inner shrinking, with maddening shame and powerlessness. *"Wick calls love-nest only refuge . . . Mrs. Wick spurns compromise . . . Why Wick went astray . . . Wick's notes to sweetie convulse court . . . Wick's wife defends home . . ."* The newspapers trampled on the man's soul; they threw him to the mob and the mob, half lecherous, half envious, sinister, revengeful, unclean, triumphed. One could see it in the faces of readers of papers in the subway. Ah, ha, so that was the life led by these high-brows while plain honest folks had to stay home, however stale and irksome home had become! Pretty soft—to leave your wife year in and year out in a suburb and to have a little girl in an apartment in the city. Pretty soft! But why in hell should he? Serve him right! They read only the headlines—these people with sad, tight, sordid

284

mouths in the subway. In vain Dr. Wick declared in court that moral and temperamental differences between his wife and himself had destroyed their marriage in any sense that counted twenty years ago, that he was devoted to Miss X who was a lady of high culture and intelligence; in vain his counsel protested against the reading of the playful or impassioned letters which detectives employed by Mrs. Wick had stolen from Miss X's apartment. In vain it was pointed out that Doctor Wick had long ago turned over all his property to his legal wife in order to appease her. Mrs. Wick won her suit for legal separation. To divorce Dr. Wick, she declared, would be putting a premium on gross immorality and on the destruction of the American home. The judge, a learned and crabbed bachelor of seventy-eight, ordered Dr. Wick to pay alimony at the rate of one hundred dollars a week. At the same time Dr. Wick was relieved of his duties at the university where he had been teaching. Miss X was given notice by her landlord as a person of questionable morals and Mrs. Wick declared that if her husband and his mistress attempted to leave the state she would prosecute him under the Mann Act.

Herbert, arriving at his office one morning, found Dr. Markowski, at whose house he had met Wick, shaking his long gray locks and wiping tears from his cheeks which were like the cheeks of Liszt. "God, Crump, what for a country is this country of yours. The laws are everywhere stupid. That I know. But public opinion and good healthy human reason mitigate them everywhere else. Last night after dark Tom Wick and that dear girl Margaret came to me. What shall we do? they asked. What? Our pictures have been in all the papers; so we can't get a place to live in even under assumed names. Together no one will take us, yet we would rather die than be separated. Tom —you should see him—he has aged twenty years. He tried to be dignified. He said: 'Margaret, darling, it's an academic question anyhow. I've lost my position and I can't get another. While most of my friends pretend to be sympathetic, they are a little shy and a little cool. Well, how will I pay the alimony? I'll have to go to the Ludlow Street jail. You must grit your teeth and forget me!' And then"—Markowski gave a sob at the recollection—"and then he suddenly broke down and cried like a little child." Markowski took out an enormous handkerchief of cream silk and wiped his eyes and cheeks. "What for a country," he repeated. He shook a finger at Herbert. "In some ways you Americans are a very kind people but in others you are the most cruel savages in the world!"

Herbert felt stunned. That eerie dread dug into his vitals again. He had half agreed to meet Anne at luncheon. He kept the appointment and found her already waiting for him in a small Village restaurant. She had on the gray raincoat in which she had followed him that day on Fifth Avenue when he had been on his way to the Brevoort to meet Rachel. She held her glasses with one hand on the boneless bridge of her fleshy nose. She held a newspaper in the other.

"So you've come, Bertie. By the way, the contractors tell me we can move back home in three weeks. Aren't you glad? Luella is much better too."

A waitress came up and they ordered some food.

"Have you been following the Wick case?" Anne asked quietly. He nodded.

"It just goes to show," she said, "that men can't always get away with their dirty lechery. What right had that girl to take Wick away from his wife? He says he stopped loving his wife twenty years ago. A fine excuse, I must say. I wonder Mrs. Wick didn't sue him for desertion long ago. If he had known he'd lose his job he might have gone back home before he had a chance to meet this dirty little trollop. But women are so slavish. They make me sick. He wanted new flesh, I suppose. That's about the size of it. Well, how do you know Mrs. Wick wouldn't have liked that too? But did she take a lover? No! She was too decent. Oh! I think men are disgusting."

Herbert couldn't eat. Neither could he think. A hopeless chill pervaded him. He watched Anne eating. He watched her with the absorption of his gradually overmastering fear. She was a woman; and did that not mean patience and mercy? She was an old woman, a mother and a grandmother: and did that not mean a touch at least

286

of the kindly wisdom and long resignation of mankind? Old women sat in the sun, did they not, mellow, a little detached, counselors, healers, reconcilers of strife? He watched Anne. The powerful jawbones moved dourly under the rouge and flabby flesh; the eyes had their look of stone: that concentrated, frozen fury of determination to make her will, her desires, herself prevail—a determination that knew neither hesitancy nor scruple, neither shrinking nor quarter, that had never stopped at anything nor ever would. The cold and stealthy trickery of the detectives threw a long fierce light upon the past. She had plead the impulsiveness of her nature. She had said that she, a poetic temperament, had never grown up. Tricks as vile as the hundred lies and subterfuges by which she had diverted from their proper uses the very many dollars which, in the course of the months, she had paid to the detective agency. No, Anne had always known. She had always known precisely what she was doing. She had known when she gave herself to him in her husband's house; she had known when she manoeuvered the discovery of their guilt and pursued him to his paternal home and when she had perjured herself to get a divorce and when she had dragged him forth into the world to be provider, slave and scapegoat for herself and those children of hers whom she felt to be extensions and parts of her self and its necessary indomitableness. Anne had known when she refused food and refreshment to his aged father. She had known why she had hired the detectives—not to get evidence in order to set him free. But to confuse him and discourage him and daunt him with the show of her knowledge and her power; to wear him out and whip him back like the mad dog she called him by implication, to the foul straw of her kennel. A great desolateness swept through him. But at the core of it glowed immediately a tiny spark of hope. There must be an error in all this. People weren't that way. It wasn't so far as he could see that kind of a world. He must find the error. He spoke. "Wick is a friend of Markowski's and I've gotten some insight into the story. Long ago Wick turned over all he had in the world to his wife; long ago there had ceased to be any love or good or blessedness in their union. Say it was the fault of both or say, if you prefer, that it was a fatality and the fault of neither. Now why should either one of these human souls want to wound or disgrace or hound the other? Why should either want to rob the other of such flickers of happiness as may still come? Should there not be peace for each other in both their hearts? Why, because mortal words were once spoken over two people which fate and their own characters could not make true—why should one of them, guilty or guiltless, desire to crush the other? Isn't life difficult and tragic enough without such things? What does it profit Mrs. Wick to ruin two other lives? She is no less alone. Do you think her loneliness happier for what she has done?"

Anne looked up. Anne spoke. "You're very eloquent, Bertie. And maybe you think I don't see through you. But your subtleties don't confuse me. Men like that ought to be driven out of human society and out of life. He's to gallivant about with his mistress! What has she left in life? Well, at least she has her revenge. She can live for that. As for me, if you want to know it, I would have followed him and the woman in person. I would have seen to it that they hadn't a place to lay their heads, that no one spoke to them or gave them a bite of bread or a drink of water and I would have moved heaven and earth and appealed to the decency of all men and women to strip and to beat that vile adulteress within an inch of her life! Aren't there men enough in the world? Did that slut have to take another woman's husband? Well, let anyone try to take mine. Let her try. That's all I say."

Herbert bowed his head. Anne had spoken. And curiously enough there, in that restaurant in Greenwich Village with plates and broken food between them, there came to him, unbidden and unsummoned, a vision of a white road somewhere in the East along which walked a man, a tall, grave man, who had eyes of an unbearable strength and sweetness. Beside the road was a palm and a saint's tomb that mark a well in that land and under the palm, in the straight shadow of it, crouched an old woman holding a jar of water. The tall man turned

288

aside from the white burning road and held out his hands to the woman in a gesture that was half a gesture of beseeching and half of benediction. The woman sprang up and hurled her earthen jar against a gray stone so that it broke and the water was spilt. She tossed back her dark shawl from the forehead and jaws and eyes of Anne and spat full into the unbearable sweetness of those eyes. . . .

2 THE house had been repaired and rebuilt. Anne bought some more new rugs and chairs and pictures and hung curtains of gold-tinted silk in the windows. She developed a passion for candlesticks and other ornaments of brass and made excursions to Allen Street from which she returned with a cabful of strangely shaped bundles. She seemed to feel that, after the horrors of the summer, some concession was due to Herbert. She tried to make the house attractive. She would not or she could not keep it clean. A slovenly charwoman came once a week to sweep and scrub. But food was again forgotten in the kitchen and soiled dishes were stacked up and from the foundations which had been shaken by fire and water mice appeared. One entered the kitchen or the hall that led to the kitchen and heard scratching and scrabbling and swift scurrying away. The mice's tiny black droppings were not swept up unless the charwoman appeared. A thin, penetrating stench floated from hall and kitchen and pantry into the well-decorated drawing rooms with their curtains of gold-tinted silk. Into the upstairs rooms the dust sifted. Washing was as accidental as it had been in Central City. Towels were constantly bought and never to be had; the bed linen was habitually grimy. Anne speculated with heavy judiciousness on how much of a thief Maggie, the charwoman, was. She appealed to the police and visited the poor Irishwoman's home on Sixth Avenue in company of a plain-clothes man. Nothing was found. Anne was eloquent on the inefficiency of the police and the astuteness of knaves. Now there was not even a charwoman and the house settled deeper and deeper into dirt. Eileen,

searching for a mislaid frock one day, came upon all the things supposedly stolen. Anne was loudly surprised but unabashed.

Luella, having recovered, returned to Central City to go to college. Eileen and Elmer remained in the house. Herbert had quietly begged them to stay. He had come back. He saw no immediate alternative. He did not want a foul and rancorous scandal. He was too weary and too sick at heart. But he could not bear the notion of being alone in the house with Anne. The presence of Eileen and Elmer put a distance between them. Also those two relieved Herbert of small annoyances and worries and duties and mitigated the dust and disorder in which Anne seemed to take a fierce and stubborn satisfaction. Occasionally, of course, they were drawn into outbreaks of reviving turmoil. With a well-known music scholar who admired his work Herbert was having luncheon at the Harvard Club. A page came with the message that Mr. Crump's stepdaughter had just telephoned. Mrs. Crump was dreadfully ill and would Mr. Crump come home at once. Herbert nodded. "We'll finish," he said to his friend. "I'm sure it's not so bad." The man looked at him with a courteous but knowing glance. He drove home and found Anne's eyes wide and terror-stricken. She was artificially struggling for breath. "I can die here for all you care," she said. Dejectedly he went upstairs to his study. In the upper hall he met Eileen. He put his hand on the girl's arms.

"How could you, Eileen?"

"Wasn't it better than to have her run there after you? That's what she threatened to do."

He agreed. These two strangely-assorted friends looked into each other's eyes.

"But why should she do such a thing?" Herbert asked.

"You remember you said to me casually that you had a luncheon engagement at the Harvard Club?"

"Yes. What of it?"

"Mamma thought it was a deliberate blind and that you were going to see some woman."

"My God!" he cried, "and if I did!"

"She'll try to destroy you and the woman even if she destroys herself in the process. She'll go as far as suicide and murder. I don't know that I ought to say this to you about my own mother but I don't understand her and you've always been awfully kind to me."

Herbert leaned against the wall.

"By the way," Eileen said softly, "she tried to get Elmer to take cash to the detective agency the other day. He refused, of course. She'll probably try to get you to put us out now."

"I understand," he said. "Don't worry at all. I——"

He couldn't finish. Anne's harsh voice rang out through the house.

"What are you two whispering about there? Up to your old tricks again? I always thought there was something dirty between you. I've got a good mind to warn Elmer."

Sorrowfully Herbert and Eileen looked at each other. She started downstairs; he went into his study.

Rehearsals were in full swing; Markowski's health was indifferent. The suicide of Dr. Wick in a Mills Hotel had worn upon his mind and broken the last inner bond which, despite the bitterness of the war, he had bravely struggled to maintain with his adopted country. He talked about resigning. He had no heart for conducting. Hence the great part of the society's work fell to Herbert who was grateful for the intensity of his professional preoccupations. The directors of the society informed him that the plan, so long close to their hearts, of a great performance of the Ninth Symphony must be carried out before the end of the season. They implied that, in case Doctor Markowski did resign they would not look very far for his successor. Herbert sat in his office staring at the cordial letter of the president of the society. How futile, he thought, were the triumphs of the world, even its nobler triumphs, to a heart oppressed and desolate and in fear. If he were given the directorship of the society he would be more, not less the slave of that sordid and relentless woman to whom his life was in pawn. A scandal would be more than ever out of the question. She would have more money to spend on detectives and on other forms of hounding him than ever; she would maintain all the Vilases in luxury. Such to him would be the fruits of his success. He laughed to himself. The society would have to look for a director elsewhere. He could count, by the end of this season, on having saved nearly ten thousand dollars. He would simply flee. To Europe. To the uttermost isles of the ocean. But first he would give these friends who admired and trusted him a few sound and memorable performances. . . .

Preparations for the Ninth Symphony were not simple. A large chorus had to be assembled and trained. Soloists had to be found. The latter task proved especially formidable. Herbert did not want operatic singers. There was always a touch of the meretricious about their personalities if not about their actual performance. Of the concert artists available many had more art than voice. He wanted both intelligence and vocal accomplishment. The society, moreover, preferred to choose among the singers available in America. On a day of great discouragement Markowski telephoned that he was sending over the most brilliant pupil of an old friend. The young woman had already given a number of concerts that had been of a singular distinction. She had a voice of extraordinary range—one of the longest voices in the world. Its quality too was first rate. In addition the girl had brains. Herbert was to use his own judgment. . . .

Less than an hour later Barbara Trent was announced. He went into the reception room and found a dainty, shapely little figure with a mass of deep golden hair bent absorbedly over a book. She had put her hat and bag on the table beside her. She looked up. Her eyes and brows were both darker than her hair warranted. But what at once smote upon Herbert's heart was not all this, nor the childlike purity of the complexion, nor her firm little nose, nor the ripe and generous sweetness of the lips. It was that from this lovely mortal vestiture there came to him a breath of earnestness and of devotion. Art or life or both. This girl was eager for the consuming flame—for great sacrifices, for heroic giving, for worlds well lost. She met him with a frank warmth. She said with a wistful little smile that he would probably not take her because her reputation was still very small. He led her to the rehearsal room and sat down at the piano and felt her vibrancy beside him like the involuntary throbbing of a bird. He asked her to sing something simple, something definitely for the voice.

" 'Care Selve'?" she asked.

He assented and played the accompaniment. Her voice floated free and effortless in that large noble melodic line of Handel; it was both resonant and liquid—a great, rich, young voice. He thought of a tall jar of honey with the sunlight streaming through it. He swung around and faced her earnest glance.

"Marvelous," he said. "I see no reason why we shouldn't give you a job."

"Oh!" It was almost like a little sob in her throat. "I've always wanted to sing with a symphony orchestra. You're sure you'll want me—me?"

There was an exquisite humility about her now. He took her back into his office and they talked about herself and about music and books. She thirsted for the fullness of life. All she had known or experienced hitherto seemed to her meager and thin.

"You're going to singe your wings, Barbara Trent," he said. "You're too pure and too impassioned at the same time."

She looked up into his eyes. "If I can't fly I'd just as soon singe them in a good cause. But tell me—am I hired?"

He nodded sadly. "Oh, yes, I can't let you go."

She took his hand and pressed it impulsively to her bosom. Then she flitted out and left him dazed.

3   WHEN the black curtain seemed to have fallen forever upon the tragic farce that was his life, it appeared to Herbert Crump that in the vast and incalculable economy of things a compensation had been meant for him. This compensation was the three months which followed his meeting with Barbara Trent. He didn't lose the sense of danger or of doom. He knew despite hours of faint hope or voluntary forgetfulness what force, like a strong circling bird

of prey, hovered about Barbara and himself. He knew that he could not protect either himself or her whom he loved. All the more avidly he pressed upon his tongue the grave of every moment. . . . His compensation was not only magic and delight. It was knowledge, a knowledge rarely reached by men, though embodied for the memory and the self-recollection of the race in myth and legend. And the name of that knowledge was what Dante called long ago "intelligence of love." He remembered likewise the fable of Plato concerning those lost halves of a primordial world which sometimes meet and are severed no more. These and other poetic and legendary dealings with love which he had always taken to be the mere expressions of fancy and of hope, he now knew to be the record of an experience which had from time to time visited and exalted the forlorn hearts of men. This knowledge and this experience were intuitive and immediate. They were incontrovertible facts of consciousness from the start. In a world of freedom and cleanness Herbert and Barbara would have arisen on the day of their first meeting and left friends and home and set up their tent somewhere under the benignant stars. . . . No shadow ever fell between them except the shadow of the hatred and the cruelty of men—hatred and cruelty that arose from frustrated hopes and perverted emotions and sickly repression and the dwelling with ugliness and want. . . . A conductor's affair with a singer. Harmless enough, a few wiseacres said, more than excusable in this case. But Herbert knew that dwelling with ugliness and spiritual squalor and hatred and treachery had not withered his soul or made dry his heart. He was not—ultimate indignity of words!— having an affair with Barbara Trent. He had at last found his way home in a homeless world: beauty was intelligence; both were harmony, both were passion, pulsing as a star, clean as a flame. . . . They stood together by the window of his office and looked out upon the people and the traffic of the street. His arm was about her; she leaned her head lightly against his shoulder. They spoke no words. It was as though they had in very fact become one consciousness that opposed itself as a unity to the world as object and also bathed the world in

294

the magic of an undivided light. They saw a single radiance which was not and could be forever for them upon land and sea. It was not and was yet as real as sunlight and could be extinguished for them only by hopeless separation or by death. It was a heavenly radiance but it shone strongly upon the earth. Barbara was full of a sweet serviceableness to him. If she could only have helped and tended him in the common humble needs of daily living; he had an equal impulse toward her. The fancied rancorous sense of inequality that disturbs the ill-mated never rose in their thoughts. Each would have kneeled instinctively beside the other to bathe the other's travel-weary feet. Each would have felt that act to be an act of the highest spiritual freedom and dignity. . . .

What was it that protected these lovers for even so brief a space? The contract with Barbara had been signed. Her presence in the offices and rehearsal halls could not be questioned. Herbert gave her a key to his private office. Concealment and subterfuge seemed like an affront to the quality of their feeling and their relationship. They were justly proud of each other as artists, as human beings and as fellow pilgrims. They bore this affront bravely. They endured its humiliation together. It did not luckily tear at Barbara's soul as it tore at Herbert's. Her imagination could not at once envisage Anne as stripped of all claim, all moral rights, all need for pity or compunction on their parts. She asked Herbert indeed how such a thing were possible. He begged her to take that ultimate truth of his past on faith. The facts would seem unbelievable to her. He told her the one anecdote of Anne openly grudging his father food. She grew pale and her eyes filled with tears. He said that he knew it was inconceivable, but that it was precisely Anne's quality to convert the morally inconceivable into facts as concrete as brass.

"How unhappy she must be," Barbara said.

"Terribly," he agreed, "but quite beyond human help on account of the badness of her heart. Because the only thing that could break the fierce strain of her misery would be humility, self-abnegation, the love that is charity. And these instincts, if she ever possessed them, have withered in her nature."

"You're describing a lost soul."

"She is a lost soul," he replied.

"And what will be the end?" Barbara asked. "Not that I'm afraid or sorry, Herbert," she added quickly, "but tell me what you think."

He stood before her with outstretched arms. "I can't tell. Nothing but evil, I'm afraid, will come from her. And men and their laws give her power. But I believe that our love has not hurt you. As for me— if she destroys me now I shall at least have known and loved you and so cleansed and justified my life."

He lived for his hours with Barbara. They stood in a circle of light around which the world lay silhouetted in sharp-edged blackness. Visible dark fell upon the house in which he lived. Mechanically he went through gestures and spoke words in that house. But only the body of this death—the Pauline phrase haunted him—visited these rooms and halls. He would have found it difficult to project his inner state to anyone. For to say that he had fallen in love was but to touch the outer edge of it. To understand that state one would, he reflected, have to conceive of the soul, the psyche, the mind, as of a tangible and concrete substance or as an organ which in his case had been deafened with alien clamor, smudged by alien touches, wrenched, stabbed, scraped, wounded and violated incessantly for twelve long years and which now lay in the hollow of Barbara's healing hand. Or, one had to conceive of the psychic life as having its orders of beings like the physical life—beings who could live healthily only in certain atmospheres or media. The thrush cannot burrow with the mole nor the deer swim with the shark. So great and so flagrant can be the moral divisions between man and man. . . . If ever he were to be permitted to live with Barbara as a man and a woman live together amid the complex business of the world, disagreements and temporary disharmonies would arise between them too. But each would understand the other, since even their disagreements would be based upon certain fundamental and common perceptions and assumptions. But you cannot reason concerning color with those born blind nor concerning tone with those born deaf. Except from Eileen in more recent years Herbert had never, literally never, heard a phrase on the lips of Anne or her children which he understood except in its outer and verbal sense. A thousand times he had strained his ears and mind in vain. He and these people talked at each other into a hollow void. . . . He had learned as a matter of long experience to be able measurably to predict Anne's actions in giving situations. Their groundwork of motive and character was as dark to him as ever. . . .

He watched her now in that gray and shadowy house. She kept on buying things and filling the house with them. By secret trickery or open insolence she succeeded in not spending her housekeeping allowance for the purposes for which it was meant. A stranger might have thought this a pathetic striving not to be left penniless. Herbert knew better. Anne had no intention of being left at all. She knew in addition that Herbert would buy his freedom if she would only sell it to him, at any material sacrifice. Herbert did not wonder at her actions. He could have predicted them, without understanding their inwardness. . . . She filled the house with decorative objects and let it lapse more and more into dirt and disorder. A poisoned mouse lay rotting in the pantry. Anne stormed when Elmer and Eileen pleaded to throw it out. No, Anne said, it was to remain till Monday when the new charwoman came. The filthy creature had not removed it and must be taught a lesson. . . .

On many afternoons she went to call on what few common friends they had. Or else she pretended to have done so. And she came back and told Herbert how they had wondered at her story of her loveless and sex-starved and unhappy state and how they had commiserated with her and had shaken their heads over Herbert's cruelty to her. And from one brash and youngish woman, with whom she had formed one of her sudden, shallow and self-interested alliances she came back with the report of the woman's saying that if her old man treated her so, undoubtedly consoling himself elsewhere, she would use a knife on him. . . .

Herbert's horror deepened and he clung to Barbara not only as a man clings to his best-beloved but as one driven by the furies clings to a sane and saving hand. . . . At an unavoidable evening party Anne, screamingly bedizened, flaming with rouge, shouted across the room: "What do you think of a husband who has not known his wife in the flesh for eleven weeks?" . . . Herbert closed his eyes in that crowded place. He could hear the rich, soft voice of Barbara as she had said to him two hours before: "I shall feel it when you're suffering most and I shall say a little prayer for both of us." He clenched his hands. Verses half forgotten since his boyhood stole into his mind. He saw Barbara as clearly as though she were beside him. "There may be heaven!" He opened his eyes and saw Anne flaunting herself. "There must be hell" . . .

4   ABRUPTLY Anne stopped running about the city; abruptly she stopped her half threatening, half falsely triumphant talk. Herbert came home and entered the rear living room and found her sitting upright in the dusk. By the glint of the hearth fire he could see that she was uncombed, unwashed, dressed in the same kimono in which he had left her at breakfast many hours ago. She moved her head a little and he could see her eyes—stony and yet wild, drunk with an exhaustless fury checked only by a rein of fear. The eyes were lifted; they met his and he knew that she knew. . . . For a swift second a kind of madness overcame him. He felt like shrieking with terror. He had a vision of those withered, brownish claws stretched out after Barbara's eyes even as in that old dream of his, so long ago, he had seen the fangs of wolves closer and closer to his mother's breast. And instantaneously the memory of that old dream blended with his present vision and the two terrors became one and there leaped from his subconscious into his mind the knowledge that in ways deeper than eye could search out Barbara was like his mother and was meant in the very eternity of the blood itself to be flesh of

298

his flesh and heart of his heart. . . . He sat down opposite that strange old woman with the wild, sinister eyes and the silence yawned between them like a serpent's maw. Anne's jaws of steel were set. She was the stronger and he knew it even as the first word that was spoken wrung itself from the tightness and drouth of his throat.

"Well?"

Fiercely she looked at him. "What do you want of me?"

He did not answer.

"What?" she repeated, and her voice was like a harsh hot flame. "You've forbidden me—" a somber taunt stole into her tone—"to know."

He kept his voice level. "But you do know."

"Everything."

He was cold. He shivered and leaned nearer to the fire.

"I will put this house in your name and assign my royalties to you and give you half my salary. Will you divorce me?"

"Never!"

"Why not?"

Her voice was deep and harsh. "Because I won't."

He got up; he walked up and down; every now and then he stopped and leaned for a moment upon the back of the chair opposite Anne's in which he had been sitting. Words came to him, words poured from him as though he were but an instrument, as though a force not himself wanted these words to be spoken.

"Anne," he said, "I want to put aside all pride and all thought of any blame or guilt. I want to go farther. Perhaps in all these years it has not always been given me to see the right and I may have sinned more than I have known and been cruel and unjust to you. Do you hear me, Anne?"

The tight jaws barely moved. "I hear you, Herbert."

"If that is so and in the measure in which it is so," he went on, "I beg you to forgive me. Say then, though to save my soul I can't see it in that light—but say that, in the beginning, we both made a mistake. That's not so very terrible. Many people commit these errors.

299

But you do know, do you not, that I have suffered very terribly for mine?"

He stopped. No answering sound came to him through the gloom.

"I swear to you by all that either you or I hold sacred that every day of these twelve years has been a day of livid agony to me and every night a night of torment, that when my mother died my first thought was: she is safe from the crucifixion of this life, and when my father died I was relieved at the cessation of his pain over my inexpressible wretchedness. Perhaps I am oversensitive, perverse, even mad. Call me what you like. Think me what you like. The fact of my suffering remains. Isn't it time for my expiation to be at an end?"

He peered at her and thought he saw a softening, a relaxation in her rigid face.

"You have, after all, had everything that life can offer: young love and motherhood and twelve of my best years."

Her wild, shrieking, ironic laughter broke in upon his words. "I? You say I have had everything? O you fool! You fool!"

"You have had much that I have never had," he said as gently as he could. "I have had no home of my own and no child."

"I thought you didn't want children," she flung at him. "And why haven't you had a home? I've tried to make one for you."

He curbed himself. "Let's not quarrel about details, Anne. I didn't say you had been happy. I meant to say that you have had the normal and natural chances of life. And that I haven't. I want them before it is too late. Let me go."

"To that green girl? Never!"

He folded his hands and bowed his head. "You have daughters of your own. Barbara is younger than Eileen. Doesn't that make you compassionate? Doesn't it?"

No answer came. The last glow of the fire had died and in the gloom he saw Anne still upright in her chair like a gray gnarled shaft of stone. Only from a dim lamp in the yard a faint pallid shimmer seeped in. He leaned against the wall. He had a sense of something ultimate in this hour. He must wrestle with Anne's soul. He must

300

reach a depth in her that was hidden but could not be wholly dead. Under this rancorous female there must be a human being. If he could reach that, if some word of his could revive that . . . He began softly. He spoke humbly. "I am sorry myself that Barbara is so young. It makes my position doubly difficult. It makes it even more difficult that she is so entirely unspotted from the world. You will say that that doesn't concern you and you will be quite right. Barbara doesn't concern you. I am pleading with you for my life—for mine—for my freedom to live and choose. I am pleading to be set free from a compulsion that began when Barbara was a small child. I ask you to think over the years with me. What joy, what satisfaction, what blessedness has it brought you to join the forces of the world to your own strength and keep me in unwilling bondage? Can you remember one good day—one day of beauty or even of peace?" He gazed through the gloom. He thought he saw a scarcely perceptible shaking of that rigid head. "You see, Anne, force is of no avail—literally of none. You keep me in this house. You keep my body here—an empty shell. What is that to you if my heart rebels and flees and my mind judges and condemns? What have you? And if this evil compulsion goes on the hatred and the bitterness will become so great that the body of whatever was between us once—that body of it which has for years lain dead at our feet—will begin to rot and grow putrid and we two tied to that noisome thing, will poison the whole world about us and die of the agony of its utter loathsomeness ourselves. Let us bury that body; let us part in freedom and in peace. It may be that even now, at this late hour, there will arise from such a liberation forgiveness and forgetfulness of all evil and a shadow of human kindness."

Her head was bowed now. Dry, hard sobs came to his ears. He went over to her in the darkness. He kneeled before her; he raised his folded hands. "For your sake, Anne, and for mine, and for the sake of goodness and mercy—let me go!"

She dried her eyes. She spoke in a hoarse whisper. "I'll try. But I must have time to get used to the idea. I have to grow strong enough gradually to bear it. Give me time, time." He got up. He stood before her. She raised wild eyes to him. "Do you want to throw me out this minute?"

"You will stay here, Anne," he said gently. "This is your home."

She too arose. She faced him. "Listen, Herbert."

"Yes, Anne."

"If six months from today you feel exactly as you do now, I'll try to do what you want me to—yes, yes, yes, yes!" Her voice rose to a wild, forlorn shriek. "I will, I will! I promise, unless I kill myself first!"

Strange grotesque leaps brought her to the door. He heard her sob as she dragged herself up the stairs. He heard doors open and close and heard Eileen go into her mother's room and heard the long, low murmur of muffled voices. . . .

5   HE TREATED her gently and courteously. He did not remind her of her promise. With a wan smile she asked him for money with which to buy a few more things to complete the furnishings of the house: another rug, a small table, a brass and cast iron fire-set for the rear drawing room. Implicit in this wan smile of hers was the pathos of these being his last gifts to her which she would treasure the more because they came from him. He denied her nothing she asked for. He went farther. Out of his hope and gratitude he asked her whether she did not need this thing or that. His creative vigor, long paralyzed or dormant, returned and he wrote songs for Barbara and began to plan an orchestral work of new and epic proportions. Barbara and he were together daily. Being both moderate spirits and capable of the grace of humility they were not triumphant. Patiently they awaited and expected annoyances and difficulties and dangers. But they had each other and some day, whether it was one year later or two, they would be able to have and make a home for each other. And the anticipation of that was a happiness so profound and magical that it had almost the piercingness of pain. They were

utterly united, body and soul. Their cup was full. Peace and strength flooded their hearts. Herbert felt as though he must propitiate the jealous gods. He "loaned" money to Bronson Vilas and sent a gift of money to Luella and promised Anne that he would not quite abandon Luella in the days when she herself would be no more. . . .

Then the first shadow fell. He had a headache one day and came home an hour earlier than was his custom. Perhaps he was impelled by the slight discomfort which he had felt all day on missing the key of his desk from his key-ring. He must have left it in the lock. He let himself into the house and went wearily and quietly upstairs. He wondered, as he had done so often, what he was doing in this place. Thus, he thought, a simple man innocently condemned might suddenly stare at the unimaginable walls of his prison, unable to believe, despite all evidence, that the walls would not melt away and leave him in a sunny meadow amid the winds of his homeland. Was his own long term of imprisonment and degradation truly coming to an end? . . . The door of his study stood ajar. He pushed it open and entered and saw the back of a crumpled, yellowish kimono bent over his desk and heard a faint, feverish crackle of paper. He tapped on the floor with his foot. Anne straightened and turned with a motion like that of a stealthy animal and their eyes met. The expression in hers was hard and furtive. He opened his lips but she slipped past him and he heard the thump of her slippered feet upon the stairs. . . . He sat down at his desk which had been pushed open and looked through the little drawer in which he kept the few things, such as everyone has, which symbolized the life of his heart: a tiny gold locket of his grandfather, a small photograph of his mother, a lock, burnished as old gold, of Barbara's hair. Everything was there. But his neat order had been destroyed. Hasty and hateful fingers—long but blunt fingers with the flesh growing too far up the nail—weak and yet treacherous fingers had rummaged here. With a perceptible trembling of the hand he tried to pull out another drawer in which he kept a few notes that Barbara had written him. The drawer stuck. It had been taken out and hastily and unskilfully thrust back in. It yielded at last. Thank God, the letters were there though crinkled and in disorder. . . . He swept the shadow aside. To his incurable lack of suspiciousness the whole thing began to seem almost pitiful. Anne was morbidly torturing herself. . . .

Two days later the incident took on a new significance—a significance more in harmony with the real Anne. Frank Conrad called Herbert up at his office. He had made an observation which in his opinion should be communicated to Herbert at once. He had recently had occasion to consult an old college classmate of his who was a lawyer on matters connected with Agnes' property. On the same floor of the same building as his friend's offices were also those of Burg, Kleinman and Freeburg. "Do you happen to know those people by reputation?" Frank asked. "Never heard of them." "Well, they're notorious for dirty divorce and separation and breach of promise cases. Moral blackmail is their middle name. The firm is never mentioned without a ribald pun that has been made on its name." "Yes, yes," Herbert said, "what of it, old man?" "Why, just this, that every time that I've been in to see David Newman I've seen Anne either go into or come out of the offices of those scavengers. You'd better get a lawyer damned quick."

Herbert felt himself turning pale. Yes, he thought he saw what was coming. Instead of waiting the six months and then co-operating with him in a seemly fashion, Anne intended to spring a clamorous and scandalous suit for divorce on him and of course name Barbara as co-respondent. . . . Of course, of course. That foul and treacherous old hag would try to drag him into her own slime. And not him only; that didn't matter. But Barbara, the innocent, impassioned, gifted—sacred to him as the girlhood of his mother—she too was to be spattered and blasted by the ordure native to that inconceivable woman and her brood. Did not the universe have pillars that one could shake like Samson, and bring crashing down? Was there no God who had a bolt of justice? Did one have to sit still and let the mud of her seep and splash and ooze and poison and choke all things decent and kindly and not ignoble and of good report?

304

Men babbled of goodness and justice and character. Who was the conqueror in this world? The unscrupulous of mind, the black of heart. . . .

Telephone messages and telegrams confused him and drowned the cry of his soul. The orchestra was to play in Chicago the following night. The men were already there. Doctor Markowski had suddenly come down with influenza. Herbert must take a night train to Chicago. Accommodations for him had already been procured. He must. He promised. He could not leave his friends in the lurch. It was only five o'clock now. He drove to his house and let the taxi wait while he hastily packed his suitcase and a Boston bag. The house was empty, silent, ominous. He telephoned to Barbara, found her at home and begged her to wait for him. He left his bags in her apartment and they went out to dinner. He told her his story. Her eyes which always grew dark and glossy at night had a troubled look.

"Will we be separated?" she asked.

"Not while I live and am free," he replied quietly.

"Then it can't really hurt us," she declared.

"It will be more horrible than you imagine."

"I shall learn to bear it."

"Thank God for your courage," he said. "The worst, the newspaper stories and the gossip, will be brief. So soon as the decree is pronounced we'll get married and go to Europe."

Her cheeks glowed. "I think we should be so grateful," she said. "If we didn't have some trouble we would grow too proud and self-satisfied in our happiness."

She accompanied him to the train. She waited till the engine pulled out. Leaning from the window he watched her till she became a black speck in the distance. He settled back in his seat and felt like a child who has lost sight of its mother in a crowd. . . .

It was remembered afterwards that during these two days in Chicago Herbert Crump had been alternately absent-minded and feverish. A corroding anxiety seemed to possess him and he had sent almost hourly telegrams of love and reassurance to Miss Barbara

Trent in New York. He had been a trifle late to the concert and had kept his orchestra and his audience waiting. At last he had appeared, pale and erect, and had conducted superbly, but with a passionate abandon, an emotional emphasis which were far from being his wont. After the concert he had stayed in his room at the Congress Hotel until it was time to meet his train for the East. . . . The truth was that he had been tormented during all these many dragging intolerable hours by a premonition of evil greater, more monstrous, more hideous of aspect, than any he had ever known. From depths of a half mystical perception came to him images of that evil and of a personified malevolence: faceless, contorted creatures, blind, white heads, half woman, half serpent, dreadful racial memories of some primordial hell. . . . A fear for Barbara shook him. He had left her unprotected in the same city with Anne. . . .

It was nine o'clock in the evening when he leaped from the train in New York. He almost ran up the dim stairs in the Pennsylvania Station. A shabby man with a furtive foxlike head that reminded him of Harry Vilas', barred his way.

"Mr. Herbert Crump?"

"Yes, yes."

The man thrust a thick roll of paper into Herbert's hands. "I'm servin' them on you, see?" he said, and slipped away into the crowd.

So soon, Herbert muttered to himself, so soon. He stopped and controlled himself and summoned his reason. He must examine the papers quietly and calmly somewhere. He thrust the thick roll into his overcoat pocket, checked his bags, jumped into a taxi and drove to a favorite chophouse of his in the Forties. He found his hands trembling violently as he undid the roll of paper. He ordered and drank down a whisky and soda and read the twenty-eight type-written pages of an affidavit in support of an action not for divorce but for separation on the grounds of cruelty and neglect. For separation. . . . For separation. Ice seemed to trickle into his veins. For a moment he thought he was going to be violently sick. No, no, he struggled and overcame. He must read; he must find out. The

306

plaintiff, Anne Bronson Farrel Crump declared that she and Herbert Crump had been married on a certain date of 1906 in the city of Queenshaven. It had been a love-match pure and simple, in proof of which she herewith adduced letters written by her husband in the course of their courtship and engagement. Although the earlier years of the marriage had been lean years and although Herbert Crump, like many artists, had always had sick nerves and had indulged in violent fits of temper, the union had been a radiantly happy one. She, the plaintiff, had always recognized the defendant's potential genius and had hesitated at no form of help, however menial, or of sacrifice, however great. Thus no shadow had clouded their marriage until Herbert Crump had been called to teach at the Central City College of Music and Expression. Here the presence of the young women students had evidently and unfortunately aroused the defendant's morbid tendencies. He had declared himself no longer satisfied with his devoted wife, had insultingly compared the plaintiff to the young students at the college, had grudged her money for the expenses of their home and had offered her physical violence on a number of occasions. All these things the plaintiff had borne patiently and lovingly and devotedly in the hope of better things. When the defendant had finally been called to his present commanding position in the world of art the plaintiff had hoped that his duties and responsibilities would steady his eccentric character and that he would give his faithful helpmate the affection and consolation which were her due after all these many years. Only too soon did the plaintiff's tragic mistake become clear to her. No sooner had the couple arrived in New York than the defendant ran after every immoral woman he met, neglected the plaintiff ever more grossly and insulted and slighted her in every conceivable way. In spite of this the plaintiff had never quite given up hope and had redoubled her devotion. In the last few months, however, she had been unwillingly forced to the conclusion that hope of amendment was indeed at an end. The defendant had made the acquaintance of a young woman named Barbara Trent, of whose character and antecedents the plaintiff professed no knowledge. She did not even know whether the defendant sustained illicit relations with the aforesaid Barbara Trent nor did she care to ascertain. It sufficed her to declare that since that fatal meeting with an obviously designing woman, the defendant had utterly refused to have marital relations with the plaintiff, had tried by both threats and chicanery to wring from her a promise to divorce him and had ended with an oath to kill her if she did not abstain from inquiring into and thus having a knowledge of his adulterous and criminal activities. Under this heavy burden of neglect, terror, anguish of mind and body, the plaintiff's health, long undermined by her faithful services to her husband and their common home, had broken down. And nothing was left her but to pray the honorable court for a decree of separation with such alimony as her love and constancy merited and her husband's total income from all sources of about $15,000 justified. . . .

Herbert laughed and stopped abruptly as he saw the scared faces of the waiters above their scarlet waistcoats. He ordered another whiskey and soda and drank it down. The affidavit was of an infernal and triumphant astuteness. It flattered every prejudice of the mob against the artist and soothed all its unappeased feeling of inferiority. No more perfect or credible newspaper story, with the right heroine and the right villain, had ever been concocted. It would be believed with glee and with righteous indignation. American manhood and American womanhood would once more be vindicated. It was the case of Wick over again. Barbara and he would be broken and destroyed and there was no way out. For if he contested the suit and told the story of Anne and the Vilases and she—though this was questionable—lost the action, what would it avail him, him or the woman he loved? What? What? He paid his bill, giving the waiter a generous tip. He felt suddenly grave and exalted. The long years flashed before him. He saw Anne in a hundred attitudes which had stamped themselves forever on his mind. That stupid, treacherous and ferocious creature must not triumph. He mattered little. Even the precious spirit of Barbara mattered little. Justice mattered. The honor of God—if there was a God. . . .

6 HE FOUND her crouching over the hearth fire in her favorite rear drawing room. Her grizzled hair was hanging down in oily strands; a fleck of soot was on the huge bulge of her forehead; her jowls drooped heavily forward. Dourly she looked up at him. He sat down opposite her before the fire. He tapped the roll of paper which he held in his hand.

"You promised to divorce me. You must withdraw this."

She looked up at him sidewise, with a somber cruel curiosity. "Like hell I will."

"You must," he repeated.

She shrugged her shoulders. "The affidavits were given out to the reporters this afternoon. The story is coming out in the papers in the morning."

He began to tremble in every nerve and sinew and muscle. He felt his very skin quiver and felt his blood leaping into his head like a geyser.

"Do you know," he panted, "that you are destroying two human beings?"

Her voice croaked like her mother's. "Easy enough to avoid. Give out a statement that it's all a mistake, that you love no one but me and behave yourself as a husband should!" She leered.

"Never!" he cried, and she saw the look of unbelievable horror on his face. "Never! I'd rather die."

"Oh, you would, would you? Well, you'll often wish that you had. I'll win my suit hands down. I know that there will be a non-molestation clause. And I won't personally approach either you or that girl. But I'll know where you are and I'll be there to tell people what you are and what she is. I'll cry it from the housetops of every city that

I'm your wife and that she's your mistress. I'll get the children to howl it after you in the streets. If you go to Europe I'll go too—on your money—and I'll see if even there such vileness is tolerated. I'll take good care that you two don't have a roof over your heads, that you're driven from place to place like the criminals you are and I wonder how much of this boasted love will be left after a few years; I wonder whether you two won't turn on each other and hate each other even more, you dog, than you ever hated me. And by the time I'm dead or too weak to crawl after you, you'll be old too and you'll both be so jaded that you'll curse the day you met and the day on which you were born!" Her yellow teeth were bared like fangs. He trembled so that the chair on which he sat shook under him and shook the room. "And now go," she shrieked suddenly. "Go to your God-damned who——" He did not know that he had grabbed the brass handle of the poker. He knew nothing until he heard the grinding impact of his blow and saw Anne crumple and then tumble forward and strike her forehead against the fender. Slowly blood came forth from the bald center of her skull and oozed slothfully over the gray of that dishonored head. . . .

Herbert Crump trembled no more. Quietly he went to the window and opened it and looked up at the stars. If the universe was a mere mechanism and we but acidental crawlers on this planet's crust, neither deeds done nor undone mattered and love and hate and cruelty and mercy and rancor and justice were indistinguishably one. But if this were not so, if—were it only by a slow process of becoming —the universe strove, like man himself, for values beyond the dust, then he had helped to reestablish the shaken moral equilibrium of the world, to save cosmos from chaos, to make justice to prevail. Though his body would be imprisoned, his mind would be free. Ah, he was human. Already at the thought of Barbara tears scalded the corners of his eyes. He would have to learn to transcend longing and desire and regret and to dwell upon the blessedness of having known and loved such a one as she. . . . He turned and looked at that huddled, shrunken, sack-like bundle on the floor. Where now were her gibes and her malevolence and her ferocity, her lusts and treacheries and hates? How strong and unvanquishable she had been. . . . Goodness might have made her almost great. Evil is both destroyer and destroyed. . . . Slowly he went to the telephone, took up the receiver and asked for police headquarters.